ACKNOWLEDGMENTS

The story marches on with another meaty installment! Thank you for following along. And thank you to my editor, Shelley Holloway, my cover illustrator, Jeff Brown, and my beta readers, Sarah Engelke and Cindy Wilkinson. I appreciate all the help!

Now, let's go find some dragons!

CHOSEN FOR POWER

DRAGON GATE, BOOK 4

LINDSAY BUROKER

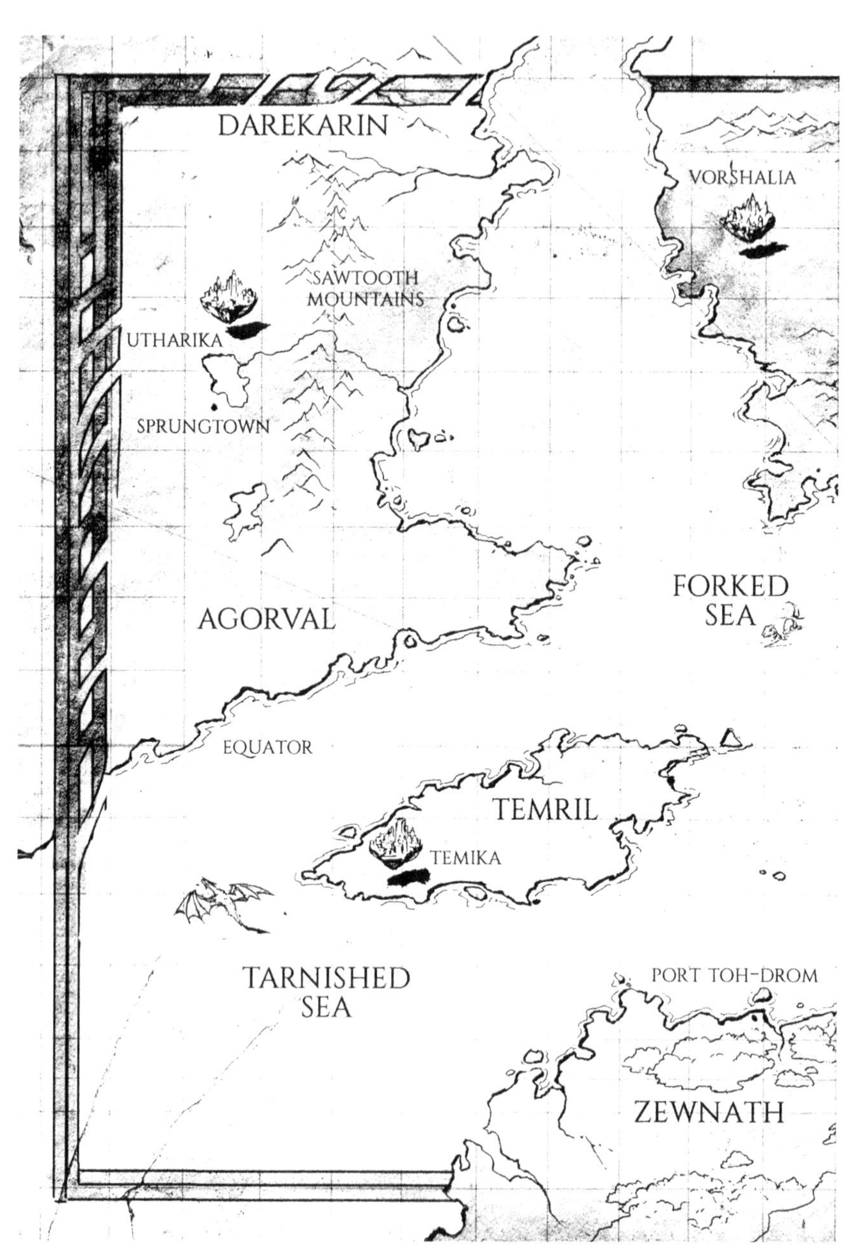
DAREKARIN
VORSHALIA
SAWTOOTH
MOUNTAINS
UTHARIKA
SPRUNGTOWN
FORKED
SEA
AGORVAL
EQUATOR
TEMRIL
TEMIKA
TARNISHED
SEA
PORT TOH-DROM
ZEWNATH

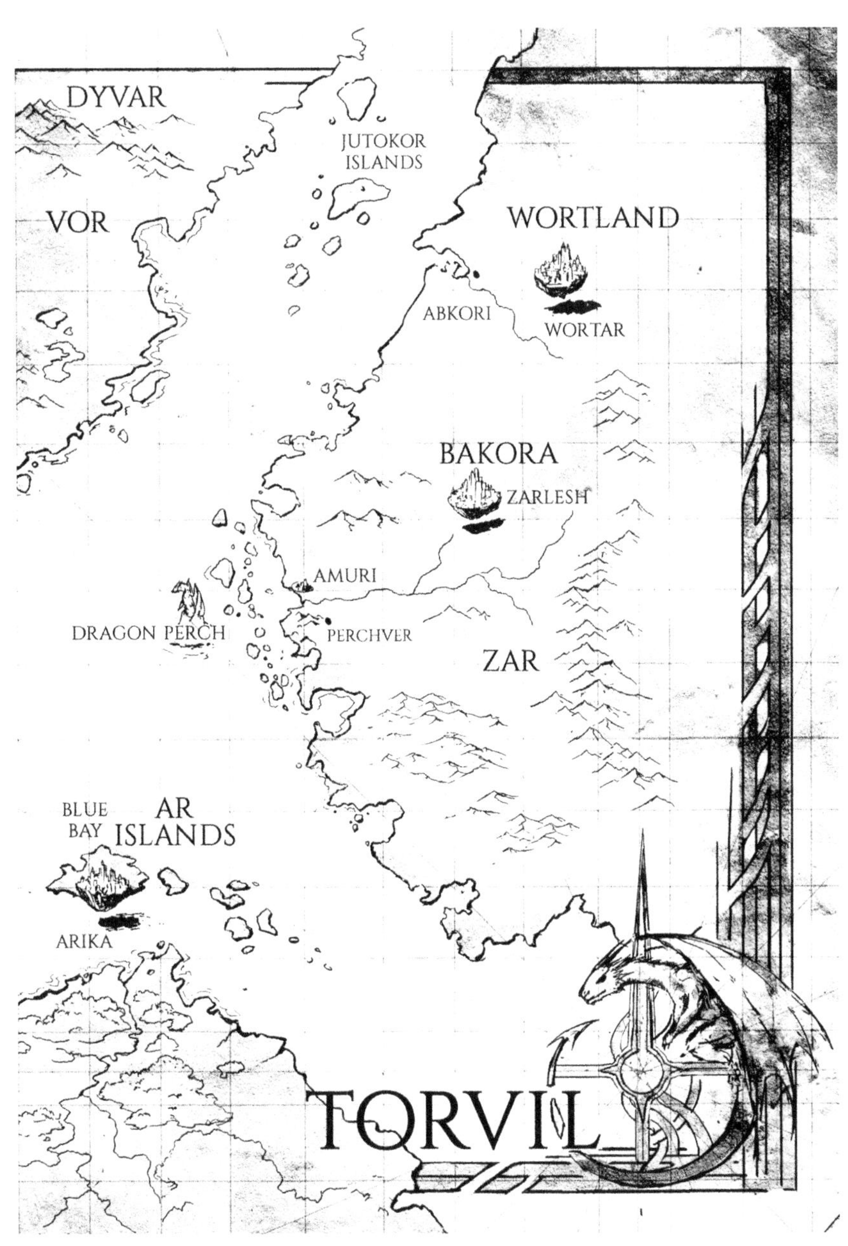
DYVAR
JUTOKOR ISLANDS
VOR
WORTLAND
ABKORI
WORTAR
BAKORA
ZARLESH
AMURI
DRAGON PERCH
PERCHVER
ZAR
BLUE BAY
AR ISLANDS
ARIKA
TORVIL

1

JAKSTOR FREEDAR LEAPED FROM THE ROCKS AND FLAPPED HIS ARMS like chicken wings before splashing down into the clear jungle pool. He felt like an idiot, but if it got the point across to his young charge, it would be worth it.

As he came back up, someone's laughter rang over the roar of the waterfall, and Jak knew that more than *his charge* had witnessed the jump. At least the young dragon was paying attention. Shikari perched on a boulder, a puzzled tilt to his blue-scaled head as he peered at Jak.

The laughter came from some of the mercenaries lounging around the sprawling camp that was set up in the shadow of the ancient dragon portal. Not all of the men were amused. Many watched Jak with narrowed eyes and hard tattooed faces. He didn't see many of the Thorn Company women. Too bad. They didn't usually glower or mock him overmuch.

Shikari scampered to the rock Jak had used to launch himself into the water. He'd grown from parrot-sized when he'd hatched a few weeks earlier to coyote-sized, and his leathery blue wings had gotten large enough that Jak thought he might be able to fly now.

This was his latest attempt to teach the young dragon how to do something that he was physiologically incapable of himself.

As Shikari flung himself from the rock, concern washed over Jak, and he swam closer. Earlier, the dragon had been wading around in the shallows, but Jak hadn't seen him attempt to swim yet and didn't know if he could. Just because some animals picked it up instinctively didn't mean dragons did.

Shikari squeaked in the air, sounding more excited than alarmed by his decision, then splashed down and disappeared underwater. Jak frowned. Shikari hadn't even *tried* to flap his wings.

He surfaced, splashing and floundering. Jak swam closer in case Shikari couldn't figure it out, but he was hesitant to get close to those flailing limbs. As he well knew from the scabs healing on his shoulder, Shikari had sharp talons.

After several seconds, the dragon got the hang of swimming and dog-paddled around the pool. He spread his wings, giving himself more surface area and making it easier to float.

"That's not the use I had in mind for those wings, but I guess it's a start." Jak pushed wet hair out of his eyes. It had gotten shaggy after weeks in the jungle and traveling through the portal to explore other worlds. He would have to ask his mother to trim it.

Maybe Captain *Rivlen* would trim it for him. Jak hadn't seen much of her since they'd returned from their last mission, the mission where she'd kissed him after they'd battled dragons together. He had no idea if it had meant anything, especially after all the times she'd called him *kid,* or if she'd simply wanted to thank him for his help, but she'd replaced Tezi as the star in his dreams. Not that he should have been dreaming about either of them.

"She'd light my hair on fire to trim it, anyway," he muttered.

"You look like an idiot," a man said from the rocks.

He wasn't alone. Two other male mercenaries with swords and magelock pistols belted at their waists glowered down at Jak, no hint of humor in their eyes.

"When I jump into the pool?" Jak asked. "Or just in general?"

"*Always*." The speaker fondled the hilt of his pistol.

"Huh. That must be why I haven't managed to get any of the ladies here to have a drink with me."

Not that there were many places to *have a drink* when one was a thousand miles from the nearest city, not unless one counted the dozens of mageships anchored in the air above the trees. Thanks to the mages who crewed them, and their cheerful willingness to force their terrene human slaves to climb trees and pick fruit, they had fresh juice every day. But those beverages never made it down to the camp on the ground. Maybe the mercenaries would have been less grumpy if they could have enjoyed papaya juice now and then.

"Maybe the *ladies*—" the speaker said with scorn in his voice as he glanced toward one of the Thorn Company tents, "—don't like having drinks with boys who think they're *better* than us."

"Uh, trust me. I don't think that." Feeling vulnerable in the water, Jak swam to the bank to climb out. He angled away from the men, not wanting to come up at their feet. He didn't know what he'd done to irk them, as he'd hardly spent any time in the camp, but from the way they were looking at him, he wouldn't be surprised if one kicked him in the face. "When it comes to jungles full of dangerous creatures, enemy mages, and druids who would like to see us all eaten by animals, you mercenaries are a lot more capable of handling yourselves than I am."

Alas, a true statement, though he was encouraged that under Lord Malek's and Captain Rivlen's tutelage, his new aptitude for magic had turned into the ability to do a few useful things.

"That's right," the man agreed as Jak dripped on the rocks in nothing but his underwear. Taking his clothes off before swimming had seemed wise, but he felt even more vulnerable with his hat, shirt, and trousers draped over a boulder twenty feet away. His pistol was over there too. "We're a *lot* more capable than a scrawny kid who's still in school. A scrawny kid who's turning his back on his own kind and trying to become one of *them*." The mercenary thrust a finger upward at the closest mageship, the black-hulled yacht that belonged to King Uthari.

"Ah." Jak didn't know what else to say. He hadn't been openly and brazenly learning magic, nor could he remember using it around any of the mercenaries, but the word might have gotten out.

"I thought they *killed* wild ones," another mercenary said, the one with a fondness for caressing the butt of his pistol.

"If they won't, *we* could," the third man said.

Jak blinked. That had escalated quickly.

"That's not necessary. I'm not a threat to you, and I'm delightful and entertaining. Perhaps you'd like to see me perform? I had to memorize several passages from *The Retribution of the Vexing Vixen* by Egarath the Eternal for my World Cultures and Literature class. I remember most of the words, though I was admittedly more interested in drawing maps while the professor was lecturing. Do you need anything mapped? That's what I was studying before I got swept up in all this and dragged off against my will. I'm not even getting paid to be here, not like you fine mercenaries are." Jak smiled as he babbled, hoping they would see him as charming, or at least too unthreatening to bother harassing—or killing.

"How long until you start ordering us around, boy?" The original speaker curled his upper lip. "Forcing us to do things just because you think you can. Because you've got magic."

Jak, doubting any amount of charm would work on the men, made his way toward his clothing. He knew how to make a magical barrier to defend himself, but he hadn't yet tried to keep it up while someone was shooting at him. The idea of having to do so made him nervous.

Thus far, he'd always had someone nearby to protect his back in a fight, and he'd mostly battled well-defined enemies, such as attacking wizards or ferocious predators or evil dragons. Even though those foes had been more powerful than these men, the idea of facing his own kind—people he was supposed to be working with—made him uneasy.

"Not so quick, kid." The mercenary blocked him from reaching his clothes. "We've decided there are already too many mages in the world, and it's our duty to cut the population down."

Splashes came from the water. Shikari had discovered the delight of swimming and wasn't paying attention to Jak and the burgeoning trouble on the bank. Having a two-month-old dragon at his side wouldn't necessarily drive fear into his enemies' hearts, but Shikari had proven useful in battles before. He was smart and had inherent magic.

"Listen, fellows." Jak lifted his hands. "We're on the same side. I'm no different from you." He lowered his voice. "I'd also like to see the mage kings overthrown and our people given the right to rule themselves."

"Sure, you would. That's why you're trying to become one of them." The mercenary threw a punch at Jak's face.

Jak ducked and scrambled backward. His first instinct was to keep running, but he made himself pause to envision great snow-capped mountains emerging from the ground all around him. It was his mental tool for summoning a magical barrier.

The man's first punch had swept through empty air, but when he lunged closer and threw a second one, he found the barrier fully formed—and adequate for blocking him. Though nothing was visible in the air, his knuckles bashed against the obstacle as if they'd met a brick wall.

The mercenary cried out, but the yelp of pain quickly turned into curses as he gripped his battered knuckles. "Mage!"

His two buddies drew their pistols and pointed them at Jak.

He crouched, instincts again yelling at him to sprint away or at least fling himself behind a rock for cover. Doubt made his barrier waver, and he stepped back, his heel catching on a rock. He flailed, almost ending up on his butt. A squawk came from the water—Shikari—and the mercenaries glanced over instead of pulling their triggers.

Jak scowled at himself and used their brief distraction to re-form his barrier, making the mountains so dense and thick around him that they knocked the men backward. One stood close enough to the pool that when he stumbled, he slipped off the rock and pitched into the water.

Another man scowled fiercely at Jak and fired. Filled with magical charges, the pistol lacked the boom of a black-powder weapon, but that didn't make it any less deadly. Fortunately, Jak had found his concentration, and his barrier remained intact. The blue charge bounced off and dissipated before striking anything.

Shikari squawked again. Maybe it was supposed to be a roar. His young, reedy voice wasn't ferocious in the least. Still, having him swimming toward the men encouraged them to leave the area with only backward glares. The one who'd fallen in the water glared particularly icily at Jak.

He dragged a bare arm across his face as Shikari climbed out of the water and padded through Jak's barrier as if it weren't there to stand at his side.

"Thanks for the help." Jak glanced around the camp and up at the mageships, afraid Malek or Rivlen or someone else whose good opinion mattered would have seen how clumsily he'd defended himself. He'd fought against *dragons.* Why had he been nervous against mundane humans with no power beyond their fists and firearms?

Because it hadn't been long since he'd been exactly like them, and the idea of his own kind hating him and casting him out was distressing? He sighed.

Shikari shook himself like a dog, flinging water droplets everywhere.

"We need to find an elder dragon to teach you." Jak looked wistfully toward the portal, but from what he'd learned thus far, all of those elder dragons might be dead, leaving behind only the younger dragons, the brown-and-gray mottled ones that liked to slay humans. The last thing he wanted was for one of them to teach Shikari how to be like them. "How are you going to learn how to fly without a nice mama dragon to teach you?"

Shikari sniffed at Jak's boot and nibbled on the laces. He'd started eating more than insects as he'd grown larger, but he hadn't lost his interest in chewing on everything from boots to hats to tent flaps.

Movement by the portal caught Jak's eye. Two mages in green uniforms—Queen Vorsha's troops—gripped the arms of a familiar man, marching him toward other green-uniformed mages, some with oval skyboards tucked under their arms.

"Uh oh," Jak whispered.

Their prisoner was Zethron, the man who'd helped Jak and the others on Vran and who'd returned with them because he was an explorer who'd wanted to see the *First World*. He'd helped Mother learn more about Jitaruvak, the plant King Uthari wanted her to find, and Zethron had also helped her discover the secret of working dragon steel. He'd been a guide for them and even brought Jak the map of their world that they'd used to navigate there. They owed him a lot.

Since arriving, Zethron had been lying low, trying to avoid the notice of any of the mages as he learned the language and earned funds for his travels by gambling with mercenaries. As he'd promised, Malek hadn't turned him over to Uthari, but it looked like it hadn't mattered. Someone else had found him.

"What do you think they'll do to him?" Jak whispered as the soldiers directed Zethron onto a skyboard and flew toward one of the green-hulled ships with him. A split lip and disheveled clothing suggested they'd already *done* things to him.

Shikari wasn't paying attention. Instead, he pounced on a butterfly that had made the mistake of landing within his reach. He chomped it down.

Jak grimaced. "That's exactly what I'm afraid they'll do to him."

"I've turned the acidic gas into a liquid," Jadora said, "and done a few experiments to prove that if you bathe dragon steel in it for at least ten minutes—ten minutes and twelve seconds to be precise—the surface will become malleable. If you leave it in the solution for longer, the acid somehow permeates it further, and eventually the whole bar can be manipulated. A blue glow comes over it, indicating the process is working. Interestingly, the dragon steel can continue to be manipulated for approximately two hours after it's been taken out of the acid bath—the glow gradually fades away, as does its softness, and it returns to its ultra-hard state, unable to be affected by any degree of heat or damaged by contact with the hardest substances."

"Fascinating," the blacksmith mage Homgor said, watching as she demonstrated.

They were in the laboratory tent that King Uthari had ordered set up for Jadora, the amount of equipment inside now rivaling that of any university lab back in Uth.

"I've long fantasized about being able to manipulate dragon steel." Homgor adjusted his spectacles as he peered at the bar from all sides, the corner recently melted by the liquid compound.

He had the powerful muscles and broad shoulders of any blacksmith, mage or mundane, but his head reminded her more of her fellow professors back at the university. He had curious eyes, a pencil tucked behind his ear, and wispy gray hair combed straight back from his forehead. "I can't tell you how much I look forward to making weapons and tools out of it."

Jadora made herself smile, though the idea of mages gaining even *more* weapons and tools with which to enslave terrene humans made her insides churn. The fact that she was *helping* them brought tears to her eyes when she let herself dwell on it.

She still wished she could grab Jak and disappear into the jungle, but where would they go, with civilization so far away? And how long would it be before King Uthari sent Malek to hunt them down? After all, she hadn't yet found the one thing Uthari truly wanted: Jitaruvak and the life-extending formula that could supposedly be synthesized from the plant.

The tent flap stirred, and Jak ran in so quickly he almost tripped over the black-uniformed mages standing guard inside. They were another reason that Jadora and Jak couldn't have escaped into the jungle, even if she'd thought it wise. Thanks to the extreme value of the bars of dragon steel they'd brought back from Vran, dragon steel that now sat in a chest next to her worktable, her tent was guarded around the clock, not only by mercenaries but by powerful mages.

"Mother, we've got a problem," Jak blurted before noticing the blacksmith.

Homgor straightened, adjusted his spectacles again, and regarded Jak with a flicker of annoyance. His fingers reached protectively for the acid formula, as if to gather it to his chest and protect it from the excessive exuberance of youth.

"A new one?" Jadora attempted a smile, but it fell flat. Jak was in nothing but his underwear, with his clothing clutched to his chest, and concern haunted his eyes. "What is it?"

Jak glanced uncertainly at Homgor, then whispered, "It's about Zethron."

"Allow me to take these items to protect them from young elbows, and perhaps, while you speak, I can also protect your notes from mishaps." Homgor plucked up the bar, her vials, and her papers related to the acid, then headed for the far side of the tent. He paused along the way to slide a loving hand over the locked chest, but only for a moment before finding another table and hunching over it to peruse the papers.

"What is it?" Jadora asked quietly, doubting they had to worry about Homgor gossiping—or even being aware of their discussion. The guards might be another matter.

"Two of Vorsha's mages caught him somewhere. They just took him up to their ship."

Jadora closed her eyes. All along, she'd feared that some of the mages would stumble across Zethron, realize he was from another world, and suspect him of being a spy.

With dozens of mageships in the sky from eight different kingdoms, all here in Zewnath to try to gain access to the portal and the valuable resources that might be found on other worlds, it had seemed that Zethron might escape notice. In addition to all the mageship crews, there were hundreds of mercenaries from different units and even a coalition of roamer pirates stationed around the portal to patrol the area and keep druids from getting close—and to keep an eye on each other.

"We have to help him." Jak gripped her arm. "He helped *us*."

"I know." Worse than that, Zethron seemed to have a crush on Jadora. She worried that he'd followed her back to Torvil for more reasons than wanting to explore their world. Even though she'd warned him of the dangers, she knew she would feel guilty if something happened to him. However inadvertent, it would be partially her fault. "But it's not as if we can stage a rescue. We would need help."

Without a mage, they couldn't even get up to the flying ships. Storming past dozens of soldiers to break someone out of a cell would be impossible.

Jadora rubbed her face as she debated how to get in touch with Malek and how to ask him to help with Zethron. But even if he could help, *would* he? He'd said he wouldn't mind if Zethron and Jadora had a romantic relationship, that it might keep Uthari from suspecting she and *Malek* had a relationship, but she hadn't believed him. Malek glared at Zethron every time he was in the tent with her. Zidarr weren't supposed to fall in love or even have relationships with women, something Uthari had reminded her of several times, but…

She rubbed her face again. She was a widow in her forties, and the sexiest thing she wore was a lab coat, the pockets bulging with tools and vials. How had she ended up with two men interested in her?

"I can ask Malek." Jak touched his temple, indicating he meant he would use telepathy.

Jadora hoped he wasn't mentioning that ability to everyone he passed. Her father had been in the tent earlier, lecturing her on the evils of using magic instead of doing honest work with one's hands, and how only those who dedicated their lives to that honest labor earned a place in the Eternal Paradise. The words had been prompted by Father learning that Jak was being tutored by Malek. For some reason, *she'd* gotten the lecture. Not that she wanted Jak to have to endure it. It wasn't as if he'd had any choice in developing the ability to use magic.

"Or I could ask Rivlen," Jak added, unaware of her thoughts.

Jadora lowered her hand. She hadn't thought of asking Captain Rivlen and was momentarily taken with the idea—Rivlen had no love for Zethron either, but she wouldn't care if the man had feelings for Jadora. Still, what could Rivlen do? For that matter, what could *Malek* do? It would be one thing if Uthari's troops had captured Zethron, but would either of them risk an international incident by rescuing him from another kingdom's fleet?

"I don't see how Malek or Rivlen could get Zethron back from Vorsha's people," Jadora said. "Just because the various kingdom fleets have a putative truce at the moment doesn't mean they'll hand over prisoners to each other."

"But Malek helped us rescue a prisoner from an enemy before. Tezi."

Jadora glanced at the guards, worried they were listening to the conversation and Jak's revelation of what was not, as far as she knew, widely known information. But they were nudging each other and pointing to Homgor as he dribbled acid onto the block of dragon steel. Maybe they hoped to be given some of the first weapons made with the stuff.

"He and Tonovan are in the same fleet. They aren't enemies," Jadora said, though she didn't deny that Malek and Tonovan were far from friends.

"Yes, but you know what I mean. We have to get his help and do *something*." Belief shone from Jak's eyes, the belief that Malek would be able and willing to solve their problem.

Jadora wasn't so sure. Just because Malek had taken Jak under his wing to teach him—believing Jak could eventually be of use to his master, Uthari—didn't mean he would risk starting an international incident because his pupil wanted a favor. Or because *she* wanted a favor.

"They can't have captured Zethron for any good reason," Jak added. "They may torture him just because he's not one of us. Or because they want to know all about the mission we went on and what's out there."

"I know." And Jadora did want to help Zethron. She just didn't think they would be able to get any of Uthari's mages involved in a rescue. "I—"

The tent flap stirred again, and she broke off.

"Malek is out there," Jak whispered, his eyes brightening again. "We can ask him. Uhm, maybe. He's with someone else. Someone with an aura as powerful as his."

"Tonovan?" Jadora grimaced, but her son would have been able to identify Tonovan.

Jak shook his head. "Someone I don't know."

Someone held the tent flap open, and the side of Malek's brown jacket was visible. Jadora could make out his voice. It sounded like he was explaining something, or maybe giving a tour, though his tone was cool and aloof rather than congenial. Not that zidarr were known for their congeniality.

Malek stepped inside, followed by a shaven-headed, bronze-skinned man in a silver uniform with black trim. Those were King Jutuk's colors, weren't they? Jadora had seen a few of their silver-hulled ships sail into the area, but thus far, they hadn't fielded any of the mercenary teams or made demands regarding the portal. As the ruler of a small island kingdom in the north, Jutuk might simply have sent troops to see what was going on and make sure he wasn't left out.

"Lord Malek, Admiral Bakir," the mage guards at the entrance said, saluting both men.

Malek twitched a finger to acknowledge them. The admiral ignored them and looked around.

In contrast to his shaven head, he had eyebrows like caterpillars that appeared ready to crawl off his face at any moment. When he squinted, they drew together into a single long furry brow. His clean-shaven jaw drew attention to numerous old scars, and the breadth of his shoulders suggested he could go toe to toe with Homgor in a smithing contest. As fit and muscular as Malek was, he seemed small next to the boulder of a man.

"This is the laboratory where the research on manipulating dragon steel is ongoing." Malek spread an arm to indicate the equipment and Homgor. He only met Jadora's and Jak's eyes briefly, as if he didn't want to draw attention to them. Maybe there was a reason for that. "Lord Homgor will attempt to make something soon."

"Something simple, yes," Homgor murmured without looking at them. "The king has already made a request."

Malek stepped back toward the entrance, as if he was already done with this portion of his tour, but the admiral lifted a hand and stepped farther into the tent.

"And are these the archaeologists who helped you find and activate the gateway to the stars?" Bakir pointed at Jadora and Jak.

Helped him find it? Jadora knew it wasn't important, but she couldn't help but feel indignant that others believed she and Jak had voluntarily come to work for Uthari—and Malek—and that they'd only *assisted* in locating the portal. She'd devoted the last five years of her life to finding it. Her husband had devoted even *more* years to it before being killed for what he knew.

"They are archaeologists working for King Uthari, yes." Malek held Jadora's gaze longer this time, and she tried to stifle her indignant thoughts. With his mind-reading abilities, he already knew all about her feelings, and she didn't need to ooze them all over this new admiral, who was doubtless as adept at mind reading as Malek. "Professor Freedar and her son Jakstor," he added, reluctantly giving the introduction.

Bakir smirked at Jadora. *If you want more credit and a place in the history books, you should come work for King Jutuk,* he spoke into her mind. *Whatever Uthari is paying you, we could pay more. And I'd personally protect you if his loyal servants were miffed at your departure.* Bakir glanced at Malek.

Malek squinted. It wasn't likely that he could hear another mage's telepathic words for Jadora, but he would know from her response that something was going on. And her response was to grimace and think about how little she desired to trade one master for another.

No, thank you, she replied.

Just because you're born into one king's realm doesn't mean you have to stay there. Where did you find all that dragon steel? And how exactly is it manipulated? Bakir's eyes closed to slits as he held her gaze, and he sent some magical compulsion that prompted her to want to thrust all the answers he sought toward him.

She clamped down on that urge, well aware by now how mage manipulation worked. Even being aware of it, she struggled to resist it, to keep from thinking about Vran and the people there, the ziggurat made from dragon steel, and the acidic gas that wafted out of a slit in the top.

Annoyed, she pushed the thoughts aside and blanked her mind. Bakir's squint deepened, and pain accompanied his compulsion. Something like razor-sharp fork tines raked through her mind.

She didn't think she gasped aloud, though the abrupt pain made her stiffen and want to, but Malek gripped Bakir's arm, and the pain halted.

Jak stepped forward and blurted, "What are you doing to my mother?"

Bakir was the one to gasp and stagger back from Malek, though Malek didn't release his grip on the man's arm. Fury contorted Malek's usually calm and hard-to-read face, and for an instant, murder burned in his black eyes.

Bakir spun to face him, anger replacing his pain as he seemed to get a protective barrier up around himself.

All trace of the admiral, including the pain, disappeared from Jadora's mind, and she sucked in a relieved breath, though she didn't relax. The two powerful mages were doing more than glaring at each other. Though it was hard for her, a sense-dead woman with no aptitude for magic, to tell *what* they were doing, even she could feel the magical power crackling in the air around them as they challenged each other. Or were they full-on attacking each other?

Jak shifted uncertainly from foot to foot and lifted a hand, as if to help Malek. Jadora stepped forward and gripped his shoulder in warning.

Even though an admiral was surely powerful and might be a real threat to Malek, she didn't want her son getting involved. *Especially* because the admiral was powerful, she didn't want her son involved. Jak didn't need any more enemies. Only if it looked like Malek would lose would she let him step in. Maybe. She would prefer to step in herself and throw a vial of acid at Bakir's face instead of letting Jak garner a powerful mage's wrath.

She dipped a hand into one of her pockets to make sure she had a vial handy. With so many enemies about, she tried to ensure she was ready to defend herself at all times.

"If you want an alliance with King Uthari," Malek said, his tone an icy growl, his face tight with tension, "I'd think you would know better than to attack one of his guests, especially while I'm *right here* watching you."

Bakir scowled, his own face tight, the tendons in his thick neck standing out, as if he were trying to lift hundreds of pounds, not trading magical jabs with an opponent. "A *guest?* That's not how *she* sees herself. Don't try to tell me that these aren't prisoners that he's forced into working for him. Forgive me if I thought they might prefer a more generous benefactor."

Malek scoffed. "And that's Jutuk? Has he started paying all the concubines he keeps to service his ravenous appetite?"

"Of course not, but he donates to the Church of Thanok and ensures his universities are among the best in the world. Any scholar would be honored to work for him."

"Step outside, Admiral," Malek said. "Now that your tour is

complete, I'll take you to Uthari. If an alliance is truly what you wish."

"You had better hope it is, zidarr. Uthari has Vorsha, Zaruk, and Dy all working together and angling for him and that portal. He needs help."

"Rarely. We've thus far defeated their combined forces without trouble."

Bakir allowed himself to be shooed out. Malek strode out after him, the tent flap closing behind them.

Jak swore and whispered, "I wanted to talk to him about Zethron."

Jadora touched her head, a headache lingering though Bakir's attack had disappeared. "I think he's busy and we'll have to figure something out by ourselves."

She'd no sooner voiced the words than Malek spoke into her mind.

I apologize for reacting so slowly to the admiral's attack. I'm not surprised that he hoped to steal information from your mind, but I didn't think he would so brazenly try to extract it while I stood next to him.

It's all right. Jadora thought his reaction had been impressively quick, especially since the admiral hadn't outwardly done anything to indicate an attack.

It is not. You are still under my protection.

I'm glad.

I must, however, inform you that Uthari wants to see you after his meeting with Bakir. I'll return shortly to take you to his yacht.

Is it about Zethron? Jadora asked.

No. Malek seemed surprised by the question. *I am not sure what it's about, but he didn't sound pleased this morning when he demanded to see you. I will accompany you to make sure...*

Jadora raised her eyebrows at the long pause. To make sure... what? To protect her? Against his own master? Would he?

I will accompany you in case you need someone to speak on your behalf, Malek said.

That didn't sound promising. *Is it a trial?*

He probably just wants information.

Jadora didn't let herself think about the kerzor, the disc she'd brought back from Vran that could be inserted into a person's skull to keep them from accessing their ability to perform magic. She'd kept it, aware that if it could be replicated, the discs could be a powerful weapon against mages. If Malek found out that she still had that thing and had been contemplating how more could be made, he would be irked. Uthari would be furious and would punish her. He'd already threatened to *get rid of* her if she succeeded in drawing Malek into a romantic relationship. What would he do if she fomented rebellion and created the tools to make such a rebellion a possibility?

Any chance I can opt out of going to visit him? Jadora asked.

I'm afraid not.

She shook her head. She'd liked spending time with Malek a lot more when they'd been exploring other worlds and he hadn't been at Uthari's beck and call. Oh, he was always loyal to his king, no matter where he was, but sometimes, Jadora could forget that he wasn't his own man. She could believe that, if Malek were forced to choose, he would choose her over Uthari.

A fantasy, alas.

2

Captain Xeva Rivlen stood in King Uthari's office on the *Serene Waters* with her hands clasped behind her back, listening as Lord Malek, General Tonovan, and Uthari discussed the portal and how the various kingdoms wanted access to it with Admiral Bakir and Zidarr Prolix, representatives from King Jutuk's fleet. The yacht's captain was also in the cabin, but like Rivlen, he listened and did not speak.

Uthari and Bakir were doing most of the talking while Prolix, a man far terser than his name implied, watched Lord Malek intently. Malek appeared unperturbed, but he also kept a steady eye on Prolix. Maybe the two zidarr were fantasizing about squaring off against each other. Their impressive auras promised that would be quite the battle.

Rivlen was aware that everyone in the cabin, with the possible exception of the yacht captain, was more powerful than she. It surprised her that she'd been invited to the meeting.

"You realize, Your Majesty," Bakir said, "that *I'm* the only one making an overture of friendship toward you, on my king's behalf, of course."

"Is that what this is?" Uthari didn't seem tense, not here in his domain, with his officers prepared to back him up if Jutuk's men tried anything, but he also didn't appear pleased by the situation. "An overture of friendship? You started the meeting by saying that if I didn't heed your advice, I'd find myself and my fleet annihilated by the end of the week."

"Yes. It was friendly advice about annihilation." Bakir smirked tightly and tilted his head. "And I thought you would appreciate that we're risking the wrath of the rest of the fleets by coming to warn you that every other ruler is contemplating putting aside their differences and banding together to end you and your control over the portal."

"They would be foolish to make such an attempt while we have enemies here in Zewnath, enemies who threaten to take the portal away so that *none* of us may use it." Uthari stretched a hand toward his large porthole, the lush greenery of the jungle visible below.

He meant the druids, of course. Since Rivlen had been with Malek on Vran, she'd missed their attacks on the camp—their attempts to steal the portal—but her officers on the *Star Flyer* had filled her in.

"None of us can use it currently," Bakir said, "so it would hardly matter to us if the druids captured it."

"Which is no doubt why your fleet, as well as every other fleet, stood aside and did nothing when they attempted to get it," Uthari said coolly.

"We have no grievances with the druids. Besides, it was clear as soon as you started using the portal to shoot extremely powerful lightning out into the jungle to slay your enemies that you needed no assistance. If you had, we would have been pleased to offer it, assuming you agreed to do what you promised from the beginning." Bakir's eyes closed to slits. "Let mages from other fleets go through the portal to explore with your teams. Your *team.*" He glanced at Malek.

Uthari leaned back in his chair. "I'll assume from your presence here that your people have been unable to find the druids and the other key to the portal." His eyelids drooped. "I know you've been looking."

"Many have, Your Majesty. You can hardly blame us. But you're correct that we haven't yet located their base or acquired the key. What can we offer you to be allowed to send officers through the portal with your zidarr and his team?" Bakir flattened his hand to his chest and tilted his head toward Prolix, making it clear which officers he had in mind.

Rivlen watched Malek, wondering how he would feel about such men going along with him, powerful magic users who might place themselves at odds with his and Uthari's desires instead of obediently following commands as Rivlen and the mercenaries had. She wouldn't have minded more mage allies along when they'd faced off against those dragons, something that seemed inevitable on these other worlds, but mages from other fleets might be more inclined to hinder than help Malek.

Throughout the discussion, Malek's face remained a mask, giving away nothing of his thoughts.

"What can you offer? I would want a written promise of assistance against the druids and any other fleets who might take action on this *annihilation* plan you've spoken of, as well as a promise that you would agree that my chosen team leader—" Uthari nodded toward Malek, "—would be in charge of the mission and that your officers would obey him as they would a senior military commander."

Uthari must have been thinking similar thoughts as Rivlen. She was surprised he was offering to work with Jutuk's people at all, regardless of what they might promise. Maybe Uthari had spies among the other fleets and knew that Bakir spoke the truth, that the others truly were planning to move against him. Even though he'd found a way to force the portal to shoot out lightning, the way it voluntarily did for Jak, Uthari and his officers couldn't stand against the might of so many other powerful mages. New ships arrived every day. By now, there were hundreds, if not thousands, of mages in the area.

Bakir sneered as he glanced at Malek, whose face remained impassive as he stood with his back to a wall, his arms folded over his chest.

"Though I'm not convinced a *zidarr* is an appropriate team leader—I'd argue that a military commander with vast experience leading men should be in charge of an excursion—I agree that one of your people could lead the missions." Bakir forced his sneer to change into a smile. "As long as King Jutuk receives a share of the spoils and equal access to any knowledge that might be acquired by your *guests* in the laboratory tent below." Bakir bowed to Uthari, letting him know how much he'd learned of the goings on around here.

Malek's face seemed to grow a touch frostier at the emphasis on *guests*, but that might have been Rivlen's imagination.

"You think we'll find more chests of dragon steel out there?" Uthari asked dryly.

"It's clear that you believe you'll find *something* of value, or you wouldn't continue to send your team through the portal, especially when powerful magical creatures like to fly or trundle out of the thing to attack your ships and kill whoever's in the area."

"We're coming up with a solution for that," Uthari said.

Rivlen arched her eyebrows. She hadn't heard about that but hoped it was true. Even though she enjoyed going into battle and pitting herself against powerful enemies, she liked it to be for a reason, to gain something personally or for the good of the kingdom. Risking their men to kill dumb animals—admittedly powerful dumb animals—was not what she had in mind when she envisioned glorious battles.

"Will it be crafted by the other *guest* you've acquired?" Bakir arched his eyebrows. "I hear Zaruk has learned that you've got one of his valued engineers slaving away, building a little boat to sail through the portal for you."

"His *valued* engineer? Even his own brother has been happy to cast him away. Not very noble for a zidarr." Uthari eyed Prolix, though he was talking about Night Wrath.

Bakir opened his mouth, no doubt to again show off how much intelligence he'd gathered, but Uthari lifted his hand.

"Enough, Admiral. If you agree to the terms I've set, you may participate in the next excursion. Choose no more than two men to go along with Lord Malek. *If* they are obedient and helpful on the trip, I will agree that you'll receive a share of the spoils."

"An *equal* share of the spoils," Bakir said.

"Very well."

Bakir and Prolix bowed to Uthari and headed for the door, Prolix keeping an eye on Malek the whole way out. Bakir ignored Malek in favor of contemplating Rivlen's chest on his way out.

She clenched her jaw, immediately dreading going on a mission with the man. He was as powerful as Tonovan and might be as much of an ass.

"I trust you expect Malek to ensure those two meet with an untimely end on the mission, Your Majesty?" Tonovan drawled from his seat, his leg flung over the armrest. He wasn't wearing an eyepatch today. Maybe he'd decided to show off his scar.

Uthari snorted softly. The thought must have crossed his mind.

Rivlen glanced at Malek, whom she'd always perceived as being honorable, and wasn't surprised that he gave no indication that he would relish arranging the deaths of teammates, even teammates who had manipulated themselves into being invited along.

"They may be useful," Uthari told Malek. "You keep running into dragons out there."

"Yes, Your Majesty."

"Useful to throw in the dragon's maw while the rest of the team gets away, right? Bakir would look good dangling from fangs." Tonovan tapped one of his canines and grinned.

"Are you still irked at him for getting the best of you at Mount Crown Fire?" Uthari asked, referencing a war that had taken place before Rivlen had been old enough to join the fleet.

"Not at all, Your Majesty. And I got the best of *him*."

"I shall hope that you have no trouble working with him, General," Uthari said. "I'm sending you along with Malek on this next mission."

Malek's face had been bland and indifferent up until that moment. At this news, his eyes sharpened, and he looked intently at Uthari.

Rivlen couldn't tell if it was because he disapproved and didn't want to work with Tonovan or if it was because he was imagining the *general* dangling from a dragon's fangs.

"Oh?" Tonovan eyed Malek warily.

"While I admit that having more firepower along could be useful, Your Majesty," Malek said, his tone giving away nothing of his thoughts, his face already regaining its neutral expression, "don't you think you should keep as many of your strongest mages here with you as possible? As you've admitted, many of the other fleets aren't happy with you."

"I can handle them." Uthari clasped his hands together, set them on his desk, and leaned forward in his chair. "If you and Professor Freedar are correct, you now know which symbol leads to a world called Nargnoth, and what I want is there."

"We believe so," Malek said.

"I want to stack the odds in your favor. I *want* you to succeed."

Rivlen couldn't tell if Uthari felt the team hadn't succeeded thus far. They hadn't brought back the plant he sought, but dragon-steel weapons, a chest of the magical metal, and the secret of working it were even greater prizes, as far as she was concerned. Uthari had to be pleased with his senior zidarr.

"I understand and will, of course, work with whomever you deem best for the team." Malek looked toward Rivlen. "Will Captain Rivlen also be accompanying us?"

She didn't know whether to hope for that or not, given that she hated the idea of being in close proximity to Tonovan, but if the mercenary Tezi came along with her magic-repulsing battle-axe, maybe they would get the opportunity to do something Rivlen had wanted to do for years. End Tonovan's career—and his life.

He deserved that fate, and perhaps Uthari would even believe her worthy of taking his place as fleet commander. If she received such a promotion at such a young age, it would ensure her family was proud of her.

Tonovan smirked over at her. Judging by the way he openly ogled her chest—it was even worse than the admiral's speculative gaze—he wanted her to come along for reasons that had nothing to do with her competence as a mage and an officer.

She bared her teeth at him. *Let* him try something. Oh, she knew he was still more powerful than she—unfortunately—but if she had Malek and a mercenary with a dragon-steel axe nearby, she might finally get her revenge.

"Not this time." Uthari turned his contemplative gaze toward Rivlen. "I have another mission for her, one for which a ship's commander is better suited."

Though the thought of a special mission was intriguing, Rivlen didn't feel the instant elation that she normally would have. For one thing, Uthari's gaze wasn't that friendly, and it made her wonder if he was irked with her for not performing as adequately as she should. For another, if she wasn't along with the team, Malek wouldn't have an ally against the potential enemies going with him—*powerful* enemies. Even though Tonovan worked for Uthari, he hated Malek and would destroy him if he could. And while she didn't know if Jutuk's men felt the same way, they might try to get rid of Malek simply because it would be an opportunity to deprive a rival kingdom of its most powerful zidarr.

If that happened, what would befall Jak and Jadora? Rivlen assumed they would also go along on the mission. Jak was developing his talents, but he was still young and had only started training his mage skills recently. Tonovan could flick a finger and end his life. Though Jak was young and impetuous, he was loyal to his comrades, and Rivlen had come to like him. The thought of his death disturbed her.

"A mission, Your Majesty?" Rivlen asked, realizing Uthari might expect a response from her.

The way he kept gazing at her—studying her—made her think uneasily of the Vran mission. Facing those extremely powerful mages had left her with feelings of inadequacy, and she longed to prove herself worthy of her current command and future promotions. Jak, Jadora, and Malek would have to watch out for themselves. Malek was more than capable. He wouldn't let anyone outmaneuver him. And Jak and Jadora... They would just have to stay out of Tonovan's way. She didn't even know why she was worrying about them.

"We have a druid problem," Uthari said.

"Yes, Your Majesty," Rivlen said.

"First off, they keep trying to take the portal. *My* portal." Uthari pointed his thumb at himself. "Not only is it vexing, but any victories they have against us, no matter how small, make us look weak in front of the others. I want you to take the *Star Flyer* and two other ships and deal with them. Find their base and drive them out of the area. Kill them or burn the jungle down around them so that they have nowhere to hide. I don't care which, but I don't want any of them within hundreds of miles of here."

"Yes, Your Majesty."

"I also want you to find their key—the dragon-headed medallion that operates the portal." Uthari slid the one he had, the one he'd taken from Jak and Jadora, out of his pocket to show her. "I don't believe theirs is hidden under gold plating, but it should look the same as this one and feel the same to your magical senses. I don't know where they got it, and I don't care. *I* want to be the only one to control access to the portal."

"I understand, Your Majesty."

It was a daunting mission, since the druids had magic users as powerful as the zidarr, but Rivlen was up for it. She relished the challenge and loved the thought of being trusted to command this mission. Not only would she captain the *Star Flyer*, but she would have two other ship's captains and their crews working under her. This would be her first multi-ship command, and she intended to succeed.

"Good, Captain," Uthari said softly, holding her gaze and smiling for the first time.

Rivlen didn't think she'd let her mental guard down so he could read her thoughts, but maybe her face was betraying her and letting everyone know exactly what she craved. Tonovan must have caught the gist for, unsupportive ass that he was, he rolled his eyes.

"I know what you want, Captain," Uthari added. "*Who* you want to prove yourself to, and I want to facilitate that."

She almost said that he was the only one she wanted to loyally serve and impress, but Uthari switched to telepathy to put an image in her mind. Her stern father who'd always wanted a boy and had gotten a girl instead, who'd hoped that she might, even with that handicap, as he'd called it, impress Uthari enough to gain entry into zidarr training. But she'd failed the tests. She'd only been twelve at the time, but her father hadn't forgiven her. He'd barely spoken to her since then, even though she'd trained hard, entered the fleet as soon as possible, and climbed the ranks faster than any woman and all but a few men in the kingdom's history. She'd long hoped to bring enough honor to her family to have him say that he loved her and was proud of her.

Her throat tightened at this reminder of emotions that she tried to keep buried deep.

"Yes, Your Majesty," Rivlen whispered, ignoring Tonovan, wanting to pretend he wasn't in the office instead of peering over at her, fiddling with a pencil as he watched her with intermittent interest.

"Take some of the mercenaries with you on your mission, Captain. The ones with those axes that nobody's stolen from them yet." Uthari snorted and glanced at Malek, as if they'd had a previous discussion on the matter. Had they? "They might as well put them to use. You'll likely need to send parties down into the druid tunnels to find them and get the key."

Rivlen nodded in agreement, though she would lead such a party herself. She wouldn't risk *mercenaries* being responsible for whether she succeeded or failed.

"See if you can find where Colonel Sorath went while you're out there." Uthari's expression turned sour, and he looked at Malek. "He's been missing since before you got back. All the interrogator I sent to the Thorn Company camp learned was that Lieutenant Vinjo made another of those damn stealth devices that can hide a person, even from mage senses, and those women gave it to him. They keep saying he fled to the coast, but even they don't believe that when you pry into their minds. He's around here somewhere, plotting something. I'll bet Tonovan's other eye that he's working with the druids."

"Really, Your Majesty." Tonovan's finger twitched toward the mangled scar on his face. "I'd prefer to keep my remaining eye.

And find a dragon and see if I could talk it into rebuilding my other one. The legends say they're powerful healers."

"If that's true," Uthari said, "you should be kissing the grimy talons of Jak's hatchling instead of harassing his mother."

"Harassing? Me? I wouldn't dream of giving her anything she doesn't want." The ass didn't even try to hide his salacious smirk from the king.

Rivlen wished Uthari would punish him for his transgressions against women, but he seemed content to look the other way. So long as Uthari looked the other way when Rivlen took her revenge on the man.

Judging by the frosty look Malek delivered to the back of Tonovan's head, a rare glimpse behind the stoic zidarr mask, Rivlen wasn't the only one fantasizing about doing away with Tonovan. She had a hunch that one of those two wouldn't be coming back from their mission.

As the sun sank below the horizon, turning the western sky orange and the clouds pink, Sorath stood on a cliff near a mountain peak. From his position, he looked down on the dragon portal, the mercenary encampment, and more than forty mageships hovering in the area.

Behind him, a cave led into a tunnel, one of many in the labyrinth of passageways that the druids had hollowed out beneath the earth. Some had existed for millennia, and others had been newly excavated with the help of their magical boring crystals. They'd expanded their underground warren in the area around the portal, but they could use the crystals to close the entrances after using them, making the tunnels difficult for even mages to find.

It had been several days since the druid leaders had elicited from Sorath a promise to assassinate not only King Uthari, a man he'd longed to kill since he'd played a role in the annihilation of his company, but also the zidarrs Yidar and Malek. Sorath had recovered from the torture he'd endured at Uthari's hands and had been ready to start on his mission immediately, but the druids wanted him to wait until they retrieved their ally, Tovorka, who was now being held captive on one of Uthari's ships.

Days earlier, Sorath had helped capture the druid. If Sorath hadn't detested Uthari so much, it would have bothered him that he'd agreed to switch sides, but he believed the world would be a better place with Uthari dead. He wished he could kill *all* the kings and help Jak and Jadora with their dream of freeing terrene humans from mage rule. But killing a powerful wizard was no easy task, and if he wasn't very careful, he would die attempting it. As it was, he highly doubted he could survive this mission. All three men were extremely powerful, and Yidar and Malek were also gifted weapons masters. Getting the best of them would take a great deal of luck as well as skill.

Though he didn't hear anything or catch movement out of the corner of his eye, Sorath's instincts told him someone was approaching. He turned in time to see Kywatha walk out of the cave.

"Is it time to go?" Sorath touched the dragon-steel dagger he'd given a place on his belt next to his black-powder pistol.

Normally, he eschewed magical weapons, preferring reliable mundane technology that always worked, but he knew the value of the blade the druids had lent him. At least *some* of its value. Such weapons were so rare in this world that few grasped all of their secrets. At the least, he knew it would keep druids and mages from reading his thoughts. It should also protect him from many magical attacks.

"If our team succeeds tonight, you may go tomorrow," Kywatha said, speaking in Dhoran so he could understand.

She joined him on the ledge and clasped her hands behind her back as she looked out toward the camp. She had a voluptuous figure under her woven grass tunic, but lately, when Sorath thought of women, Captain Ferroki's face came to mind. He hoped she and Thorn Company found a way to escape Zewnath alive. Even if he didn't.

"Your team? Druids going to rescue your friend?" Sorath didn't know if Tovorka was still alive and wondered if the druids even knew, or if they were hoping for the best.

"Yes."

"I could go with them. If they're caught or discovered, the distraction might help me complete *my* mission."

Kywatha shifted her gaze to him, then glanced down at the dagger. She'd been the one to give it to him.

"They won't be caught," she said, "and as good as you are, Colonel, I expect you to be able to slip in and kill your targets, regardless of distractions."

"I'm good at commanding troops on a battlefield, not assassinating mages."

"No? I find it hard to believe you haven't done your share of both."

"I haven't," Sorath said coolly. "I'm an honorable man."

An honorable man who'd allowed himself to be talked into an assassination mission. He gritted his teeth, missing the days when life had been simpler, when it had been easier to be honorable.

"That's good. Our team will retrieve our comrade, and then one of us will lead you close to their camp for your part. We don't want anything to happen to Tovorka if you're discovered prematurely."

"Is that truly the only reason you don't want me to go with them? Or is it that you don't trust me? Do you think I'd alert the mages to your team's presence?"

"It crossed our minds, especially since we can't read your

thoughts anymore." Kywatha waved to the dagger. "The elders feel we can't trust you."

"Why would I betray you? You've promised to assist Thorn Company in escaping the mages and getting out of the jungle, no matter what the outcome is for my mission. It behooves me to help you. I care about them."

"Good. And *I* believe you mean what you say. You did help me when I faced the two zidarr. I haven't forgotten that. The elders are the ones who aren't willing to trust you, but have no fear. The delay won't be much longer."

Sorath sighed but didn't object further. What did it matter to him whether he tried to assassinate Uthari tonight or the night after? It was likely he would die in the attempt, so maybe he ought to appreciate the extra time, the scent of the jungle foliage all around him, the call of wild animals in the night. The memory of the kiss he'd shared with Ferroki before he left.

"You'll get your chance soon, Colonel." Kywatha patted him on the shoulder and headed back toward the cave. "And we'll be ready to capitalize on it."

Sorath frowned after her. Maybe they intended for *him* to be the distraction. What if they didn't believe he could succeed, and they planned to use whatever chaos he created in his attempt to attack the camp to take another stab at stealing the portal out from under the mages' noses?

He supposed it didn't matter. His only concern was for Thorn Company. They were still working for Uthari, whether they'd wanted to be finagled into that contract or not, and if the druids attacked again, they would be forced to defend against them.

3

As polite as always, Malek offered Jadora a hand as she stepped off the skyboard and onto the deck of Uthari's yacht. She shouldn't have noticed the warmth of his skin, the roughness of his callouses, and the strength of his grip, nor should she have thought about the kisses they'd shared in that cell under the gladiator arena, kisses that couldn't entirely be blamed on that drugged juice.

Malek, no doubt aware of her thoughts, withdrew his hand. It was a normal thing to do, since her feet were now on the deck, but she couldn't help but feel stung. He'd seemed to withdraw it hastily. Lately, he'd been more aloof with her on the rare instances when he'd come into the laboratory tent. Even though she knew it was for the best, she couldn't help but wonder if he believed he'd made a mistake and regretted letting himself develop feelings for her. Maybe Uthari had *made* him regret it.

"Have you recovered from Admiral Bakir's mental intrusion?" Malek asked quietly, nodding toward the ornate double doors that led to Uthari's suite.

Guards stood there, watching them with more curiosity than

boredom, and Jadora straightened her face and attempted to lock her thoughts in a vault, as *The Mind Way* taught. More than once, she'd read the chapter on hiding one's contemplations from mind-scouring mages, but it was an elusive skill.

"Yes." Jadora walked with him toward the doors and reminded herself that her relationship with Malek wasn't what she should be worrying about this evening. Zethron was a prisoner on another ship, and Uthari wanted *information* from her. "It wasn't that bad. It just startled me."

That wasn't entirely true. Admiral Bakir's attack *had* hurt, but it had been thankfully brief.

The doors opened automatically, letting them into a magically cooled interior that was refreshing after the humidity of the jungle.

After the doors swung shut, leaving them alone in the short corridor, Malek said, "We'll be traveling with Bakir on our next mission. Zidarr Prolix is coming too. They made a deal with Uthari. I'll do my best to stay close to you and Jak, but if either of them tries anything, let me know." Malek paused and lowered his voice almost to a growl as he added, "If Bakir hurts you again, I'll challenge him to a duel and kill him. I don't care whose fleet commander he is."

A little shiver went through her at that growl and at the intense look in his eyes. Malek's aloofness had disappeared, along with the implication that he didn't care.

"Thank you." Jadora licked her lips. "I'll hope it doesn't come to that. I assume he's powerful and dangerous."

And if the admiral would have an equally powerful zidarr at his back, any challenge Malek made might not go well, not if they ganged up on him.

"Will Captain Rivlen be coming with us?" she asked.

"No." Malek took a breath and smoothed his face, tucking his emotions away once more, and continued down the corridor toward Uthari's suite. "She's going on another mission. General Tonovan will be accompanying us."

"*What*?" The polished wood floor was utterly smooth, but Jadora tripped anyway as horror gripped her limbs. She caught herself on a pedestal adorned with the bust of some powerful dead wizard. "*Why*?" she added as Malek turned to look at her.

"King Uthari wishes it."

"Why?" she couldn't help but ask again. "Your king has to know what an *ass* he is."

"Something that does not preclude his ability to be useful on a mission that may once again pit us against dragons."

"If he kills you, what will it *matter* if you've defeated dragons beforehand?"

"I'll stay alert so he doesn't get the opportunity to do that."

Jadora hadn't been looking forward to her next trip through the portal, but she'd been able to hope they might finally find the Jitaruvak, and it could be her last time risking her and her son's lives on another world. Now, all she could do was worry. It sounded like every mage who was going along was a potential enemy for Malek. And if he were killed, she and Jak would be left at Tonovan's mercy.

Malek had continued down the corridor, but she merely stared bleakly at his back, her legs numb. Her whole body was numb.

"You know how these past trips have gone," Jadora whispered, sweat breaking out despite the cool air in the corridor. "I can't imagine you found it easy to *stay alert* while you were unconscious after falling from a dragon's maw. Or while having your brain operated on by a hatchling. Or while having that needle *shoved into your skull*." Her voice cracked on those last words, and she clenched her fists in frustration, both at the situation and at the fact that she couldn't keep her emotions in check.

That damn Uthari was probably magically spying on them

from his suite. She didn't want to break down into a weepy puddle outside his door.

"I was quite alert during the needle insertion," Malek said in a dry voice.

He smiled, but it quickly turned into a frown as he watched her face. He walked back to her and lifted an arm, but he hesitated. Maybe he'd meant to offer her a hug, but he'd also remembered how easily Uthari could spy on them.

Jadora took a deep breath, straightened, and blinked several times to keep tears from forming. She had to hold it together. As strange as it seemed, she was more surrounded by enemies here than when they were out on foreign worlds teeming with man-eating monsters.

Malek didn't hug her, but he did rest a gentle hand on her shoulder. *I'm not happy about Tonovan's inclusion either,* he spoke telepathically, *but I understand why Uthari made the choice. Tonovan is more powerful and experienced than Rivlen and can be a boon in a battle against superior forces.* He grimaced, probably thinking about the Vran mages as well as the dragons they'd encountered there. *When we're fighting for our lives, he should be too busy worrying about that to conjure up betrayals, but I'll protect you from him, just as I will from Jutuk's men if needed.*

Jadora forced herself to smile and think, *I appreciate that*, though she was tempted to point out that he was only one man, no matter how powerful, and he couldn't be awake and guarding her all the time.

She and Jak would have to watch out for themselves. Before leaving, she would peruse her lab *very* thoroughly and gather formulas, explosives, acids, and anything else that came to mind that could be used against enemies.

The corners of Malek's eyes crinkled with a smile, and she knew he'd caught that thought. He squeezed her shoulder, touched her cheek, then let his hand drop and headed for the doors.

They opened, and Jadora braced herself to follow him into the suite. They walked through the foyer and turned into Uthari's office, the only room Jadora had ever seen him in.

An orange-glowing orb rested on a pedestal on the desk—a dome-jir for distant communications. Uthari sat back, removing his hand from it, and waved them toward the two seats opposite him. As its glow faded—with whom had he been speaking?—he drank from a glass of juice with ice cubes clinking inside.

"Thank you for coming to see me, Professor," Uthari said.

Jadora fought the urge to ask if she'd had a choice. Sarcasm wouldn't get her anywhere, and despite his promise that he would send her father back to the kingdom, he was still here, a prisoner on this very ship. She had to be on good behavior, just as Uthari no doubt wished.

She made herself perch on the edge of one of the chairs and say, "You're welcome, Your Majesty."

He smiled.

At least it wasn't a cruel, leering smile, not like the ones Tonovan gave her. If Uthari hadn't been a powerful wizard and the supreme ruler of a kingdom, he might have passed as someone's mostly easygoing grandfather. Too bad he was a three-hundred-year-old megalomaniac who wanted to live forever.

"She's judgmental, isn't she?" Uthari asked Malek, who'd chosen to stand behind one of the seats rather than sitting in it.

"Opinionated and full of conviction," Malek said.

"I should have known you'd approve."

Malek didn't smile. His face was once again carefully masked, and Jadora trusted he was walling off his thoughts so that nobody could read them. If only she could do that.

Though she had no desire to be able to use magic, and was still distressed that the gods had granted Jak the ability, protecting her mind was one thing she wished she could do in this world full of mind readers. *Worlds* full of them.

"That is, of course, why I wanted to speak with the professor myself." Uthari sighed and gazed a little sadly at Malek. "I do not wish to put your loyalty to the test by asking you to question her and bring me any information she might be trying to withhold."

A chill went through her. Was Uthari fishing, or did he truly believe she had information she'd been withholding? Was this about Zethron? The disc? She blanked her mind and hoped Uthari wouldn't probe her the way the admiral had started to.

"My loyalty is to you, Your Majesty," Malek said quietly. "Whatever command you give me, I will carry it out. You know this."

"Of course," Uthari murmured, though the sad gaze remained.

Jadora worried about what Uthari might learn from poking around in her mind, but a part of her was glad that it didn't appear that he would force Malek to do it. She was almost surprised, having no trouble imagining Uthari putting Malek to a test, forcing him to prove where his loyalties lay by performing some cruel act on her. The mere idea made her shudder. Better to be tormented by an enemy than a friend.

Or a lover? Uthari asked into her mind, his eyebrows raising.

We aren't that, Jadora hurried to reply, keeping herself from glancing at Malek. *He's complying with your wishes. Your Zidarr Code.*

Good. "Tell me, Professor," Uthari said out loud, "your theory on how the mages on Vran came to be so much more powerful than the mages in our world. Malek believes you know the answer, but oddly, he didn't poke around thoroughly in your thoughts to learn it." Uthari slanted a look of censure at his loyal zidarr.

Oh. *That* was what Uthari wanted to know? Jadora wasn't relieved, as that wasn't a secret she'd wanted to hand the mages, but it wasn't the most condemning one swimming around in her mind.

"It's more of a hypothesis," she said. "A weak one. I don't have any evidence to back it up, and only one case that has led me to form it."

"It's based on Jak developing magical powers," Uthari said slowly, looking at her—looking into her mind, "even though you're positive his father didn't have any aptitude for magic. And we *know* you don't." His expression grew condescending, a reminder that he believed she and every other terrene human were lesser beings, people who wouldn't be worth keeping alive except that they did all the work in the world while serving the mage class.

"Don't be so melodramatic, Professor. I've offered you a comfortable position in my sky city, the opportunity to continue to research and teach, and I've gone through great lengths to keep you alive because of your value."

She barely kept from snorting. *Malek* had gone through great lengths to keep her alive. Uthari wouldn't shed a tear for her passing—or her violent murder.

"Who do you think commanded him to protect you?" Uthari flicked his hand, as if to wave away this tangent, and peered into her eyes.

His mental touch wasn't as painful as Bakir's had been, but she sensed him rooting around in her mind. Even if he didn't mean it to be, it was unpleasant, like ants crawling all over the inside of her skull.

She didn't think of the dragon steel or how she believed that it, over time, altered something about the cellular makeup of people close to it. But he got the information anyway.

"Ah," Uthari said. "Interesting. And the alterations are something passed along to children? We know that to be true, that powerful mages are more likely to have powerful children. There's so little dragon steel in our world that I can see why people might not have noticed a connection between proximity to it and the development of magical ability before. Especially if it takes years for that change to occur. You say your son carried the dragon-steel medallion for five years before developing any power?" He raised his eyebrows.

"Actually, I *didn't* say," Jadora said.

"Heh. Quite. But I see that in your mind. As well as... something about a dragon-steel pillar on Agathar Island leading to everyone living there evolving into powerful mages. Fascinating." Uthari scribbled a note for himself.

"Evolving and then killing themselves off with their great power," Jadora said. "Sadly, the dragon steel doesn't impart wisdom as well."

"Few things except age do." Uthari set down his pen. "And that's not a given. Though perhaps the world will be a better place when I'm able to give a longevity formula to those who *are* wise, while we allow the substandard to die after their typical short lifespans."

"The *mages* who are wise."

"As I've told you before, I'll be happy to pluck scholars such as yourself up from the terrene cities and extend their lives, so long as they don't vow to work against me." Uthari gazed frankly at her, then looked at Malek. No, at his temple.

The injury he'd received from the kerzor had healed, leaving only a faint scar behind.

Jadora shifted uneasily on the edge of the chair.

"You know she still has that dreadful device that robbed you of your power?" Uthari asked Malek.

Jadora couldn't keep from checking Malek's expression. He knew about the world she dreamed of, one where terrene humans weren't enslaved and could govern themselves, but she didn't think she'd thought about how the kerzor could be a tool for fighting mages, not in his presence.

"I'm aware," Malek said. "It's in her laboratory."

"I'm surprised she hasn't foisted it off on someone to try to make more yet. You must know what she's thought of doing with it —with *many* of them." Uthari's tone had turned colder than the ice floating in his glass.

"I know what she's mused about." Malek's flat tone lacked surprise.

Jadora doubted that meant he didn't care. Did he feel betrayed? Or had he truly already known about her thoughts on the matter?

"And you've *let* her muse? You've deliberately looked the other way when she's contemplating something that could endanger our people? Zidarr, wizard, and mage alike?" Uthari rarely lost his temper, at least in Jadora's presence, but he was on the edge of it now, his voice full of exasperation. "Don't presume she's not capable of finding someone able and willing to make those devices. That idiot Vinjo is in the tent adjacent to hers and has already proven he'll happily build magical devices to vex mages. How do you think Sorath disappeared from our camp without a trace?"

"Had she taken the step to attempt to have more made, I would have stopped her." Malek stood tensely, with his hands clasped behind his back, as he gazed over Uthari's head at the wall behind him instead of meeting his eyes. "Right now, it's simply in her lab with every other sample and specimen she's brought back. She collects *everything.* That doesn't mean she's fomenting rebellion."

Uthari made a disgusted noise. "You can see her thoughts as easily as I can. You *know* what she wants. Just because she's a middle-aged female professor doesn't mean she's incapable of *fomenting rebellion*, as you put it. And her son. What of him? A teenager brimming with potential with a chip on his shoulder because one of my people killed his father. This willful shortsightedness disappoints me, Malek. You are choosing to look the other way because of your feelings for her. And *you*." For the first time in several minutes, Uthari turned his scowl on Jadora. "I have offered to bring you into our realm and give you all that you could wish. And yet you persist in fantasizing about our downfall. You have more in common with us than the mindless peons who work in farms and factories, people you've never even interacted with. Do you really think such idiots would be capable of governing themselves? They're like chimps throwing dung at each other in the wilds."

"Intelligence is just as likely to arise among terrene humans as mages," Jadora couldn't keep herself from saying, though she should have kept her mouth shut, "and is not, regardless, a stipulation as to whether a person should have free will and the same freedoms and rights granted to mages, including the right to participate in a government of their own choosing."

The disgusted noise came again. It was reminiscent of a cat hacking up a hairball.

"I'm afraid this *negligence* calls for punishment," Uthari said.

Jadora struggled to swallow as fear spread through her body. What *kind* of punishment?

Some kind of magically inflicted torture, she thought she could endure, but what if his idea of punishment was to hand her over to Tonovan for the gods knew what sexual torment? That might break her in a way that the simple methodical application of pain wouldn't.

Uthari's lips thinned as he pressed them together. "I'm not a deviant, Professor. Punishment is delivered as a method to correct wayward behavior, not to destroy a person with value. Regardless, I'm certain my loyal zidarr would be furious with me if I presumed to punish *you* while he watched." The look that Uthari slid toward Malek was one of continuing exasperation.

Malek stood in the same position, not even his eyes moving. It didn't look like he was even breathing. He might have been a statue.

"Leave us, Professor." Uthari flicked a finger toward the doors, and they opened, revealing two guards waiting outside. "My men will take you back down to your tent."

"You can't punish him," Jadora blurted, barely able to keep from leaping to her feet and wrapping her arms protectively around Malek. As if *that* would do anything. "He's been loyal to you and done everything you've asked. He's done nothing wrong."

"Except for choosing to be oblivious to your plotting and machinations. What might you have done if I hadn't peered into your mind today?"

"I've done nothing *either*. You can't punish a person for their thoughts."

"I can, and I will. *Go*." Uthari thrust his arm toward the door, and magical compulsion forced Jadora to spring from her seat and stride toward the exit.

Damn it, Malek was going to be hurt because of her, by the man he thought of as a father and who he least wanted to disappoint. And it was her fault.

I'll try to find out about Zethron, Malek spoke into her mind as the doors closed behind her and the guards directed her out of the suite.

Jadora hadn't asked him to or even explained that Zethron had been captured, but Malek must have seen it in her thoughts. That he worried about helping her when he was about to be punished only made her care for him more. Damn it. Her throat tightened so that she couldn't have spoken aloud, but she didn't need to, not with him.

Malek, I'm so sorry. Don't let him do this. Can't you leave? Run away. You don't have *to let him hurt you.*

He is right, and it's a punishment I deserve. Do not worry for me. I have endured punishment before.

A second later, a wrenching scream of pain sounded through the walls. *Malek's* scream of pain.

Jadora lurched to a stop and spun, wanting to run back inside and throttle that horrible old man.

"Continue," one of the guards said.

They gripped her arms and forced her to keep walking away from Malek. Away from his pain.

There was nothing she could do, but she couldn't help but feel she'd betrayed him.

Malek didn't know how much time passed, how long he writhed on the floor, first on his hands and knees and finally curled up in a ball as he gripped his head, willing the pain afflicting his mind and his body to end. He could hear his ragged breaths scouring his throat between the cries of agony that escaped his mouth, and he hated that he couldn't endure the punishment without making a sound. He always longed to be stoic, the dragon-steel-like epitome of the Zidarr Code, but the pain that a wizard could deliver was like no other.

Perhaps Malek could have fought back, something that crossed his mind more than once, but that would only make it worse. Should he prove stronger than Uthari and manage to cast aside the punishment, his king would only find another way to hurt him—likely, he would hurt Jadora. Malek knew that was what Uthari would have preferred.

Oh, Malek had skated the edge, just as Uthari said, choosing not to pry into Jadora's mind when he knew there were plots developing in there, but he hadn't brazenly defied his master. *He* wasn't the one contemplating rebellion. She was.

But Uthari was correct that Malek would react badly if Uthari punished her. He didn't know what he would do, if he would truly turn on his king, but he'd been enraged every time Tonovan had suggested he might torment Jadora, and he'd barely kept himself from trying to kill Admiral Bakir when he'd hurt her. Malek never should have let himself come to care about Jadora, but he doubted it was possible for him to withdraw those feelings now.

Gradually, the pain subsided, and Malek grew aware of the office around him, the texture of the rug under his hands, the taste of blood in his mouth. At some point, he'd bitten his tongue. That small pain lingered after Uthari's punishment wore off, as did an ache in his entire body as he rolled up to his hands and knees. Darkness encroached on his vision, and he rested there, needing a moment before he could stand without passing out.

Uthari's black silk shoes came into view, and he rested a hand on Malek's back.

"I am sorry, my son," Uthari said quietly. "As I said, I would rather punish her, but I'm not blind to how you feel about her."

No, he wasn't. And that was the problem.

"That is my fault," Uthari continued. "I do not regret giving you the task of protecting her, for others have tried numerous times to kill her and her son, or to acquire the information in their minds, and you are my best zidarr. My best *man*. There is no other I would want to give such an important task, but I should not have asked you to get close to her, to attempt to earn her trust. Though I wouldn't have guessed she was your type, or that you even *had* a type." Uthari patted his back before stepping away.

"Nor would I." Malek blinked a few times and managed to kneel back.

"It's possible I'm not as intelligent and wise as I'd like to think."

"If I agreed with that, I might be opening myself up to further punishment."

"You know *criticism* isn't what I object to, as long as its respectfully delivered."

Malek started to say more, but a soft *bing* came from the dome-jir on Uthari's desk. A premonition flashed through him, the certainty that it was about Zethron. He wasn't sure whether the insight was simple human intuition, or if it had been imparted to him by one of his lesser-dragon-steel blades.

Uthari touched the device to activate it, and the head and shoulders of a senior officer in a green uniform appeared above the glowing orange orb. Fleet Commander Veygeroth, the man in charge of the six mageships that Queen Vorsha had sent. They'd arrived one morning, nobody bothering to send a message to Uthari, no acknowledgment that Vorsha's people had been working hand in hand with Zaruk's fleet scant weeks earlier to attack Uthari's ships in an attempt to steal the portal. Like so many others, they were lurking in the area now, watching everything that developed and waiting for an opportunity.

Why did Malek have a feeling that opportunity had come?

"King Uthari." Veygeroth's head half-disappeared as he bowed. "My officers found a suspicious stranger lurking among the mercenaries below. We captured him, questioned him and, to our surprise, found that he not only is from another world but returned through the portal with your team. Are you aware of this?"

"I am aware of everything that happens when my people visit other worlds," Uthari said smoothly, though he flicked a we're-going-to-talk-about-this-shortly glance down at Malek.

Malek sighed, tempted to sink back down to the floor. He'd told Uthari about *most* of what had occurred on Vran, everything from the battles with the dragons to the great power of the mages there to the kiss he'd shared with Jadora in that cell. He'd even told Uthari about Zethron and how the explorer had assisted the team in acquiring information about dragon steel and Jitaruvak. What he *hadn't* mentioned was that Zethron had returned with them. It had been a favor to Jadora, who'd feared he would be captured and interrogated, perhaps accused of being a spy.

Malek hadn't gone out of his way to hide the man, and enough witnesses had been around when the team returned that he'd thought someone would have reported the extra person to Uthari, but in the aftermath of a battle that had occurred between the mages and the druids, things had been chaotic. He wasn't surprised that Zethron had slipped away before anyone noticed him. The last he'd heard, the man had been blending in with the mercenaries and doing his best to learn their language so he could pass as a native.

Maybe I should have you make a list of all the secrets you're keeping from me these days, Uthari spoke into his mind, though he'd returned his focus to Veygeroth.

That wasn't a secret, Your Majesty. It was an omission.

That earned him another flat, disapproving look even as Uthari asked Veygeroth why he was contacting him about this.

Malek looked bleakly at the rug. He felt like a juvenile delinquent. After decades of unwavering loyalty, he was allowing himself to be less than the zidarr he'd always striven to be, less than 100 percent loyal to Uthari. And why? Because of a woman. This was why marriage and romantic relationships were forbidden by the Zidarr Code.

Malek didn't blame Jadora—it wasn't as if she'd been trying to seduce him—but he did blame himself. He was relieved that this next trip through the portal could be the last, that their information—the information *Zethron* had helped them get—suggested Nargnoth contained the plant Uthari sought. After they delivered those green fronds to Uthari's hands, there would be no need for Jadora to continue going on missions through the portal. There would be no need for Malek to interact with her. It would make it easier for him to distance himself from her and return his full attention to Uthari and his duty.

He firmed his jaw and nodded to himself. Yes, that would be for the best.

"Even though we knew he had to have come back with your

team," Veygeroth was saying, his tone turning dry, "we didn't expect to learn that he had feelings for your archaeologist."

"Professor Freedar?" Uthari quirked an eyebrow toward Malek. "Given her age and bookish nature, she has a fascinating ability to attract men."

"I've spoken about him to my queen, who you may have heard is en route."

"Yes," Uthari said. "It's become fashionable for rulers of entire realms to visit this previously forsaken continent."

"A trend you started, Your Majesty. Queen Vorsha wants to know if you want this prisoner back and, if so, what it would be worth to you to obtain him."

"I can't imagine why we would need him, as we've already obtained the information in his mind for ourselves, but let me consult my zidarr."

"Certainly."

Uthari switched to telepathy when he looked at Malek. *I don't appreciate being blindsided.*

I apologize, Your Majesty. Malek winced. *Again.*

Do we know everything in this man's head? I assume you don't believe he's a spy or any kind of real threat, else you would have told me about him.

He's an explorer who wants to visit the ruins of our world and learn their ancient secrets.

Apparently, he also wants to visit your professor's bed and learn its *secrets.*

That is immaterial.

But not untrue?

Malek hitched a shoulder, then regretted it. His body still hurt, and any movement brought a twinge of pain.

Is there any reason I should give up something to acquire him? By joining forces with Zaruk, Vorsha has made it clear she currently considers me an enemy. I have no desire to give her alliance anything. I already have a handle on your professor, so I don't think I need anyone else around to ensure her compliance. I assume from the fact that you neglected to mention this Zethron was here that it was to please her.

Malek clenched his jaw, but he couldn't deny it. It hadn't been so much about *pleasing* Jadora as not wanting to cause her pain. It had been a favor. That was all.

As Uthari's eyebrow climbed again, Malek sighed and shook his head. Yes, he definitely needed to distance himself from Jadora. His... friendship with her was affecting his decision-making process. And not in a good way.

I agree that you don't need another handle *on the professor.* Malek thought of but didn't point out that Uthari had said he would send Jadora's father back to the kingdom but hadn't yet arranged for that. *But it may be better if Zethron isn't in an enemy's hands. He was the one to tell Jadora on which world the Jitaruvak may be found, and given enough time, interrogators might stumble across the information in his mind and wonder why the archaeologist working for you is so interested in a plant.*

Uthari bared his teeth. *Damn it, Malek. You should have thought of that, and that he might be captured, before you turned your back and let him wander off.*

I agree, Your Majesty. It was an error.

Uthari pointed toward the door. *Go prepare for your mission. I want that plant in my hands as soon as possible, and I want the professor hard at work synthesizing that drug. This is my legacy, Malek. I'll not have a competitor beat me to it or sabotage my efforts.*

Yes, Your Majesty. Malek rose stiffly to his feet.

And Malek? Destroy that disc before the professor can hand it off to those mercenaries or the engineer or anyone else who would like to make her fantasies a reality.

Yes, Your Majesty.

4

THE MAGESHIP THAT THE ENGINEER HAD DESIGNED TO FLY THROUGH the dragon portal was the strangest-looking ship, flying or sailing, that Jak had ever seen.

It was made from wood and had a deck up top that was exposed to the elements, but that seemed more of an afterthought than part of the original design. The ship was essentially a long tube with a narrow corridor that ran through the middle. Everything from the engineering room, with all the magical devices that powered the craft, to small cabins with double bunks built against the hull, to a navigation chamber with a huge forward-looking porthole were inside. There was a large hatch in the side for loading cargo, and a smaller round hatch on the deck, with a ladder descending to an alcove attached to the corridor.

After gazing wistfully up at the green-hulled ship that held Zethron prisoner, alert guards visible on deck, Jak climbed inside the new vessel. He found Lieutenant Vinjo working in the navigation cabin, his head and torso under a console as he made adjustments to a glowing yellow orb that pulsed erratically.

Rookie Tezi and Lieutenant Sasko from Thorn Company stood

nearby. They carried wrenches and toolboxes as well as their weapons, so it was unclear whether they were acting as bodyguards or assistants. Maybe both.

Jak cleared his throat as he stepped inside, Shikari trailing behind him, his long blue tail whacking the walls as he peered through doorways and sniffed at and licked everything. For someone who preferred an all-protein diet, he was oddly content sampling all manner of random and presumably inedible items.

"You called for me, Lieutenant Vinjo?" Jak asked, nodding at Tezi and Sasko.

Tezi's dragon-steel battle-axe glowed a faint blue, either acknowledging his presence or letting her know it wanted to cleave him in half. Since Jak had communicated with the weapon before, he hoped that wasn't the case. Maybe the axe was pleased that a dragon had entered the room. Little did it know that Shikari would inevitably lick it.

"Is that one of the archaeologists?" came Vinjo's voice, echoing from under the console.

"Yes," Sasko said, "but that's the only clue you're getting. We're not telling you which one."

"I'd like to think he can tell the difference between my voice and my mother's," Jak said.

"I wouldn't count on it," Sasko said. "He's absent-minded. I was surprised he knew you two existed."

Vinjo scooted out from under the console, with baggy pants rucked up to his knees. They'd been made from grass. Had he woven them himself? Or bartered with a druid?

"Be glad he's *wearing* pants," Sasko told him, guessing Jak's thoughts. "He wasn't for a while."

"Only because I refuse to wear one of those odious red uniforms supplied by King Uthari's torture-happy mages." Vinjo sneered distastefully and wiped at a grease smudge on his cheek. He didn't succeed in removing it, only smearing it around.

"They're not torturing you when they ask you to wear pants," Sasko said. "That's a normal thing."

"They've tortured me other times." Vinjo grimaced and touched an old bruise on the side of his face.

Sasko's expression grew more sympathetic. "I know," she said softly. "They like to do that."

"How are you doing?" Jak asked Tezi quietly.

In between trying to teach his charge to fly, swim, hunt, and refrain from eating people's bootlaces, he'd been busy training with Rivlen and Malek. He hadn't seen Tezi for a few days and was glad she still had her axe. He wondered if Sergeant Tinder had hers. Every time those weapons appeared in camp, dozens of mercenaries eyed them covetously.

"I'm training a lot." Tezi hefted the large double-headed weapon. "I really want to master it."

"A good idea."

"Jak?" Vinjo asked. "That's your name, right?"

"Yes."

"Good. You've been to the other worlds, and you're becoming a mage, yes? I can sense your burgeoning aura." Vinjo waved vaguely at Jak.

"His burgeoning what?" Sasko asked.

"His aura. Of power."

Sasko looked Jak up and down skeptically.

"It's there," Vinjo assured the mercenaries. "He's going to be a strong one, if the other powerful mages don't find him a threat and kill him first."

"Yes, I've been to other worlds and I'm learning how to use magic." Jak didn't want to comment on—or contemplate—the rest, but he couldn't help but glance out the large porthole. All that was visible was the portal and part of the camp, but he sensed Uthari's *Serene Waters* floating almost directly overhead. It worried him that Mother had been called up there for a meeting and hadn't returned yet. He hoped Zethron's capture hadn't turned into trouble for her.

"And you're acting as the mama to that little dragon." Vinjo pointed behind him to where Shikari's tail was visible in the narrow corridor as the rest of his body investigated the tiny kitchen. It hadn't appeared to be stocked yet when Jak had passed it and peered in, but perhaps someone had brought in some dragon delicacies and tucked them into a cabinet. Or maybe a delicious spider was spinning a web in a corner.

"I'm acting as his *papa* actually," Jak said. "I'm lacking in mama parts."

Tezi snorted softly.

Vinjo waved dismissively. "Regardless, you may be the closest thing to an expert on dragons here."

Jak started to shake his head, but maybe it was true. In addition to his hatchling-raising duties, he'd spent years studying his father's archaeology books and learning everything he could about the portal—and the dragons who'd created it.

"What do you want to know?" he asked.

"I attempted to weave some magic into the hull of this ship. It's intended to camouflage it from dragons and mages, or at least make it seem boring and uninteresting to them. It relies upon one of the power sources, so it won't work until it's fired up, but once it is, the ship *should* seem to lack magic. It may even mask the auras of those riding inside. I thought you might appreciate it if, when visiting worlds, you didn't beam out power like a lighthouse beacon."

"I would appreciate that, yes." Jak wondered if there was a way he could use the ship to rescue Zethron. Probably not. It didn't sound like it would make them invisible. Besides, the guards stationed outside would notice if the ship took off prematurely.

"I thought so," Vinjo said. "Can you help me test it? I'm running out of time, and I want to make this as good as I can."

"Or maybe you could actually get some sleep tonight," Sasko suggested. "The bags under your eyes are so pronounced that it looks like someone punched you. Again."

Vinjo's next wave was airy. "I can catch up on my sleep the next time a pissed-off mage throws me in a jail cell. Which could be any time now. Sooner or later, Zaruk or some of his high-ranking officers will find out that I'm building this for another king, and they'll capture me. Or send assassins."

"Your zidarr brother is out there and could be hunting you right now," Sasko pointed out.

"Yes, thanks for the reminder."

"Why *are* you building this ship?" Jak asked curiously. "I appreciate it and think it'll be a tremendous help, but was it only because of… the torture?"

It crossed his mind to wonder if a mage engineer who'd been forced to build the ship by threat of pain might have sabotaged it. But if that were true, would Vinjo be putting extra time and effort into adding camouflage?

"The torture was *highly* motivating, but mostly I was promised Lieutenant Sasko's love and adoration." Vinjo beamed what seemed a sincere smile at her.

Jak blinked.

"I only promised to hold your tools and listen while you babble about your projects."

"Do you know how *few* women are willing to do that?" Vinjo beamed at her even more.

"Technically, Captain Ferroki was the one who promised I would do those things," Sasko pointed out.

"But you agreed to go along with her, because you value me and realize what a joy I am."

"She's my commanding officer and can withhold my pay if I don't follow orders."

Despite these efforts to squelch his adoration, Vinjo didn't stop beaming. Maybe because Sasko's squelching attempts weren't that heartfelt, and she smiled faintly as she delivered them.

Jak shrugged. As long as the ship he would be traveling on hadn't been sabotaged, he didn't care about whatever relationship they had.

Jak? Malek spoke into his mind from Uthari's yacht. His usually strong telepathic voice sounded weary and drained.

Yes? Are you all right?

We're working on getting Zethron, Malek said without answering the question. *In the meantime, don't do anything rash.*

Who was the *we*? Malek and… Uthari?

Jak winced but made himself reply with a polite, *Yes, my lord.*

He hadn't figured out a rescue plan anyway. Still, if Uthari was the one to negotiate Zethron's release, Jak couldn't help but feel that it would come with catches.

Malek's presence disappeared from his mind. Jak hoped he was all right.

"Anyway," Vinjo said, wrenching his gaze back to Jak. "Can you and your scaled charge help me test it?"

"What do you have in mind?" Jak envisioned them all going outside, Vinjo throwing an extremely long blanket over the ship, and then asking Shikari if he could still find it.

"I'm not sure exactly." Vinjo scratched his jaw with a screwdriver that glowed silver. "I know he's young, but dragons are supposed to be smart, right? Can you *ask* him if he can detect my camouflaging magic? Or maybe if he's struggling to detect the magical elements that power the ship?"

"Uhm. Maybe." Jak considered how he might convey that, since it was a complicated concept. True, he'd guided Shikari through helping with Malek's brain surgery, but that had mostly involved him thinking of the strands and hooks inside Malek's head and envisioning them being incinerated.

A wrenching noise came from the little kitchen. Uh oh. Shikari's tail—and the rest of him—had disappeared inside.

"Be right back." Jak lunged out of the navigation cabin, almost cracking his head on the low frame of the hatchway, and jumped into the tiny kitchen.

Shikari had ripped a cabinet door off the hinges and stuck his head inside. Someone had indeed brought in a few staples for the trip. Ration bars, hardtack, limes, and plantains were now scattered on the deck. With Shikari's head inside the cabinet, it was hard to see what remained in there—and what had his attention. Clearly not the plantains. He'd stepped on one and squeezed the pale insides out onto the deck.

"Shikari," Jak said, saying the name telepathically as well as out loud, "that food is for *humans*. You like insects and small animals, right? Not biscuits and limes."

The dragon withdrew his head and turned to look at Jak. Something dangled from his jaws, the tips of his sharp teeth clamped down on whatever he'd snatched.

"Is that... a mouse tail?" Jak asked.

Dragons didn't grin, no more than crocodiles or alligators did, but something about the glint in those yellow eyes conveyed both triumph and amusement as Shikari chomped on his prize. Soon, the mouse disappeared into his gullet. Shikari's tail swished cheerfully across the deck, knocking biscuits in all directions.

"This is the smart and superior dragon that's going to advise our mage engineer on the ship's construction?" Sasko asked dubiously from the hatchway.

"Now that he's properly fueled himself, yes." Jak knelt on the deck and closed his eyes, doing his best to communicate with Shikari what Vinjo wanted to know.

His charge responded by sharing an image of the two of them cavorting through a field, sticking their heads into holes and catching mice. Seeing himself through Shikari's eyes was odd. It was even odder when the Jak in the vision lifted his head and had a mouse tail dangling from his lips.

"Ew," he muttered, finding it strange, not for the first time, that he'd ended up as a surrogate father to a member of another species. "We need to find you one of your own kind to raise you."

Shikari cocked his head, managing to look sad and hopeful at the same time.

Jak wondered if there *was* hope or if all the elder dragons were extinct. He didn't know what he would do if they were. Even if he somehow managed to teach Shikari to fly, there was no way he could teach him to speak the dragon language or about their culture or any of the hundreds of other things a parent would pass along to offspring.

After about ten minutes of going back and forth, Jak managed to get some images from Shikari related to the ship. The dragon was indifferent to the magical engine, navigation equipment, and other devices Vinjo had made, but Jak didn't know if that meant they were camouflaged. They might not find out until they were flying through the air on another world and encountered dragons.

A throat cleared in the corridor, and Jak recognized Rivlen's aura. She peered into the kitchen, her dark hair back in a professional bun, her red uniform clean and pressed, her black boots gleaming. Even though night had fallen, she looked like she was ready to leave on a mission. *Their* mission?

Jak smiled at her and raised his eyebrows, but she shook her head, and he suspected he still wasn't doing a good job of walling off his thoughts from mages. He was getting better at it—it was becoming more of a habit to keep that mental protection up around his mind—but he'd had his guard down as he'd attempted to communicate with Shikari.

"I was up at a meeting with the king earlier," Rivlen said. "You're leaving in the morning with your mother and Malek."

Jak nodded. With the ship finished, he'd assumed they would depart soon.

"And Tonovan," she added.

Jak groaned. "*Why?*"

It came out sounding like the petulant whine of a seven-year-old, but he didn't care.

"And an admiral and zidarr from another kingdom," Rivlen said. "And... not me."

"Not you?" Jak frowned.

He supposed there was no reason he should have assumed Rivlen would continue to go along with them on missions. It wasn't as if she'd gone on the first one, and she had other duties as a ship's commander. But he'd gotten used to having her around. And she'd kissed him. Whether that had meant anything or not, he liked her. He liked her a *lot* more than General Tonovan.

I'm glad to hear it, Rivlen told him, switching to telepathy. The others were conversing quietly in navigation. They might not have been listening, but Rivlen understandably didn't want to discuss the subject where others could overhear. *He's a horrible kisser.*

She might have meant to make it a joke, but the grimace and pain that flashed in her eyes ensured it didn't come across that way. Given what he knew about her past with the general, Jak doubted she would ever be able to joke about him.

He's horrible all around, Jak said with passion.

"What will you be doing while we're gone?" he asked aloud.

"I have my own mission." Rivlen lifted her chin, looking pleased.

A chance to prove herself? Something that she considered an honor?

"Yes," she said. "I'll be commanding the *Star Flyer* and two other ships. King Uthari is personally sending me to rout the druids, get their key to the portal, and ensure they don't threaten our people anymore."

Get their key? As in *steal* it? And what did rout mean? Kill them? Drive them away from their home?

Jak tried to hide his thoughts and keep his disapproval off his face, but he couldn't help but feel disappointment. Not only did that sound like a cruel mission, but it disturbed him that Rivlen was pleased to have been assigned it. Uthari was the invader here. To attack the druids when all they wanted was to protect their homeland was loathsome.

He must not have succeeded at hiding his feelings, because Rivlen frowned at him. "Several mages, Uthari's and those from other fleets, died when that druid girl led five magic-resistant animals back through the portal."

"They were *awful*," came Sasko's voice from navigation. "A bunch of companies lost mercenaries too. I almost took a dagger to the eye."

Jak hadn't witnessed the events, but he'd seen the creatures' bodies when he'd returned, and he didn't doubt that the battle had been fierce, but weren't the druids justified in defending their homeland by whatever means possible?

"Wouldn't it be best for everyone if Lieutenant Vinjo focused on building something that could prevent travelers—including aggressive and powerful magic-resistant creatures—from coming through the portal to our world?" Jak asked.

"I don't know if that's possible, but the portal isn't my mission. The druids are, and I intend to excel at my duty." Rivlen looked toward the navigation cabin. "And Thorn Company will be coming with me."

"We will?" Tezi asked.

"King Uthari said I could take some of the mercenaries," Rivlen said. "I choose you and your dragon-steel axes."

"Do you choose us *because* of our dragon-steel axes?" Sasko asked dryly.

"It's one of the reasons. They'll be useful weapons against the druids."

"We only have two of them," Tezi said.

"That's two more than any other mercenary company here has. Besides, you're already in King Uthari's employ."

"Yes," Sasko muttered. "Lucky us."

"You should be *honored* to come on this mission with me and do more than lounge around the camp, twiddling your thumbs."

"Twiddling?" Sasko asked. "We've been running patrols every night, keeping fit, and jumping into action whenever a threat comes through the portal."

"And letting your colonel wander off to plot shenanigans," Rivlen said coolly.

"He left because your ass of a king was *torturing* him."

Rivlen's eyes flared with anger, and she stepped out of the kitchen. "You will show *respect* when you refer to King Uthari."

Sasko gasped. In pain?

Jak lunged out and grabbed Rivlen's arm. Whatever she was doing to Sasko stopped as Rivlen spun back toward him, her eyes narrowed.

He felt like he'd grabbed a hungry tiger but forced a smile as he met her eyes. "We're all on the same side here, right? Let's see if we can get along and finish the mission. *All* of the missions." Even though Jak didn't approve of Rivlen's assignment, he made himself tamp down any further thoughts of disapproval. "Thorn Company and their axes will be great. They'll be a big help for you. And Tonovan, uh, maybe we'll get lucky and he won't talk to me and my mother. Or maybe the railings up on the deck will prove weak, and as we fly over a volcano, he'll trip, fall through, and plummet into molten lava where he'll be instantly incinerated."

Rivlen held his gaze through this babble, her expression softening little.

"My railings are *not* weak," came a whispered protest from Vinjo.

"Ssh," Sasko hissed at him.

Why do you defend them? Rivlen finally asked, switching back to telepathy. *You're one of us now. They're beneath you.*

They're people, the same as mages. They also deserve our respect.

I'd give them respect if they gave us respect. They mouth off at every opportunity. That one called our king an ass. If someone less lenient than I had heard her, she would already be dead.

It's a good thing you're such a softy. Jak risked lifting his hand from her arm to her shoulder to give her a pat. Though her sternness wasn't in the least inviting, for some reason, he remembered her lips pressed against his outside the ziggurat, and the bizarre urge to kiss her came over him. Which was ridiculous when she was defending Uthari and berating the mercenaries and glaring at him, but she was also beautiful, even when she was frigid and standing close enough to him that he could feel the power coiled in her body.

Rivlen's lips parted slightly, and a surge of anticipation went through him. Was it possible she was *also* thinking of kisses? No, more likely she meant to yell at him. Her eyes were still narrowed and her body tense, as if she wanted to punch something—or unleash a gout of fire.

"Is she going to incinerate *him*?" Tezi whispered from navigation.

"Maybe his dragon will protect him," Sasko whispered back.

He might have if he hadn't been rooting in the cabinets and looking for more mice.

Rivlen stepped back and closed her mouth. She took Jak's hand from her shoulder, and he half expected her to fling it away, but she squeezed it instead.

"Be careful on your mission," she said. "You've learned a few things, but you're no match for Tonovan. Do your best to avoid getting in his way or challenging him in any manner. It'll be hard, since he's such a bastard, but be *respectful.*" She slanted a cool look toward the mercenaries.

"I'll do my best," Jak said. "Thanks for caring."

"I haven't spent hours training you only to see you killed by friendly fire."

Jak snorted. If Tonovan fired at him, it would be anything but friendly.

Watch out for Malek too, Rivlen said, switching to telepathy again. *Tonovan hates him and may try to use the fact that there will be few witnesses around as an opportunity to scheme against him. Tonovan is* not *honorable.*

I've noticed.

Malek is. I don't want that to be his downfall.

I don't either.

Good. Rivlen leaned in and kissed him on the cheek before leaving.

He'd been fantasizing about lips pressed against lips, but he caught himself touching his cheek as she climbed the ladder. His skin tingled where she'd brushed it. His brain knew that he shouldn't want anything to do with someone who would happily destroy natives in order to do her king's bidding, but his heart and the rest of his body weren't that wise.

"Did she *kiss* him?" Sasko sounded stunned.

"I'm not sure," Tezi whispered. "Maybe she tripped and fell against him."

"Lips first?"

Embarrassed, and feeling like he was betraying terrene humans everywhere, Jak wanted to hurry away. But he realized that the mercenaries' mission would be as dangerous as his and that he might not see them again, so he made himself stay long enough to bow and wish them luck. They would all need it.

~

Darkness filled the tent when Tezi woke, gasping at the intensity of the dream she'd been having. She'd been back on the deck of Tonovan's ship, trapped under him as his degenerate men watched. Despite all her struggles, nobody had arrived in time to help.

Sweat drenched her nightshirt, and she could feel her heart pounding. She sucked in deep breaths, wishing the air were crisp and cool instead of muggy and stifling with the promise of rain.

The vestiges of the dream and Tonovan's leering face made her reach for her axe, needing the comforting solidity of its haft in her hand. It was still next to her. Thankfully. She'd had nightmares about losing it too.

Her mouth dry, Tezi patted around until she found her canteen. The sounds of other women breathing—and Corporal Basher snoring—filled the tent along with the darkness. It was peaceful breathing. It didn't sound like anyone *else* was having nightmares.

The water was warm, and Tezi wrinkled her nose, thinking of the cool waterfall and the stream that flowed out of the pool on the far side. With axe and canteen in hand, she went out to relieve herself at the camp latrine that Thorn Company used, then headed to the water.

She stepped warily and quietly, not wanting to wake any of the mercenaries who slept outside, not bothering with tents even though rain was frequent in the jungle. Every time she went anywhere alone, she was nervous. The axe made her better able to protect herself, but it also made her a target. Ever since Sorath had disappeared, there'd been more skirmishes between the mercenary companies, more men trying to talk—or force—the women of Thorn Company into having sex with them. Even though Sorath wasn't the belligerent, bellowing type, for whatever reason the men had been on better behavior with him around.

As Tezi knelt on the rocky bank to fill her canteen, the feeling of being watched came over her. Many of the trees and much of the foliage had been cut back from the pool, or outright destroyed in the various monster attacks, but the jungle was still dense enough on the far side that someone could have been spying on the camp from over there.

Tezi peered into the foliage, looking and listening for movement. Patrols circled the camp constantly throughout the night, the teams made up of mages as well as mercenaries, so enemies should have had a difficult time getting close, but the druids had proven themselves powerful opponents and skilled at eluding the troops. It wasn't that surprising, given that this was their homeland and they knew every nook and cranny. They could also spy through the eyes of animals.

Tezi didn't detect any movement, but her senses crawled, and she was certain someone was over there. Certain enough to wake Captain Ferroki and the others to investigate?

She looked up at the mageships hovering high overhead, wondering if their crews were watching the area. Lights burned on Uthari's black-hulled yacht, and a red-uniformed mage walked along the railing before disappearing from view. He wasn't looking down toward the camp.

On another ship, all of the lights were out. If anyone was up there, Tezi couldn't tell. The darkness was atypical. Every other ship in view had some kind of magical lamps active.

Her focus on the mageships almost made her miss hearing the rustle of clothing behind her.

A man whispered, "Get the axe."

Tezi had set it down to fill her canteen, but she grabbed it and rolled to the side. The person who'd been reaching for her missed her arm but managed to snag her shirt. The fabric tore as Tezi flung herself away while swiping the axe behind her.

Her assailant blurted a startled curse and let her go. Surprisingly, it was a woman.

The axe whipped through the air, not making contact, but at least it had forced Tezi's attacker to release her, giving her time to spring to her feet. She spun to face her attackers, her weapon gripped in both hands, the sharp double-bladed head gleaming blue in the night. It reflected in the water of the pool—and the eyes of the two mercenaries who faced her, a man and a woman in sleeveless gray uniforms. The man pointed a magelock pistol at Tezi while the woman snarled and drew a knife.

Tezi didn't recognize them, but the uniforms marked them as belonging to Moon Guard, a company contracted to King Dy.

"Toss us the axe, girl," the man said. "You're not worthy of it."

"Just shoot her." The woman glanced nervously toward the rest of the camp.

Tezi thought about shouting for help, but she was as likely to draw enemies, people who wanted the axe, as allies.

The woman lunged in, slashing with the knife. Though Tezi wasn't as experienced as most of the mercenaries here, she *had* been training hard. And the axe seemed to help her, guiding her arms to connect accurately with the dagger and deflect it. She struck harder than the woman expected and knocked the weapon out of her hand. It splashed into the water.

The axe flared brighter blue in warning. The man fired his pistol, the soft *thwump* making Tezi duck as she swung the blade up, hoping the charge would strike it instead of her. But the magical projectile never reached her. The axe's power deflected it as readily as it did attacks from mages.

"Hurry up," the woman growled. "We only get the bonus if we get the thing."

Bonus? Someone was *paying* these two? Who? Their captain? Some random mercenary with a big purse?

Growling, Tezi lunged toward them and swung, hoping to scare them out of this lunacy. *She* might not be ferocious, but the axe was.

They skittered backward. The woman pulled out another weapon, a pistol, but she hesitated and glanced over her shoulder. The man also looked worried, but then his eyes widened, and he smiled with confidence.

Tezi glanced back, certain some ally had arrived, but she wasn't quick enough. A second man had crept up without making a noise, and he grabbed her from behind, pinning her arms with his own massive muscular limbs. He crushed her in a bear hug that drove the air from her lungs and made her ribs creak. Tezi kept her grip on the axe, but she couldn't swing it.

The smiling man lunged in and gripped the haft, trying to yank it free. Tezi couldn't free her arms, but she still had her legs. She kicked him in the groin and managed to twist in her captor's grip enough to get the axe thief from another angle. Her second kick sent him flying into the pool with a splash.

The woman fired her pistol at Tezi's face, and her heart nearly stopped. But even down at her side, the axe protected her, sending the charge bouncing away as surely as a mage's barrier would have.

"Stop fighting, girl, or you're dead," the bear of a man behind her snarled. "That thing's worth a fortune, and *I'm* going to get it. You don't deserve—"

The man's voice cut off abruptly with a gurgle. Something warm and wet struck the back of Tezi's neck, and his grip slackened.

Though confused, she had the presence of mind to squirm away. The woman fired again, not at Tezi this time but at something over her shoulder. The charge zipped close enough that the axe's protection deflected it. Though hesitant to take her gaze from the woman, Tezi turned partway. She had to know who or what was behind her.

The man who had bear-hugged her lay on the ground, his arms and legs akimbo. The blue glow from her axe provided enough light to see his slit throat and the blood gushing from his arteries.

A wiry man with two knives crouched behind the body, his green hair a wild carrot top, his cheeks covered in tattoos, and his eyes gleaming in the light.

Splashes came from the pool as the man Tezi had kicked climbed out. Barely glancing at him, the newcomer—the *druid*—threw one of his knives. With horrifying accuracy, it thudded into the man's eye. He pitched backward, landing in the water again. A new knife replaced the first in the druid's hand, and he threw it as well.

At first, Tezi thought she was the target, and she jumped aside, her foot slipping on the edge of the pool. She flailed and kept her balance—barely. In the half second she was distracted, the blade found its target. It lodged in the woman's throat. Her pistol clattered to the rocks as she stared in stunned surprise at the druid before crumpling to the ground, as dead as the other two mercenaries.

The druid grinned, a feral glint to his eyes as he held Tezi's gaze. He moved like an animal, light on the balls of his feet—his bare feet—and never rising from a crouch. He lifted his remaining knife, the blade dripping with blood from his first kill, and licked it.

Tezi stared in horror, her grip vise-tight around her axe's haft. Would the crazy druid attack her next?

He sprang, not at her but to the woman he'd killed. He pulled his knife free from her throat, then lunged toward Tezi.

She jumped to the side, swinging her axe to keep him back. But again, he wasn't trying to reach her. He stepped into the pool and pulled his other knife free. The one he gripped in his right hand was the only one he hadn't thrown. It was made from bone, bone stained with blood.

"What do you want?" Tezi whispered, still wondering if he would attack her.

He'd *saved* her, but that didn't make him an ally. He might be getting rid of the people around her first so he could study the axe and figure out how best to steal it from her.

But he looked up at the dark mageship instead of answering her. Movement stirred at the railing.

Without any lights, Tezi couldn't tell what was going on up there, but a shout rang out from one of the cabins. Several dark figures leaped over the railing.

Some magic slowed their descent, and they landed lightly ten feet behind the crazy druid. One of the men was naked and could barely walk. The others, clad in grass and hide garments—druid clothing—hurried toward the jungle on the far side of the pool.

The crazy druid lingered and lifted a finger to his lips, meeting Tezi's eyes again.

Realizing this was a jailbreak, and that she was standing dumbly by and letting it happen, Tezi opened her mouth to shout and warn the camp. But the druid jerked his arm in a circular motion.

She hefted the axe, prepared to defend herself from a thrown knife. But all that appeared was a great puff of green smoke. It spread rapidly, obscuring the druid and everything for several feet around him.

Tezi lunged at the smoke and swung. It wasn't a fully committed swing, not when the crazy man had saved her life, but she feared the repercussions that would befall her when her superiors—and the mages employing the company—found out that she'd watched a team of druids steal back their ally and hadn't done anything to stop them.

Not surprisingly, her axe whistled through the air without connecting with anything.

The druids were gone.

5

Rain pattered on the roof of the tent as Jadora finished packing for the trip. She tucked everything, from the scant spare clothing she had to her homemade smoke grenades and vials of acid to her microscope and sample jars, into the magical backpack that Malek had made for her. The backpack that held far more than should have been possible.

She'd slept little the night before as she stared up at the ceiling of the tent, worrying about Malek and envisioning him being tortured by his bastard of a king. Every time she'd dozed off, she'd dreamed of Malek in an ancient castle dungeon, hanging from shackles bolted into mildewy walls, naked in a cell with one of the slavemasters from Hell whipping him as he screamed in pain.

The reality, she was sure, hadn't been so grisly, but she'd heard him cry out more than once as her guards had taken her back to camp, and she knew genuine pain when she heard it. It appalled her that Uthari could treat him so. She hated him, hated that Malek was loyal to a man who didn't *deserve* his loyalty. Even worse, she couldn't help but blame herself for his predicament.

As much as she wanted the world to change, she shouldn't

have allowed herself to contemplate ways to make that happen. Not here in a camp full of mages. Not when it could get Malek in trouble.

Her gaze snagged on *The Mind Way*, the monk book that he'd given her to study. She grabbed it, looked at the cover, and lamented that she hadn't yet succeeded in mastering protecting her thoughts. Was it delusional to believe she ever could? Or would someone like Uthari always be able to twitch a finger and rip them out of her mind?

No, the book said in the introduction that the exercises took practice, that the monks spent years mastering them. She tucked the tome into her backpack. It might take a long time, but she would keep working on it. It would be worth it to keep mages from reading her mind.

It would be worth it to keep Malek from getting into trouble because of her.

The tent flap stirred, letting in the sounds of camp, of mercenaries practicing at swords and of someone yelling about an intrusion in the night and a missing prisoner. She would almost be glad to escape this enemy-filled place and visit a new world where she had orders to study exotic plants. If only Tonovan weren't going.

Malek walked into the tent, ready for the trip. He wore a backpack, with his weapons at his hips, and a couple of magelock pistols in his hand. There was a stern, aloof set to his jaw.

"Malek," Jadora whispered, searching his eyes for pain—and for signs that he resented her for what he'd endured.

His cool facade should have made it easier to keep her emotions in check, but its presence only made her more certain that he'd been hurt badly. That he wanted to distance himself from her so he wouldn't have to suffer that treatment again. She drew in a shaky breath. She would do nothing to thwart his wishes.

"Professor Freedar." Malek stopped in front of her. "The ship is ready. Have you finished packing?"

He glanced at her backpack, the top of her disassembled microscope and the monk book visible.

"Yes. I'm ready."

"I must ask for the kerzor," he said.

"Per King Uthari's orders?" she guessed.

"It's not safe to leave it in your hands."

"I suppose not." Jadora kept her mind empty, not letting herself lament that she hadn't taken the opportunity to ask someone to make more of them. Who would she have asked, anyway? What mage would have willingly built weapons that could be used against their kind?

She tugged the metal disc out of a case on a shelf and gave it to him. Malek set it on the table, and a second later, it burst into flames.

Jadora flinched, startled. Why, she didn't know. Of course Uthari would want the thing destroyed. And judging by the brief savage look in Malek's eyes, he delighted in doing it. Understandable, since the device had taken his magic from him.

As the flames died away, leaving only a melted lump behind, she couldn't help but gaze at him and wistfully remember the Malek who'd had no power, the Malek she hadn't had to guard her thoughts around.

Since that Malek was no more, she took care not to think about the schematics she'd made when she'd had the kerzor disassembled back on Vran. With luck, he wouldn't remember that she'd been studying it, and Uthari wouldn't find out.

With his task done, Malek held the pistols out to her.

"I brought these for you and Jak." They were surprisingly ornate, the hilts engraved and gilded, the metal gleaming with fine craftsmanship. Were they magical? She couldn't tell, but they were of a fine quality. "They'll do until such time that Lord Homgor can figure out how to make firearms out of dragon steel."

"Are you sure it's a good idea for us to be openly armed?" Despite the question, Jadora accepted the weapons.

The firearms wouldn't be effective against Tonovan or the other mages, but she had no doubt they would face dangerous creatures on Nargnoth. She put one aside to give to Jak and attached the other to her backpack where she could reach it easily.

"Yes," Malek said firmly. "I also rummaged through the *Serene Waters*' armory, hunting for anything that might be of use to you in case you need to protect yourself and I'm busy being attacked and can't manage." He reached into his pocket and opened his palm to reveal a silver ring with an exquisitely cut emerald embedded on the top.

"You scrounged priceless jewelry in your ship's armory?"

And he was giving it to *her*? The emotions she'd tamped down threatened to overflow again.

"In Uthari's armory. The *Star Flyer* possesses nothing so glamorous. But this is more than a bauble. If you twice tap the gem to someone's flesh, it will give them an electric shock. I'm afraid it's unlikely to take down a powerful mage, but perhaps it will assist you if you need to get away from an enemy." He shook his head, as if he lamented that he couldn't give her something better.

"Won't Uthari miss it? And be angered if he sees it on my finger?"

"I doubt he remembers it's in his armory. It's likely some doodad that he won in a battle decades past. He has many treasures."

"Right. I remember he decorates his lavatory with dragon-steel artifacts."

Malek snorted softly and took her hand. He gently slid the ring onto her finger, its magic making it a perfect fit.

An ache filled her at this tenderness, and she drew a shaky

breath to resist the urge to lean into him and rest her cheek against his chest. She glanced at the book and again vowed to study it. To protect him.

"Jadora," Malek said with a soft sigh.

She couldn't help it. She leaned against him. And he rested an arm around her shoulders and breathed in the scent of her hair.

"I vowed not to touch you again," he murmured.

"And I vowed not to grow weepy and dribble tears all over your shirt."

"Well, you're not doing that. I don't believe."

"No." She sniffed and wiped his shirt.

He laughed softly.

"Where's our fearless commander?" came a bellow from outside.

Tonovan.

Jadora pulled back as Malek dropped his arm. She wiped her eyes, grabbed her pack, and nodded her readiness.

The tent flap stirred again, and she tensed, certain Tonovan was barging in. She blanked her mind. She definitely didn't want any feelings for Malek brimming in her thoughts when he lurked nearby.

But Jak was the one to enter, his pack slung over one shoulder, and he didn't comment on their closeness. "Did you hear? There were druids in the camp last night. They stole back the prisoner who was being kept up on one of Uthari's ships."

"I heard." Malek headed for the exit. "Captain Rivlen and Thorn Company have been charged with dealing with the druids."

"Think that'll be better or worse than our task?" Jak looked at Jadora.

She could only shake her head. She didn't know about the mission, but the people—the *company*—would be better on the *Star Flyer*. The mercenaries hardly ever threatened to brutalize, apprehend, or kill her and Jak.

Jadora walked outside with him and found the long narrow mageship ready for departure. It faced the gate, propped on legs that she first thought were independent of the craft. As they got closer, she realized they were built into it and had folded out for the purpose of keeping the curved bottom of the hull level and off the ground while it wasn't in the air.

Shikari was sniffing around the base of the portal, still small in comparison to it, though he'd grown much in these past weeks. Jadora couldn't tell if the ancient artifact interested him, or if some wolf or coyote had prowled through during the night to scent-mark it.

When she spotted King Uthari as well as Tonovan, Lieutenant Vinjo, and King Jutuk's men standing beside the cargo hatch in the side of the ship, Jadora slowed to a stop. Uthari was speaking with Vinjo, who wore a grass skirt that left his knees bare, while the other men watched impassively.

Several of Uthari's bodyguards had come down with their king, but they stood back, not participating in the conversation. Two attractive young women with slavebands around their heads wore glazed expressions as they waited near the hatch as male servants carried cargo into the ship. Were the women coming along? Bed slaves for the officers? Tonovan's or the admiral's? Or maybe they would share.

Jadora couldn't keep from frowning with distaste. There was also a willowy, green-uniformed lieutenant with short blonde hair leaning against the hull with her arms folded across her chest. Had Queen Vorsha also finagled a person onto the crew?

"That's Lieutenant Harintha, a helm officer and mage of modest talents," Malek said quietly. He'd stopped when Jadora had stopped and noticed where she was looking. "She's also been tasked with keeping an eye on the prisoner that King Uthari and Queen Vorsha are now sharing custody of, per their latest negotiations."

"Prisoner?" Jadora asked. "Zethron?"

She winced, realizing she'd almost forgotten about him the night before. She'd been worried about *Malek's* torture, but Zethron might have been suffering a similar fate.

"Yes," Malek said.

Zethron stuck his head out of the open hatchway and peered around. Relief at seeing him alive and capable of standing upright washed through Jadora.

He'd retained his hat, one not that different from the one Jak wore, and wasn't noticeably wounded, but his clothes were rumpled, and he hadn't been given a chance to shave. He managed a smile when he spotted her, the gesture reminding her, as it had when they'd first met, of her dead husband. Despite the smile, he looked beleaguered, as if he'd had a long night.

A long *painful* night?

After returning Zethron's smile and waving to him, Jadora looked at Malek, wondering if he knew if Zethron had been tortured. He might not, since whatever had been done to him had been at the hands of Vorsha's officers.

I do not know, Malek spoke into her mind. *I only know that Uthari wasn't pleased with me when Vorsha's fleet commander contacted him and he learned that Zethron came back with us and I'd failed to mention it.*

Jadora slumped, regretting again that she kept getting Malek in trouble with his king. She hadn't *asked* him to hide Zethron, but she'd expressed concern that exactly this would happen, that Zethron would be captured and tortured for information. She hadn't envisioned officers from one of the *other* fleets stumbling across him, but perhaps she should have.

I'm sorry, she replied.

I believe our rulers came to an agreement that he'll act as a guide on the mission and that anything we learn will be shared between Vorsha and Uthari.

And King Jutuk? Jadora looked at the admiral.

Yes. Uthari would prefer to keep everything to himself, but the other fleets—and their rulers—are pressuring him with the threat of banding together against him. It was difficult enough dealing with Zaruk's and Vorsha's and Dy's combined forces. Fighting off the combined fleets of all *the other kingdoms... Even with the portal's help, Uthari doesn't believe he could do that.*

The portal's help. Jadora looked at the ancient artifact. She'd heard that Uthari had called forth lightning from it, the same as Jak could, to drive off the druids. She shivered to think of that man with access to even more power.

Maybe he was monitoring her thoughts, for Uthari looked over at her, then met Malek's gaze.

"Come," Malek said quietly, touching the small of her back and nodding for Jak to follow as well.

She would have preferred to go straight into the ship to check on Zethron, but she doubted she had a choice. She raised a finger toward the hatchway, hoping she and Zethron would get a chance to talk privately later.

"Wait, *I'm* going along?" Vinjo was saying as Jadora and Malek approached. "I just explained everything about the operation and maintenance of the power supply, navigation orb, and engine for *their* sake." Vinjo gestured with both arms toward Tonovan, the admiral, and the helm officer. "They can perform any repairs that might be necessary."

"I don't believe these officers have engineering experience," Uthari said dryly.

No, Jadora highly doubted Tonovan had experience doing anything except barking orders at people.

Tonovan had been watching Vinjo with a bored expression on his face, but he gazed over at her and smirked. Reading her thoughts, no doubt. Jadora practiced the exercise from *The Mind*

Way, envisioning her mind within a turtle shell, protected from hurricane gales battering at it.

"I left instructions," Vinjo said. "And diagrams. *Simple* diagrams. I'm sure they can figure it out."

"You'll go along," Uthari said, his tone switching from dry to cool. "Perhaps, if the mission succeeds, I'll allow you to return to your fleet."

Vinjo peered wistfully toward a blue-hulled ship visible over the trees in the distance. Some of Zaruk's ships had joined others in the area, but they were giving Uthari's fleet a wide berth.

"Also," Malek said, "if you're not here, you won't be a target for the druids or anyone else who wants to remove you as a resource for King Uthari."

"It's true that I didn't enjoy being targeted by the druids. They have *no* love for mechanical devices. They blew up my first power converter." Vinjo's gaze shifted to where the Thorn Company women were gathering, preparing to be loaded onto the *Star Flyer* for Rivlen's mission. "Can Lieutenant Sasko come along too? She's wonderful at holding my wrench."

"I'll bet," Tonovan said with a snort.

"She has a more important mission than holding your tool," Uthari said.

"Fighting druids? I heard they're going to fight druids. That sounds deadly." Vinjo gazed at Sasko, distress twisting his mouth. "I made her a clandestineness creeper, but she gave it *away*. She has no way to protect herself now except with her fists and that weak pistol and knife."

"Yes, she gave it away to *Colonel Sorath*." Uthari stepped forward and gripped Vinjo's shoulder to pull his attention back. "I was *not* pleased about that. Why are you making those at *all*, you fool?"

Some magic must have flowed from his fingers, for Vinjo

gasped, his back going rigid. Tonovan smiled his approval at his king's actions—or maybe at seeing someone else in pain.

Jadora clenched her fists, barely able to keep from envisioning driving one of those kerzor into Uthari's temple to rob him of his powers. But Tonovan was still watching her, a smile playing across his lips, so she banished such thoughts. Besides, Malek had destroyed the only kerzor she had.

At her side, Jak also fumed, looking like he wanted to test his burgeoning magic skills by doing something. Jadora gripped his arm. He wasn't a match for any of the men singly and he certainly couldn't attack all of them en masse.

Jak clenched his jaw and looked over at his charge, as if hoping Shikari would rush over and break things up with powerful dragon magic. But their scaly ally was rolling around on his back in the vegetation near the pool, a reminder that he wasn't yet two months old.

Unfortunately, judging by the amused smirk that flirted with Admiral Bakir's lips as he watched the engineer's torment, he and Tonovan might be cut from the same cloth.

"You'll make no more of those," Uthari growled as Vinjo gasped and writhed under his power. "*Ever*. You may be King Zaruk's man, but I'm positive he wouldn't want you making devices to give our mundane minions the ability to strike at us. Use your powers for the good of our kind. For *your* kind." He released Vinjo, whose knees almost gave out as he blinked several times, fighting his body's desire to black out. "You're one of us, not one of them. Don't forget it."

Vinjo bit back whatever retort he wanted to make and looked over at the mercenaries again. Sasko must have heard his gasp and seen him being tormented by Uthari, for her expression was sympathetic as their eyes met.

"If you help us come back with all that the king wants," Malek told Vinjo quietly, "you can reunite with her. Perhaps we'll finish our mission first, and you can use your resourcefulness to help the mercenaries find the druids and render them a non-threat."

Tonovan scoffed. "Why wheedle with and coddle him, Malek? It's not very zidarr-like."

"The promise of a reward can motivate a man as much as the promise of pain," Malek said.

"Please. *Fear* ensures compliance far more than greed."

"But it also cultivates resentment."

"Any man who resents me is welcome to challenge me to a duel." Tonovan eyed Vinjo. "If he's not busy wetting himself at the thought."

"Enough." Uthari stepped back and pointed to the ship. "Waste no more time. Board and depart, and bring me back what I want." He looked toward Malek when he said that.

Jadora wondered if the others knew what Uthari wanted, or if they were only coming along because their rulers had vague notions of finding treasures out there.

"Yes, Your Majesty," Malek and Tonovan said together.

Malek walked toward the portal to insert the key and activate it while the others filed into the ship.

"Hate them," Vinjo muttered under his breath as he walked beside Jak and Jadora. "Hate them *all*."

Jadora hadn't spoken often to the engineer, but she couldn't help but think that this was someone who might indeed be willing to make devices that could rob mages—powerful mages who lorded over the lower-ranking magic users like him—of their power.

Jadora... Malek whispered into her mind, though he was near the portal and not looking at her.

Damn it, she'd been doing the turtle-shell exercise.

I implore you not to scheme in this group. I would prefer you not to have to test that ring immediately.

I'll do my best to think about plants instead of rebellion. Jadora hoped Malek hadn't figured out yet that she had schematics for the kerzor.

A far safer subject, but given that Uthari hasn't shared his hopes for the Jitaruvak with the other rulers or anyone else on this mission, perhaps you could avoid thinking about plants as well. Malek slid the key into the portal and activated the symbols that would open a magical passageway to Nargnoth, the world where plants like Jitaruvak originated, at least according to what she'd seen in the greenhouse on Vran.

You're not leaving me many safe topics to think about.

I know. I'm sorry. Perhaps you could contemplate that dragon parasite and whether we're likely to run into affected dragons on Nargnoth.

I've already contemplated that a great deal but need to gather further specimens to learn more. It's unfortunate that thinking about you would probably also be frowned upon.

About me?

When Tonovan was inserting cruel thoughts into my head before, I repelled him by thinking of you shirtless.

I suppose that would effectively repulse him. Malek didn't mention if he liked the idea of her having such thoughts about him. *But let me know if he torments you again. I'll put a stop to it.*

Of course, Jadora said, though she knew she wouldn't. She was already worried that Bakir and Tonovan were similar souls and, despite having allegiance to different rulers, might well gang up against Malek. The last thing she wanted was to set up a situation where her hypothesis was tested.

As soon as the mageship flew out of the portal on Nargnoth, Jak climbed up to the open deck. Shikari scrambled up the ladder after him, somehow navigating it far better than most four-legged creatures would.

Once outside, the first thing Jak noticed was the scent. The air smelled of unfamiliar foliage, fungal spores, and tar. Huge evergreen trees grew up from islands amid a swamp layered in lily pads the size of mattresses. They floated on murky water gleaming with an oily sheen that made Jak glad they'd brought plenty of their own water to drink. The tree trunks rose hundreds of feet into the air, the needle-filled branches spreading wide and blocking out the sky and most of the light that struggled to filter down.

Something about the place made him think of the primordial climate of Torvil that scientists theorized had existed long before the first animals had crawled about on land. But Zethron had warned his mother that dangerous creatures lived here, so Jak had no doubt that they would encounter animals of all sorts. Animals that probably liked to eat people—and young dragons.

Jak dropped a hand down to reassure himself that Shikari was close. His charge chirped uncertainly. This past week or two, his voice had deepened a little, and he'd developed a fledgling roar, but when something had him worried, he still emitted noises more akin to a chicken than a mighty predator.

"Don't you recognize this place?" Jak whispered.

He knew full well that Shikari had never been here, but in the past, he'd shared imagery suggesting that he could remember things that he hadn't seen, things that his *ancestors* had experienced and somehow passed along in their blood.

Another uncertain chirp followed. Jak hoped they hadn't been led astray and come to the wrong place.

Mother, Zethron, and Malek came up on deck to look around. Before they'd flown through the portal, she'd been talking to Zethron, asking if he was all right and apologizing to him about his capture and treatment at the hands of mages, but this new place inevitably drew her attention.

"Fascinating," she whispered after stepping from one side of the ship to the other, grasping the railing as she peered into the gloom in all directions.

The others observed the world from the navigation cabin below. Jak could sense them down there. Poor Vinjo was wedged in between Tonovan, Bakir, and Prolix while the helm officer sat in one of two seats and guided the ship slowly into this new world. She probably wasn't delighted by the company either.

Giant gray birds squawked and screeched as they flew between trees with branches draped by vines that stretched all the way into the swamp below. Some of the vines hung so densely that they created curtains around the islands. Elongated mushrooms several feet high peeked out from behind them, blue- and purple-speckled caps providing rare spots of color among the browns and dark greens.

Mother peered down at the mushrooms, her fingers twitching, as if she longed to collect specimens. She doubtless did, though there wasn't anything like the Jitaruvak in her drawings. Aside from the trees and lily pads, Jak didn't see much foliage. They might have to fly somewhere else to find plants with the fern-like fronds that were supposed to proliferate on this world.

"Someone had best mark the location of the portal," Zethron said, pointing behind them. He spoke in Dhoran, his command of the language having improved much over the past couple of weeks.

The ship was sailing away from an island dominated by two towering trees with the ancient portal glowing blue between them. It was as draped with vines as the nearby branches, as if it had been forgotten and hadn't seen travelers for a long time. But that couldn't be true. A skiff and a canoe were pulled up on the shore below it, as if waiting for new adventurers to arrive and explore.

Of course, it was also possible they'd been used by people who'd gone through the portal to *escape* this world. Jak tried not to dwell on that possibility.

The constellation of stars in the portal—the Dragon's Tail of Torvil—winked out, and the glow disappeared, leaving the monolith dark on the island.

"We won't get lost." Malek stood in the center of the deck, his hands on his weapons as he surveyed the area, his gaze lingering on another of the large birds as it flew near the ship. No, that wasn't a bird but an insect. A *huge* insect. It had four leathery wings instead of two and looked like a giant dragonfly.

"Many do," Zethron said.

"You're not being cocky, are you, Malek?" Mother asked with a faint smile.

"Zidarr can find their way with their senses and are taught not to get lost," Malek said.

"So... yes. Cocky."

Malek's eyebrow twitched. "Rightfully so. Besides, we have Jak, and he's a cartographer, isn't he?"

"Nobody's mapped this place yet," Jak said. "At least nobody from our world."

"Then you'd better get started."

"Given the speed with which we're flying away from the portal, that could be challenging." It didn't help that everywhere Jak looked was the same. He spun a slow circle, searching for landmarks, but aside from the portal itself, little stood out. "We might want to fly up above the trees and look around."

"*Yes*," Zethron said and snapped his fingers, as if something had occurred to him.

Everyone looked at him.

"The natives here come down to the swamp to hunt and forage when they must, but they otherwise live on islands above the trees. When I visited before, they said it was safer up there, that predators and other dangers were less likely to find them."

"You'd also be able to see for miles," Jak said. "Maybe there are lakes or mountains or other landmarks that would be visible."

"Islands in the sky?" Mother asked. "Magical islands like our sky cities?"

"I'm not sure, actually," Zethron said. "The one I visited was supported by great posts even taller than the trees."

"How do the natives get around?" Jak asked. "Mageships?"

They hadn't existed on Vran, but he supposed it made sense that people on other worlds could have developed such craft, especially if there were a lot of dangers near the ground.

"No," Zethron said. "From what I saw, the people here don't have powerful magical devices or the technology to fly by mundane means. They domesticate and ride the *nakka*. Large birds."

"Ridable birds? That sounds intriguing. Not as fun as riding a dragon, but I'd try it." Jak patted Shikari on the head.

He was still cheeping quietly to himself and peering all around, nostrils twitching as he inhaled the scents.

"I'll tell Lieutenant Harintha to take us above the canopy," Malek said.

"Are you in charge of her?" Jak asked. "Of everyone?"

Did lieutenants in other fleets take orders from zidarr? For that matter, did Admiral Bakir believe himself of equal rank to Malek? And Tonovan? Would they end up butting heads?

"I am leading the mission," Malek said.

"Oh, good."

Mother had returned to gazing at the mushrooms, but she looked over at Malek again, uncertainty flashing in her eyes. Maybe she didn't believe the others would treat him as the absolute leader. Jak hoped they would, but he could envision trouble erupting. They had officers from three different kingdoms along, three different kingdoms that weren't, as far as he knew, officially allied with each other.

Instead of climbing down to give the order in person, Malek merely closed his eyes. Jak couldn't blame him for not wanting to squeeze into navigation with Tonovan and the others. Or maybe it was that he wanted to stay close to protect Jak and Mother. If so, Jak appreciated that. His last interaction with Tonovan had involved the cruel general smashing him to the floor and contemplating killing him.

The ship rose slowly, avoiding outstretched branches that threatened to claw at the hull. As the water and the portal receded from view, Jak wondered if he had missed his guess and the trees were thousands of feet tall instead of hundreds. Was that possible?

He didn't sense any magic emanating from them. Beyond the ship and those on it, the portal was the only thing magical that he detected.

Realizing he might have access to a resource beyond their guide, Jak closed his eyes and reached out to the portal with his mind. Maybe this one would also consider him a *Favored Traveler* and deign to communicate with him.

Before he got far with his attempt, Shikari butted his legs with his head.

"If that means you're hungry," Jak whispered, "I brought along a jar of delicious tarantulas for you, but I need a few minutes first. Maybe one of those giant dragonflies will get close. Why don't you work on your hunting skills?"

Shikari shifted to rubbing his head against Jak's leg. He had two fuzzy nubs on top that reminded Jak of antlers but would eventually turn into horns. Maybe they itched.

"Better than teething, I guess," Jak mumbled, trying not to feel like a cat tree.

"I wonder if we can convince our navigator to fly close enough for me to get a sample of one of those." Mother had taken out binoculars and was leaning over the railing, looking at some of the vines—or perhaps something *on* the vines.

"Don't fall over the side," Jak said.

"I'm not the one with a dragon ramming me in the hip."

"Not *now*, but he'll probably rub against anything nearby."

Malek must have finished communicating with the helm officer, for two little bursts of magic came from him. They sliced through one of the vines, and a sample floated toward Mother, the piece as thick as her wrist and more than three feet long.

"Oh, thank you." She dug one of her vials and a sample spatula and debated how to cut a specimen small enough to fit.

"There are plants like your Jitaruvak along the rivers here," Zethron said, "but not in these stagnant swamps. If we can find some locals, they may recognize your drawing and direct you to the exact place."

"That would be ideal," Mother said.

Jak shifted his attention back to the portal. It would be easier to communicate with it before they flew farther away.

Hello, portal friend, he thought at it. *I'm Jak Freedar, an explorer from another world, and I've come across this young dragon. I'm taking care of him inasmuch as I can, but I'd like to find some adult dragons—ah, friendly* elder *adult dragons—who would be more appropriate to care for him. Have you by chance seen any?*

Long seconds passed without a response of any kind. The portals usually spoke to him with images rather than words, and he sensed an entity within this one, as he had with all the others, but he also sensed it was distant and aloof.

It flashed an image of the dragon eggs embedded in the glacier back on the first world Jak had visited. Then it spoke in a stern male voice. *It is not yet their time.*

The words boomed in Jak's mind, startling him. Between that and Shikari shoving at his leg, he stumbled and caught himself on the railing. It was a good thing the barrier was there because they were hundreds of feet above the ground now.

Why did you take the egg, human?

The portal on that world asked me to. It showed me how to get to the eggs. Shikari's was half sticking out of the ice, and the portal gave me the sense that he might hatch in the spring and die alone there with nobody to take care of him. Emotion welled in Jak's throat at the idea.

Esylenara has always been melodramatic.

Uh, is that a name? The name of the portal? Did they *have* names?

She who gave herself to the Cydora gateway. You should have left the egg. Better to die than to be taken and become one of them.

One of them? The younger dragons? Or... something else? Jak thought of the parasite his mother had discovered, the parasite that had left the dead dragon on Vran and tried to infest Shikari. At least, that was what they'd believed it had been doing. They had stopped it before they'd found out for certain that the hatchling was the target. Thankfully. Jak shuddered to imagine some weird parasite infesting him and his mother.

Many seasons have passed, the portal said, *but they remain a threat, a problem for which we have no solution.*

Will you tell me more about it? Maybe we can help. We like challenging problems.

Humans are still very primitive. We'd thought that perhaps in time, they might become more of a resource, but they would rather war among themselves than evolve as a race.

Yeah, some of us are into war but not all. Let us try to help. My mother is a scientist. She may have ideas. Jak pointed at his mother, who'd sliced off a piece of the vine and was peering at it with a magnifying glass she'd removed from one of her always-stuffed pockets. A sappy purple substance dribbled from the cut vine, and she took a separate sample of that.

The portal fell silent, but Jak feared that meant it was underwhelmed. Too bad Mother hadn't been doing something a little more impressive than looking at a purple-sap-oozing plant.

We have observed her, but you humans are too primitive. There is no hope.

Jak sensed the portal withdrawing from him. "And he calls the other one melodramatic," he muttered.

"Jak?" Mother asked as she tucked her tools away.

"Just chatting with the portal. It says we're primitive."

"Really."

"I attempted to communicate with it, and it ignored me," Malek said, an eyebrow raising. "Have you figured out yet why you're a *Favored Traveler* and what that entails?"

"No, and this one was unimpressed by me."

"At least it spoke with you."

"Are you jealous?" Mother smiled at Malek.

"I am not. I am befuddled."

"Because portals should naturally prefer to speak with powerful zidarr and not boys?" she asked.

"Naturally."

Jak lifted a finger. "I'm a man these days, remember. Nineteen. I had to shave this morning."

Malek gazed blandly at him.

"*And* the day before yesterday," Jak added. "Pretty soon, it'll be every day, or I'll turn into a gorilla."

Malek shook his head and looked at Mother. "Befuddling."

A beam of sunlight slashed across the deck. They were finally nearing the top of the trees, and blue sky was visible above the branches.

Malek looked sharply upward, but he appeared more alarmed than pleased by their progress. "I sense something magical."

"There are flying creatures here called *myvlarii*," Zethron said. "They are naturally magical and prey upon the *nakka*."

"I believe it's a dragon," Malek said.

Zethron frowned. "*They* prey on *everyone*."

"No kidding," Jak said.

"I sense several dragons," Malek said, "and they're heading this way."

"*Several* dragons?" Mother looked gravely at Jak.

"I believe six," Malek said.

Six?

"Is there any chance we can hide from them?" Mother asked.

"That hasn't worked yet," Jak muttered.

"Thus far, we've sought them out. Whether intentionally or not."

"I don't think hiding behind vines is going to fool them. Oh, wait." Jak snapped his fingers. "Vinjo was trying to put some camouflage on the ship. Maybe we *can* hide."

"I saw his attempt at camouflage." Malek didn't sound impressed. "I doubt it'll fool a dragon, but I'll attempt to use my own magic to further the effect. If we have to fight six dragons, this mission will end before it begins."

6

OUTSIDE, THE SUN WAS SETTING, BUT THE DRUID TUNNELS HAD THE same green glow no matter what the hour. Sorath had been summoned, Kywatha's telepathic call saying only that it was time, and he was heading to one of their meeting areas.

Before leaving the clifftop, he'd seen Malek, Jak, Jadora, and several other mages leave through the portal on their new ship, so he knew one of his targets was out of reach. That suited him. He believed Malek would be the hardest to kill.

Would the druids want him to take out Yidar tonight? Sorath hadn't seen the zidarr since he'd been living in the camp, but he assumed the man was on one of the mageships. He had a feeling it didn't matter, at least not tonight. The druids would want him to prioritize the assassination of Uthari.

His stomach fluttered at the thought. He had agreed to it, and he had Vinjo's stealth device and the druids' dragon-steel dagger. He was as prepared as he would ever be, but he couldn't help but find the mission daunting. Still, he wouldn't shy away from it. He wanted that man dead, even if he had to trade his own life to make it happen.

Numerous men and women waited in the meeting area. They all wore deadly weapons, an interesting juxtaposition to the flowers braided into their green hair and their homespun tunics and trousers made from coarse plant fiber. An older man with white hair was wearing a cloak made from matted grass.

Sorath spotted Kywatha speaking with two other women and headed toward her, but another group arrived, four men helping a fifth out of a tunnel. Sorath paused as he recognized the druid prisoner who'd been tortured in the same tent as he. Tovorka.

Their eyes met, and the druid's widened. He pointed at Sorath in alarm and spoke rapidly to the men in his group. Three of them were dressed similarly to the other druids in the room, but one was a younger man with wild eyes, bare feet, and short green hair that stuck out in all directions.

He dropped to a crouch with a dagger in his hand as he studied Sorath with assessing eyes. Unlike most of the druids here, he had pale skin that suggested he was from Tezi's part of the world. There might even have been a few freckles under the grime and tattoos covering his cheeks.

The freckles didn't make him appear any less fierce and intimidating. Not that Sorath was easily intimidated. He narrowed his eyes and met the kid's gaze.

"Kywatha," one of the newcomers called and waved her over.

She spotted them, smiled, and jogged to the group, then gave Tovorka a hug. The former prisoner patted her on the back but didn't take his gaze from Sorath. He whispered to her. Judging by the alarmed pointing, Tovorka wanted to know what Sorath was doing here and possibly how he'd acquired the dragon-steel dagger.

Sorath rested a hand on its sheath, hoping none of the druids would demand that he give it back, not before he'd gone on his mission. To his surprise, the weapon warmed his hand through the leather sheath. A faint blue glow seeped out around the hilt, and a vision popped into his mind.

In it, he lay injured on the floor of a luxurious room with a four-poster bed, silk sheets, and a white sheepskin rug. Blood spattered that rug. His. His and someone else's. A crumpled form sprawled across the bed, more blood turning the sheets dark. Was it Uthari? No, the wounded person's back was to him, and he couldn't rise from the floor for a better view, but it wasn't the old wizard.

Before he could investigate further, someone naked climbed out of the bed to glare down at him. *That* was Uthari. And he didn't appear injured, just furious. Not good.

Uthari spread his hand, and lightning streaked from his fingers. It slammed into Sorath, delivering intense pain, making him cry out and writhe helplessly on the floor. Where was the dragon-steel dagger? He needed it for protection and to kill that bastard.

But it lay on the floor, too far away to reach. Lightning pummeled Sorath, and all he could do was writhe as the agony intensified, as his death approached.

A raised voice nearby caused the vision to shatter. Sorath was back in the underground chamber and looking at the wild man, the wild man who'd crept closer and was pointing angrily at him while speaking loudly to the rest of the group. No, to Kywatha. The accusing words seemed to be for her.

Sorath didn't recognize the kid—he appeared to be nineteen or twenty behind those tattoos—and wondered how he'd wronged him. Then he realized the wild-haired druid wasn't pointing at him but at the dagger.

Kywatha held up a conciliatory hand as she walked over to join Sorath. The young man growled like a panther. From the way he crouched, ready to spring away at any sudden movement, he *acted* like a panther too. He was animalistic even for one of the nature-loving druids, and Sorath found *himself* crouching and raising his pickaxe hand, not certain if the crazy kid would attack him.

He bared his teeth at Kywatha as she approached, and she grimaced and stopped a few feet away. Even the *druids* didn't seem to know if their wild man would attack them.

"Part of your rescue team?" Sorath asked mildly, though he didn't rise from his defensive crouch or lower his pick.

"This is Grunk. He's... a strong warrior and an asset."

"There's grass stuck between his toes."

"That happens when you don't wear shoes."

"So I hear."

Though Kywatha was speaking to Sorath, she kept her eyes on the wild kid, her hands raised, palms out, as if she felt she needed to show him that she didn't carry weapons. "He believes the dragon-steel dagger is his and feels betrayed that you're carrying it," she explained before switching to her language and firing off a rapid series of words to the kid.

"It's not, is it?"

"Technically, he was the one responsible for bringing it to our community."

"Oh?" Sorath's hand strayed possessively toward the hilt, but he stopped himself. As handy as it would be for this mission, he knew it had been lent temporarily to him. He just hadn't realized *how* temporary it might be.

"He was originally an outsider," Kywatha said, switching back to Dhoran, "from one of the few families of druids who live in the Kingdom of Vor. He had to leave and flee here. He brought the dagger and offered it as a gift to our people in exchange for being allowed in to become one of us."

"But he opted not to adopt the dress code?"

Kywatha gave him a flat look at the joke, but all she said was, "He wouldn't mind if one of our people were holding the dagger, but he objects to you using it."

"Does he object to my mission?"

"He doesn't know about it. I haven't told him."

Grunk jumped up and down as he whipped two knives out of belt sheaths. He darted in close, and Sorath shifted to put his pick between them, but it was a feint, and the druid sprang back out, landing in a crouch again as he spoke rapidly to Kywatha.

"Would it *help* if he knew?" Sorath asked, not fazed by what he perceived as a challenge. If the kid wanted a fight, Sorath would give him a fight, but if the rest of the druids didn't treat it like a duel and piled on, that would be problematic. "I assume he's not a fan of Uthari."

Sorath hadn't yet met anyone who *was*, unless one counted his loyal and brainwashed zidarr.

"He's not," Kywatha said, "but Queen Vorsha is the one he truly loathes."

The kid recognized the name, and his eyes widened again, pure fury burning in them. He leaped in the air again, though he didn't close on Sorath this time. He landed in a crouch facing a wall and slashed and stabbed at the air with his daggers. Shadow fencing? Imagining Vorsha was standing in front of him?

The kid had fast feet, his legs a blur as he darted and dodged, fighting with his imaginary opponent. It was more than mindless swatting. Sorath recognized experience and skill in the way the kid attacked and guarded his blades. Scars on his arms suggested he'd been in numerous real fights.

With a snarl and a finishing flourish, he spun back toward them.

"You said he's from Vorsha's continent?" Sorath asked.

"Yes. We don't know everything about his past, or even if Grunk is his real name, but he told us he lost his family and was taken prisoner. For years, he was tortured and forced to fight." Kywatha frowned. "And perform other demeaning tasks."

The kid flashed his teeth again. His canines were strangely

sharp, as if he or someone else had filed them to make him look more like an animal.

"I'll bet," Sorath said.

Grunk eyed him, and it occurred to Sorath that, if he was from Vor, he might understand Dhoran after all. That and Wizards' Common were widely spoken languages, and Dhoran was the main language of the northern continents.

Grunk rattled off what sounded like a command—or maybe an ultimatum—to Kywatha.

She sighed and explained something to him. Sorath's mission?

The kid settled somewhat, but he ultimately shook his head and pointed at Sorath's chest.

"He doesn't trust you," Kywatha said, "and he doesn't want the dagger to be let out of our community with a foreigner. To ensure it's not lost, he wants to go with you to assassinate the mages."

Sorath blinked.

"He's heard that Vorsha is on the way here, and he wants to kill her while you're killing the others."

"Oh, sure," Sorath said. "Killing a wizard and two zidarr was going to be extremely easy, so we should naturally plan to visit another well-guarded mageship and kill another wizard."

Grunk nodded firmly.

"Just see what you can do," Kywatha said. "With his help."

Sorath rubbed his face. "I have a device that can hide me from eyesight and mage senses." He touched the clandestineness creeper attached to a leather bracelet on his wrist. "How's *he* going to sneak in?"

Kywatha shrugged. "I don't know. Maybe you can hold hands."

The kid's lip curled. Sorath's did too. While he wouldn't have minded taking a few capable and trustworthy allies on this mission, especially if they were also armed with stealth devices, the thought of sneaking onto the well-guarded mageships with an unknown and untested jungle child was as appealing as camel dung smothered in flies.

"It's the only way he'll let the dagger leave the tunnels with you," Kywatha said. "He'll probably stay here if you leave it behind."

Judging by Grunk's frown, that might not be true.

Even if the kid had nodded firmly, Sorath didn't know if he would have left the dagger. Based on what little he'd seen of Tezi's new axe, protecting him from mind readers was the least the magical weapon could do. He trusted it had been responsible for the vision he'd received. He hoped it had been a warning and not a promise of an immutable future.

The last thing Sorath wanted was to die writhing on a rug at Uthari's feet.

"We're not that far from the portal." Jadora gripped the railing of the ship, glad Malek stood at her side but worried about his promise that *six* dragons were on the way. "Maybe we should fly back down and flee home before they get here."

As much as she wanted to find the Jitaruvak and study the other interesting flora here, if this world was overflowing with dragons, they dared not explore.

"Wouldn't they follow us back?" Jak whispered. "We don't want to lure them home."

"We could go somewhere else," Jadora said. "The world with all the ice, maybe."

"*No.*" Jak gripped her arm. "We can't lead them there. We can't lead *anyone* there."

"Ah, right. I remember." She'd been thinking of its frigid barrenness, not the eggs trapped—hidden—in the glacier. "Another world, then."

"If they're after us, they'd still be able to follow us and get us."

"*Are* they after us?" Jadora looked at Malek, but his eyes were closed, his face rigid with concentration.

Could he truly camouflage the ship from dragons? Given their immense power, it seemed unlikely.

"It might be a coincidence that they showed up," Jak said.

"This isn't right." Zethron peered up at the canopy and the sky beyond it. "When I visited before, the people here said dragons hadn't been seen for a long time. They spoke of dangerous animals, birds, and insects, but they were able to protect their people from them and survive."

"That may have changed," Malek said.

Shikari had been nibbling at the vine, but he sat back on his haunches and peered upward. He issued an uncertain squeak. A dark winged shadow flew through the blue sky, but the branches made it difficult to tell much about it, except that it was large.

"Any chance he's sensing friendly elder dragons?" Jadora looked at Jak.

Shikari ran and hid behind his legs.

"I don't think so," Jak said grimly.

A soft clang sounded as the hatch in the deck opened. Admiral Bakir and Prolix climbed out, followed by Tonovan. Normally, Jadora wouldn't have been pleased to see him—any of them—but they would need the help. Was it possible that with more mages on their team, they might effectively drive off the dragons?

If there'd been only one, she might have had hope, but with so many…

A thunderous screech came from above, the terrifying sound raising every hair on Jadora's arms and making her want to drop to the deck, curl up in a ball, and wrap her arms around her head and neck. As if that would do anything against dragons.

"Shit, Malek," Tonovan said. "What are we supposed to do against so many?"

Eyes closed, Malek didn't answer.

Tonovan cursed again and drew his weapons. The admiral and his zidarr did the same, Bakir wielding a sword and dagger and Prolix lifting a mace and short sword. The men crouched, ready to fight, but they exchanged nervous, daunted glances. Seeing such an expression on a zidarr did nothing to bolster Jadora.

Now, she wished the ship had stayed near the ground. What would happen if the dragons destroyed it? The team wouldn't even have the opportunity to fight. They would all plummet to their deaths.

Zethron touched Jadora's arm and pointed to the hatch. Suggesting they should hide below and let the mages battle the dragons? It wasn't a bad idea, but she couldn't imagine leaving Jak and Malek to fend for themselves. Besides, her little explosives might be able to distract one of the dragons, however briefly.

She waved for him to go below. He had no magic or even a weapon. There was nothing he could do.

Zethron hesitated, as if he didn't want to leave her.

She opened the hatch and gestured again for him to go below. "It'll be safer down there," she said, though she couldn't know that. "Don't endanger yourself. You've suffered enough."

"It was my choice to come," Zethron said.

"To our world perhaps, but not *here*." Jadora pointed at the deck, well aware that Uthari had forced Zethron to join them.

Zethron smiled wistfully. "It's true that this isn't the world I dreamed of exploring. I've already seen *their* ruins."

Up above, the branches stirred, and the first dragon flew fully into view. As Jadora had feared, it was one of the brown-and-gray mottled creatures, its yellow eyes cold and reptilian, so different from Shikari's curious gaze. So alien.

The dragon wasn't looking at the ship—yet—but that didn't mean it didn't know they were there.

Seeing it convinced Zethron to leave, and he eased quietly

down the ladder. Jadora resisted the temptation to follow him, instead silently closing the hatch and going to stand beside Jak and Malek.

Two more dragons streaked between the branches behind the first, their wings furled to their sides as they dove. A few hundred feet away, the other three dragons came into view, also arrowing downward.

Even as a sense-dead human, Jadora could feel their tremendous power and how easy it would be for them to destroy the ship. She locked her knees to keep her legs from giving out and, with a shaky hand, drew the pistol Malek had given her. Little good it would do.

Surprisingly, the dragons didn't alter their course and veer toward the ship. They didn't look at it at all. They kept flying downward toward the swamp. Toward the *portal*?

Jadora eyed Malek, wondering if he—with whatever Vinjo had built into the ship—had managed to keep the powerful creatures from sensing them. Given the lengths that previous dragons had gone through to draw the party to them, it was hard to believe these six were simply ignoring a ship full of humans. Humans and Shikari. The dragons at the ziggurat on Vran had wanted him. Badly.

Jak peered over the railing.

"The portal is activating," he whispered so quietly Jadora almost missed it.

"I thought a key was needed for that," Tonovan said, also speaking in a low voice as he watched the descending dragons.

"For humans," Jak said. "I think the dragons can wave a hand. A talon."

"Check the constellation," Malek murmured, his eyes still closed.

Alarm flashed in Jak's eyes, and he peered over the railing

again. "It's hard to tell from this angle and so far above... but..." He swore.

"Torvil?" Malek asked.

Fresh fear charged through Jadora, not for herself this time but for her world. For her father, who was still with the mage fleet surrounding the portal. And for Thorn Company and all the other terrene humans who had no hope of defending themselves against dragons.

"Yeah," Jak croaked. "They're going to our world."

The first two dragons reached the island with the portal but landed instead of heading through it. Were they waiting for the others to all fly through at once?

The rearmost dragon spread its wings to halt its descent. It was still more than a hundred feet from the ground, and as it leveled out, its long sinuous neck twisted, its head turning like an owl's to look back the way it had come. Its large reptilian eyes peered toward the ship, and Jadora held her breath.

That one might have seen or sensed them through the camouflage—or caught their scent.

The other three dragons landed next to the first two. They looked at the portal, the passageway still open for them, but also at each other. Two flicked their tails, as if in agitation. Because one of the dragons had delayed? Jadora had no idea. Those five weren't looking up at the ship or at their delayed comrade. Unfortunately, the dragon that had halted its descent banked and flew back up toward the ship.

"Uh oh," Jak breathed.

The dragon's eyes weren't focused on them, but they were flicking about, searching in their area. The camouflage had to be helping, but it might not be enough.

"Think we can take that one down?" Tonovan whispered.

Every time Jadora had heard him speak before, he'd sounded

arrogant and cocky. This time, he was uncertain, and he eyed Malek and the others uneasily.

"The other five would come help," Malek murmured.

I sense something out here to hunt, a sinister voice spoke into Jadora's mind—into *all* of their minds.

"Do not answer," Malek whispered, still concentrating on the camouflage. "It does not know exactly where we are. It may not be certain who or what is up here."

I sense a youngling, the dragon said, flapping its wings lazily as it headed toward the ship. *One of our kind but not yet one of us.*

Shikari nosed the vine, as if he wanted to crawl under it to hide. Jadora couldn't blame him.

She slid her backpack off her shoulders. None of the smoke bombs, homemade explosives, or vials of acid inside would bother dragons, but she would throw everything she had to try to distract it, to help the magic users.

He will soon be one of us. And those with him will soon be food.

Humans, one of the dragons on the ground spoke. *They are humans. Our favorite prey.*

A blue flash came from far below. The portal?

Jadora peered over the railing in time to see the connection to Torvil wink out. The dragons next to it noticed and all turned their focus to the portal. It flashed blue again, the symbol for Torvil on the inner wall reappearing, but the typical swirling stars didn't appear in the center. The gateway didn't open.

The portal is denying us passage to the human world, one dragon said.

It defies us? Another dragon roared, and every bird and insect in the swamp fell silent.

Maybe what we were told was incorrect; maybe the portal there is not open once more.

It is. Others have gone there.

The dragon that had been flying toward the ship was no longer looking in their direction. It circled, watching the portal and the others. If the dragons' conversation continued, they stopped sending their words out wide so Jadora and the others could hear.

The portal flashed, and stars swirled in the center. Jadora winced. She didn't want the dragons to stay here and hunt for them, but she also didn't want them to fly to Torvil and attack everyone she knew.

But the constellation that formed in the center wasn't the Dragon's Tail. They'd opened a passageway to another world. Four dragons flapped their wings and sprang through the portal.

The remaining one on the island looked up at the one that had sensed the ship. *Come, before this old malfunctioning heap denies us passage to* all *worlds. Worry not about the natives here. Soon, we will hunt far more humans than you dreamed existed.*

The flying dragon glanced upward again, and Jadora held her breath. Shikari cowered behind Jak's legs.

Finally, it banked again and flew downward. The two dragons disappeared through the portal after the others, and the constellation vanished, closing the route behind them.

Jadora slowly let out her breath. This didn't mean they were safe, as the dragons could turn around and come back, but for the moment, the threat was gone. At least to them.

"Do we know where they went?" Bakir asked.

"They were trying to go to our world. The portal stopped them for some reason, but…" Jak shook his head. "They may still be on their way there. Just because this portal stopped them doesn't mean the others will. They could travel to another world first and use its portal to reach Torvil."

Bakir looked sharply at him. "They can do that? You're sure?"

Jadora nodded. Their own party had done exactly that to get home from Vran.

"Six dragons is a lot," Malek said, "even for the combined might of the fleets. We should go back and help."

"We were sent to find what's *here*," Tonovan said, regaining his bravado now that the dragons were gone. "We won't return until we find it." He looked frankly at Jadora, making her think he knew about the plant.

Did Bakir and Prolix? She suspected their ruler had sent them because of the promise of finding dragon steel or other more obviously valuable treasures.

"Our people need us back there," Malek said.

"I'm not sure if it was intentional," Jak said, "but the portal helped us. It distracted that dragon and kept the others from going to our world."

"*Temporarily*, you think," Bakir said.

Jak spread his hand. "I think the portal may want our assistance. I did kind of offer it."

Malek gazed at him.

"It spoke of an ongoing problem, and I pointed out that Mother is a scientist, and we like to solve problems."

Malek's gaze shifted to Jadora. *Everyone's* did.

She wished Jak had consulted her before volunteering her services to an ancient artifact.

"Are you communicating with it now?" Malek asked.

Jak shook his head. "It feels dormant now. At the least, it's ignoring me."

"Then how do you know it wants your help?" Bakir snapped.

"I don't," Jak admitted. "It's a guess."

Zidarr Prolix rarely spoke, only watching the goings on, but he managed to radiate disapproval as he frowned at Jak.

Jadora touched her son's shoulder, hoping he would drop it. If there was any possibility that those dragons were heading to Torvil, they had to focus on that. They had to go back and help their people.

But Jak lifted his chin mulishly. "We should look around here and try to learn more. If we *could* find a way to help the portals, and through them, the elder dragons, we might be rewarded. Greatly." He was looking at Tonovan and Bakir, saying what they might want to hear.

Jadora doubted Jak cared about rewards. He wanted to find elder dragons to raise Shikari, and he wanted to be a hero. Jadora understood that, but she couldn't support Jak in this. Her father's face flashed in her mind. Portal travel didn't take long. Those dragons might already be attacking the camp.

"King Jutuk doesn't care about the *portals'* problems," Bakir said. "We're here for dragon steel and whatever other prizes there are to be found."

"Helping the portals may result in you getting those prizes," Jak said.

"You just said it isn't talking to you, kid," Bakir said.

"It *did*."

"The portals do communicate with him," Malek said.

Tonovan squinted at Jak. "I can't read his thoughts anymore."

"Darn," Jak muttered.

"But I'm sure if I tormented him a little, he would drop his mental barriers."

"Yes," Jadora said, "tormenting each other is what we should be doing at this crucial time."

I have no trouble reading your *thoughts, Professor,* Tonovan spoke into her mind.

"I imagine they're quite boring." Jadora took a step closer to Malek.

Mostly, he agreed. *Though I'm sure I could find a way to stimulate them.*

"We'll return through the portal." Malek didn't address Tonovan's comments—it was possible he hadn't heard them—but he did rest a protective hand on Jadora's shoulder. "We can search for *prizes* after we've ensured our people are safe."

Bakir grimaced. Why did Jadora have the feeling he would prefer not to return and jump into a battle with six dragons?

Because I'm not a fool, woman. Bakir squinted at her.

"Of course not," she murmured, not pleased that another mage was sauntering through her thoughts. Or *more* than sauntering. She well remembered him striding into her tent and trying to tear information from her mind.

Bakir smiled at her. *A simple matter. I learned enough to know you're here for more than shiny battle-axes. When your zidarr protector isn't nearby, I intend to find out what.*

"Admiral," Malek said, ice in his tone. He must have caught some of that.

Bakir merely turned his smile on him. "Your king should have chosen a mage archeologist if he wanted his secrets kept. Removing her meager defenses is easier than peeling clothes off an eager woman."

Jadora didn't care if King Jutuk's people *did* learn about the Jitaruvak and Uthari's plans for the plant, and she wouldn't have fought that hard to keep the secret, but she worried about what else she might reveal to mages probing her thoughts. If she ever hoped to see some of the kerzor devices made, she would have to set something into motion soon. But dare she?

The ship started descending again, and Bakir's focus shifted toward the portal. Malek must have ordered the helm officer to take them home.

"It would be nice if *we* could wave a hand and activate the portal without a key," Malek said, then hopped over the railing. He dropped more than thirty feet to the ground and landed in a deep crouch before striding up to insert the medallion. Then he eyed the constellation on the inside of the ring, the one for their home world.

Surprisingly, it didn't light up the way it usually did. A fish jumped in the murky water between the islands, and a bird screeched from the branches. The portal remained dormant.

"Uh oh," Jak said.

"Why isn't he pressing it?" Bakir asked.

"He is." Jak's brow furrowed as he studied the portal. "But nothing's happening."

"What does that mean?" Tonovan asked.

"That we can't go home," Jak said.

7

The magelights along the railing of the *Star Flyer* grew brighter as night deepened, but Rivlen could have seen her sparring opponents even in the dark. Sergeant Tinder and Rookie Tezi attacked her with their dragon-steel axes, the weapons glowing blue as they swiped through the air. Tinder's axe was a single-header and Tezi's a huge double-headed weapon that was ridiculously large in her hands, but thanks to its light weight, she could wield it effectively. Effectively and far less awkwardly than she had a few weeks earlier.

Tinder, a veteran mercenary, had no trouble with her axe, even though she admitted a short sword and pistol were her preferred weapons. As Rivlen parried their blows with her lesser-dragon-steel sword, she tried not to think about how badly she would like to relieve Tinder of the axe. A year earlier, she'd been proud of defeating a ship's captain from King Dy's fleet in a duel and taking the sword as her battle prize, but it was hard not to long for a more powerful weapon, especially when such was whizzing through the air right in front of her eyes. It didn't belong in the hands of a sense-dead mercenary who would never be more than cannon fodder in any battles of significance.

"Almost got you there, Captain," Tinder called after her axe swiped within an inch of Rivlen's chest. "This big blade wants to shave off your nipple. Can mages still perform magic without their nipples?"

A sense-dead mercenary prone to mouthing off and failing to show proper respect for mages…

"Yes," Rivlen said coolly and counterattacked, tempted to bring her power to play so she could do *more* than shave the mercenary's nipples. She'd said their sparring match would involve physical attacks only, thus to make it fair, but it was difficult to resist the temptation to smother her opponent with magic and remind the mercenary who was the superior warrior.

Rivlen stifled the urge. She wouldn't go back on her word, nor would she use her power to steal an axe. The honorable Lord Malek, whom she wanted to prove herself to as much as she did Uthari, would be disappointed by such an act. And so would Jak.

Not that *Jak's* opinion should matter, especially when he was a naive do-gooder who didn't realize that he was no more like terrene humans than a tiger was like a dung beetle, but she remembered how disappointed in her he'd been when she'd used a small amount of pain to discipline the mouthy mercenary on the new mageship. He hadn't voiced the words, but he wanted her to be *kinder* to those she commanded.

Kindness could be perceived as weakness by her fellow mage officers, those who coveted her captaincy, and might get her killed. She admitted, however, that hurting people might not always be necessary to ensure obedience and respect. She didn't want to turn into someone like Tonovan, who enjoyed others' pain. She had to prove herself a hardened and competent officer, but she ought to be able to do that without losing her temper or being cruel.

Or, she gazed wistfully at the axe as it whizzed past, by taking things from allies.

Of course, if Tinder fell in battle, Rivlen would make sure to swoop in and pluck it up before an enemy could grab it. That would just be practical.

"Captain?" one of her lieutenants called over the clang of weapons clashing. Most of Thorn Company and a number of Rivlen's crew were on deck sparring, practicing the battles they hoped to engage in as soon as they found the druids. "Captain Ular from the *Moon Spear* is reporting in on the dome-jir."

Rivlen stifled a grimace. When Uthari had given her this assignment, she'd been delighted at the chance to demonstrate that she could competently command a trio of ships. She hadn't realized the *Moon Spear* would be one of those ships.

She and Captain Ular had been promoted at the same time, but she'd received command of Lord Malek's *Star Flyer*, a newer and far superior ship to the *Moon Spear*. A zidarr would never deign to call that moth-ridden relic home, even for a short excursion. Ular had always been a condescending bastard to her, but he'd been more openly snide and bitter in their interactions since their promotions.

Rivlen couldn't help but wonder if Uthari knew about their rivalry and wanted to see how she dealt with commanding a subordinate who resented her. She lifted her chin, vowing to deal with it adequately. *More* than adequately.

She resisted the temptation to tell her lieutenant to take a message. After all, it was possible Ular had a lead.

After leaving camp that morning, the three ships had spread out and spent the day searching independently for signs of civilization or anything that would hint of druid activity in the area. Thus far, they'd seen and heard nothing but wildlife in the jungle below. Numerous mages were stationed around the ships, using their power to scan for magic, but none had reported detecting anything anomalous. As Rivlen knew from experience, the druids liked to build their sanctuaries underground and were experts at insulating and protecting them from outsiders, even *mage* outsiders. She might have to come up with something clever to draw them out.

"We'll continue this later." Rivlen stepped back from the mercenaries.

"We'll be here," Tinder said, "anytime you and your nipples are up to the challenge."

Tezi lowered her axe and poked the sergeant. "I don't think mages like it when you talk about their anatomy and forget to call them by their titles."

"I didn't *insult* her anatomy. She shouldn't be offended. Right, Captain?" Tinder smiled at Rivlen.

"Sergeant Tinder," came a calm voice from the side.

Captain Ferroki was frowning over at the conversation and waved for her mouthy sergeant to come over. Rivlen hoped it would be to berate her for her impertinence.

Leaving it to the mercenary captain, Rivlen headed to the small communications cabin near her own cabin. Captain Ular's face floated above the dome-jir, though he was looking down at something at his feet or perhaps in his lap and wore an idiotic expression of bliss on his face. It confused Rivlen until the top of someone's head—presumably some *woman's* head—came into view for a few seconds. Ular noticed Rivlen and pushed the head back down and wiped the stupid expression off his face, though he couldn't—or didn't bother to—hide a lingering smirk.

"Do you get your cock sucked while reporting to King Uthari too?" Rivlen asked.

"Only if he makes me wait for a long time," Ular drawled, no hint of shame or embarrassment diminishing his smirk.

Rivlen shook her head, feeling nostalgic about the time she'd served with Malek, however briefly. *He* acted like a professional when he was on duty. She found it embarrassing for Uthari and the rest of his fleet how few of his officers embraced that kind of professionalism. But their lack of focus was to her advantage. It was why she would excel and outrank them all soon.

"What do you have to report, Captain?" she asked.

"We found a grouping of stones in the jungle, nearly hidden by vines and the canopy overhead, but one of my men sensed its magic. It's druid magic."

"One of their stone formations." Rivlen nodded, well aware of them. They were ancient and numerous across the continent of Zewnath. The presence of one in the jungle didn't mean druids would be nearby, but it could. "Have you checked it out yet?"

"I didn't send a team down, no. I've been..." Ular's eyes rolled back in his head, and there was a long pause before he met her eyes again and finished, "busy."

Rivlen ground her teeth. "Send the location to my helm officer. If you can't be bothered to leave your ship, I'll handle it."

"Relax, sweetie," Ular said. "There's no hurry to find these grubby druids. It's peaceful being out of that crowded, chaotic camp without worrying about generals or zidarr showing up for a surprise inspection at any moment."

"Your ship should always be in tiptop shape so that you don't need to worry about surprise inspections."

"Don't be so uptight, Rivlen. Why don't you bring the *Star Flyer* over, and we'll have an officers' dinner together? If you can manage to turn those frigid lips into a pouty smile, we could have an entertaining evening together. I can have my girls give you some pointers."

Rivlen knew he was deliberately goading her, but that didn't keep her from wishing she could cast a fireball through a dome-jir to wipe that oily smile off his face.

She forced herself to loosen the grip she hadn't realized she'd locked on the desk under the orb. If she couldn't find a way to work with and gain the respect of the officers who served under her, it would be nobody's fault but her own. She couldn't roast everyone in Uthari's fleet, however much she would like to.

The reasonable thoughts didn't keep her from imagining punishments for the lax captain. She envisioned stabbing one of those discs from Vran into Ular's temple and stealing his power. That would teach him a lesson.

The thought startled her into leaning back, a hint of fear icing her anger. That she'd thought wistfully of that thing chilled her. She shouldn't want to see *any* mage lose his or her power. It was akin to blasphemy. Turning on her own kind.

And yet… it was hard not to envision Ular with the disc seated at his temple. Without his power, he would be relieved of his command and probably kicked out of the fleet entirely. His family might disown him, and then he would be left to find his way in the world by begging for the charity of others.

"Ah, that's better," Ular crooned. "Not exactly a pouty smile, but a smirk isn't bad. Softens that frosty bitch face of yours."

"Thanks for the tip. I do so seek to soften myself."

"As all women should. Nobody wants to serve with a stone. I'll have my helm officer send over the coordinates for that monument, but I'm sure there's nothing there. It looked like an abandoned heap of rocks when we flew over it. But if you want to waste your night scouting around it instead of having some fun, that's up to you." Ular stood up to rest a hand on his dome-jir and cut the link, intentionally giving her a view of his crotch as he did so.

"Just what I want to haunt me in my nightmares tonight," Rivlen grumbled as the dome-jir went dark.

She glowered at the orb, fantasies about teaching the man a lesson returning. But she shook her head and made herself focus on the mission. It might be worth diverting to check out the monument—it wasn't as if much else in the jungle promised clues to their quarry's location—but why had he tried to minimize the value of the sighting?

What if he *had* sensed druids and magic around the monument? So much so that he'd been wary about investigating it on his own? Was it possible he wanted her to go in alone, for the *Star Flyer* to run into superior numbers, and for her to need to call him for help?

Rivlen growled, having no trouble imagining Ular setting something like that up. He would *love* to report to Uthari that she hadn't been able to handle this command and had needed to beg him for help.

Her mission, however, was to find the druids, so it wasn't as if she could ignore a potential opportunity to do so. She would have to fly in carefully.

It crossed her mind to send the *Sky Talon*, the third ship in her command, in ahead to take the brunt of what might be a surprise attack, but that would be cowardly. She *would* order it to join her at the monument, so it could back up the *Star Flyer* if necessary.

Rivlen touched the dome-jir and envisioned the *Sky Talon* in her mind, Captain Gyarth's ship. It only took a few seconds for someone to answer, Gyarth himself. *His* uniform wasn't rumpled, unbuttoned, and slumping off his shoulders. It was as pressed and proper as hers, and he was still clean-shaven, despite the late hour. Not a piece of his short salt-and-pepper hair was out of place.

"Captain Rivlen," he said with a curt nod. "What can I do for you?"

"Any sign of druids over there?"

"No, ma'am." A slight twitch to Gyarth's lips was the only indication that he would have preferred not to *ma'am* a captain twenty years his junior. He was a powerful mage, flirting with the designation of wizard, so it had to gall him, but he accepted his orders in stride. "All I can sense is those two axes."

Rivlen arched her brows, surprised he could sense anything on her ship from dozens of miles away. "The dragon-steel battle-axes?"

"Yes. You were smart to pick that mercenary unit to go along with you, if only for their weapons." One of his eyebrows arched. "I assume you or Lord Malek or King Uthari has plans to make them *our* weapons eventually."

"Possibly," Rivlen said, though neither of those two had brought up the subject with her. If anything, Malek nobly giving Tezi back her axe after slaying that giant worm was the reason so few people had dared challenge her for it. "But the king has the means to have more made now, so he may not bother."

"Ah, yes. I'd heard about that. I hope I can get my hands on one."

Rivlen leaned forward. "Work with me to your utmost on this mission, and I'll do my best to see that you're rewarded with one."

Gyarth snorted. "You have Uthari's ear, do you?"

"He put me in charge, didn't he?" Rivlen hoped Gyarth wouldn't imply she had slept with him for the command—or the mission.

Gyarth paused, eyeing her speculatively. "I've sensed your power, and I heard you took down one of Zaruk's ships in Port Toh-drom single-handedly while Lord Malek was fighting their cowardly zidarr below."

"My crew helped, but we did utterly destroy that ship." Rivlen lifted her chin.

"As we'll utterly destroy the druids?"

"That's the plan. Once we find them. Ular is sending the location of one of their monuments that he found but couldn't be bothered to investigate. I'd like the *Sky Talon* to join me in checking it out."

"Did Ular say he sensed druids there?"

"He said he *didn't*, which makes me suspicious."

Gyarth's brows drew down but only for a moment before he caught on. "You don't trust Captain Ular?"

"Let's just say that I'm giving him the opportunity to prove to me that he *is* trustworthy."

"I see. I'm prepared to divert our course."

"Good." Rivlen lifted a hand to end the communication but paused. "Thank you for being respectful and maintaining your military decorum with me."

"Of course, Captain." Gyarth bowed in his seat.

Rivlen sat back, relieved that *some* of Uthari's officers were professional. She just had to hope that whatever trap Ular wanted her to bumble into wasn't so dastardly that two mageships couldn't handle it.

Lord Yidar clasped his hands behind his back as he directed his skyboard toward the *Serene Waters* and kept a neutral expression on his face, not wanting any of Uthari's guards to suspect he was nervous. Unfortunately, it was his new regular state whenever he interacted with the king, and he resented the dance he had to do to stay in Uthari's good graces. Or at least to keep from straying further from them.

Maybe currying favor with Uthari wasn't worth it. The notion that Uthari would help him carve out—or take—a kingdom for himself was laughable. The old man might simply be humoring him. If so, why continue to work for him?

But what alternatives were there? Even a zidarr couldn't conquer an entire kingdom by himself.

He'd contemplated contacting the druids again, but after they'd brought in all those magic-resistant animals to attack the camp while they attempted to steal the portal, Yidar hadn't dared. The woman he'd spoken to, that Kywatha, had led the charge, cementing herself as an enemy to all mages. Yidar didn't have another potential contact.

He hadn't given up hope entirely that he could make a deal with the druids, but they were single-minded in what they desired. He wanted a kingdom, if not an *empire*. They wanted a hunk of metal. How could he nudge their goals into alignment with his?

Another yacht had sidled up to the *Serene Waters*, Queen Vorsha's sleek *Dominion*. It was a personal yacht roughly equivalent to Uthari's vessel, complete with dozens of mage guards as well as slaveband-wearing servants wandering the deck. Uthari's guards were paying more attention to it and their counterparts stationed near the railing than Yidar's approach.

As Yidar hopped onto the deck, tucking his skyboard under his arm, he spotted Uthari and Vorsha strolling side by side with their bodyguards trailing them. Uthari pointed at the portal and waved toward the jungle. Was he... giving a tour? To a woman who'd been his enemy the week before? At the least, Vorsha had been allied with King Zaruk, who'd ordered numerous attacks on Uthari's fleet in his attempt to get the portal for himself. Had something changed when Uthari had come down here personally to oversee the mission?

Yidar didn't care who was allied with whom this week, but it surprised him that Uthari had called him to report when he was clearly busy. Unless he wanted Yidar to be a part of this meeting for some reason? That would be surprising, as the zidarr were rarely asked to engage in politics.

Vorsha and Uthari stopped at the railing and gazed down at the portal, which had been dormant since Malek and his team left that morning. Vorsha, clad in flowing green silks with gold trim, was an attractive woman, despite thinning hair that hadn't been dyed recently enough to entirely hide the gray. She used her magic to radiate sex appeal as well as power equal to Uthari's, and it briefly crossed Yidar's mind that if he were to seduce her, he might turn her into an ally.

He snorted at himself, recognizing her magic having an effect, even on someone as well trained as he.

As Uthari gestured, indicating the lightning he'd commanded the portal to throw at his enemies, Vorsha gazed blandly down at the camp, as if the ancient artifact were only mildly interesting. As if *Uthari* were only mildly interesting. But something had brought her all the way down from her kingdom in the north. What did she hope to achieve here?

Uthari kept smiling and acting the role of gentleman and guide, but her expression changed little. Maybe *he* wanted an alliance, but she, knowing well that all the other rulers were displeased with his hoarding of the portal, did not. If so, it was surprising that she'd come onto his yacht.

Uthari glanced at Yidar, and he straightened, exuding suitable zidarr attentiveness and eagerness to please, but Uthari only held up a finger, silently asking him to wait.

"The helm officer you lent to the mission will be well protected," Uthari said, speaking out loud. "I'm certain Lord Malek will protect him."

"Protect *her*, you mean," Vorsha said. "Lieutenant Harintha is a competent officer. She does not need a babysitter."

"Nonetheless, these worlds we are visiting are dangerous even for a zidarr. I am surprised how many rulers want to send troops along. Let us hope that Admiral Bakir and his zidarr survive."

Vorsha looked sharply at him.

Uthari's choice to converse out loud surprised Yidar. The two rulers no doubt trusted their bodyguards and other minions completely, but when they could communicate telepathically, why risk being overheard by someone who might be a spy? Unless Uthari *wanted* to be overheard. Maybe he was planning something and wanted one of Vorsha's people to blab his supposed secrets. Yidar wouldn't put it past the crafty old man.

"Do you think that's likely?" Vorsha asked.

"Perhaps. As I said, these worlds are very dangerous."

"If you were worried about that, you should have allowed me to send more of my people along. Such as the zidarr I suggested when we negotiated." Her lips thinned as she glared at him.

"A zidarr who might have worked against my people?"

"You trust that *Jutuk's* zidarr won't?"

"Jutuk has not been assisting Zaruk against me of late." Uthari smiled at her.

"If you don't want more rulers to work against you, you should put effort into appeasing them."

"Would allowing you to send a zidarr along with Lord Malek have appeased *you*?"

"It would have been a start, though I would prefer access to the portal to send my *own* teams through to explore rather than hoping for a pittance of whatever valuables your team brings back."

"There is, alas, only the one key, and Malek must take it with him on his journeys so that his team can return."

"The druids have a key," Vorsha said.

"True. That is a recent revelation. Perhaps if we're able to raid their tunnels, we'll be able to acquire it."

"Is that what you sent those three ships off to the south to do?"

"Nothing gets past you, my dear." Uthari smiled again and rested a hand on her sleeve.

Was he *flirting* with her? When he was hundreds of years old? Could he even get his prick up anymore?

Yidar kept his lip from curling upward, since zidarr weren't supposed to have opinions on their rulers' pricks any more than their rulers' political machinations, but it was difficult.

"Nothing indeed." Surprisingly, Vorsha's indifferent facade

faded, and she smiled at Uthari as she met his gaze. "Perhaps, if you acquired a second key, you would see the wisdom in letting an ally hold it. The two keys shouldn't be on the same ship where some enemy zidarr could sneak in and steal both at the same time."

She didn't look at Yidar, but since he was the only zidarr within hearing range, he couldn't help but wonder if they had him in mind.

"Indeed, indeed," Uthari said. "I shall keep that in mind. If I could *trust* anyone here to be an ally, I would have to consider that suggestion."

"You know that alliances change rapidly among the rulers. We must be open to new possibilities and people and willing to bury old grudges… if we wish to get what we want."

Yidar wondered if she had ships of her own out looking for entrances to the druid encampments. Surely, she would prefer to get a key without having to kiss up to or even work with Uthari.

Zidarr… Yidar, isn't it? The female voice that spoke into his mind almost startled Yidar into losing his mask of indifference. It was Vorsha. She was still looking at Uthari and exchanging some murmurs with him that didn't reach his ears, but that didn't mean she couldn't carry on a telepathic conversation at the same time.

Yes, Your Majesty, Yidar replied, carefully pinpointing her mind so there was no chance the nearby Uthari would detect the words, though he was tempted not to reply at all. Whatever Vorsha wanted, it could only get him in trouble.

I understand you've had some difficulties with your current employer.

You're mistaken, Your Majesty.

Is that so?

Yes.

If you ever felt you were being treated unfairly, I could use another well-trained and capable zidarr in my employ.

Yidar hesitated, surprised by the suggestion, since she didn't even know him. Had she been a true ally of Uthari, Yidar might have suspected the king of talking Vorsha into testing Yidar for him, but that wasn't Uthari's style, and she still seemed more aloof to than aligned with him.

"It would also behoove us to have a second key," Vorsha said, "in case anything happens to your Lord Malek on his missions, and he's not able to return."

"He is one of the most powerful and resolute zidarr in the world," Uthari said. "Nothing will happen to him."

"You can't be certain. You just told me how dangerous it is out there, and I've heard he came back gravely wounded from his first two missions through the portal." Vorsha shifted to telepathy to speak again with Yidar. *Your master never praises you so openly to others or even speaks of you. Are you* sure *you are content with him?*

Yidar made himself reply, *I am content, Your Majesty. I am young and must prove myself to him, as I will in time.*

It was the correct response, but it made him want to gnaw his own tongue out of his mouth and spit it onto the deck. Youth shouldn't matter. Power and deeds should, and he'd been performing capably since being officially made zidarr. It galled him that Uthari didn't praise him to others the way he praised Malek. But he would never admit that to another ruler. She was trying to play him like an instrument. Why she wanted him to defect to her, he couldn't imagine. The offer was surprising for its rarity. From what he'd heard, rulers widely believed that a zidarr who was willing to switch allegiances wasn't worth having, for such an act would brand them as untrustworthy. That was one reason why Yidar had never considered it. Besides, he wanted his *own* kingdom, not to exchange one employer for another.

"Malek will always come back to me," Uthari said confidently. "He is nearly indestructible."

Vorsha chuckled. "I hear that he was quite recently as mundane as the servant who scrubs your ass in the tub."

Uthari twitched an eyebrow but didn't reply.

Yidar frowned, not sure he grasped what she meant. Whatever she was speaking about was new information to him. He eased a couple of steps closer, not wanting to miss anything, though he kept his hands clasped behind his back and gazed down at the portal, pretending disinterest.

"As you know," Vorsha said, "we had a long chat with the human explorer who came back with your team. Apparently, on the last world they visited, the mages there had small devices that they inserted into the skulls of their servants and travelers who irked them, devices that instantly removed all of their magical power. I suppose I don't have to tell you about this. Your Malek came back with a scar on his temple from one of these devices. I'm certain he filled you in."

"Mm," was all Uthari said, neither confirming nor denying.

But Yidar's heart skipped a beat. He had *seen* that scar. At the time, he hadn't thought anything of it, since Malek had been injured in battles with dragons on both worlds he'd visited. The scar had since faded, but the thought that Vorsha might be speaking the truth was intriguing.

"Such a device is both horrifying and titillating, isn't it?" This time, she rested a hand on *Uthari's* arm.

"Titillating, Vorsha?" he asked.

"Don't you have enemies that you loathe? Who are too powerful for you to challenge openly but whom you'd dearly like to see disappear? I still remember King Temrok negotiating with my father for my hand in marriage to solidify an alliance between our two kingdoms. The king was quite boorish and cruel when we spent time together." Vorsha bared her teeth in an unladylike smile. "He had greater power than mine, at least back then, and I wasn't able to protect myself from his crude advances. I told my father that he was unacceptable, and there was no way I would marry him. Do you remember what happened then, dear Uthari?"

"I recall your father dying suddenly and you taking over his realm."

"Indeed. Such drastic measures wouldn't have been necessary if I could have taken Temrok's power away and ensured he was no longer an appealing candidate. At that point, his own people would have done him in. As it was, I had to fight a costly and tedious war with him a few years later to keep him from taking over my kingdom by force."

"I remember, Vorsha," Uthari said patiently, though he probably wanted her to get to the point.

Yidar was barely listening to the history lecture. He was thinking about the possibility that a device existed that could remove a mage's powers.

If Yidar had encountered the sanctimonious Malek when he'd been without power, he would have been tempted to take advantage of that. If Uthari were deprived of his favorite zidarr, maybe he would be forced to lean more heavily on Yidar and Gorsith. Not that Yidar cared about being Uthari's right-hand man anymore. Still, it was pleasing to contemplate a world without Malek in it.

"If I were given a key to that world, or you let me send people along with your team when they return to it, I could acquire some of those devices for myself," Vorsha said.

"Such devices are too dangerous," Uthari said. "Slaves, or those feckless mercenaries who hate us even as they work for us, might be tempted to rise up and start a rebellion. They would be emboldened by such devices, believing that if they used them, they could nullify our advantage." His eyes narrowed. "It's possible they would be able to."

"I find that highly unlikely. There are too many of our kind to allow that or to truly be threatened by a few devices, but imagine..." Vorsha leaned closer to him, pressing her shoulder to his.

"Imagine if we worked together and used them to nullify the power of the other rulers. The prisoner implied it's *very* difficult to remove the devices once they're implanted. It takes a dragon to perform the surgery."

"What are you proposing, Vorsha?"

"Why should we endure a world that is split up into twelve tiny kingdoms when there could be one vast empire with two powerful wizards ruling it together?" She smiled at him. "Have you named an heir yet, Uthari?"

"Who my heir is is none of your business."

"It could be, if we were to rule one vast empire together. We could even work together in the bedroom to conceive an heir. With a little magical assistance, I could do so. I'm not too old for such things, and I trust *you* aren't either." She looked pointedly down at his crotch.

"You've always been an interesting woman with interesting ideas, Vorsha."

"I trust that's not a rejection and that you'll contemplate my suggestion." She rested a hand on his chest, and several long minutes passed as they gazed at each other. Not surprisingly, their eyes were full of calculation, not lust or romantic feelings.

Yidar realized they were finishing their conversation in private. Not unexpected, but he wished he were privy to it. Not because he cared about their ambitions, but because he wanted to learn more about the power-depriving devices. It was too bad the foreign prisoner they'd captured had been sent on the mission with Malek and the others. Yidar would have been tempted to try to get to him and question him himself.

"Excellent." Vorsha lowered her hand and stepped back. "I'll see you later tonight."

Uthari bowed politely to her and waited until she and her entourage had departed before facing Yidar.

Though Yidar had long ago learned to protect his thoughts

from other mages, he wiped any lingering notions of finding those devices out of his mind.

"Come." Uthari gestured for Yidar to join him. "It's time for our discussion."

"About your impending alliance with Queen Vorsha, Your Majesty?"

"I'm more interested in hearing about the alliances *you've* been attempting to solidify."

Yidar kept his face masked, but uncertainty fluttered in his belly like butterflies in a windstorm. As Uthari had made clear, he'd already learned of Yidar's meeting with Kywatha, and he knew of Yidar's ambitions. What *else* had he learned?

8

Jak walked slowly around the portal, looking at it from all sides, as if some clue might be revealed, an explanation as to why nothing had happened when Malek inserted the key and tried to push one of the buttons. Jak didn't sense anything from the portal, and it didn't respond when he asked it telepathic questions. What could have happened? He'd communicated with it right before the dragons arrived.

"Thoughts?" Malek stood on the island with Jak, his hands resting on his weapons as he stood guard.

They'd brought Shikari down with them, though he was more interested in sniffing around on the ground than in studying the portal. Mother remained with Zethron and the others on the deck of the ship as it floated nearby.

"Originally, I thought it was working against the dragons," Jak said. "But maybe they punished it or sabotaged it somehow."

"Is it possible it needs time to reset after someone travels through?" Mother called down.

"I suppose." Jak scratched his jaw, trying to remember if they had activated any of the portals back to back on any of their trips.

He didn't think so, but... "I'm not sure why that would keep it from communicating with me. It almost feels like the time a saboteur on the *Star Flyer* placed a magical device on the portal that kept me from activating it. I could sense it on the deck, but its power was locked up so I couldn't communicate with it in any way."

"Let's get that *saboteur* out here to opine." Malek looked expectantly at the ship.

He must have given someone besides Vinjo the order, for the cargo hatch in the side of the ship opened, and Vinjo tumbled out, as if he'd been pushed. He flailed when he landed in the hip-deep water, barely keeping from flopping over. He glowered back through the hatchway before wading toward the island.

Jak did another slow lap around the portal as Vinjo shambled up to join them. Once more, Jak attempted to communicate with it, but an unmanly shriek from their engineer broke his concentration.

"What are they? Get them off. Get them off!" Vinjo had reached land, but he was bent over, plucking at something long and dark stuck to the side of his bare calf.

Several of the creatures were attached to his legs. Leeches? This world's equivalent? If so, the little suckers had attacked fast. Vinjo had only been in the water for seconds.

He yelped and flung the leech away. It splatted against the portal. He grabbed another one on the back of his knee, tore it off, and cast it to the earth and stomped on it, but only for a moment before shaking his hand and scowling at it. Had the leeches bitten or stung him when he'd grabbed them? Though wincing, Vinjo tugged at another one stuck to his kneecap. This one resisted his efforts to yank it off.

"They *hurt*," Vinjo complained, trying to get a better grip so he could tear it free.

Malek sighed and focused on the engineer's legs. All at once, the remaining leeches burst into flames. That prompted another shriek from Vinjo, and he sprang away from the area, as if he could escape Malek's magic that way.

The tiny fires soon burned out, leaving only smudges of darkened matter—leech remains—on Vinjo's legs. Panting, he clasped a hand to his chest.

"This is why I go outdoors as seldom as possible. And would *not* visit other worlds of my own volition." Vinjo glowered at Malek, then looked at the leech that was still stuck to the portal, waiting for gravity to overcome whatever slimy ichor held it there, and shuddered.

Shikari ambled over to investigate the leech that Vinjo had smashed under his boots.

"Check the portal, Lieutenant, and see if you can figure out why it isn't working," Malek said.

"How would *I* know? Aren't those two the ones who've studied it for years?" Vinjo pointed at Jak, then up at Mother.

"Check the portal to see if the dragons or someone else put a device on it since we arrived," Malek said.

"Like the one you made." Jak smiled at Vinjo, trying to encourage him. "It was clever. I couldn't see it and didn't notice it until I found it with my hands."

"Hm. Yes. It *was* clever." Vinjo took a bracing breath and walked up to join Jak in investigating.

"May I have that organism?" Mother called down and pointed at the leech affixed to the portal.

Malek raised his eyebrows. "For one of your vials?"

"Yes. You know I brought my microscope so I can study the local flora and fauna."

"Those are Hell-spawned creations sent by the slavemasters to torment us, not flora or fauna," Vinjo said.

Malek lifted a hand, as if to physically pluck the leech free, but maybe he decided Vinjo might have genuinely been hurt by the thing. He ended up using his magic to pry it off and float it up to

Mother. Meanwhile, Shikari decided the one on the ground was edible and licked it up.

"This woman is Uthari's *archaeologist?*" Bakir asked as Mother produced tweezers to capture the hopefully dead leech. He stood at the railing with Prolix, his eyelids drooping thoughtfully as he watched her. "What kind of archaeologist travels around with a microscope and tweezers?"

"Such equipment is not inappropriate for the field," Mother said, though she gave him a concerned look, as if worried she had given away a secret.

"She is talented in *many* fields of study." Zethron smiled broadly at Mother. "She learned our language in days and spoke eloquently on many subjects to me. She adores plants."

"Plants?" Bakir squinted at Mother's head—trying to read her thoughts.

Speaking of giving away secrets…

Jak frowned at Malek, not sure how close an ally King Jutuk was to Uthari and if they should try to keep information from the admiral.

Malek was intently watching the exchange on the deck. Bakir frowned fiercely at Mother, as if he wasn't getting what he wanted. She stepped farther away from him and closer to Zethron.

Are you protecting her thoughts? Jak asked silently.

Both of their thoughts, Malek replied without looking at him. *But the admiral is a powerful mage, Tonovan's equal, I'd wager, so it is not easy.*

Does it matter if they find out about the Jitaruvak?

Uthari would prefer nobody else learn about it until he's synthesized his drug. Concentrate on the portal, Jak. We need to go home to help.

I know, but that may not be possible right now. Unless Vinjo sees something I don't.

Vinjo had paused his examination to poke at something on his shin.

Malek sighed. *Do you truly think the dragons did something? Even if they'd known exactly who and what we were*—especially *if they had —they wouldn't have believed us a threat or worried about us following them back.*

I don't think they would either. It's possible... Jak thought of his conversation with the portal. It hadn't seemed interested in humans or believed they would be able to help it, but had it grown slightly thoughtful when he'd mentioned Mother was a scientist? Or had that been his imagination?

What?

It's possible the portal doesn't want us to leave.

That seems a poor way to treat its Favored Traveler.

I agree, but it never called me that. I'm not sure any of the portals did. That was the ambassador's term on Vran.

But the portals do *treat you differently than the rest of us. They don't communicate with us.*

I know. Jak could only shrug.

"I don't see any devices or anything obviously wrong with the artifact," Vinjo said.

"How about your shin?" Jak wondered how much studying of the portal the engineer had actually done. "Anything wrong with it?"

"Oh, yes. And my calf and kneecap and ankle. Look at the bloody bruises those things left behind. Also, someone singed me." The glare he gave Malek wasn't very heartfelt, perhaps because he remembered he was dealing with a powerful zidarr, a man one shouldn't irk.

"I can leave them be next time," Malek said in a flat tone.

"I believe I shall avoid the swamp going forward. Perhaps all water on this world. I see no need to bathe while adventuring in swamps."

"His mercenary lieutenant is a lucky woman," Malek murmured.

Before Jak could reply, Malek spun to look toward the canopy and drew his sword and main-gauche.

Jak groaned. Not *more* dragons.

"Just one this time," Malek said. "It was flying this way, but it's turning now."

"Because it sensed our great prowess and knew it was no match?" Jak forced a smile.

A distant scream reached their ears. Jak dropped the smile. That hadn't been a dragon screech. It had sounded human.

"Are there *people* up there?" Bakir asked.

Everyone's eyes were toward the canopy now.

"It could be the natives," Zethron said. "I told you they ride birds."

Another human scream sounded, one of pain.

"I don't sense anything magical up there besides a single dragon," Tonovan said.

"A single dragon is a large threat. Most of the people on this world aren't mages. They're like me." Zethron tapped his chest.

"Come on." Malek sprang more than thirty feet to clear the ship, the railing, and land on the deck beside Mother. "We'll see if we can help them."

As Malek levitated Jak, Shikari, and Vinjo up to the deck, it occurred to Jak that if most of the people here weren't magical, there might not be a lot of dragon steel around. There might be even less here than there was back on Torvil. If that was true, and it was what King Jutuk wanted, Bakir and Prolix would be disappointed with this trip.

"*Help* them?" Tonovan asked.

The ship was already rising, Lieutenant Harintha receiving telepathic commands from Malek.

"We didn't come here to be do-gooders on another world and risk ourselves fighting *dragons*," Tonovan said.

Malek, his weapons in hand as the ship continued upward, didn't look at him.

Jak drew his pistol and wished Rivlen were with them instead of Tonovan. Even though she'd learned enough about dragons and their power on Vran to be wary of them, she would have agreed to fly off to help people. He was sure of it. Even if she wasn't exactly a *do-gooder*, she always wanted to prove herself in battle.

"That's a good way to get yourself killed," Tonovan growled at him.

Jak huffed in annoyance and carefully wrapped a mental bandana around his mind to protect his thoughts. He was getting better at remembering to keep it up whenever he was around mages, but it was still a challenge to do it while concentrating on something else.

More screams of pain echoed down from above. What might have been war cries also rang out, but there was a frantic edge to them. Jak couldn't tell how many people were up there facing the dragon, but they sounded outmatched.

"Malek." Tonovan thrust his hand toward the portal. "Get your people back down there, and fly us out of here. We're not going to get injured or die for someone else's problem."

"You're not in command of this mission, General," Malek said coolly. "I am."

"If we help those people, they may be grateful," Mother told Tonovan. "They may give us the information we need to succeed here and be able to go back home."

"Or to figure out *how* to go back home," Jak said, still confused about why the portal had gone silent on them. He refused to believe that they wouldn't be able to figure out a way to return home, but if it ended up being contingent on them finding a way to help the dragons with a ten-thousand-year-old problem, he would have no one to blame but himself for that. *He* was the one who'd hinted it might be a possibility. "Idiot," he muttered.

"Mind your manners, boy." Tonovan's eyes locked onto him. Had he thought Jak was talking about him?

The label applied, but...

"We can tear the information we need out of people's minds *without* risking our lives to help with their problems," Tonovan said.

The ship broke through the canopy, and more screams sounded, clearer now that there weren't trees in the way. Afternoon sun in a cloudless blue sky shone upon a brown-and-gray dragon twisting and snapping in the air as more than twenty giant birds with human riders flew about it. The men and women all wore bronze skullcaps and simple leather armor that couldn't possibly be effective protection against dragons.

As Jak watched, a mental attack sent five of the riders and their birds tumbling away. As they spun, the men hung upside down, but they must have been attached by harnesses, for they didn't fall. One struck the top of a tree hard enough that wood snapped and bones crunched. The bird cried out as its wing twisted, maybe breaking, and it was caught up in the branches.

Several riders who hadn't been targeted hurled spears at the dragon. Jak shook his head, sensing only the faintest magic about the weapons. Whatever they were made from, it wasn't dragon steel.

Certain they would be ineffective, Jak was shocked when two spears made it through the dragon's protective barrier. They slid in under its wing and stuck in its side.

Maybe there was more magic to them than he'd believed. Several other spears protruded from its scaled body. They didn't keep the dragon from flying about with the grace of an eagle and catching a rider in its snapping jaws, but Jak was stunned that the simple weapons had slid through its scales.

"How are they hitting it?" Tonovan asked as their ship headed toward the battle. "I sense that the dragon has a barrier up. A *powerful* barrier." He shot Malek another dark look, reminding him that this was a bad idea.

"One we'll have to take down to harm it with our magic." Malek pointed his longsword at the dragon, and Jak sensed a strong blast of power shoot out.

It struck the dragon's barrier. Unlike the spears of the human riders, it didn't slip through. It did, however, gain the dragon's attention.

The scaled creature wheeled in the sky until it faced them. For a few seconds, it didn't seem to know what had struck it—the ship's camouflage had to be helping to obscure them—but it soon figured it out. The dragon's yellow eyes focused on them, and after batting at another rider with its tail, half-knocking the woman from her mount, it flapped its wings and flew straight at the ship.

Bakir swore, but he lifted his hands and hurled a fireball at the dragon as Prolix raised his weapons, an eager glint in his eyes. *He* hadn't objected to the idea of going into battle with a dragon.

Malek hurled another magical attack, this one striking hard enough to make the dragon's wingbeats falter, if only for a second. Tonovan, Bakir, and Prolix also cast attacks, but theirs didn't seem to bother their powerful foe. Prolix jumped up, waving his weapons in invitation, as if he wanted the dragon to come within blade range.

Its cold reptilian eyes gleamed as it flew closer. Prolix would get his wish.

Behind it, the riders took the time to regroup rather than giving chase. Other than the spears that had pierced the dragon's scales and might be hurting it a little, Jak and the others would be on their own against this enemy.

"Jadora," Malek said without looking at her. "Take Zethron and go below."

"And Vinjo," Vinjo said, darting for the hatch.

Mother, with a vial in one hand and a grenade in the other, opened her mouth to object.

"*Go*," Malek ordered, compulsion in the word. More softly, he added, "It'll be safer."

The dragon was almost upon them. Mother hesitated, then nodded. She ran to the hatch, pushing Zethron before her, but she paused to give Jak the vial and grenade.

He juggled his pistol so he could put them in his pockets, though he wondered when he'd become useful enough that Malek wanted to keep him around during a battle. He couldn't yet hurl fireballs. When it came to attacks, all he could do was help by channeling some of his own power into other mages.

The dragon opened its maw, and an ear-splitting screech of fury flowed out. The mages combined forces to raise a barrier around the ship, but their enemy's raw power tore it away.

A blast of energy that Jak sensed an instant before it hit them had him scrambling to brace himself against the railing. The attack struck the craft and hurled it through the air like a piece of flotsam on a tsunami wave. The ship flipped over, leaving Jak dangling from the railing and Shikari shrieking in alarm.

Fingers tight around the railing, Jak tried to grab for his charge with his magic. He willed Shikari not to fall, but the ship kept rolling. Jak smashed back down to the deck only to have it flip over again three more times. His grip threatened to give way. Wrenching noises came from the ship's frame, and terror filled Jak as he envisioned it breaking to pieces and all of them plummeting to their deaths.

As it rolled back into an upright position, he spotted Shikari using his tail to grip the base of one of the railings, but his relief was short-lived. The mageship smashed into a treetop. That halted its tumbling with a thunderous *crash*, and Jak almost lost his grip again.

Someone in black tumbled past him and broke through the railing. Prolix.

The zidarr issued an uncharacteristic terrified shout. He landed in the branches, wood snapping as he fell through, struggling to find a handhold sturdy enough to support him.

Something fell from above—it looked like a piece of a wall or maybe an old stone tablet. Gravity took it past so quickly that Jak couldn't tell. He had no idea where it had come from. It wasn't as if the dragon had *pockets*.

A shadow blotted out the sun as their enemy whipped past right above, but it shrieked in pain instead of launching another attack.

Something else fell and clattered to the deck as Jak struggled to rise and get his balance. Though the ship was still now—caught in the tree—the deck had an alarming tilt to it. A huge piece of brown-and-gray metal skidded down the incline to knock into Jak's boots.

No, that wasn't metal. It was a dragon scale. Blood smeared the deck under it.

Shikari cried out in distress, but he still had his tail wrapped around the railing, and nothing appeared to be harming him. Not yet. It was possible the dragon had threatened him telepathically.

"Keep attacking!" Tonovan shouted from the other end of the long ship.

He and Bakir gripped the railing there, struggling as much as Jak to find their balance.

"You'll hit him," Bakir responded.

"I don't *care*. Just attack while it's distracted. *Kill* that thing." Tonovan cast an attack at the dragon as it swept through again, its defenses down for some reason.

The blow knocked their foe sideways. Surprisingly, it didn't look at Tonovan. Its neck was craned as it tried to bite something on its back.

Jak sucked in an alarmed breath. Malek.

At some point, he'd leaped onto its back. He used his main-gauche and sword like pickaxes on a glacier, plunging them between the dragon's scales and into flesh as he advanced toward its more vulnerable head. *He* was the one who'd cut off the scale.

Unfortunately, with its flexible neck, the dragon could reach him even on its back. Somehow, it managed to fly and snap at him at the same time. The other mages' attacks struck, but they weren't enough to knock the dragon out of the air or distract it.

Malek dodged as much as he could with his legs dangling free, the dragon whipping around and rocking left and right. It wasn't above the ship anymore, and only Malek's grip on the blades plunged into its back kept him from falling to his death.

The dragon snapped for his head, fangs glistening as they caught the sun. Malek raised a barrier around himself, one strong enough to deflect the bite.

A wave of magic crashed into the dragon and caught Malek as well. His barrier faltered.

Jak glanced at Tonovan. That bastard had done that, and he was grinning maniacally. He'd included Malek in the attack intentionally; Jak was sure of it.

Oh, how he wished he had mastered fireballs. Instead, Jak closed his eyes and envisioned a torrent of water that was the power within him. He created a chasm for it to rush through, funneling it and pouring it into a huge lake that represented Malek.

A roar came from above. It was Malek this time instead of their scaled enemy. Reinvigorated by Jak's magic, he reinforced his barrier, yanked one of his blades out and plunged it in higher up on the dragon's back. He climbed quickly toward the neck and was soon too close to its head for the dragon to reach him with its jaws. It tried to flick its tail at him, cracking it like a whip, but it wasn't long enough to reach.

Jak funneled more power into Malek, willing him to be able to keep his barrier up, to keep climbing and smash a sword into the dragon's brain.

Shikari squeaked a warning. A stab of pain struck Jak in the side of his head, making him gasp. Had that been the dragon? No, it was too busy with Malek to pay attention to anyone on the ship. Jak looked over and spotted Tonovan staring at him.

Let him fight his own battles, kid, Tonovan growled into his mind.

We're a team, you ass, Jak snarled back, not caring the least about respecting mages, not at that moment. *You'll never get back home without him and without me.*

Blood spattered the deck as if someone had upended a bucket over them. It startled Tonovan as much as Jak, and they both looked up in time to see Malek pull his sword from the dragon's throat. It issued a final gurgling screech and pitched sideways.

"Jump!" Jak yelled, terrified that Malek would go down with their foe.

Before the dragon tumbled out of sight below the ship, Malek sprang from its neck. A normal human wouldn't have made it, but his magical zidarr muscles took him over the railing to land in a crouch on the deck.

Jak slumped down in relief. The ship still hung precariously in a treetop, and he had no idea if it could navigate—or fly at all—under its own power, so his relief might have been premature, but he couldn't help it.

Shikari galloped over to check on him, putting a taloned foot on Jak's thigh.

"I'm all right," he said. "Thanks."

Shikari looked at the bloody scale and hissed.

Meanwhile, Malek eyed Tonovan, looking like he wanted to hiss too. His face was frostier than the glacier Jak had been imagining.

I think he hit you on purpose, Jak told him silently, not wanting the bastard to get away with anything. Why hadn't *Tonovan* tumbled through the railing and fallen to his death?

I'm aware. Malek held Tonovan's gaze—the heartless general stared back at him with no sign of guilt or regret—before cleaning and sheathing his weapons and walking toward Jak.

There was no sign of the riders or their feathered mounts. Jak didn't think they'd all been hit, but it looked like they'd fled as soon as the dragon was focused on a new target. He couldn't blame them, not when they'd had so little magic of their own, but it did feel like they'd been abandoned.

Malek paused in front of the dislodged dragon scale. Teardrop shaped and more than four feet by four feet wide, it looked like a warrior's shield. One of the edges was ragged, blood glistening along it. More of the crimson liquid spattered the deck, and Jak wondered if dragon blood had any special properties.

"Perhaps your mother will want to come up and collect a sample," Malek said.

"Oh, I'm sure of it. Do you think it's safe to call her up?" Jak eyed the tree they were stuck in. It was a *large* tree, but they were at the very top of it. If a wind came up, or someone jumped up and down on the deck, the ship might be dislodged.

Malek opened his mouth, but the hatch creaked on its hinges. It hadn't done that before, but Jak suspected a lot of things on the ship would creak now.

Mother stuck her head out and peered warily around.

A grunt came from the tree, and Malek rested a hand on his sword hilt as he gazed toward shivering branches.

"Prolix survived." He lowered his hand.

"It looks like everyone did." Jak glanced over at Tonovan and Bakir. Their heads were together, as if they were deep in a private —and possibly mutinous—conversation, but their lips weren't moving. Of course not. They had telepathy. Even better for conspiring. Jak shook his head in disgust.

"Not all of the natives did," Malek said. "I saw several killed in the air. Some of the birds they rode too."

"I wonder why they went after a dragon," Jak said as Mother crawled out, spreading her arms for balance on the slanted deck. Her backpack wobbled on her shoulders, vials clinking inside. "Do you think it attacked one of the island cities Zethron mentioned?"

"Maybe they wanted what it held in its talons," Malek said.

"I didn't see it holding anything," Jak said before remembering that flat rectangle that had tumbled past. He'd only glimpsed it but had thought it was a stone tablet, the kind of thing humans had used for recording information before they'd invented paper.

A thunk sounded as something heavy landed on the deck. Jak jumped.

The very tablet he'd been thinking about clattered before coming to a rest not ten feet away.

"Did the tree spit that at us?" Jak glanced over the railing as Prolix climbed into view. Blood smeared the side of his face, his clothing was ripped, and either the tree or the dragon had taken a gouge out of his jaw.

"A zidarr tree, perhaps." Malek jogged over to give Prolix a hand onto the ship.

"Less than an hour on this world, and we've found more trouble than anyone could want," Jak muttered as Mother stopped beside him, her gaze locked to the scale.

"We thought you might like some dragon blood," Jak said.

"Yes." With empty vials already in hand, Mother knelt and swept her spatula through some of the crimson liquid. "I want to check it for signs of that parasite."

"You think the dragons on every world will have it?"

"We'll find out. I also want to look at *this*." She rested a reverent hand on the scale.

"I don't think that's going to fit in your vial. *Or* through the hatchway."

"I'll see if I can scrape off a sample to put on a slide."

"Dragon scales are kind of impervious."

"Not to Malek's blades."

"You want him to use an invaluable lesser-dragon-steel weapon to prepare a slide for you?"

Mother nodded firmly. "Yes."

She looked over at him, but Malek and Prolix stood gazing down at the tablet with similar thoughtful expressions on their faces.

"What is that thing?" Tonovan asked as he and Bakir approached. "And more pertinent, how are we going to get out of this tree?"

"We don't *want* to get out of the tree," Vinjo's voice came from the hatchway as his head poked up. "At least not for a few hours."

"*Hours*?" Tonovan asked.

Vinjo nodded. "The engine and the power supply need repairs. I'll work quickly—thank Shylezar I thought there might be trouble and brought spare parts—but I came to say it would be best if you don't make any sudden movements."

A branch snapped under them, and an ominous creak came from the ship's framework.

"You don't say," Tonovan said.

"I can levitate the ship to the ground if necessary," Malek said.

"That might not be a bad idea," Vinjo said, then glanced beyond the ship. "Assuming *they* don't have a problem with us leaving."

Several of the riders had reappeared in the sky, their bird mounts carrying them toward the ship.

"They better not after we saved their asses," Tonovan said.

"*We*?" Jak couldn't keep from scoffing. What had Tonovan done?

"More than you, kid," Tonovan growled. "Can't you even throw a fireball yet? The way Yidar spoke, I thought you were some great threat."

Jak clenched his jaw, vowing to ignore the general as much as possible. Though if he ever got a chance to pay him back for all the people he'd hurt—and for trying to kill *Malek* in the middle of a battle—he would.

Tonovan smiled. *Go ahead and try it, brat.*

Jak bit back the urge to deliver an insulting retort. Tonovan wasn't above hurting him to teach him a lesson. Or hurting him just because he enjoyed it. As long as Malek was at Jak's side, Malek would put a stop to it, but the day would come when he wasn't around.

While they waited for the riders to arrive, Jak walked over to check out the tablet.

There was no writing on it, as he'd expected there would be. The flat stone—no, that was hardened clay, such as the Ancient Zeruvians had once used—held something that made his breath catch. It was a map.

Jak gripped his chin and studied it, immediately recognizing the ring-shaped portrayal of a portal in an empty field. Something that might have represented a large plateau stretched along one side of that field and a lone butte rose up on the other side of the portal. It was a crude map, and he was sure he hadn't seen a similar one before, but an unsettled feeling came over him. There was something familiar about it.

Then he saw it and froze, forgetting to breathe. That butte—it could be the icy butte that had held the dragon fortress on the first world they'd visited. And that might not be a plateau but a glacier.

When they'd visited, the portal had been *inside* the glacier, albeit at the very edge. But glaciers moved over time, and this map might have been carved long ago. By whom? And why?

The possible answer came like a punch to the face. What if someone had made it to indicate the location of the dragon eggs? All those hapless unhatched dragons had been embedded in the glacier at some point in the past—perhaps *hidden* in the glacier.

Jak didn't see any markings to represent eggs or any other kind of treasure, but the fact that this map existed made him believe he was right. Aside from the portal itself, there hadn't been anything else of value in the area. And everyone from humans to other dragons had wanted to know where his hatchling had come from.

Shikari came over and sniffed the corner of the tablet. Jak shook his head bleakly. What if the dragon they'd battled had stolen this map to show the rest of his kind? So they could find those eggs and destroy them?

9

Though Uthari had called Yidar to the *Serene Waters* and said he wanted to speak with him, long minutes passed as they stood at the railing. A bead of sweat slithered down Yidar's spine. Due to the jungle humidity, of course, not nervousness. Still, he wished Uthari would get on with it. Didn't he have a date with Vorsha to prepare for?

A screech sounded in the distance. Uthari strolled to the opposite railing to gaze out over the jungle and the mountains instead of the portal.

Two brown-hulled mageships were chasing after a pair of large birds as mages on the deck hurled fireballs at them. The birds twisted in the air, attempting to avoid the attacks, but flames caught one. It screeched in pain, its wings gave out, and it plummeted into the trees below.

Yidar had seen similar birds in the area before. They were fearsome predators but nothing that could bother a competent mage. He didn't know why other mages would bother chasing after them, unless for sport. People did enjoy hunting the large and deadly creatures of this continent.

Uthari smiled faintly, glanced at Yidar, and pointed at another ship. Orange-uniformed mages on skyboards were flying from the deck and toward the jungle. One blasted a lightning strike at a target on the ground.

"Are they attacking druids or some other threat?" Yidar asked, though he wanted to ask Uthari to bring up what he wanted to discuss so they could get their talk over with.

"Just animals, I believe. Animals that I suggested might be spies for the druids and should be obliterated at every opportunity."

"They *could* be spies."

"True. And that possibility has many of the ship commanders distracted. The busier they are dealing with minor threats, the less likely they are to conspire against and attack us. But I trust you are ready to fight if it's required."

"I'm *always* ready to fight, Your Majesty."

"Good. Perhaps it won't be needed, but we must remain vigilant."

"Unless you and Queen Vorsha can work together to nullify the magic of your enemies?" Yidar raised his eyebrows, wondering if he could get Uthari to give him more information on those devices, such as if any had been brought back along with that chest of dragon steel. Yidar could travel to other worlds to acquire resources, if he ever found a key that he could use, but he would rather get them more easily.

"That won't happen," Uthari said coolly.

"The devices don't exist?"

"Oh, they exist. But I had Malek destroy the only one that was brought back, and from what Malek said of the world where they came from—Vran—their mages are more powerful than ours, so it wouldn't be wise for us to visit again with theft in mind."

Yidar rocked back. "More powerful than ours? Than *us*?" He touched his chest.

"So it seems. We're fortunate they're not invading our world right now."

"Was that a possibility?"

"It was. They've told Malek that they won't, but I don't trust their leaders. Their world is infested with dragons. Ours isn't. So they covet ours."

"If they are truly... more powerful than we are—" Yidar had a hard time imagining that, especially when one was talking about *zidarr* instead of simple tinkering mages, "—how would we battle them?"

"By shutting down and burying the portal once again so that enemies can't come through."

"I thought you were opposed to that."

"Not once I have what I seek. It would be wise to ensure no enemies from other worlds can threaten us in the future."

"Wasn't there a discussion at one point about whether that engineer could make a device that could nullify the portal without the need for burying it? So that its magic couldn't be activated except on our terms?"

"There was a discussion—while we tortured him. He didn't know if he could create something that would override the magical link sent from another portal. I am tempted to have him try anyway, as it's unlikely he could damage the artifact, but he's away now with Malek. Regardless, once I have what I want, there's no need for the portal to remain open. I am thinking of taking it back to our kingdom and putting it up somewhere for decoration."

"Because you worry about threats from other worlds or because you don't want anyone else to be able to find dragon steel and other valuable resources out there that they might use against you?"

Uthari squinted at him. Perhaps Yidar had spoken too frankly.

"Despite the foolish decisions you've made in the past, you're not that dull, are you?" Uthari mused.

"I am ambitious," Yidar said stiffly. "Not stupid."

"Ambition can make one stupid."

So could the desire to obtain a bunch of magical *stuff* from worlds full of dangerous people and predators.

Yidar kept that thought to himself, but maybe Uthari guessed it anyway. He smiled.

"Do you know where an entrance to the druid lair is?"

Yidar shook his head. "No, Your Majesty."

"Are you sure that didn't come up when you spoke with the female who led the attack on our camp?"

"No, Your Majesty. As I told you, I only met with her briefly because she gave one of my crewmen a communication stone and an offer of seduction if he would spy on us. I used it to lure her to a meeting and to let her know that neither my lieutenant nor I would be her spy." Yidar tilted his head. "I explained this to you before, Your Majesty."

He'd been forced to when Uthari had first called him in, wanting to know about it. Apparently, Sorath had been the one to blab about Yidar's meeting. Yidar would like to hammer a metal device into *his* skull as well. Oh, the mercenary had no magic, so it wouldn't do anything, but it would be pleasing.

"You did," Uthari said, "but that was before the druid woman sneaked through to another world, brought back all those animals, and nearly led her people to get away with *my* portal."

"I haven't spoken to her since then. As I reported the other day, I did find *Sorath* speaking to her in the jungle. Perhaps you should question him again. Maybe *he* knows where their hideout is."

"I would love to question him again, but he's disappeared from camp."

"Unfortunately."

"Yes." Uthari watched him carefully as they spoke. He might have been probing Yidar's mind, as well, to see if any revealing information slipped out. His touch was too deft for Yidar to know that for sure, but he wouldn't have been surprised.

Finally, Uthari turned his attention back to watching the other mageships hunt. "Before the team left, I told Tonovan that I wouldn't mind if Admiral Bakir and his zidarr didn't return. If they were lost in battle, perhaps their fleet commanders and rulers would be less insistent about threatening, bribing, and blustering at me to get people on the team and out there spying on Malek and what our people find."

"What *is* it that you hope to find, Your Majesty?"

When Malek had come back with that chest of invaluable dragon steel, Yidar had thought that might be it, but they were out there looking for something else. Others speculated that Uthari wanted to find dragon allies that he could coerce into working at his side, but Yidar didn't think that was it.

"Nothing that I want to share with the other rulers," was all Uthari said.

"Even your new ally, Vorsha?"

Uthari snorted. "Let her believe what she wishes, and if she wants to entertain me in the bedroom tonight, I'll allow it."

"Magnanimous," Yidar muttered. The idea of Vorsha stirring up potions in an alchemy lab to allow her to become pregnant at her advanced age was almost as disturbing as that of his hundreds-of-years-old king having sex.

"I understand she's quite talented." Uthari smiled again. "I trust you've slept with other mages and know how stimulating magic can make things."

"I'm not inexperienced," Yidar said, hoping this wasn't a trap. He worried that Uthari believed his conversation with the druid lady had gone much further than it had.

"It is a wonder that Tonovan enjoys being served by all those mundane humans." Uthari waved an indifferent hand. "To each his own."

"If you'll pardon my saying so, Your Majesty," Yidar said, "General Tonovan is more likely to try to arrange that *Malek* not come back." There. Hopefully that would steer the conversation away from everyone's sex lives. Yidar was far more interested in learning more about those devices. Had Uthari spoken the truth that the only one brought back had been destroyed? Or was it possible the king had a stash?

"He won't do that. I've let him know what's at stake if he conspires against Malek." Uthari closed his eyes to slits. "And the possible reward he could receive if he serves me faithfully and does as he knows I wish."

"What more reward could he want? You've given him three sprawling mansions, great wealth, and as many slaves as he wishes."

What was left? For Uthari to name Tonovan as his heir to the kingdom?

"Like you, he has ambitions. As talented men often do. I'm not blind to that or unwilling to accommodate, should rewards be warranted." Uthari slid him a sidelong look, and Yidar had little doubt that Uthari referred to his own ambitions.

"Oh?" he asked carefully.

"It peeves me that Colonel Sorath skulked off into the jungle."

"Oh?" Yidar repeated, not sure what to think of the topic change.

"I sent a couple of mages after him, but another of those stealth devices has been made." Uthari pressed his lips together in disapproval. "Were that engineer here, I would punish him by chopping off his fingers. He was supposed to be working on my ship, nothing else."

"It's strange that he would work against his own kind," Yidar said, though Vorsha had just been fantasizing to Uthari about those devices and stealing power from mages.

Uthari squinted at him. "Retrieve Sorath for me, Yidar. As a highly trained zidarr, I trust you can find him." Uthari lifted a hand. "No, don't retrieve him. Just kill him. He's outlived what paltry usefulness he had to me. Bring me his head."

Ah, so *that* was what Uthari wanted. Yidar relaxed an iota. This was a perfectly reasonable request for a zidarr. He hadn't expected it, but he wasn't surprised by it.

"The druids may be helping him hide," Uthari added. "I trust you can sweet-talk your way through them, if necessary, to get to him."

Yidar's muscles tensed again from the implication that he'd formed a relationship with them, with that woman who'd refused to do what he wished.

"Sweet-talking isn't my specialty, but I *can* get through them to reach him. One way or another." Yidar touched the hilt of his sword.

"Good. If Vorsha gets her way, kingdoms may be opening up soon. Kingdoms need leaders." Uthari held his gaze, making his meaning clear.

Was he truly offering Yidar a kingdom of his own? Even after his betrayal? Yidar had come to doubt that Uthari would help him.

"I thought *her way* was to establish an empire that you two would rule over jointly." Yidar hadn't thought Uthari was entertaining that idea at all.

"A global empire isn't realistic. Perhaps I could combine a few choice kingdoms into one, but all twelve? What a headache. It would be more practical to place amenable rulers on the thrones of the other kingdoms, rulers who would be happy with what they have and not plot against me." Uthari raised his brows and looked frankly at Yidar.

Interesting that he'd said *me* instead of *us*. Was he going to let Vorsha believe what she wanted while acting in his own interest?

"I would be quite happy with a single kingdom of modest size with reasonable resources." And Yidar truly would. He didn't need the world, just a place to relax and make a name for himself. And to be a servant to no other man, even a king.

"Good."

"Are you actually entertaining Vorsha's idea of using those devices to figuratively castrate the other rulers?" Yidar wondered if he would get *that* task as well. The thought was daunting, but it might be a way to prove himself capable and *worthy* of a kingdom.

"I hadn't originally planned on it, but it's an interesting notion, one not without merit."

"And will Vorsha find one of those devices inserted into her brain while she's sleeping with you?"

"That would be a rude way to thank a powerful mage for thinking of aligning with you when everyone else is plotting against you." Something about Uthari's smile made Yidar believe that he *did* have some treachery in mind. At the least, he was likely trying to foresee numerous possible futures while setting himself up to prosper in each one. "Besides," Uthari continued, "the only device *was* destroyed. Malek did it, and you know I trust his magic."

Yidar kept from sneering.

"But perhaps," Uthari said, "when that engineer returns, he and I will have a chat about the possibility of creating more such devices."

"Will that be before or after you chop off his fingers?"

"During. He has power. He doesn't need his fingers to make anything. And after I've removed a few of his digits, he'll know what a bad idea it is to cross me."

"Yes, Your Majesty."

"Now, go find and kill Sorath before he can align himself with the druids or whatever else he has in mind to cause trouble. I don't believe for an instant that he's left the area and is done with us."

"Yes, Your Majesty."

Uthari gripped his shoulder and looked into his eyes. "Do this for me, and I'll ensure you gain a kingdom of your own."

A zing of pleasurable energy flowed from his fingers and into Yidar's body. It felt good, but it was the promise in Uthari's eyes that was far more intriguing.

"Yes, Your Majesty." Yidar bowed and hopped onto his skyboard to head back to his ship.

As he flew away, two things occurred to him. First, he was excited to hunt down the mercenary colonel, best him in battle, and earn the most promising reward he'd ever been offered. Second, Uthari had played him expertly, promising Yidar exactly what he wanted.

So be it. As long as he got a kingdom of his own in the end. Even better would be if Tonovan arranged for Malek's death while they were out on that mission, and Yidar no longer had to listen to *him* getting all of their king's praise.

Jadora was torn between wanting to examine the dragon scale and blood as soon as possible and being curious about the newcomers. The riders on their winged mounts, green-feathered birds far larger than any avian creatures back on Torvil, had flown close enough for Jak to see their faces under the identical bronze skull-caps they all wore, no hint of hair escaping them.

They hadn't yet tried to speak to Jadora and the others. They were circling the ship, which was still caught in a tree hundreds of feet above the ground, looking warily at Malek and the other mages.

Between the skullcaps that hid their hair and the armor that hid their curves, it wasn't that easy to distinguish males from females, but Jadora spotted a few women. They wore leather cuirasses identical to those of their male counterparts, and they all carried spears. *Multiple* spears. A combination of saddle and harness attached each rider to his or her mount, and long containers behind their seats held the pointed weapons.

A few of the riders flew side by side and whispered to each other, but Jadora couldn't hear the words, couldn't tell if they, as had been the case on Vran, spoke a derivative of Ancient Zeruvian. Zethron, probably terrified after the dragon battle, hadn't yet come up on deck. Clangs echoed from the open hatchway, indicating Vinjo working on the repairs. He might have enlisted Zethron's help, though he also could have grabbed the helm officer or the two servants the admiral had brought along.

"Can you understand them?" Malek asked quietly.

He'd sheathed his weapons and stood at her side, his arms folded over his chest as he kept an eye on the riders. One flew closer, and Prolix started to draw a sword, but Malek told him to stand down and wait to see what they did.

"I can't hear them well enough to tell," Jadora said. "You may have to communicate telepathically with them."

"I'll see if I can. I'm not able to read their thoughts."

"They're not mages, are they?" Jak looked up from the clay tablet that had ended up on the deck of their ship.

He'd been staring at it for several long minutes and hadn't seemed to notice the riders' approach. It was amazing that he could interpret anything on it, since Shikari had come over and plopped down on one side, his tail swishing back and forth.

"I don't sense any power coming from them, though now that they're closer, I can tell there's some in their spearheads. I'd wondered how those pierced the dragon's barrier when *we*—" Malek waved to indicate himself, Tonovan, Bakir, and Prolix, "—struggled to get through it with our magic."

"The metal doesn't look like dragon steel," Bakir said, "and the spearheads have a weak magical signature. I'd like to know what spell has been applied that's so effective on otherwise nearly impervious dragons."

"Yes," Malek agreed, glancing at the scale.

The riders looked off in one direction as two more of their kind appeared, flying low over the canopy. Their great avian mounts were bright blue instead of green and larger than the others. Maybe the riders were leaders in the community.

Distant white-capped mountains were visible far behind them —the landmarks Jak had hoped would be visible from above the canopy. Jadora hoped it would help him make a map—or at least ensure they could find their way back if they managed to repair the ship and explore farther. In the swamp below, she hadn't seen much in the way of plant life, nothing with fronds such as the Jitaruvak had. Maybe these people would be familiar with the plant and willing to share information.

"There's some magic about their skullcaps too," Malek added.

"It's very subtle," Bakir said. "I can't imagine it does much beyond keeping rain out of their eyes."

"Or mages out of their minds?"

Bakir glanced sharply at him. "You can't read them either?"

"No."

As the two new riders approached, a middle-aged man and woman, one of the nearby riders called what sounded like a greeting and possibly a question. Jadora shook her head slowly and with disappointment. She didn't recognize the words.

"I'll get Zethron. He's been here before." She stepped toward the hatchway, but Malek lifted a hand to stop her.

"I told him to come up here."

Jadora raised her eyebrows. "Politely, since he's our guide and not in your chain of command?"

"Actually, he's Vorsha's prisoner, on loan to us for this mission."

"So… there was no politeness?"

"I didn't threaten to incinerate any of his body parts if he didn't hurry. I'm not an animal." Malek glanced at Tonovan. The general wasn't paying attention to him.

"That must be what I like about you," Jadora murmured. "Your un-animalness."

"I thought it was my blade skill and willingness to use it to protect you."

"I suppose. You also look good in battle panties."

Malek dropped his arms and gave her a startled look. "In *what*?"

"That's the term I've been using for the skimpy leather undergarments you wore in the Vran arena."

"Dear Shylezar, *why*?"

"It amuses me." Jadora smirked at him and might have patted him on the back, but Tonovan squinted over at them. She sighed, wishing he were anywhere else besides along on this mission. Stuck in a glacier where he would be frozen for ten thousand years, perhaps.

"As long as it's not what their term for it actually translates to." Malek eyed her suspiciously. "It's not, is it?"

"No. The natives called them *chitoka,* which translates to *challenging* or *advanced armor*."

"Catchy."

"Yes. My term is better."

"Your term is loathsome."

Zethron stuck his head out, spotted Tonovan standing near the hatch, and looked like he wanted to disappear back into the ship. But then he saw the winged riders.

"Oh," he blurted, sounding pleased, and climbed out. He waved vigorously to them and called out in their language.

"I'll take that as promising," Jadora said. "He doesn't seem to believe they're enemies."

"They better not be after we helped them kill that dragon." Malek lifted his chin, meeting the male leader's gaze across the distance. Malek emanated power that even Jadora could sense and looked like a haughty and supremely self-confident zidarr.

She hoped the riders didn't mind that.

Perhaps the leader knew what Malek had done, for he nodded firmly back at him. Zethron called to them in their tongue and pointed grandly at the dragon scale, at Shikari, at Jak, and expansively at Jadora. She hoped it wasn't a bad sign that Zethron wasn't introducing or even acknowledging Malek, Tonovan, Prolix, or Bakir.

Malek clearly picked up on that for his eyes narrowed as he looked at the back of Zethron's head.

The leader pointed at the deck in front of Jak. At the tablet? Or at the young dragon lounging on it?

"I think they want to come aboard," Zethron said.

"You think?" Malek asked.

"I didn't spend enough time on this world to fully master their language."

"Those giant birds might add too much weight and break the branches holding us up," Tonovan said.

Prolix eyed the tree he'd climbed out of earlier and shook his head.

"Birds," Jadora said, "at least birds on our world, have hollow bones and are generally lighter than they appear."

The two blue birds landed with thumps that did not sound *light*. Snaps came from the branches under the ship, and the deck tilted further. They dropped several feet before the vessel caught again in the branches.

Jadora's heart tried to leap out of her throat, and she lunged and grabbed Malek's arm for support. As if *that* could keep them from crashing to the ground.

"Are the riders also lighter than they appear?" Malek asked dryly.

"Perhaps not." Jadora cleared her throat when her voice came out squeaky.

The leader pointed at the tablet. Shikari had shifted to cover up almost *all* of it. Accidentally or intentionally? Jadora hadn't gone to look at it yet and didn't know what it held.

"He says that belongs to their people," Zethron said, "and that they only challenged the dragon because it flew into their city and stole it."

"Did they expect to be able to *beat* the dragon to get it back?" Tonovan asked. "Or are they human sacrifices that their people didn't care if they lost?"

"Uh, he's the chief, and she's his wife," Zethron said. "I don't think I should ask your question."

"Is there any way to tell if they're telling the truth?" Jak knelt with a hand on the corner of the tablet. He looked at Malek.

"I can't read their thoughts." Malek eyed the skullcaps on the riders' heads, his gaze lingering on the chief.

"It might not be a good idea to steal the headwear of the natives," Jadora whispered to him.

"I don't want to steal it. I only want to hold him down and peel it off."

"So much more congenial."

The chief looked at his wife. She shrugged and pointed down to the jungle, saying a few words. He nodded and repeated them to Zethron.

"To thank us for helping them defeat the dragon and retrieve their valuable possession," Zethron said, "they're inviting us to a feast in their village."

"*Helping* them defeat the dragon?" Tonovan asked. "We defeated it by ourselves while they wet themselves as they watched from a distance."

Jadora rolled her eyes. For all his power and bluster, Tonovan hadn't seemed to do much in that battle. She supposed it would be immature and uncouth to suggest a check for evidence that *he'd* wet himself.

"We accept the invitation." Malek flicked a finger at the tablet. "Jak, remove your dragon from that and let them have it back."

"Uh," Jak said. "Do you know what it's a map of?"

"I see that you do." Malek shrugged. "If it's their map, they may already know all about that place."

"What if it's not theirs, and they're lying? What if they stole it from the dragon, and it was stealing it back?"

Jadora frowned at her son, doubting he believed that. He was certain that the younger dragons were pure evil.

"We'll find out at their feast," Malek said. "We'll also find out if they know why we weren't able to activate the portal and leave."

Jak's expression was dubious, but he made shooing motions at Shikari.

Shikari obeyed, but more because he was interested in another huge winged insect flying low over the deck, drawn by the dragon scale—or the dragon blood. He sprang into the air and tried to chomp on it, but the insect was faster than it looked. With an angry buzz, it evaded his snapping maw.

Instead of giving chase, Shikari looked expectantly back at Jak.

"Oh, right." Jak screwed up his face in concentration and used his magic to push or pull the insect toward his charge.

This time, when Shikari leapt up, he caught the big bug, gnashing cheerfully down on it.

The riders exchanged startled looks at each other, some openly gaping at Jak.

Jadora hoped it hadn't been unwise of him to demonstrate that he had magical power. But the riders had witnessed the battle with the dragon. They had to know the team contained mages.

"Are you his hunting partner?" Malek asked mildly. "Or his servant?"

"Well, he's young," Jak said. "He still relies on me to get food. I assume he'll one day be able to magically swat his own insects toward his jaws."

"In the old days, weak-willed humans supposedly prostrated themselves before dragons," Tonovan said, "worshipping them and bringing them whatever they wished, like faithful dogs retrieving their master's slippers."

"I didn't know you were a student of history, General," Jak said, forcing himself to smile pleasantly.

Jadora thought about contradicting Tonovan, giving three factually correct examples to the contrary of his idiotic statement, but she didn't want to pick a fight with him.

But Tonovan must have been keeping an eye on her—on her mind—for he sneered over at her. *Those who don't want to pick fights with their superiors should keep their thoughts suitably meek and respectful.*

I'll keep that in mind. Though it was difficult, Jadora carefully did not fantasize about having a kerzor to jab into his skull. She wore the ring Malek had given her, and appreciated his thoughtfulness, but robbing degenerate mages of their power would be far preferable to giving them a little shock.

Do. It would be a shame if I had to punish you in front of strangers.

Malek shifted to stand beside Jadora, blocking her from Tonovan's view. "Tell them we look forward to this feast," he instructed Zethron.

Zethron must have caught the fact that Tonovan and Jadora were conversing—and that it hadn't been pleasant for her—for he gave her a sympathetic smile before obeying the order.

"Are you starting to regret leaving your world?" Jadora asked him softly.

They'd not yet had an opportunity to speak privately, but she'd apologized to him for whatever torment he'd endured at the hands of Vorsha's people. He'd given her a good-natured shrug and said he'd known it would be a possibility. That didn't mean it hadn't been horrible for him.

"I was perhaps a touch impulsive," Zethron admitted, stepping closer. "I could have waited a few months, until all the mages congregating around your portal had perhaps moved on, but then... you might not have been there either." He smiled quickly, though he cast a wary glance at Malek.

"I could have given you my address in Sprungtown." Jadora returned the smile, though she made sure it couldn't be misinterpreted as a flirtatious gesture. "You could have stopped by for coffee at a future date."

"Sprungtown?" Zethron asked. "Is that close to your portal?"

"No. To reach it, you'd have to walk a thousand miles across a continent, swim across an ocean, and walk another thousand miles or so." And then there would be no guarantee that she would be home. Who knew if Uthari would ever let her return to her old life?

"That's a long trek for coffee."

"It is." Her smile turned sad as she wondered if she would ever get a chance to do such a normal thing as meeting a colleague for coffee again.

The chief picked up the tablet, and he and his wife climbed onto their birds, said a few words, and took to the air.

"They say to follow them," Zethron translated. "They'll take us to their city where we can relax until it's time for the feast."

All Jadora wanted was the opportunity to look for the Jitaruvak. The thought of having to endure a meal with Tonovan making more snide comments in her mind was enough to make her cringe. She hoped she could learn where the Jitaruvak was and that they could leave this world as soon as possible.

~

Tezi gazed over the railing of the *Star Flyer*, wondering how they would find sign of druids in the dense jungle below. The camp and all the mageships hovering near it had long since disappeared behind them, and with clouds blotting out the stars, there was no hint of light anywhere. Even the running lights of the other two ships that had joined the *Star Flyer* for the search weren't visible at the moment.

"You ready for some practice, Tezi?" Sergeant Tinder asked, coming up beside her. She clunked two large wooden axes against the railing. "I had Corporal Smith make these for us so we don't risk lopping off each other's heads with our real weapons."

"It's probably not a bad idea."

"Of course it's not. My ideas are all brilliant."

A soft snort came from nearby, Dr. Fret sitting on the deck against one of Lieutenant Vinjo's collapsible defensive bulwarks with her knitting bag out and a new project in the works.

"I don't know if you're officially back in the company yet—" Tinder raised her eyebrows in inquiry, "—but if you're working with us, you've got to keep up with your training."

Tezi didn't know if she was back in the company yet either, so she only nodded in agreement. She would *like* to be invited back in, and Rivlen, at the least, seemed to consider her a part of it, but Captain Ferroki hadn't said anything to make it official.

"Here you go." Tinder thrust one of the axes toward her.

The double-headed weapon was heavier than the dragon-steel version but otherwise a decent approximation. Tezi held it up to look at colorful braided thread—or yarn?—dangling from the end of the haft.

"Is this a tassel?" She glanced at Fret, wondering if the company's knitting doctor had helped design the axes.

"It's a wrist strap," Tinder said. "To keep it from going flying if you lose your grip."

"My real axe doesn't have one."

"Because the original crafter was short-sighted," Fret said without looking up from her project. "You *definitely* don't want that deadly thing flying from your grip."

"A weapon attached physically to you could allow an enemy to grab it and yank you off balance," Captain Ferroki said, walking up to join them. "Also, if you lodged your axe in an enemy's shield, your shoulder could be pulled out of the socket as they raced away."

"*Captain.*" Tinder swatted Ferroki on the arm. "Quit being so practical. You know Fret has to decorate things. Like this. Look." Tinder turned to show off an ammo pouch attached to her belt. The belt *and* the pouch had tassels as well as—

"Is that beadwork?" Ferroki asked.

"Yes. Fret found a mercenary to trade craft supplies with. She got a bunch of colorful beads and quills that she's working with now. There are some pretty green ones. If you ask nicely, maybe she'll do a dragon for your sword scabbard. Nothing drives fear into the hearts of enemies like dragons."

"Even dragons made from beads?" Tezi asked.

"Well, it helps if you're shooting at the enemies while running at them with the beadwork dragons."

"Tinder, give us a moment of privacy, please," Ferroki said.

"Sure. I'll be waiting when you're ready, Rookie." Tinder held up her wooden axe and wandered off to shadow spar with one of the bulwarks. Through the various battles, Thorn Company had managed to retain all the ones Vinjo had sold them.

"Yes, Captain?" Tezi stood at attention and faced Ferroki.

"Before we left, I caught wind of some rumors about what happened last night."

Unease swirled into Tezi's gut. She'd worried that someone would accuse her of doing nothing while the druids rescued their comrade.

"I'm sorry, ma'am," she blurted, guilt swamping her. "Some of the mercenaries attacked me and were trying to get my axe. I didn't even realize the druids were there until they were on their way out of camp with the prisoner. Well, I sort of did, because one jumped in and helped me against the mercenaries. I mean, he didn't *help* me specifically. I don't think. But..." Tezi trailed off because Ferroki's eyebrows were climbing her forehead. "This *is* what you wanted to talk about, isn't it, ma'am?"

"It is. I just hadn't heard this version. The one that came to me via other mercenaries was that you walked out to the pool, waved to the druids to let them know the way was clear, and stood by while they sneaked into the camp and killed three mercenaries from Moon Guard."

Tezi rocked back. "That's not even close to true, ma'am."

"I didn't think it was, or we would be having a much sterner discussion. I also heard another version from one of the roamers who woke up when he heard sounds of fighting. He said you and the Moon Guard mercenaries were fighting against a druid invasion."

A druid invasion? Just one crazy man with spiky green hair and a tattooed face...

"That's not quite what happened either, ma'am. The Moon Guard people were trying to get my axe." Tezi took a deep breath and started from the beginning, meeting the captain's gaze and speaking earnestly in the hope that Ferroki would believe her.

"It sounds like I need to have a talk with the Moon Guard commander when we return," Ferroki said. "But you're sure the druid boy was helping you? Not simply that he killed the others first and didn't have time to get to you?"

"I'm not sure he *intended* to help me, but that was the end result, ma'am. He didn't at any point try to kill me, but he did notice my axe, I'm sure, so it's possible he realized it would have protected me and didn't think trying to get to me would be wise." Admittedly, Tezi hadn't seen the druid use any magic. He'd killed the Moon Guard mercenaries with his blazing-fast knife work, something the dragon-steel axe wouldn't necessarily have protected her from.

"I can see why witnesses would have been confused and might have thought you were in allegiance with him."

Tezi winced. "I'm not. I guess I'd owe him one if I met him again, but I don't *want* to meet him again."

She frowned down at her boots, reluctantly admitting that she *did* owe the man a favor. Whether it had been his original intent or not, that druid had saved her life.

"Thank you for clarifying, Tezi. I hope no further trouble will arise due to the event." Ferroki's expression was bleak.

That made Tezi wonder how many versions of that attack were floating around camp. What if, while Thorn Company was gone, the rest of the mercenary units banded together and decided that Tezi was a traitor? Or what if they tried to somehow convince the others that the Moon Guard company should receive her axe?

"I hope so too, ma'am," Tezi said glumly. "I just want to be a good mercenary and for mages and axe thieves to leave me alone."

Ferroki smiled. "You had better go practice with Tinder. The more competent you are with the weapon—the more competent everyone *believes* you are—the less likely people will try to prey on you."

"Yes, ma'am," Tezi said, though unless she single-handedly killed one of those giant flying worms in front of the camp, the way Malek had, she doubted any of the other mercenaries would believe her too ferocious and deadly to take advantage of. Too bad.

10

THE CHIEF AND HIS WIFE AND THE OTHER RIDERS FLEW IN FRONT OF and alongside the mageship, leading them toward what Zethron promised was a *city in the treetops*. Jak watched his mother lean over the railing and use a spyglass to peer into the canopy as they skimmed above the needles and leaves. He didn't know if she was able to glimpse anything through the branches. Clearings were scant. Zethron stood nearby, occasionally mentioning some distant landmark or offering information about the local culture.

Jak sat with his back to the railing, worrying about that map and that the mottled dragons had gotten an opportunity to look at it. Later, he would ask Malek if they could stop in that world on the way home to make sure nothing bad was befalling those eggs. The thought of the mottled dragons melting the ice and destroying the unborn beings inside—dozens of brothers and sisters to Shikari—filled Jak with horror and chagrin. And guilt that he hadn't—hadn't yet—figured out a way to ensure the safety of the eggs. It seemed that in guiding him to them, the portal had been appointing him surrogate guardian. Or father. Or something.

The others would doubtless mock him for such thoughts.

Maybe not Malek or his mother, but Tonovan and the new people. The new *mages.*

At least for the moment, there was little chance of anyone burrowing through Jak's mind. After Malek had levitated the dragon scale through the cargo hatch and into the kitchen for Mother to study later, he'd joined Tonovan, Bakir, and Prolix in the navigation cabin below. The poor helm officer, Lieutenant Harintha, was wedged between them down there. Jak doubted Malek wanted to spend time with the other mages, especially Tonovan, and had a feeling he'd led them below for Mother's sake, so that Tonovan wouldn't be on the deck with them, tormenting her with whatever cruel thoughts he liked to thrust into her mind.

Jak had never been the kind of person to fantasize about killing people, and it bothered him that he kept catching himself envisioning throttling Tonovan or sticking a dagger in his chest while he slept. He'd killed in self-defense but never in cold blood, and the idea of doing so repulsed him, but that man also repulsed him, and he hated that Tonovan *liked* tormenting his mother.

The hatch clanged open, and Lieutenant Vinjo climbed out.

"Thank all the gods in the heavens and even the slavemasters in Hell." He spread his arms and looked at the sky. "Fresh air, free of arguing wizards."

Shikari galloped past, dropping a translucent wing at Vinjo's feet.

"What is that?" Vinjo lowered his arms.

"He's playing with his food," Jak said. "I don't know how to discourage it or even if I should. Maybe mama dragons regularly toss giant insect wings to their hatchlings to keep them entertained."

"Hm, I wonder if I could make something with it." Vinjo picked up the somewhat mangled wing but quickly dropped it again and shook his hand. "It's damp."

"Dragon saliva," Jak assumed.

"A lubricant I'm not interested in incorporating into my projects." Vinjo ambled over to join him. With grease smearing his cheek, and his short hair sticking up in several directions, it didn't seem like a little dragon saliva should bother him. He pointed at Mother and Zethron, who were murmuring quietly nearby as they peered down at marshy water visible through the canopy. "Is that romance happening?"

Jak blinked and looked at them. "I don't think so." He almost said that his mother was more inclined to spend time with Malek than Zethron, but his mind shied away from the thought of them together, or his mother having *romance* at all. "They're old."

He supposed someone in her early forties wasn't *that* old, but the idea of his mother being intimate with a man made him want to furl up like a zanga flower before an impending rainstorm.

"Oh, good. I didn't want to interrupt a date." Vinjo flopped down between Jak and his mother, putting his back to the railing and letting his head clunk against it. He didn't look like he'd slept since long before the mission started. He probably hadn't. "And just so you know, old people like romance too."

"Ew."

"And they're not that old. *I'm* not that old." Vinjo rested his palm on his chest, though Jak hadn't suggested he was. The lieutenant appeared to be in his early thirties. Admittedly, the weariness and general seedy scruffiness about him made him seem older. "I like romance."

"Ah, sure." Jak didn't know what to make of the bewildering conversation. He barely knew the engineer. Was he supposed to commiserate with him about the lack of suitable women onboard to attempt to woo? For some reason, Rivlen's stern face popped into his mind. Stern but not uncaring.

"I do not believe Lieutenant Sasko would have wished to come along on this mission," Vinjo said, "but I selfishly wish she'd been assigned to it. She was acting as my bodyguard while I built this ship, you know."

"A terrene human was acting as the bodyguard for a powerful mage?" Jak hadn't spoken often with Thorn Company's second-in-command, but she was another woman he would classify as stern. Stern but not uncaring? Maybe she was a softy with Vinjo, though that was hard to imagine.

"Certainly. Terrene humans can watch your back for hurled wrenches—and daggers—as well as the next person."

Jak preferred having Malek, with his power and weapons skills, protecting him and his mother, but he supposed a zidarr bodyguard wasn't an option for most people.

"Are you and she having a romance?" Normally, Jak wouldn't pry, but he was curious if Vinjo might be sympathetic to terrene humans in general. Such a talented maker of magical devices would be a good ally if Jak ever had the opportunity to enact his wish—his *plan*—of overthrowing the mage oligarchy. Would Vinjo work against his own kind?

Jak glanced up at Mother and caught her gazing down at them—at the top of Vinjo's head—and wondered if she had similar speculations. Now and then, he caught a whisper of her thoughts—of the thoughts of many terrene humans—and assumed he was developing more of the typical mage abilities. Perhaps if he focused, he could read her more clearly, but he wasn't sure he *wanted* that ability. He knew how irritating it was when mages read *his* mind.

"I *hope* we get to have a romance." Vinjo gazed wistfully off toward the clouds. "She kissed me once. Before my first prototype engine blew up in the druid attack. But I'm not sure that means she's smitten with me."

Jak couldn't imagine any of the tough Thorn Company mercenaries being *smitten*.

"I made her a clandestineness creeper, and she seemed to

appreciate it, but then she gave it to Colonel Sorath." Vinjo's forehead creased. "What do you think *that* means?"

"That Sorath needed it more than she did?"

"What if she didn't like it? What if she found it repulsive and was foisting it off on the first likely person?"

"I'm positive that wasn't the case. Any human, terrene or otherwise, would *love* to be able to turn invisible, especially when grumpy mages are all around." Jak remembered that he was *talking* to a mage—with Vinjo, it was easy to forget—and hoped the comment didn't earn him a glower or some stupid punishment.

"Mages *are* grumpy," Vinjo said with a sigh. "Do you know that my own brother has threatened to kill me? And he *has* used his power to hurt me. Grumpily."

"That's the zidarr Night Wrath, right?" Jak scratched his jaw. Vinjo *did* seem like a candidate to help them. Maybe he would be willing to make more of his stealth devices. Clandestineness creepers, as he called them. A *lot* more. Jak thought about asking, but with Malek, Bakir, and Prolix below, this wasn't the time to plot rebellion. Maybe once they reached the city, the important officers would be taken off to speak with the chief while Jak, Vinjo, and Zethron were left behind.

"Yes. He was grumpy even before he started zidarr training, but that made it even worse. Now he's grumpy *and* full of himself. As all zidarr are."

"Malek isn't like that."

Vinjo shuddered. "Malek beams power like a sun. I would not want to provoke him in any way and risk finding out personally how grumpy he can be."

"Probably wise," Jak said, though he had stopped seeing Malek that way. Oh, he was aware of that power that Malek emanated, but he didn't believe Malek would use it against him or was a threat to him. Maybe it was a mistake to think that way, but since Malek kept helping him and Mother, and since Jak had been training with him, it was easy to see him as a mentor. A friend.

Maybe he hadn't protected those thoughts sufficiently, for Vinjo turned a perplexed expression on him. He looked like he might say something, but Zethron spoke first.

"We're heading into a swarm of dagger darters." Zethron pointed toward a black cloud hovering above the trees ahead of the ship. More insects? If so, they were dense. "They're not usually above the canopy."

The riders split to go around the cloud. *Far* around the cloud. Their bird mounts were also flying faster now. Hurrying to get past the insects?

"Should we all go below?" Jak asked, figuring they would be safe inside the ship.

"I'll warn the helm officer." Zethron headed toward the hatch.

"Are they a danger?" Mother asked. "To us?"

"They *can* attack people, but they prefer birds, flying lizards, and other large airborne targets." Zethron thumped a boot on the wooden deck. "I'm not sure if their threat extends to people who are *riding* airborne targets."

As Zethron climbed below, Vinjo jumped to his feet and scowled fiercely at the cloud. "Airborne *targets*? My ship is in danger? From *bugs*?"

Jak also stood, tempted to go below but curious about the insects. "Maybe that camouflage you mentioned will keep them from seeing it."

"Maybe a fireball hurled into the middle of the swarm will keep them from seeing it," Vinjo grumbled.

Shikari squeaked. He'd seen the insects and wasn't afraid of them. He crouched at the front of the ship, his tail swishing on the deck as he stared intently through the railing at them.

The cloud parted, but not to let the ship pass through. Both halves buzzed toward them, as if the insects intended to flank the vessel. And attack from both sides?

"Vinjo," Mother said quietly, easing over to stand next to him.

"Yes?" Vinjo asked.

"I have something I want to show you. Something I'm curious if you could… replicate." Mother glanced at Jak.

A bout of nerves assailed Jak's gut as he had a premonition that she was going to ask Vinjo about the kerzor. If so, why *now*? The mages might be distracted from monitoring the minds of the people up here by the encroaching insects, but wouldn't there be a better time?

Admittedly, Jak had been thinking about asking if Vinjo would make stealth devices. Ultimately, the devices could be used toward the same goal, but the Vran discs seemed a lot more nefarious. Jak doubted Malek would care that much, other than to waggle a finger at them, if he found them plotting to have stealth devices made, but Malek had a very good reason to detest the kerzor. And he would find the idea of terrene humans plotting to make them treasonous at best. He might be driven to punish someone contemplating such a plan, even someone he cared about.

"You want me to build something?" Vinjo asked curiously.

"If you could, it's something that might be useful to terrene humans, including your Lieutenant Sasko."

"*My* Lieutenant Sasko," Vinjo said, his eyes growing wistful and dreamy.

Mother grimaced, probably not liking the idea of using the woman as a tool to manipulate Vinjo, but for whatever reason, she felt compelled to bring this up here. Maybe she believed their time with access to Vinjo would be limited. Or—a chill went through Jak—had something happened that made her feel it imperative to make some of those discs now? Had *Tonovan* threatened her? Or one of the others?

Mother pulled a folded piece of paper out of one of her

copious pockets. "The original was destroyed, but I did my best to make a detailed schematic of a magical device from Vran."

"It was destroyed?" Jak whispered.

He knew Shikari had bitten one in two, removing the needle and tendrils from the metal disc when he'd *eaten* it, but Jak had given the mostly intact one that he'd taken from Malek's temple during the magical surgery to his mother.

She nodded grimly at him. "Malek did it."

"Oh," Jak mouthed.

"After Uthari found out about it and ordered him to do so."

Vinjo had been reaching for the folded paper, but he hesitated. "Do you want me to build *contraband*, Professor?"

"Something like that, but having a number of these could help Thorn Company. And the rest of us." She smiled and waved at herself.

Vinjo eyed her dubiously. Perhaps he didn't yet consider Mother and Jak people that he wanted to help.

Jak admitted that now that he'd been developing magical power and was on the verge of being able to do useful things with it, like defending his mother and himself, he found the thought of making such devices unappealing. But if one could be driven into Tonovan's skull, would he object to that? No. Nor would he volunteer to entice Shikari into helping him remove it.

Vinjo's fingers twitched several times, as if common sense were warring with curiosity, and finally grabbed the paper and opened it. "What does it do?"

A thump sounded, and Jak flinched. He glanced toward the hatch, certain Malek or one of the others knew what they were talking about and was coming to punish them for it.

But when another thump came, the sound caused by something striking the hull, he realized it wasn't the hatch. A bug almost as large as his forearm, with a proboscis that reminded him of a drill, flew past and landed on the railing. The thing was huge, as all the insects on this world seemed to be.

It touched that long proboscis to the railing. Vinjo squawked and waved a hand. Jak sensed him flicking it off the railing with a burst of power. It landed on the deck, momentarily disoriented, and Shikari galloped over and pounced on it. Bug blood and guts spattered, and Jak frowned and looked away.

"Ugh," Vinjo said. "The dragon blood maligning my freshly varnished deck was bad enough."

More thumps sounded, and Jak leaned through a gap in the railing in time to see numerous bugs burst into flames before they could damage the ship. "Looks like Malek and the others are on it."

"Good."

"The schematic, Lieutenant?" Mother tapped Vinjo on the shoulder. "What do you think? Is it something you could make?"

Vinjo glowered at Shikari devouring the large bug for another moment, then turned his attention back to the paper. "Without knowing what it's supposed to do, I wouldn't know what kind of magic to infuse it with."

"Given how much Uthari likes to have you tortured, it might be better for you that you *not* know," Jak said, eyeing his mother.

"Then you'd get a large thumbtack." Vinjo squinted at the drawing. "With strange little threads on the end."

"Those are tendrils with hooks," Jak said.

"They burrow into the subject's brain," Mother murmured.

Vinjo gaped at the paper, then held it at arm's length. "You insert this into someone's *skull*?"

"A mage's." Mother pointed to notes she'd written on the back. "You can read everything we know about it here. I'd prefer not to spend a lot of time dwelling on it." She grimaced as more insects thudded against the hull, but Jak doubted they were the reason for her expression.

"I am horrified," Vinjo said, skimming the notes.

Jak also grimaced. What if he was so horrified that he handed the paper over to Malek and the others and pointed out who'd given it to him? This might have been a big mistake.

More bugs buzzed past, making Jak and Mother duck, though Vinjo, with his gaze locked on the paper, barely seemed to notice them. Shikari leaped up and dragged another insect from the sky. The wings and proboscis were all that was left of the first one, the remains scattered on the deck.

"Although... is it wrong that I'm already fantasizing about shoving one of these into my *brother*'s skull?" Vinjo mused. "Does it do any damage to the person? Besides stealing their magic?"

"Not that we saw," Mother said.

"Malek wore one on Vran, and he's fine now. Did you see his scar?" Jak touched his temple, though the scar on Malek's face had faded and wasn't too visible anymore. "When he first came back?"

"Horrifying." Vinjo's gaze remained toward the paper. "But I could see..." He licked his lips.

The appeal? Jak met his mother's eyes.

"Of course, the idea would be to only use them on truly reprehensible mages," Mother said. "Not good, hard-working people who don't ensl— *hurt* others."

She'd been about to say enslave, but Jak understood why she'd switched to another word. Almost all mages either had slaveband- or mageband-wearing servants, or at least made use of them in some capacity, so it might be best not to make that the defining factor on whether someone deserved having a kerzor shoved into their skull. Though Jak dearly hoped that a revolution would result in everyone being freed of those awful bands.

Vinjo's head jerked up, and he looked at the hatch. He folded the paper and slipped it into his pocket a second before it opened. Malek, Prolix, and Bakir climbed out. Malek stalked to the bow, spread his arms, and bugs everywhere burst into flames. Their charred carcasses fell out of the sky.

"That's a relief," Vinjo said. "I was worried my ship would be damaged. Maybe I should give it some weapons in case bugs attack again and there aren't mages around to protect it."

Malek gazed over at him, his face unreadable.

"Like harpoon launchers. That could work. Or cannons. Or have I ever told you all about the magical fireball-producing and slingshotting apparatus that I designed?" Vinjo sounded nervous, and he kneaded the hem of his tunic, looking at Malek's collarbones instead of his eyes as he spoke.

Jak resisted the urge to rub a hand over his face. However helpful Vinjo was when it came to engineering and crafting devices, he might have been a poor choice for a confidant. Like all mages, he seemed able to guard his thoughts—at least, Jak didn't sense any of them trickling out of his mind—but his worried face and body language might give everything away.

Mother pulled out her spyglass again and faced the railing, going back to searching for signs of her plant.

As Vinjo kept babbling about his inventions, now muttering under his breath and talking to the deck instead of Malek, Malek shifted his gaze to the back of Mother's head. Jak feared it wasn't because he admired the way she'd braided her hair that morning.

Hopefully, she was having loving thoughts of finding the Jitaruvak and delivering it to Uthari, but Jak knew how difficult it was to avoid thinking about something one shouldn't be while a mage looked on. He hadn't yet tried to guard another person's thoughts, but Malek did it all the time, so Jak knew it was possible. Maybe if he imagined his mental bandana, the one covered in imagery of mountains capable of walling off one's thoughts from prying minds, wrapped not only around his head but around his mother's head, he could keep Malek from seeing in.

Prolix and Bakir, who were looking toward the distant riders while having a conversation of their own, didn't seem to be paying attention to them. But on this particular subject, Malek could be as much of a threat as those two.

He walked toward Mother, barely glancing at Jak and Vinjo as he joined her at the railing.

"I need to work on something," Vinjo blurted and ran toward the hatch, his grass skirt flapping around his legs.

"I hope we can fly lower later," Mother said, her eye pressed to the spyglass. "From here, it's rare to catch a glimpse of the ground below, and even when I do, it's nothing but swamp water. There could be plants growing on the banks under the trees, but who would know? It's a foregone conclusion, however, that they don't grow in treetops."

Mother didn't sound as nervous as Vinjo as she babbled, but Jak knew her well and recognized her unease, her attempt to distract Malek with a different topic. Would he find it suspicious? Again, Jak tried to wrap a protective mental bandana around her mind.

What are you doing? Malek asked him silently.

Erg, maybe *Jak* was the one acting suspicious. *Trying to learn how to guard my mother's thoughts. It seems wise, given the enemy mages skulking about on board.*

Uthari has an alliance, however temporary it might be, with King Jutuk and Queen Vorsha. Their mages shouldn't be a threat.

I was talking about Tonovan. Jak smiled, though Malek was looking over the railing with Mother, not at him.

I see. Malek didn't sound amused. *Is there something in her thoughts that you don't want... Tonovan to see?*

Usually.

This time, Malek did look at him, a cool assessing gaze.

You know she has an irreverent streak. It runs in the family. Just a few minutes ago, when you walked up, she was having irreverent thoughts.

About me? Malek touched his shirt.

About Vinjo and his grass skirt.

That skirt deserves irreverent thoughts.

True. But it's dangerous to be irreverent with mages. Will you teach me how to effectively guard the thoughts of others? Jak smiled hopefully at Malek, trying to do a little distracting of his own.

The hatch clanged open again, and Tonovan climbed out. He stood and sneered toward the riders. "Nothing but bird butts up here again. When do we get to this vaunted city for a feast?"

"What do you care?" Bakir asked. "I thought you were busy checking out your bunk and using my slave."

"I was, but having giant thuds sounding as those bugs struck the hull irritated me. I'll have to talk to our engineer about adding soundproof insulation."

"I'm sure we'd *all* appreciate that," Bakir said.

"Your slave also wasn't very stimulating. I'd expect an admiral to have his choice of beautiful women, but perhaps Jutuk's offerings are inferior."

"His *offerings* are just fine."

"Then your taste is the problem. I prefer feistier women." Tonovan smirked over at Mother, heedless of Jak and Malek beside her.

Jak clenched his fists, barely remembering to keep his own mental bandana in place. He didn't want to be caught fantasizing about clobbering the man—or jamming one of the *kerzor* into his brain.

Mother kept her back to Tonovan, but her spine was stiff, and there was little doubt she knew he was looking at her. Was he saying something crude into her mind?

Tonovan snorted, looked at Malek, and made a rude gesture with his fingers. Maybe Malek had caught the gist and told him to leave her alone. Jak hoped so.

"There's the city." Bakir pointed toward the sky ahead of the riders.

The never-ending sea of treetops remained unchanged, but they could now see wooden structures built on a great platform that rose above them. A palisade of vertical logs created a wall all around the city, each one sharpened to a point. The roofs of one- and two-story cabins were visible inside.

At first, Jak thought of the floating sky cities where the mages back home lived, but then he saw the supports that Zethron had mentioned, thick posts that disappeared into the forest, presumably secured to the ground far below. Given how tall the trees were here, that was impressive, and Jak wondered if magic had been used to strengthen them.

"You call that a city?" Tonovan asked. "It's made out of *logs*. It looks like some primitive fortress built by mundanes out in a wild frontier land."

The riders should have been too far ahead to hear the comment, and couldn't have understood the language, but one of them peered back. Jak hoped he'd gotten the gist of the insult and would instruct whatever cooks prepared the feast to spit in Tonovan's food.

Tonovan frowned over at Jak. Damn it, had he let that thought slip through? He'd been so careful with the rest.

Mind your charge, Malek, Tonovan said, letting Jak hear the words. *For someone with supposed talent, he's abysmal at guarding his thoughts. I can understand when his terrene mother lets her fantasies of climbing naked into my bed leak out, but he should be better trained.*

Jak clenched his jaw.

A man who recently lost his eye to one of the women he tormented should know better than to make such comments, Malek replied, his eyes icy as he held Tonovan's gaze.

Tonovan's own gaze turned frostier than a glacier. *One of the women* you *helped.*

Malek stared stonily back at him without commenting.

Did you think I wouldn't figure it out? That you just happened to arrive seconds after we struck trees out of nowhere? Nice of you to stop in to gloat after facilitating that.

I healed your eye.

You healed nothing. I'm still missing my damn eye. Tonovan's hand jerked up as he bared his teeth, visibly seething.

Jak shifted uneasily. Would they come to blows? Magical blows that might kill innocent bystanders? Or destroy the ship they all depended on to stay aloft?

Is that why you attacked me as well as the dragon? Malek asked.

Yes, you bastard. And I'll do it again as soon as I get the chance. Tonovan stalked toward them. *And once you're dead, I'll kill the boy and screw his mother. Over and over and—*

Tonovan's head jerked back, as if he'd been punched. Fury radiated from the usually calm Malek.

Jak, burning with his own fury, wanted so badly to leap on Tonovan and hold him down while Malek punished him—no, *killed* him. He found himself taking a step in that direction, but Tonovan recovered from the magical blow, and a diamond-hard barrier wrapped around him.

Jak sensed him launching a counterattack, but a barrier also protected Malek. It was wrapped around Mother as well, and Jak hoped it wouldn't be weaker because Malek had to spread it out. Just in case, Jak funneled magical energy into it and into Malek. He might not be great at guarding his thoughts yet, but he was improving at this, at using his own power to help other mages.

"Two of the riders are coming." Admiral Bakir looked back and forth between Malek and Tonovan, no doubt sensing the power crackling in the air between them.

Would he interfere if they fought? As a fellow military officer, Bakir might be inclined to help Tonovan. Prolix was watching the two approaching riders and didn't acknowledge the test of wills going on behind him. Jak doubted he would jump in to help Malek just because they were both zidarr.

Malek and Tonovan kept holding each other's gazes—each other's *glares*—until one of the feathered mounts alighted on the deck ten feet from them. The rider looked at them, his head tilted in puzzlement, then at Jak and spoke to him.

"Unless you can understand them," Jak said to his mother, "we need Zethron."

Malek finally broke the stare with Tonovan and looked at the rider, who was speaking and pointing toward one side of the city as the mageship continued toward it. The rest of the riders had flown over the palisade and were disappearing inside, likely to the avian equivalent of a stable.

For some reason, the rider directed his instructions toward Jak. Did these people also believe him a *Favored Traveler*? Someone the portal approved of and who would have a special designation in their society?

Jak probably shouldn't hope for that, but he wouldn't mind if the chief wanted to interact with him and called Tonovan his servant. Unfortunately, Tonovan might lash out at them if they did. And they hadn't yet seen anything to suggest these people had power akin to the Vran mages. If Malek was right, they didn't have power at all.

"I can't," Mother said. "If their language evolved from Ancient Zeruvian or another Torvil-based language, it's changed too much over the millennia for me to recognize."

The hatch opened, and Zethron stuck his head out.

"Talk to him." Malek pointed to the rider. He must have summoned Zethron telepathically.

"Uh, yes, powerful mage lord leader."

"Lord Malek will do," Malek said.

Zethron bowed to him and stepped up beside Mother as he spoke to the rider. If Malek felt irritation at their closeness, he hid it. At least Jak *thought* he did. Tonovan squinted as he watched Malek, Zethron, and Mother, as if he'd picked up on something and was now plotting.

Jak hoped a stiff breeze would come along and knock him over the railing and onto one of those pointy logs. He didn't bother to hide the thought. Tonovan shifted his glare to him.

"They're inviting us to dock your flying boat outside of the city," Zethron said. "Around back, there's a landing pad where the *nakka* of visiting dignitaries alight and enter the city. Our group will be entertained at the *hydrikor*—I don't know that word, but maybe theater?—until such time as the feast is ready."

The rider nodded at him, bowed to Jak, and smiled fondly at Shikari as the young dragon ambled up to sniff his mount. The bird was several times his size, at least for now, and didn't appear concerned. It sniffed him back, then squawked as its rider climbed on, and sprang into the air.

Someone must have given Lieutenant Harintha a command, for the mageship veered to one side to fly around the city.

"I hope this feast is good," Tonovan said. "Thus far, this world hasn't been the mecca of dragon-steel weapons and other resources that I was hoping for. That our *king* was hoping for."

"Let's hope they keep them in the city," Bakir said. "And deliver them along with choice cuts of meat to their guests."

"Dragon-steel weapons typically have to be *taken*. I don't sense anyone here with power, so it would be easy to take off with whatever we wish." Tonovan eyed Malek, though they seemed to have put their notions of battle aside, at least for now. "I assume the king doesn't care how we acquire them, just that we do."

Mother flinched at this talk of open theft, but she didn't say anything to draw Tonovan's attention back to her. Good.

Tonovan strolled to the bow to watch the ship dock.

You still need to learn to guard your own thoughts better around mages, Malek spoke into Jak's mind. *You're inconsistent about it.*

I know. I'm sorry. And Jak was, but he didn't regret letting Tonovan see the fantasy of him impaled on a pointy log.

Malek snorted softly. *I will help you learn to protect the thoughts of others. I can't be around your mother all the time, and I agree that it would be good if Tonovan couldn't see what she's thinking. For more reasons than one.*

Jak worried that Malek was implying he'd caught something about the device schematics, but he would surely be more irritated if he had.

Thank you, he replied.

Shikari sat down in front of them as he gazed curiously over at the city, his tail flicking.

"Are you bringing your dragon to the feast?" Malek asked.

"Oh, he has to," Zethron said. "The rider said your Shikari would be given a seat of honor in the city."

"That should prove interesting," Malek said.

"Especially since he *eats* seats," Jak muttered.

11

TEZI LAY UNDER HER BLANKET, TRYING TO SLEEP BUT MOSTLY listening to the women snoring or chatting quietly on the deck around her. Thorn Company hadn't been given quarters inside the ship, but the weather had cleared after a brief rain, so it wasn't unpleasant. Insects chirped in the jungle below as a half-moon shined silvery light on the treetops.

Captain Ferroki and Lieutenant Sasko sat nearby, discussing what the company would do when it finally freed itself of these mage contracts and could leave Zewnath. They knew Tezi was awake and occasionally included her in the conversation, mostly to reference her axe, but she didn't mind. Being with Thorn Company was comforting. She hoped it would last.

She did miss Jak and Jadora a little—and the rapidly growing dragon hatchling—and worried because they'd gone off with Tonovan. But she didn't belong with scholars and mages and zidarr. These were her people.

"You think Colonel Sorath is out there somewhere?" Sasko asked.

"If he's wise," Ferroki said, "he'll have trekked out of the jungle and be on his way to another continent by now."

"Uh huh. So, you think he's out there?"

Ferroki snorted. "Probably."

"Trying to help us somehow?"

"I wouldn't be surprised. He doesn't seem to know how to retire. Or stop caring about people he probably shouldn't."

"Something I bet you didn't point out while you were kissing him in that tent."

"Really, Sasko. We were alone in there. You have no idea what we were doing inside."

"Judging by the satisfied smirk on his face when he came out, he approved of whatever it was."

"He was wearing that stealth device when he walked out. You didn't see his smirk."

"And yet, I know it was there." Sasko elbowed Ferroki.

"I've seen similar smirks on Vinjo's face after he's walked out of his engineering tent with you."

"Because he was in there having a good time with his tools."

"And what kind of time did *you* have with his tools?"

"Captain, are you allowed to be crude? Doesn't the mercenary handbook speak about how a leader should be a wholesome role model?"

"I've read that book enough times to memorize it, Sasko. The word *wholesome* doesn't come up once."

Dr. Fret left the blanket she shared with Sergeant Tinder, who was snoring loudly enough to drown out the insects, and came to sit beside Tezi.

"How are you doing?" Fret asked.

"I'm all right, ma'am. Just stiffening up after that weapons practice earlier." Tezi rotated a shoulder that had taken a hard thump.

"You weren't injured last night in that druid attack?" Fret peered at her. "I heard you were in the middle of it."

There was nothing suspicious or accusatory about Fret's tone —she was probably genuinely concerned—but Tezi wondered if she'd also heard rumors from other mercenaries.

"I was, but I got lucky. And the axe helped." Tezi patted the weapon that she kept by her blanket when she slept.

"That's handy. I hope it'll help if we run into more druids out here." Fret bit her lip and peered into the darkness beyond the railing. "I have a bad feeling about this mission."

"You always have a bad feeling about everything, ma'am. Isn't that how you got your name?"

"More or less. I guess working for a woman isn't bad—" Fret waved in the direction of Captain Rivlen's cabin, "—but she's still loyal to Uthari. We have to watch what we say around her and her crew."

No kidding.

"That's always the case with all mages, isn't it?" Tezi eyed the handful of uniformed guards visible. They faced outward, watching for trouble in the jungle, but she had little doubt that they also used their mage senses to keep an eye on the mercenaries.

"Oddly, Malek didn't seem to mind our irreverence," Fret said.

"You mean Tinder's irreverence, don't you? You're never irreverent."

"In my mind, I sometimes am. And I think... thoughts."

"That's vague, ma'am."

"Yes. I've learned to be vague about thinking thoughts." Fret smiled sadly.

Rivlen stepped out of a hatchway and walked toward one of her lieutenants. She spoke quietly with him, said something that caused him to draw back in surprise, then explained further. He nodded and went to pass along the orders to the other men on duty.

"Think that'll involve us?" Tezi wondered.

"If it's something bad, yes," Fret said.

Rivlen walked over to Ferroki and Sasko, who both stood and saluted her.

"We're heading to a druid monument," Rivlen told them. "It may have been abandoned long ago, but I have reason to believe we may find enemies there. Your troops will need to be ready."

"Yes, Captain," Ferroki said. "They will be."

"Keep an eye out for friendly fire too, especially if the *Moon Spear* flies in close."

Ferroki blinked. "You believe another ship in your fleet will fire at us?"

"Probably not, but Captain Ular wouldn't have been my first choice to bring along on this mission. He may be up to something." Rivlen walked off to speak with another officer.

"I'm confused," Sasko said.

"Because we might have gotten stuck in the middle of a failure in mage politics?" Ferroki asked. "It happens often."

"True. Maybe it's more correct to say that I'm *concerned*."

"As am I. I knew I was right to have a bad feeling about this mission." Fret headed off to check her medical kit.

"Wake the others, please, Tezi," Ferroki said. "I don't know how far away the monument is, but the smart rabbit is always prepared in case a fox enters the thicket."

"Yes, ma'am."

"In this case, we may need to worry about the fox *and* the wolf," Sasko said. "And maybe the panther. There are *two* other supposed ally ships out here with us, aren't there? What if they're both gunning for the *Star Flyer* for some reason?"

"Then it'll be an eventful night."

"Oh, goodie."

After she finished rousing the rest of the company, Tezi was putting away her bedding when Rivlen appeared again, heading straight for her.

Rivlen lifted a hand. “Bring your axe, and come to the navigation cabin with me.”

Tezi looked to Ferroki, not wanting to wander off without her permission. Ferroki hesitated, glanced at Rivlen as if she might object, but at Rivlen’s frosty glare gave a nod to Tezi. Ferroki might be in charge of Thorn Company, but Thorn Company was working for Uthari who’d detached them to the *Star Flyer*. Captain Rivlen was the boss.

That’s right, Rivlen spoke into Tezi’s mind. *And besides, we’re a team now, aren’t we?*

Tezi picked up her axe. It blocked all magical attacks, but it seemed to differentiate between enemy magic and friendly magic and sometimes allowed the latter through. It never viewed telepathy a threat, and Tezi had no problem hearing Rivlen’s words.

By team, you mean that you give orders and I obey, right, ma’am?

Something like that. But when we get our opportunity to take out Tonovan, we’ll do it together. We’ll share the glory. Rivlen thumped Tezi on the back before crooking a finger, commanding her to follow.

I don’t want glory, just to keep him from hurting anyone else ever again.

By embedding an axe in his chest.

I suppose that’s one way.

An effective way.

But he’s not here, Tezi pointed out as she followed Rivlen into navigation.

A young helmsman sprang up from his seat and saluted Rivlen while looking curiously at Tezi and the axe.

I know. We’ll get him eventually. Out loud, Rivlen said, “Hug the trees and alter our course slightly, Lieutenant. I want to come in from the far side of the monument. If there are druids down there, they'll probably expect any threats to come from the north."

"Yes, ma'am." The helmsman sat back down, returning his attention to the wheel and the route ahead.

Rivlen eyed Tezi for a long moment. Tezi shifted uneasily from foot to foot, certain Rivlen had more than Tonovan in mind.

You were there for the druid attack on the ship with the prisoner last night, right? Rivlen asked.

Tezi grimaced. It seemed *everyone* had that on their minds. *I wasn't on the ship but awake at the pool below when they came. I was... refilling my canteen.*

Rivlen must have caught that hesitation, for she slitted her eyes and kept looking at Tezi. *Will you show me your thoughts?*

What? Alarm surged up in Tezi. She'd come to think of Rivlen as something of an ally, but she was also Uthari's loyal officer. Would she punish Tezi for having survived—for having done nothing except gape at that wild druid boy while his comrades stole Uthari's prisoner?

We're trying to find the druids and drive them out of the jungle. If you saw something that might be useful in that goal, I'd like to know about it.

I didn't see anything useful, ma'am. Tezi should have looked her in the eye, but she found herself staring at Rivlen's boots instead. Just because the axe protected her from mind-reading didn't mean people couldn't look at her face and tell she was lying.

I'd like to judge that for myself. No offense, but you don't know much about magic or druids or anything as far as I can tell.

I know, ma'am.

Rivlen reached out and gripped her shoulder. *Put down the axe.*

If there was magical compulsion in the words, it didn't affect Tezi, but it was an order nonetheless. If she disobeyed, she might get in trouble. She might get the *company* in trouble.

Reluctantly, Tezi leaned the axe haft against the wall and stepped away.

Another step, Rivlen said, guiding her with her hand. *It seems you don't have to be touching it to be under its sway.*

Under its *protection,* Tezi thought to herself.

That's far enough. I can read your thoughts now.

Lucky her.

Think about last night, about what happened.

Though embarrassed and ashamed, Tezi didn't try to hide her memories. Maybe Rivlen would know something about the pale-skinned druid who had seemed so out of place compared to all the druids here in Zewnath.

Rivlen riffled expertly through her memories, getting every detail far faster than the events had played out.

Those mercenaries tried to kill you for your axe? What asses. Rivlen squeezed her shoulder.

Everyone wants it, ma'am.

They could have taken it without trying to kill you. It looks like that druid saved your life. Strange that he would care. You've never seen him before?

No, ma'am. I have no idea why he would have helped me or if he just had orders to kill everyone who was awake so that we wouldn't see the others sneaking aboard that ship. But if that was it, he should have killed me too. Tezi worried that Rivlen would think the same way the other mercenaries had, that she'd been colluding with the druids. If so, Rivlen might punish her. Or worse.

Relax, girl. Tezi. I'm not suspicious. I'm sure he saw your pretty face and decided he would rather date you than kill you.

Tezi blushed. *There was another woman there. I doubt that was it.*

A pretty woman?

Tezi shrugged, barely remembering the woman's face. The pistol she'd been pointing at Tezi came more prominently to mind. *I feel guilty because I didn't do anything, and the druids got away.*

You swung your axe. It's not your fault he was fast. Don't worry about it.

He flummoxed me. He looked like he could have been someone from my village, but he also seemed so… crazy.

Yeah, guys who lick blood aren't all there. He was definitely a northerner. There are druids on other continents, but they're rare. I'm not sure that will help me find and deal with the rest of them.

No, ma'am. I would have told you if I'd known anything useful.

Would you? Rivlen gazed into her eyes.

Tezi offered another shrug. *Yes.*

Good. Rivlen squeezed her shoulder again and released her.

"Ma'am?" The helmsman's voice had an odd hitch to it. "There's another ship ahead of us."

"The *Moon Spear*?"

"No, ma'am. It's not one of ours. I believe it's… one of Queen Vorsha's."

"As if things weren't complicated enough," Rivlen grumbled. She walked to a communication orb mounted on the navigation console and rested her hand on it. She must have given it some mental command, for orange light beamed from it, and a man's face formed in the air above it. "This is Captain Rivlen of the *Star Flyer*. We're hunting in this area. I suggest you find someplace else to lurk."

"I know who you are and what ship that is," came the stiff response, "and I do not care. We are not *lurking*. We are also hunting."

"Find different prey."

"Ah, but we seek the same prey, Captain. The same prize. May the best ship find it."

Before Rivlen could respond, the orb went dark.

"What prize is he talking about, ma'am?" the helmsman asked.

"Nothing you need to worry about. Continue on to the monument." Rivlen gripped her chin and gazed thoughtfully at the dark jungle ahead of them.

Tezi wondered if they would end up fighting far more than druids before the night was over.

Malek walked beside Jadora as their guides led the group from the gate into the core of the log city. Knowing Tonovan was behind him made his shoulder blades itch, especially after Tonovan had not-so-accidentally attacked him during the dragon battle, but Malek wouldn't show it. He merely kept his senses open and alert, both to his own comrades and to the natives and their surroundings.

Admiral Bakir, Prolix, Jak, Shikari, and Zethron rounded out the group. Vinjo had stayed behind with Lieutenant Harintha to repair the damage caused by the dragon battle as well as the handful of bugs that had bored into the hull before Malek had realized the insects were a threat and incinerated them.

One of their guides looked back and spoke to Zethron while nodding at Jak, who was once again receiving preferential treatment because of his association with Shikari—or perhaps the portals. It didn't bother Malek. It was easier to gather information and snoop around when fewer people were observing him.

Not that Malek believed these bird riders were a threat. Other than the skullcaps that everyone they passed wore, there was no hint of magic about them. Nor did there seem to be many magical devices or artifacts in their city. To his surprise, even the thick posts that supported the platform everything was built on appeared to be of mundane construction.

If the crude log dwellings were an example of the engineering expertise of the people, he had to assume the platform had been constructed by someone else. Dragons? Malek would have expected dragons to use magic and maybe even dragon steel, but if the ore that it was made from didn't exist here, that might not have been feasible.

"The theater is that way." Zethron pointed through an open gate in another log wall toward what looked more like an arena than a theater.

The memory of donning that ridiculous costume, having the *kerzor* stuck in his head, and battling in the Vran arena came to Malek's mind. He stifled a scowl and told himself it was unlikely they would walk into a similar scenario on two different worlds.

"They're preparing food for our feast, and while we wait, we are to sit and enjoy ourselves," Zethron said. "They will bring beverages and entertainment."

Not drugged beverages, Malek hoped. He wouldn't let himself drink anything but water from his canteen. Just because these people were simple didn't mean they couldn't be dangerous. Since Malek and his team had met them by coming to their aid and killing a dragon, they *should* feel gratitude, but he wouldn't assume that.

As the group headed into the arena, they passed numerous children playing with balls and sticks. One spotted Shikari and fell down in surprise. The others gaped and pointed, indifferent to Malek and the other members of his team but captivated by a young dragon. The children nudged each other and tried to convince someone to run up and touch Shikari, but none of them proved brave enough, even though Jak's dragon hardly appeared threatening. He was sniffing everything, as if he were a dog, and occasionally nibbling on the corner of a building, merchant stall, or something else that would fit in his maw.

Even the children wore the bronze skullcaps, the material molded to their heads for a precise fit. Not so much as a wisp of hair floated free.

"What do those do?" Malek asked Zethron.

"Last time I was here," Zethron said, "I was told they're a cultural tradition and have some religious significance. I suspect they also have a practical use."

"Such as keeping mages from reading people's thoughts?"

"It's possible. Not everybody enjoys having their mind read." Zethron smiled ruefully.

Malek squinted at him, wondering if there was more to the skullcaps than that. He might not be able to read the minds of the locals, but he *could* surf through Zethron's thoughts. Unfortunately, he didn't find anything enlightening in his head.

"Ask if there's another reason they wear them." Malek couldn't imagine someone worrying about the thoughts of six-year-olds being read. Thus far, his group hadn't even encountered any mages on this world.

Zethron shrugged, trotted to catch up to their guide, and spoke to him.

"Are you worried they're like the *kerzor*?" Jadora asked softly.

"So far, I haven't sensed anyone here with power," Malek said. "Just as I didn't with the Vran citizens who had those discs drilled into their heads."

Zethron returned to Malek's side. "He says they're for protection and that it's mandated by the gods to wear them, except when one is in one's house with the doors closed and the windows shuttered. Even then, it is suggested that one keep his skullcap on. He asked why we are risking traveling without them."

"Protection from what?" Malek asked.

"The wilds. He specifically mentioned insects."

Malek thought of the long proboscises of the giant bugs that had tried to drill into the hull of the ship. Did they also like to drill into human skulls? That would be alarming but easy enough to defend against. At least for someone like him. Maybe people with no access to magic had more trouble with them.

"Can you get some for us?" Jadora asked. "If it's recommended that people travel with them, perhaps we should."

"I will ask, but since they're magical, I believe they're considered valuable here." Zethron bowed and smiled warmly at her.

She lowered her voice. "Will you also ask about plants? You know what I seek."

"Yes, of course."

"Ask also," Malek said, "if they know why the portal would refuse to work for travelers attempting to return home."

Their guide spoke again before Zethron could get to any of that. The man stretched his arm toward a variety of seats lined up along one log wall under an awning that provided shade from the late afternoon sun slanting into the arena. They ranged from cushions on the ground to stools with cushions to an elevated seat with stone steps leading up to it. The plush golden pillow atop it was closer to a mattress with bolsters on three sides than a cushion.

The seating area overlooked a flagstone floor that, fortunately, lacked bloodstains. Whatever entertainment went on here didn't appear to be battles to the death. A number of log apparatuses stored against the far wall suggested something like circus activities might take place here. Cabinets, some with the doors open, held stacks of dozens, if not hundreds, of cushions that could be spread out.

"We're to sit down," Zethron translated. "Since we are honored guests, the chief and his wife will join us, and the entertainment will start soon."

"I'll take the spot that was clearly meant for me." Tonovan stepped past Malek and Jadora and headed for the throne-like seat.

Their guide's eyes widened, and he ran to place himself in front of Tonovan, waving with his arms as he blocked access.

"That might be for Jak," Malek said dryly, though he carefully observed Tonovan with his senses in case he needed to keep the general from lashing out.

"*Jak*?" Tonovan turned an incredulous stare on Jak, who lifted his hands in innocence.

"As someone favored by the portal system," Malek explained, "he's been perceived as a leader by the natives we've encountered thus far."

Jak grimaced, not looking like he wanted the throne or to be perceived as anything at all.

The guide frowned and pointed not at Jak but at Shikari. He bowed to the dragon, trotted up the steps to the throne, and bowed again while extending his arm toward it.

"Is he saying the *flying lizard* gets the special seat?" Tonovan asked.

"Actually, he can't fly yet," Jak said. "I've been trying to teach him, but I'm not sure how long it takes dragons to develop wings large enough for that."

"It makes sense that the people here would hold a dragon, even a young dragon, in high regard," Jadora said. "Many cultures on our world do."

Malek expected Shikari to be puzzled or to ignore the proffer of a seat altogether, but he seemed to understand. He climbed the steps, hopped on the throne, and turned around. He puffed out his chest and roared, such as it was. Thus far, his reedy roars had an unthreatening warble to them.

But the response clearly pleased the guide. He bowed to Shikari several times before directing Jak to the cushion on the stool next to the throne.

"Thanks." Jak perched on it.

Malek started for the stool next to his, but the guide lifted his hands. He touched the two other stools, shook his head, and spoke to Zethron.

"Those are for the chief and his wife," Zethron said. "The rest of us get the cushions on the ground."

"On the *ground*?" Tonovan asked. "Does he know who we are? How *powerful* we are?" He glared at the guide as if he might blast him over the nearest city wall.

"And how many battles we've seen." Bakir flexed his knees as his bushy eyebrows drew into a V. "I don't sit on floors anymore."

Prolix snorted and walked to one of the cushions, though he squatted over it, his hands near the hilts of his weapons, instead of relaxing fully. Malek nodded. He wouldn't expect anything less than alertness from a zidarr.

"You can stand, Admiral." Malek took that option himself, leaning against the log wall behind one of the cushions, until he saw Zethron and Jadora sit on adjoining cushions. An involuntary glower came to him, and he decided to sit on the cushion on her other side. In case they needed to converse about Jitaruvak.

Bakir sighed but ended up taking a cushion. Tonovan glared at Jak and Shikari before going to sit beside Prolix.

As the scents of roasting meat wafted in on a warm breeze, the two blue nakka birds alighted in the middle of the arena, the chief and his wife in their saddles. They slid off, patted their mounts, and spoke commands. The giant birds took off and flew out of sight over the arena wall.

The chief and his wife walked past all of their guests, smiling and offering what sounded like polite greetings. They did glance a little uneasily at everybody's weapons. Could they tell that Malek and the others were mages? He didn't know, but he trusted magic users of some kind existed in this world and that the mundane natives knew not to irk them. He was surprised by their decision to provide inferior seating for them but assumed it was the cultural norm and not a sign of disrespect. Malek would keep the others from, as Tonovan and Bakir were muttering about, *teaching them to respect their superiors.*

The chief sat next to Jak while his wife sat on her husband's other side, leaving Malek next to her and at a lower position. Jadora looked toward him. Afraid he would object to what a mage might consider an indignity?

No, she was eyeing a garland of leaves and flowers on the woman's head.

"When you get a chance," Jadora whispered, leaning close to Malek and resting a hand on his thigh, "will you ask her what she knows of plants such as those we seek?"

"Using my great mastery of the local language?" Malek thought about removing her hand, since Tonovan might report back any familiarity he spotted between them. A part of Malek wondered if Uthari had sent Tonovan along to do exactly that, but he hoped his liege trusted him. He'd reported everything that had happened on their missions to the other worlds, even that he and Jadora had ended up drugged and horny in a cell together. Of course, he had not informed Uthari of the *kerzor* device that she and Jak had brought back, nor had he mentioned Zethron's presence in the mercenary camp. Maybe Uthari *did* have reasons to doubt Malek.

He clenched his jaw at the thought, but he didn't remove Jadora's hand. He liked it there, and he suspected Tonovan would spin tales of Malek and Jadora's closeness, regardless of what he actually witnessed.

He rested his own hand on hers to let her know that he was only teasing her with his sarcasm. And to keep her close.

Jadora glanced down, and surprise flickered in her eyes. Maybe she hadn't been conscious of her own action.

All she said was, "You aren't able to communicate with them telepathically? The way you did with the druids?"

"I tried with the chief earlier, but he didn't respond or indicate that he heard my mental message."

"Because of those skullcaps? How odd. You're still able to

communicate telepathically with people holding dragon-steel weapons, aren't you?"

"Yes."

"I hope Zethron asked the guide to bring us one of the caps. I'd like to examine it."

"You like to examine everything." Malek forced himself to relax enough to smile at her.

"I do. I was disappointed that we were flying *above* everything. Even though the swamp held few plants, there was plenty of life. Vines, insects, animals, birds, and those intriguing giant lily pads floating on the water." Her tone grew wistful as she added, "I could have filled all of my specimen vials."

"*All* of them?"

"Well, I didn't bring that many along."

"Only two or three hundred?"

"A couple dozen," she said.

"So few? I assumed you would stuff in as many as would fit in that backpack." Malek nodded toward the pack he'd made her, still pleased that she took it on all of their missions.

"Even though you magically improved the storage area, which I appreciate, there's not *that* much room after I put in my food, water, first-aid supplies, a change of clothing, and a blanket."

"And your microscope."

"It goes without saying that I would need to bring along my chemistry tools."

"Naturally."

Malek caught Tonovan *and* Zethron looking over at them—and their touching hands. He sighed. Too bad the chief hadn't given them private booths.

Though he wouldn't have minded bantering with Jadora longer, Malek made himself pay attention to the other conversations. The chief was pantomiming to Jak and pointing at Shikari a lot. Malek brushed Jak's mind, trying to tell if he believed the chief was asking where he'd found Shikari—and about those eggs—but for once, Jak was effectively guarding his thoughts.

Malek nodded, more proud than disappointed.

As the sun sank below the horizon, barefoot men and women in topless costumes sashayed into the arena. The chief barely acknowledged them, instead calling for Zethron to come over and translate for him and Jak.

"Now this place is getting interesting," Tonovan drawled, ogling the women.

He and Bakir were the only ones to do so. The rest of the team was watching the exchange between Jak and the chief, with Zethron now kneeling on a flagstone, translating for them. The chief's eyes were intent as he asked questions. As Malek had suspected, they were about Shikari. The chief wanted to know where they'd found the dragon, if Jak had been to *Frost Palrock*, which he gathered was their name for the ice world.

Jak was evasive with his answers, clearly not wanting to tell anyone where those eggs could be found. If the chief had studied that map, and it seemed like he must have since he'd retrieved it personally, he might already know.

Are you doing all right, Jak? Malek asked telepathically during a pause.

Even though the questioning didn't involve magical coercion, Jak appeared uncomfortable. The chief's face had lost all of its earlier affability, and his tone was stern, as if he were interrogating a delinquent child, not a respected member of the party that had battled a dragon on his people's behalf.

Malek was about to tell Zethron to direct the chief's questions to him, but movement at the gate caught his eye. Out on the arena floor, the entertainers had collected musical instruments, arranged themselves in front of the seats, and started performing, but newcomers were now walking in. They were more topless men and women and carried trays of what appeared to be roasted meat on skewers. Some of the pieces were charred black and others completely pink. Malek hoped the raw ones were for Shikari. A creature who noshed on insect carapaces couldn't be that picky about his food.

One of the female servers stopped in front of Tonovan and Bakir and lowered a tray—and her bare bosom. On a mission, Malek squelched any lurid thoughts that popped up and attempted to view such things with detachment, but he *did* notice that the entertainers and the servers were attractive. Judging by Tonovan's leer, he noticed and approved.

Other servers stopped in front of Malek and Jadora, offering them skewers. Malek's stomach rumbled, reminding him that he hadn't eaten since they'd left Torvil, but he wouldn't sample the food here, not when he couldn't read these people's minds. Everything might be drugged—or poisoned.

"Uh." Jak eyed a tray that a voluptuous woman was offering him as a man spread skewers of raw meat in front of Shikari. "Are those insects?"

He pointed at a charred skewer full of lumpy shapes. Malek had assumed they were being offered meat, but as he looked closer at the tray in front of him, he realized the skewers *were* threaded with insect bodies. On some, the antennae and wings were still attached.

"They're a staple in many cultures back home," Jadora said, though her face had grown pale at the offering. "You've had cricket cookies before. Remember the Jaglorush Islands, Jak?"

"Those were made from pulverized crickets bathed in sugar," Jak said. "It's *not* the same."

The chief's wife took a skewer from the tray Jak was being offered, smiled, and used her teeth to pull a charred insect off the end. The smile appeared forced, but that might have been because she was trying to ease tensions between her husband and Jak, not due to any fault in the food. Malek couldn't tell. It annoyed him not to be able to do more than guess at these people's intentions.

Jak grimaced as he watched Jadora take a skewer and bite into something that looked nothing like a cricket. With thoughts of poison and drugs in mind, Malek almost stopped her, but the chief's wife leaned over and took a skewer from their tray. She ate without hesitation, though the smile still appeared forced.

The crunch was audible as Jadora bit down, but she chewed gamely without making a face. Malek took a skewer, but he resolved to wait before eating anything.

A startled gasp came from one of the servers. The perennially horny Tonovan had a hand on her leg and was sliding it up under her skirt.

Stop, Malek told him telepathically as the chief jumped up and spat a string of angry words and chopped at the air.

Tonovan squinted in annoyance at the man, then looked at Malek. "Do you seriously pander to the prudish sensibilities of the sniveling natives when you go to other worlds? These are terrene women, not *mages*. I assumed they were here for us." He smiled—no, *leered* up at the woman, who'd skittered back and was glancing longingly at the gate.

Jadora clenched her skewer, ready to drive it through Tonovan's heart. Or maybe his other eye.

"Don't touch any of them, General," Malek said. Silently, he added, *Let's not piss off the natives. We underestimated the locals on the last world we visited, and I ended up fighting for my life in an arena while mages more powerful than I—and far more powerful than you—watched for entertainment.*

Meanwhile, Zethron had his hands up, trying to placate the chief, though he shot Malek annoyed looks, as if Tonovan's manners were his fault.

Malek gritted his teeth, mostly because Zethron was right. Since Malek was in charge of the group, he had to keep an eye on everyone—*and* where their hands went. It irritated him that he couldn't count on Tonovan to act like a professional instead of a lust-filled baboon who couldn't control his urges.

We have similar powers, Tonovan replied telepathically, lounging back on his hands and ignoring the angry chief. *Don't try to imply otherwise. Also, I highly doubt* I *would have been stupid enough to let a stranger insert a device in my skull that stole my powers.*

Malek froze, furious that Tonovan had learned about that, about his weakness. Had Uthari given him the details? And if so, why? Maybe he'd learned about the *kerzor* from Zethron. It was also possible that Tonovan had pulled the information from Jadora's mind.

Malek forced himself to exhale his irritation. If that was what had happened, he couldn't blame Jadora. It wasn't as if the teachings of *The Mind Way* were *that* effective, especially against someone as strong as a zidarr. Or a pompous general who was almost as powerful as he believed.

Given your utter lack of tact, you would have been killed the first day, Malek replied. *Keep your hands to yourself, or we'll duel back on our ship tonight. Whether you agree to it or not.*

Terrifying. Suck my cock, Malek. While your professor watches. Tonovan looked pointedly at Jadora, though she'd withdrawn her hand and was looking at the chief and a dozen guards that had trooped in, armored men with spears.

Malek could handle any mundane warriors that attempted to hurt the group, but he would prefer to have amiable relations with these people, at least until they got the information they wanted.

Grow up, Tonovan. If you ruin this mission, I'll make sure you don't return with us.

Don't be too sure that you'll *return.*

I have the key, you idiot.

For now. Tonovan smiled.

Malek dropped it, already irritated that Tonovan had goaded

him into squabbling. Yes, they'd done it telepathically, but he had little doubt that everyone in his own group as well as the chief and the warriors knew they'd been arguing.

Two servants brought in wooden boxes and set them on the ground in front of the warriors. When the men opened the lids, a hint of magic seeped out. The warriors dipped their spears into a liquid inside, and when they pulled them out, the tips gleamed with dampness, and some of the magic stuck to them. It was the same faint magic Malek had sensed on the spears that had slipped through the dragon's barrier. It didn't strike him as strong, but *some* property allowed it to pierce magical defenses. Interesting. And another reason not to underestimate these people.

Malek wanted to ask Zethron to question the chief about the liquid, but he still stood with his hands up as he tried to placate the natives. The chief was watching Tonovan with one fist on his hip and one finger held up to the guards. Thinking of calling them to charge in?

The part of Malek that was irritated wouldn't have minded a battle, but he wanted to lash out at Tonovan, not the natives of this world.

"Tell the chief I apologize for my officer's poor behavior," Malek bit out, though it galled him to have to do so. He wished he could trade Tonovan for Rivlen.

Zethron translated. Meanwhile, with nobody paying attention to him, Shikari had eaten all the insects offered to him, left the skewers in tiny pieces littering the steps, and was now gnawing on a tassel on the corner of his cushion.

The chief met Malek's gaze, nodded curtly, and lowered his arms. He also nodded to the warriors who'd rushed in. They bowed toward him, then lined up to either side of the gate.

Tonovan sneered and looked like he was fantasizing about making an example of the warriors, and maybe the chief, by showing them what happened to a person who crossed a powerful mage. Malek would have to spend the rest of the evening keeping an eye on him to make sure he didn't.

"The chief says," Zethron said, "that he will ask if there are men and women who would like to invite your people into their homes tonight."

"Does that mean *have sex with*?" Jak whispered. He sounded more horrified than intrigued, and Malek remembered that his interest in that area was for the blonde mercenary.

"Yes," Zethron said.

"That's not necessary," Malek said.

"I'll accept that offer." Admiral Bakir lifted a finger and smirked as he ogled the nearby women.

Tonovan also smirked.

Malek would have to watch out for those two and the friendship they were developing. He believed he could handle Tonovan in a fight, but if Bakir and his zidarr jumped into it, Malek would be outmatched.

Bongos and flutes started up, the entertainers perhaps trying to smooth over the incident themselves. Several dancers delved into a chest and pulled out jangling anklets and bracelets that they donned. The chief settled down, though he murmured what sounded like disgusted words to his wife. She patted his leg and whispered soothing words back to him.

"Will you switch seats with me?" Jadora asked once the dancing started.

Malek did so, assuming she wanted to ask the chief's wife about the plant, though that left him sitting next to Zethron. The handsome man rubbed Malek the wrong way, mostly because he checked out Jadora's backside when she wasn't looking, but at least he was polite about it. Better than Tonovan.

Malek? Jak whispered uncertainly into his mind as servers came to offer Shikari more food and clean up his mess.

Yes?

I'm not sure how much you heard of our conversation— Jak tilted his head toward the chief, *—but I got the feeling he already knew about the eggs. I guess that's not surprising since he had that map, but I also sense that he's not happy that I found them and have Shikari.*

Did you confirm that Shikari came from that world?

No, but I think he knows.

It's possible these people use the portal and have been to the other worlds.

If they knew about the eggs, and they revere dragons, which they seem to... Jak looked at a woman dabbing bits of insect off Shikari's snout with a towel and giggling as she had to pull it away multiple times to keep him from chewing on it. *Why wouldn't they have retrieved the eggs themselves, brought them back here, and raised the dragons?*

Raising one dragon is flummoxing you. Would a sane human tackle raising a brood?

I'm not flummoxed. Just... challenged. And there are lots of people who'd be willing to be challenged if it meant they could raise—and maybe ultimately control—a dragon.

Malek sighed. *I know. I was teasing you. Maybe it has to do with that parasite.*

Jak's eyebrows rose. *Do you think it's on this world too?*

Your mother collected a sample of dragon blood from that scale. I'm sure she'll set up her traveling laboratory soon and find out. Malek watched as the chief's wife leaned down to look at a drawing in Jadora's hands. The Jitaruvak frond.

The woman tapped her lips thoughtfully and nodded.

It was a small gesture, but hope surged through Malek. If they found the plant here and he could bring it back to Uthari, any earlier questionable choices he'd made ought to be forgotten. Uthari might even forgive him if he returned with the Jitaruvak and *without* Tonovan.

Such scheming was beneath him, but Malek couldn't help but have fond feelings for the notion.

"Zethron," Jadora asked. "Will you see if she knows where our plant is and can provide a map of the area?"

Jak heard the question and brightened. "I would *love* to see a map of the area."

"Because of your interest in plants?" Jadora asked.

"Because of my interest in *maps*. I wonder how advanced their cartographical techniques are here. Or if they've developed *different* techniques than we have. Having access to flying mounts would be tremendously helpful for drawing maps." Jak gazed longingly in the direction the birds had flown off.

"Our family is still quirky," Jadora whispered to Malek.

"Yes." He nodded in agreement but kept himself from admitting that he liked their quirk. Especially *her* quirk.

Servers brought sweet-smelling beverages, which Malek accepted but set behind his cushion without sampling. Jadora did the same. They exchanged sad smiles.

After Zethron relayed Jadora's question, the chief's wife waved over one of the servers. The man hesitated and asked the chief a question. The chief also hesitated.

Because he didn't want to help strangers find and forage on his world?

During his hesitation, a hint of calculation entered the chief's eyes, and he finally nodded and indicated the server could go.

While Malek was debating how to interpret that calculation, Zethron translated something else for the wife.

"She says that maps of the wildland foraging areas are kept somewhere else but that she's having a rider sent to retrieve what you seek. She says it's the least they can do after you helped save their people from the dragon."

"Do you think she's being honest?" Malek asked, sifting through Zethron's thoughts. If he understood their language, he had to be getting more from his exchanges with the natives than Malek was.

"I think so," Zethron said, "but I do sense that they don't know if they can trust you and that they're being polite because their culture and ways demand it, not because they have any love for you."

"Do they trust and love *you*?" Malek said.

"I wouldn't go so far as to say that, but they like that I learned their language when I was here before. I enjoy learning new languages and studying other cultures." Zethron smiled over at Jadora. "I very much look forward to being able to explore the First World. Ideally without being apprehended by angry mages who like to inflict pain on me."

Jadora returned his smile with a sympathetic one, though when she glanced at Malek, it faltered. He hoped she didn't think of *him* as an angry mage who liked to inflict pain on people.

More bare-chested men and women walked in without trays or musical instruments or anything to suggest they were entertainers. They smiled shyly as they approached the group.

The chief cleared his throat, stood, and spoke, finishing by gesturing to his people.

"These are the citizens that are willing to entertain you in their homes tonight," Zethron said.

"Thank him for that," Malek said, "but tell him we decline. We'll stay together and sleep on our ship." He could envision all manner of shenanigans if he let his group split up and get into beds with the natives. A mage was as vulnerable as any other man while he slept, and none of them had brought bodyguards.

"Speak for yourself, you prude." Tonovan surged to his feet and wrapped an arm around one of the young women. "I'm going to sample the local culture."

The woman jumped, startled by his eagerness—and handsiness as he openly groped her—but she glanced at the chief. He hesitated, then nodded. She forced herself to smile and pat Tonovan on the chest as she looked up at him.

Malek opened his mouth to forbid Tonovan to leave—that woman didn't look like a happy volunteer—but he closed it before speaking. What did he care if Tonovan got into trouble? He hadn't even been that useful in the dragon battle. Let the woman stab him in his sleep. Uthari could hardly blame Malek if Tonovan's penis got him killed.

Admiral Bakir also accepted an invitation, and Malek didn't object. Prolix did not, merely lifting his chin and shaking his head. Malek had spoken little with him but approved of a fellow zidarr refusing to put himself into a potentially dangerous situation in exchange for fleeting carnal pleasure.

"Ah, no thanks." Jak lifted his hands and shook his head at a young woman who was trying to entice him away—she appeared more eager than the one who'd walked up to Tonovan. Jak glanced at Jadora, as if she might chastise him and make him do extra chores if he slept with strange women.

But Jadora was looking over at the chief. He knelt facing Shikari, who'd grown bored of sitting on the throne and had clambered off to investigate the arena before returning. Shikari snuffled at something in his hand. Dragon treats? More dead insects?

The chief spoke quietly and urgently to Shikari, as if expecting him to understand.

"Translate," Malek told Zethron.

Zethron hesitated. Malek searched for the translation in his mind.

The chief was asking Shikari if he wanted to leave Jak and stay here while promising that the natives would protect him. Zethron must have thought better of withholding the information, for he accurately shared the chief's words.

Jak's eyebrows flew up in alarm. "What? Shikari can't stay here.

He needs me to protect him from the evil dragons. He needs *all* of us." Jak waved at Malek.

The chief must have sensed that his words were being shared —or maybe heard the alarm in Jak's voice. He looked back at them and smiled and spoke to Zethron.

"He says he's only offering to be polite and because it would be a great boon for his people to provide a home for one of the fabled elder dragons. He's long wished to meet one and is honored by Shikari's presence."

Malek saw in Zethron's mind that he believed the chief thought Jak and the others had kidnapped Shikari—found and stolen his egg without permission from the elder dragons. The chief wanted to rescue him. He hadn't said that, but Zethron must have read between the lines.

"*I'm* honored by his presence too," Jak said. "And I can protect him. With Lord Malek's help."

"He may not realize the mottled dragons want to kill Shikari—or take them into their fold," Jadora said, "and that he would be in danger on a world where they exist."

"These people can't protect him sufficiently," Malek agreed, then pointed toward the gate. "Convince your dragon that we're leaving, Jak. We'll return to the ship and depart as soon as they bring that map."

Could they *trust* whatever map these people gave them? No, they would have to be wary. Malek was still tempted to rip off one of their skullcaps and read the person's mind. Maybe the chief's mind.

But the warriors with their magical barrier-piercing spearheads remained by the gate, and if Malek started an incident, they wouldn't get that map.

Jak waved to Shikari. "We're going back to the ship. Are you coming?"

Malek eyed the young dragon, wondering if he would go with

Jak and give up the treats the chief was trying to seduce him with. Thus far, even though Shikari could be helpful when he wished, he hadn't acted like a faithful hound who would leap to do whatever his master wished.

But after licking the remaining insects out of the chief's palm, Shikari bounded ahead of the group. He paused at the gate to sniff one of the boxes and nibble on the bottom of one of the warriors' spears. The man sprang back, tugging his weapon free, and held it over his head.

Malek prepared to throw a magical attack if the warrior tried to use it on Shikari, but his colleagues laughed, and the man only kept the weapon out of reach. Nobody here appeared inclined to harm a young dragon.

If only they felt the same way about humans. Malek caught a dark glower on the chief's face as he watched their team leave the arena.

12

MILES PASSED AS SORATH WALKED BESIDE GRUNK THROUGH TUNNELS that glowed green, the druid kid never speaking or making any attempt to communicate other than squinting suspiciously at Sorath now and then. Sorath gave him plenty of suspicious squints in return, not pleased that a new and untried person had been foisted on him.

The tunnel ended ahead of them, startling him. A purple crystal glowed from the center of the dirt and rock wall.

Sorath looked at the top and sides of the tunnel, searching for an exit. Kywatha had said this passageway would bring them out near the waterfall. Since she and other druids had sneaked into the camp numerous times, Sorath had assumed they had ways in.

The dirt appeared loose, but not so loose that he could envision digging out of the tunnel easily. But maybe that was how the druids did it, creating the tunnels, then filling them in after they used them so the mages couldn't easily find them.

As Sorath eyed his pickaxe and contemplated a dig, Grunk walked forward and rested a hand on the crystal. He closed his eyes, and long seconds passed. As he communicated with it?

Sorath didn't know if the kid had magic of his own, as not all the people who lived with the druids did, but he must have known how to manipulate their devices. The crystal flashed twice, hummed faintly, and a soft whirring noise filled the air. It tilted upward and magically started clearing away dirt, extending the tunnel they were in.

Grunk crouched, bouncing lightly on the balls of his bare feet, and watched it. He drew one of his many knives. That had to mean they were close. Sorath drew the dragon-steel dagger.

As the crystal extended the tunnel farther, angling it toward the surface, Grunk looked back and held a finger to his lips.

Sorath hadn't intended to shout and let the camp know they were coming, but he nodded.

Above the crystal, a hole formed. Dirt crumbled into the tunnel, followed by several plants and a mossy boulder that rolled down and threatened to smash the kid's bare feet. But Grunk sprang lightly aside before reaching up, tugging more earth away, and slithering out of the tunnel. A distant rumble came to Sorath's ears. It wasn't the crystal this time but the waterfall.

Nerves made his belly shiver with anticipation and concern, but he took a deep breath and climbed out after the kid. He'd accepted this mission, and he was ready for it. The fact that Kywatha had promised she would look after Thorn Company and help them get out of the area—and this miasma of mages—bolstered him.

Damp leaves batted Sorath in the face as he climbed out, tapping the stealth device on his wrist to activate it. Earlier, he'd tested it with Kywatha to make sure the dragon-steel dagger didn't nullify its magic, but for whatever reason, they worked harmoniously together. He'd also seen Tezi ride a skyboard while she carried her axe. Maybe the semi-sentient dragon steel had a way to determine which magic was friendly and which wasn't.

Sorath thought about offering to grip Grunk's shoulder to

make him invisible as well, but the kid had already disappeared. Scouting ahead? Fortunately, it was still dark out. Sorath had lost track of time in the tunnels, but they'd seemed to walk for hours.

He stepped carefully through the foliage, well aware that he would only be undetectable to the eye and mage senses, not keen ears. This close to the camp, there would be numerous patrols.

The noise of the waterfall grew louder, and he realized they'd come out on top of the cliff. That was good. It would give them an opportunity to spy from above and see if they could spot some skyboards. Without them, Sorath didn't know how they would get onto one of the ships. Even *with* a couple, he didn't know how, since he'd always heard it took magic to operate the devices. Earlier, he'd been contemplating finding a weak-willed mage, holding a dagger to his throat, and forcing him to carry him up to Uthari's ship. Now, he wondered if Grunk might be able to operate them.

As Sorath drew closer to the waterfall, the river rushing beside him, a gap in the canopy revealed numerous mageships in the air above the camp. He'd expected them, but seeing the reminder of how many enemies were about made him uneasy.

Uthari's sleek black yacht hovered directly over the portal, as if he was claiming it for himself. Had it been thirty feet lower, Sorath could have run and jumped off the cliff to get onboard, but it was out of reach for mundane legs. Further, several mage soldiers in red uniforms were visible near the railing. Despite the late hour, they were alert, and their deck was well lit. All of the mageships in view had lanterns, the magical lights glowing brighter than flame and illuminating the night for hundreds of yards around the camp.

"You sense that?" a male voice came from ahead, barely audible over the water.

Sorath paused and checked the stealth device again.

"Yes," another man spoke. "There's someone with power out here."

Mages. Sorath wasn't surprised to find them on the cliff. Even before the druid attack, Uthari and the other fleet commanders had added mages to the mercenaries' patrols.

He eased forward with his dagger in hand. If they alerted the camp—and all the mages on those ships—that someone was out here, Sorath wouldn't be able to accomplish his mission tonight.

"*There*," one of them said. "Is that an animal? Or a druid?"

"Blast it either way."

Sorath stepped out from behind a tree as one of two red-uniformed mages launched a lightning bolt at something across the river from him. Grunk? If so, why had he crossed the water?

Sorath almost traded his dagger for his pistol, thinking to shoot the two mages, but a knife flew out of the brush toward them and bounced off an invisible barrier. Of course. They were protected from projectiles. But *not* from dragon steel. Sorath crept forward as they remained focused on Grunk, though he was out of sight in the bushes and hadn't cried out, so Sorath doubted the lightning had struck him.

Thanks to Vinjo's device, Sorath closed to within five feet of the closest mage before the man noticed him. Unfortunately, the device's magic didn't work when the wearer was in close proximity to someone.

Eyes wide with surprise, the mage spun toward him, lightning crackling between his fingers. Sorath sprang, sensing the magical barrier pop like a bubble when he touched it with his dagger.

The man stumbled back, but he loosed his attack before Sorath reached him. Lightning wrapped around Sorath, and he winced in anticipation of pain, but it didn't touch him. The blade protected him from magic, just as he'd believed it would.

Sorath lunged in and drove the dagger into the mage's chest.

The lightning disappeared as Sorath pulled his weapon free, and the man tumbled to the ground.

By then, the other mage had realized Sorath was there and whirled toward him, readying a magical attack. But it never came. Grunk appeared behind the man, springing out of the foliage and onto his back. He wrapped his legs around the man's waist as he slashed his dagger across his victim's throat from behind.

Sorath lowered his blade. The two mages lay dead at their feet, having barely made any noise. But they were close to the edge of the cliff, and he eyed the mageships, worried the fight would have been visible to anyone watching from one of the decks. Fortunately, there was enough foliage to hide them.

A growl sounded. Was that the kid?

Grunk crouched over the fallen men, licked blood off his blade, and eyed Sorath as if he were next. Any rational person who valued his life would have fled.

Sorath kept his dagger in hand, so he could use it if he needed it, but he stepped forward and patted Grunk on the shoulder. He'd worked with unbalanced soldiers before and knew they had a use, as long as one directed them in the right way. Unbalanced druids probably weren't that different.

"Nice knife work, kid," Sorath said quietly.

Grunk tilted his head, puzzlement creasing his forehead, but he recovered and grinned, showing his unnaturally sharp teeth. He licked his blade again before cleaning it on one of the dead men's uniforms.

"In my first unit, we had a man who favored the knives. The captain always said he was either a crazy bastard pretending to be sane, or a sane bastard pretending to be crazy."

That earned him another grin. Grunk sheathed his weapons, then disappeared into the foliage but only for a moment. He returned with a skyboard in his hands and pointed at the black-hulled yacht above the camp. In the shadows, Sorath wouldn't have known the skyboard was nearby. Maybe the kid had sensed it.

Sorath nodded and cleaned his own dagger. "I'm ready."

He'd agreed to kill Uthari, Yidar, and Malek, but Uthari was the only one he knew the likely location of. Uthari was also the only one Sorath loathed and wanted to kill so badly that he would trade his life to accomplish the task.

"Can you make that thing work?" He'd noted that Grunk stuck to his knives in battle instead of using any magic.

The kid hesitated, then nodded firmly. Sorath envisioned them plummeting off the cliff and splatting in front of the portal.

But Grunk set it on the ground, spread his palm over it, and it rose up a few inches. He pointed at it, then pointed at Sorath and back at it.

"Are you staying here?" Sorath whispered, stepping on.

Grunk shook his head but didn't jump on with him. He backed up a few steps and scrutinized Sorath, then he slowly circled around the skyboard while continuing to face him. He stepped in and out again.

"You're trying to see how far the invisibility extends?" Sorath guessed.

The kid nodded and spread his arms, demonstrating a range of about five feet.

"That's what I figured," Sorath said. "Get on if you're coming. I think if I'm touching you, we'll both be invisible."

Grunk pointed at the skyboard and shook his head.

"That's *not* invisible to you?" Sorath guessed.

Grunk nodded.

"So, it'll look like an empty skyboard is flying up there?"

Another nod.

Maybe the stealth device couldn't make magical items invisible. Sorath wondered if the dragon-steel dagger was also visible.

At least with that, he could sheath it, and that ought to hide the magical blade.

My magic is weak, Grunk spoke into his mind for the first time. *But I'll do my best to camouflage it. My best isn't good. We'd better fly in from a direction they're not looking and stay in the shadows as much as possible.*

"Sounds good. You're the teamster in charge." Maybe Sorath should have responded silently. Most of the mages and druids had no trouble reading his thoughts, but would that work while he held a dragon-steel blade? "Can you not speak Dhoran?"

Sorath had assumed the kid had come from the north, but the words he'd spoken telepathically hadn't been Dhoran. As usual with the mental communication, Sorath had gotten the gist anyway, but he didn't know if Grunk would understand him when he spoke aloud.

The kid hesitated. *I understand it. I will not speak it.*

"Why?"

Grunk drew his knife and pointed toward a green-hulled yacht. Vorsha's vessel. He pointed his knife at the side of his head and made a circular gesture with it, then sneered, and pointed at the yacht again.

"Her people did something to you?" Sorath guessed.

Grunk shook his head and pointed emphatically at the yacht again.

"*She* did something to you?" he asked skeptically.

When would Queen Vorsha have come in contact with some druid kid? Granted, with that pale skin, he appeared to be from one of the northern kingdoms—maybe hers—but it wasn't as if druids were invited up to the sky cities of the rulers.

She made me her slave, Grunk spoke telepathically. *Many years. Many battles. Only I survived but not all the way. Not right anymore.* He waved at his head with his knife again.

"Don't worry about it. Fighting makes a lot of people crazy after a while."

The pitying look Grunk gave Sorath suggested he didn't understand. Maybe he didn't.

We kill Uthari tonight, yes?

"That's what your people want me to do, yes."

Grunk nodded. *There.* He pointed at Uthari's yacht. *Then we go there.* He pointed at Vorsha's yacht.

"Uh, she's not on the list Kywatha gave me." Sorath didn't even know if Queen Vorsha was here in person. Someone else might have flown down on her yacht. A favored fleet commander perhaps.

She is on my *list.* The knife turned back toward Grunk. *I never thought she would come here, that I'd be able to kill her and taste her blood on my blade. You will help me. With the knife I took from her when I fled.* This time, there was an evil glint in his eyes when he grinned. Or maybe a maniacal glint.

"Let's take care of one super powerful wizard at a time, eh?"

Grunk climbed onto the skyboard behind Sorath, putting a hand on his shoulder so they could share the effects of the stealth device. The skyboard rose up in the air, hovering in place for several seconds. It wobbled alarmingly, and Sorath crouched low for balance. Why did he have a feeling the kid had never flown one of these before?

Sniffing sounds came from behind him, and Sorath glanced back. Grunk crouched even lower than he and peered between the trees atop the cliff, his nose in the air.

A magical lantern glowed in the distance. A patrol or perhaps the replacements for the guards they'd just killed?

"We need to hurry." Sorath doubted they had much time before the newcomers found the dead men.

He and Grunk would never be able to kill Vorsha. They would be lucky to reach Uthari before an alarm went up.

Grunk nodded, and the skyboard settled in a horizontal position only to lurch as it moved forward.

Sorath shook his head as it flew them over the cliff high above the pool and the camp. What were the odds that they would even make it to Uthari's yacht?

In the middle of the night, Jak woke to a knock at the hatch of the tiny cabin he shared with his mother and Shikari. He peered around blearily in the dark.

Mother had been setting up her laboratory in the ship's kitchen when he'd gone to bed, her microscope going on a counter next to a crate of limes and bananas. At some point during the night, she'd finally come in and gone to sleep and now snoozed on the bottom bunk. Surprisingly, Shikari had climbed in with her and lay sprawled across her legs, his tail hanging over the side.

The young dragon wasn't as cozy as a dog or cat, but he did like to sleep with others. Jak recalled a vision one of the portals had given him of numerous hatchlings sharing a nest on the side of a cliff while their mother brought them giant spiders to eat.

Maybe dragons were meant to be raised in broods and have siblings to play with. It saddened Jak that Shikari wasn't able to have a normal upbringing, and he wondered if he'd made a mistake by not chipping more eggs out of the ice. The portal on the glacier world had seemed to want them *all* saved, but it had emphasized that Shikari was most in danger, since his egg had been hanging halfway out of the ice.

Another soft knock sounded, and Jak slid off the top bunk, careful not to disrupt the occupants on the lower one. He sensed Vinjo in the corridor outside and wondered what the engineer wanted. The memory of his mother handing Vinjo the schematic for the *kerzor* came to mind like a splash of cold water, along with the fear that someone had discovered the paper—or that Vinjo had decided to tell Malek or one of the other mages about it.

Jak sensed Malek in the cabin opposite theirs, in his bunk and possibly sleeping, though with the heightened senses of a zidarr, he might also have been stirred by Vinjo's knock.

When Jak opened the hatch, the yellow light from mage lamps mounted on the walls slashed into the cabin. Vinjo stood in the corridor, wringing his hands.

"I need your help with the engine," Vinjo blurted.

"Uh, all right." Jak didn't know which of the magical contraptions in the rear compartment of the ship *was* the engine, but he didn't want to ask questions when Malek or someone else might overhear. He kept the mental bandana locked around his mind.

After they entered the engine compartment, several glowing devices emanating yellow, blue, and green light, Vinjo closed the hatch and waved Jak to a bench with a storage area underneath.

"I think there might have been damage during that bug attack," Vinjo said. "Can you look at the devices and see if you sense any flaws?"

"I'll try," Jak said, though he assumed this was a cover and that Vinjo wanted to talk about something else.

Vinjo pulled a toolbox over and sat on it facing Jak. *I know you're a new mage and that you're learning from Lord Malek.*

Yes, Jak replied silently. *Though I'm not sure I've officially been elevated from the status of wild one to mage.*

As soon as you're taken on as an apprentice and can perform a few exercises, you're considered a mage.

So, there's no ceremony or celebration? I was hoping for cake.

Vinjo smiled fleetingly, but the worry in his eyes remained. *If you're loyal to Malek, why would you and your mother work against him?* He tapped a pocket. Was the folded schematic inside?

We're not against him, per se, but we're technically Uthari's pris-

oners being held against our wishes. Like you. Jak also smiled, hoping they could have a rapport since they were in similar situations.

Zidarr do not train prisoners to become mages. They rarely train anyone at all except at the behest of their masters.

Uthari was all right with it.

If that's true, they do not consider you prisoners. Especially you. They must expect you to serve them loyally.

I know what they expect. Jak kept his words vague, not daring to trust Vinjo as a confidant, even though he was inclined to like the goofy engineer who made stealth devices and gave them to mercenaries. Logically, Vinjo should hate Uthari and not want to help the king or his zidarr, but the time might come when Vinjo had to choose between saving himself and blurting out information. If it did, he could reveal everything that Jak told him.

Then I ask you again, why plot against them? If they find out, they'll kill you. Vinjo winced. *They'll torture you first for everything you know and* then *kill you.*

Just because my mother and I would like to see some *mages without their power doesn't mean we're plotting against Uthari or Malek.* Jak kept his face a mask and his thoughts under wraps. It wasn't an *untrue* statement, but he would cheerfully jab one of those *kerzor* into Uthari's brain. Malek... was more complicated. Jak couldn't help but think that if the head of the snake were removed, the rest of it would be less inclined to hurt them. Maybe Malek would even work with them if Uthari was no more.

What she wants me to do is very dangerous for me. Vinjo leaned forward on the toolbox, his hands clasped between his knees. *Yes, I have made the clandestineness creepers and other devices to aid terrene humans and help protect them, but that is not the same as plotting to forever rob mages of their power. Not only would Uthari be furious and vengeful if he found out, but every mage in the world would be.*

I know it's a lot to ask, but don't you agree that some *mages deserve to have their venom removed?* Jak let a thought of Tonovan slip out, though he didn't know if the general had tormented Vinjo the way he had so many women.

I agree and have longed to see people like him killed. Trust me. The idea of taking his magic and leaving him alive to endure life as a powerless peon is almost an even better torment to fantasize about. Vinjo gazed wistfully toward his glowing devices.

So, you'd like to see the kerzor *devices exist on our world? And be used as a fair punishment for mages who use their powers for evil? It wouldn't have to be done through sneak attacks. We could devise a system where mages were judged in a court system and only received the* kerzor *if there was a majority vote agreeing that they'd committed crimes and should thus have their power removed.*

Those doing the voting would have to be terrene humans, since mages wouldn't likely vote for such a punishment for other mages. An intense longing filled Jak at the thought of mages being judged by those they'd wronged, those without the power to defend themselves. If that were a possibility, mages would have to be on better behavior.

But how could such a system be enforced? They would need a lot of other mages willing to agree with it and help see it through. It was a daunting prospect. It was almost easier to imagine making enough devices to take the power from *every* mage in the world, including himself. If all that were done, humanity could continue forward with all people being equal, and they could devise a system that didn't enslave anyone. Would that be possible? Or would humans always find a way to divide themselves into groups where some amassed power and used it against those without?

Some of your thoughts are slipping out, Vinjo said. *Be careful.*

Sorry. Jak ratcheted them back down.

As someone who's never been respected, even by his own family, I understand what you want to accomplish and could even root for a reordering of the power structure, one that took the current rulers out of the equation, but I can't be the one to build these devices for you. I might be willing to risk myself—keep in mind that whoever builds them would eventually be discovered and endure the most painful death imaginable —but I have a mother and father and grandparents. I could not put them at risk. And I hope to one day have a wife and children. I'm not ready to die.

I can't blame you for that, Jak said, though he was disappointed. He didn't know anyone else who crafted magical devices, and he couldn't imagine Malek letting him take the portal back to Vran to talk the people there into giving him a few thousand *kerzor*.

I will, however, teach you how to make devices, if you wish it. With practice and the acquisition of foundational knowledge, you might be able to learn how to make these kerzor.

"Oh," Jak whispered aloud, rocking back on the bench. He hadn't considered that such might be a possibility.

But *was* it? If Malek found out, it would not only be the end of their mentor-mentee relationship; it could mean Jak's death. Malek would tell Uthari, who might kill Jak for such presumptuousness. Or he would order another mage to do it. Tonovan would gladly break Jak's neck. What if Tonovan were the one who walked in and discovered Jak making the devices? He might murder Jak on the spot, knowing that his ruler wouldn't object, not when he found out what Jak had been up to.

"Ugh." He bent forward and gripped the back of his head with both hands.

He'd been asking Vinjo to take the very risks he was now thinking about, so it would be hypocritical if he weren't willing to do this himself, but for him, it seemed like it would be such a betrayal. Oh, he didn't care about betraying Uthari, but Malek? Malek, who'd endured the *kerzor* firsthand and considered it torture and cruelty to have his power removed.

Jak didn't want to betray Malek. He wanted Malek to continue to teach him, to mentor him, to respect him, to be... a friend. The idea of losing all that nauseated him.

Still, would he be able to live with himself as he continued forward, learning from Malek so that he could loyally serve Uthari, all the while knowing that he'd missed the chance to potentially change the world and help the millions of terrene humans who endured meager existences under their mage rulers?

Jak swallowed and looked up. "I think… I've decided that engines are fascinating, and I'd like to learn from you."

"They are indeed." Silently, Vinjo added, *All I ask is that you promise not to implicate me when you are inevitably caught. I'm just the innocent mage engineer whom you begged to teach you.*

I'll do my best not to implicate you.

Very well then. Vinjo stood up and opened the toolbox. *Let's get started.*

Jak sat attentively and tried not to let the words *when you are inevitably caught* ring in his mind.

13

Even with the stealth device activated and demonstrably working, Sorath felt intensely vulnerable as he and Grunk crouched on the open deck of the *Serene Waters*. Eight mages in red uniforms stood guard around the ship, including two stationed to either side of the closed double doors leading to Uthari's suite.

One of the mages at the railing had squinted in their direction as they'd neared, so Sorath and Grunk had flown under the ship, using its mass to hide their approach. In case the skyboard was visible, they'd gotten off it early and climbed up the side of the hull. Grunk had been able to float the skyboard back down to the jungle, perching it in the branches of a tree, where it waited for them to complete their mission.

Climbing wasn't easy when one had a pickaxe for a hand and also when one had to remain in contact with another person, but they'd managed to pull themselves up and over the railing without drawing attention. The mage who'd squinted at them was still peering in the same direction. As long as he didn't start roaming the deck, looking for intruders, that was fine.

More problematic were the guards at the doors. They stood seven or eight feet apart from each other, and Sorath debated how he could slip past them without being seen. Given that the camouflage effect of Vinjo's device only worked at a range greater than five feet, there was no way to make the math work. Besides, the guards would notice the doors opening by themselves even if they didn't see Sorath and Grunk.

We're going to need a distraction, Sorath thought, not daring to speak out loud with guards so close.

Already, they'd had to move carefully on the deck, hurrying out of the way whenever the guards rotated their positions or a crew member walked past.

Grunk didn't answer. He was glaring over the railing toward Vorsha's yacht, his jaw clenched and hatred burning in his eyes.

Sorath nudged him. *Uthari first, remember?*

Uthari *only,* if Sorath had his way. As useful as it might be to deprive the world of as many overpowered wizard rulers as they could, the lantern bobbing in the undergrowth atop the cliff promised someone was looking for the missing mages. Sorath and Grunk had a very small window of time before an alert went up.

We need a distraction, Sorath repeated mentally, hoping the kid was listening. *Something that will get those guards to step away from the doors without making them believe there are intruders.*

His hand strayed toward the pocket that held his pop-bangs, but setting off explosives would alert *everyone*. And even with the dragon-steel dagger protecting him from magical attacks, Sorath had no delusions about defeating Uthari unless he caught the old wizard in bed sleeping.

Before Grunk responded, the ship started moving. Sorath tensed.

It had been hovering in one position over the portal, but now it rose upward. His first thought was that the portal had activated and some foe was coming through, but one of the mages on the cliff stood at the edge, signaling to the yacht with the magical lantern.

Uh oh. From his position, Sorath was almost positive the mage had found the dead bodies. He and Grunk should have chucked those in the river. Never mind that they would have tumbled over the waterfall, landed with splashes, and floated in the pool. The mercenaries on the night shift would not have failed to notice that.

Several of the guards walked toward the railing and peered curiously at the mage on the cliff. The door guards, too damn steadfast at doing their duty, didn't leave their posts.

Sorath would have to find another way in. There weren't any portholes in the yacht's hull, but some of the cabins above deck level had windows. He'd been aboard enough times to know where Uthari's suite was and figure out which ones matched up with it. There was little doubt that magic secured all windows and portholes, but his borrowed blade ought to let him get through.

I'll distract them. Grunk pulled out two of his knives. *You make the kill.*

Wait. Sorath gripped his arm before Grunk could pull away. *They'll wake Uthari as soon as an intruder is discovered.*

Grunk's head tilted in puzzlement again. He looked like a dog when he did that. Or maybe a wolf. Some creature of the wild.

Sorath didn't want to explain that his plan was to kill Uthari in his sleep—even if it was logical and the only thing that would likely work, it sounded cowardly, and he hated to admit it. *You hide and let me sneak in to get him. If this all blows up like a grenade... then I'd appreciate a distraction, something to draw the guards out here.*

Grunk hesitated, scrutinizing him and staring for several long seconds at the dragon-steel dagger. Maybe he feared Sorath would fail and lose it forever. It was a possibility.

Sorath almost told him to come along, but climbing while trying to touch another climber to keep him camouflaged had been difficult. They'd lost contact several times, and it had only been luck that nobody had peered over the railing, spotted them, and raised an alarm. It was possible someone on Vorsha's nearby yacht or one of the other ships had seen them but hadn't cared. None of the other fleets were that interested in helping Uthari.

Hide, Sorath urged again, giving the kid his commander's firm nod.

Though reluctant, Grunk nodded back. He looked around for a moment before pointing to the rooftop above the doors. That might be the only spot where he could lie flat and not be seen.

Sorath imagined Grunk trying to drop down behind the two guards and slit their throats. So long as Sorath got to Uthari first.

They navigated across the deck as the yacht continued to rise and floated toward the cliff. If the mages aboard and the mage in the trees were communicating with each other, they did it telepathically. All Sorath could hear was the roar of the waterfall, its fine mist wafting up and dampening the deck.

When they reached the wall, the door guards scant yards away, Sorath gave Grunk a boost up, careful not to break contact. Once on the roof, Grunk pulled *him* up. He was surprisingly strong for his size, and with his help, Sorath managed to clamber up without clunking his pickaxe against anything.

Nobody else was on the roof, nor did this ship have a crow's nest. Once they flattened themselves on their bellies, they were out of sight, at least from the mages on deck. Fortunately, since the yacht had risen up, it was now flying above most of the other mageships in the area, so their crews might not see them either.

Grunk pulled his knives and indicated that he would wait, though he kept sending those glares toward Vorsha's yacht. It was fifty or sixty feet away, so he wouldn't be able to do anything rash, not unless he called that skyboard back up.

Sorath dug into a pocket and pulled out two pop-bangs. He didn't have an unlimited supply and didn't want to waste them, but the kid might need them. He tapped Grunk's shoulder and handed them to him.

They make small explosions, Sorath thought and envisioned a time when he'd thrown one at a mage, startling the man into dropping his barrier.

His ally accepted them, though he seemed surprised by the offering. Grunk raised a finger, then delved into one of his own pockets and pulled out a few inches of green rope. Or maybe it was a vine. A *sticky* vine. Bits of fiber, dirt, and crumbs clung to it. Sorath raised his eyebrows as Grunk held it toward him.

Take it. Grunk shared a vision of it sticking to someone's face and expanding to cover their eyes.

Some magical trinket? Sorath took it gingerly. It was as sticky as it looked, and he imagined it sealing his pocket closed instead of having any value in battle, but he dropped it in and nodded at the kid anyway. One had to keep one's unbalanced troops content, lest they explode unexpectedly.

Grunk smiled at him, flashing his sharpened teeth, and pointed across the roof.

Sorath hesitated, memories of the vision the dagger had given him coming to mind, of having Uthari above him, about to kill him as Sorath writhed helplessly on the rug. Was that about to come true? Or was there something he could do to change that fate? Would the fact that he'd brought Grunk with him make a difference? Or had the future he'd seen only happened *because* he'd brought Grunk with him? And the dagger had known he would?

Sorath frowned, the speculations making his head hurt. He couldn't skulk there and dwell upon it. Whatever was to happen would happen.

As he belly-crawled toward the side of the yacht, the first words floated to his ears. The mage on the cliff was speaking to someone at the railing. He'd found the bodies and wanted the crew to send a team down. He wasn't sure if it had been druids or soldiers from one of the other fleets and didn't want to raise a camp-wide alarm.

Thank Thanok for that, though Sorath feared they would soon wake Uthari. He crawled faster until he knelt at the edge of the roof above one of the king's windows, the one he believed led to the bedchamber. That was admittedly a guess. Sorath had been in Uthari's foyer and office before, but the doors to the other rooms in the suite had been closed at the time. He did remember that there had been only one other set of double doors, located straight across the foyer from the entrance, and guessed it led to the bedchamber.

Sorath hooked his pickaxe over the edge and tried not to look down as he swung off the roof. The waterfall roared as it crashed into the pool below. *Far* below.

While hanging from his pickaxe and being careful not to let his legs dangle in front of the window, Sorath considered the other windows and scowled. One had been out of view, hidden by the curve of the hull, and he'd miscounted. He hung outside of the office. Uthari's bedchamber window was the next one over.

He almost started to navigate toward it while hanging from the roof but realized this could be better. If he made noise outside of the office, Uthari would be less likely to hear it, and the office led to the foyer which should lead to the bedchamber. As long as Uthari didn't have guards inside his suite, this could work.

Sorath drew his dagger and reached for the glass. The tip barely brushed it, but a buzz of energy ran through him before fading. Whatever magic protected the window from intruders, he believed he'd snuffed it. But there wasn't a latch or anything to use to open the window.

Awkwardly, he pressed the tip of the dagger to the glass, hoping it could cut a hole. And would he fit through that hole? He wasn't sure. It was a large window, but he was a big man.

The yacht halted movement, and his pickaxe slipped, a faint clunk sounding as he hurried to readjust himself before he fell. His chest thumped softly against the wall, but he managed to regain his grip. With his rapid heartbeats echoing against his eardrums, Sorath paused and listened, trying to tell if anyone inside had heard him.

But the roar of the waterfall made it impossible to tell. Not willing to turn back, he again pressed the dagger to the glass. Thanks to the magic and sharpness of the weapon, it didn't take much effort to break the surface. He cut a large circular opening and was debating how to push it inward or pull it out without making noise when several mages on skyboards leaped over the railing and headed toward the trees atop the cliff.

One glanced in Sorath's direction, and he held his breath, almost forgetting that he was camouflaged. Or *should* be camouflaged.

One squinted toward him. Was the knife visible? The cut in the glass?

Someone called to the mage and pointed at a gray-hulled ship lazily floating closer. That distracted the men. Sorath finished the cut, wiggling the blade and managing to tip the glass outward. He was tempted to toss it toward the pool, but there were too many men out who might see it. He shifted and managed to slide it onto the roof.

Unfortunately, he couldn't see through the window from his position, not as long as he held the edge of the roof with his pickaxe. Uthari or a pack of guards might be waiting inside with magelock pistols pointing at the window. If they were, they were hopefully more than five feet away and would be puzzled when Sorath landed and they couldn't see him.

He shifted to get his feet lined up with the hole he'd cut, then swung himself in. As he'd feared, he was too large to slip right through without trouble. His pick *and* his elbow clunked against the glass. He managed to land in a crouch with the dagger in hand, facing the desk and the door.

Knowing he'd made noise, he held his breath. The office was dark, no hint of movement in any of the shadows. The door to the foyer was closed. A few distant shouts came from the clifftop, but inside, it remained silent.

It seemed impossible that someone wouldn't have rushed in to wake up Uthari, or that he wouldn't have heard Sorath clambering around on his roof and woken on his own. Still, Sorath had little choice but to keep going. This was very likely the only chance he would get to kill the old wizard.

He crept to the door and pulled on the knob, but it didn't move. He didn't know if it was a magical lock or a regular one, but he applied the dagger once more, sliding the tip through the gap in the doors. It was slender enough to reach the bolt. He shifted the blade up and down, trying to saw through the obstacle. The magical blade cut through it easily but not soundlessly.

Sorath hefted his pickaxe as he pulled the door open, still anticipating enemies. The foyer was as dark and empty as the office had been, but a hint of light came from the gap under a door opposite the office. A single door. Sorath didn't think that was the bedchamber, but he crept across the rug to check it out.

The murmurs of two men's voices came from inside. Neither sounded like Uthari. Guards? If so, they would charge out at the first hint of trouble.

Sorath looked around for furniture that he could slide in front of the door. Even if mages had the power to hurl obstacles aside with ease, they might hesitate to knock their ruler's favorite armoire across the foyer. Unfortunately, Sorath didn't see anything that large and heavy.

Remembering Grunk's gift, he unstuck the strange vine from the inside of his pocket and pressed it to the gap between the door and the frame. That wasn't the usage that Grunk had shared with him, but maybe it could stick to wood as easily as skin.

As if it knew what he wanted, the vine not only affixed itself, but it flattened as it stretched outward and upward, covering a foot of the gap between door and frame.

Sorath had no idea if it would stop the guards for more than a second, but he felt the press of time and had to move on. He crept toward the double doors in the back.

His foot came down on something hidden under the rug, and a faint click sounded. A breeze whispered upward, stirring his hair, but nothing hurt him, struck him, or grabbed him.

A few steps farther on, he triggered another booby trap. This one flashed white, driving all the shadows from the foyer for a heartbeat, but once again, nothing painful assaulted Sorath. At least nothing that got through. The white light faded.

He was starting to think about kissing the dragon-steel blade, but then he would be almost as crazy as Grunk. Besides, he might still have trouble. What if that light had seeped under the doors and alerted the guards? Or woken Uthari?

A few seconds passed, and he didn't hear anything. Sorath gripped one of the door handles, and another little breeze whispered past him, but beyond that, it wasn't locked. He eased the door open and peered into the dark bedchamber.

It was quiet inside, the waterfall muffled by the walls, and Sorath heard the steady breathing of someone sleeping. Curtains covered the lone window, and little light filtered inside, but he could make out a lump under the silk sheets in the four-poster bed.

Sorath passed an open bathroom door and glanced in but didn't see anyone. With the dagger in hand, he advanced toward the bed.

His heartbeat was echoing against his eardrums again, rapid from his fear and exhilaration. In his life, Sorath had killed many men and more than a few mages, but it had always been on the battlefield, not skulking in the night as an assassin. He hated this, but he would put honor aside to end a deadly enemy's life and to protect Thorn Company, to make sure this bastard didn't torture Ferroki or any of the others the way he had Sorath.

As he eased closer to the pillow, prepared to slit Uthari's throat, he realized something startling. There was far too much hair strewn across the pillow for this to be Uthari.

Idiot. The vision had warned him someone else might be in the bed.

Sorath froze with indecision. Was this a simple servant woman who'd been beckoned to entertain Uthari for the night? If so, where in the jungle was *he*?

A shadow at the corner of Sorath's eye was his only warning. Something flew across the room toward him.

As he turned, lifting an arm to protect his face, a box—no, that was a *drawer*—slammed into him. It hit with such force that pain blasted his arm and shoulder as the blow knocked him into the bedside table and against the wall. The table tilted sideways, and he almost lost his footing, but he recovered and sprang in what he hoped was the direction of his attacker.

Yes, there was Uthari. Standing naked in the doorway to the bathroom. Naked but not defenseless.

Another drawer flew out of a dresser toward Sorath. He ducked it, and it slammed into the wall.

"What's going on?" a woman blurted from the bed.

She sounded older, not the nubile young servant that Sorath had imagined. He was too busy trying to get to Uthari to contemplate that further.

As more furniture flew at him, he struggled to advance. The temptation to throw the blade at that naked chest came over him, but then he would be at the mercy of the powerful wizard's magic, a force far worse than dresser drawers.

The rug was yanked out from under Sorath. He lost his footing and almost landed on his back on the floor. He managed to twist in the air, instead landing in a crouch, though his pickaxe clunked down hard.

"Assassin," Uthari said with irritating calm as he used his magic to blow the rug toward Sorath. "With a dragon-steel weapon."

Sorath was aware of the woman kneeling up in bed behind him, but he couldn't do anything. The rug swept toward him, an assailant in its own right. He dropped to his belly, trying to avoid being wrapped up in it, but Uthari manipulated it on top of him.

Snarling, Sorath sliced the rug with the blade, cutting a large gap. But Uthari, who might not have known exactly where he was before, knew now and leaped atop him. He'd found a blade of his own, a lesser-dragon-steel dagger, and he raised it to plunge at Sorath. At this close range, Uthari had no trouble seeing through the magic of Vinjo's device.

Sorath thrust upward with all of his strength, but being under the rug hampered him. The wizard's blade drove through it and into Sorath's side. Pain lanced through him, but he managed to bite down and not let out a gasp of pain. He heaved and cast Uthari aside before he could strike again.

Sorath cut his way free of the rug and jumped to his feet, but more furniture slammed into him. The entire dresser this time.

As large as Sorath was, it shouldn't have toppled him, but Uthari's magic turned it into a mountain instead of a piece of furniture. Before Sorath could scramble away, it bore him back to the floor. His hand smacked down, and he barely kept from releasing the dagger. That blade was his only hope of surviving this.

But how? Hundreds if not thousands of pounds ground into his back with bone-crushing force. Sorath heaved, using every muscle to push upward, but he wasn't strong enough to thwart the power of magic. Using the furniture to attack him worked where pure magical attacks had failed. As Uthari strolled closer, Sorath realized that he, a man who'd survived hundreds of battles in his life, might die crushed to death under bedroom furniture.

"I do believe that's Colonel Sorath," Uthari drawled in an amused tone. "I've been looking for you, Colonel."

Sorath's ribs creaked under the crushing force, but he managed to stick his dagger between his teeth and thrust a hand in his pocket. A thump came from the foyer—the guards trying to get out of that room? Sorath grabbed two of his pop-bangs and flicked his wrist.

They flew out, skidding across the floor to land at Uthari's feet. They blew, booming in Sorath's ears, and all hope that he would get out of this without alerting the entire crew to his presence vanished. All he could hope now was to distract the old wizard and escape.

But a barrier protected Uthari from the explosions even as they ripped blankets off the bed and blew wood floorboards to pieces. The weight smashing Sorath didn't falter. Damn it, how could the old man defend and attack at once? While explosions blew up at his feet?

As Sorath racked through his mind for another option, an invisible hand squeezed around his throat, cutting off his air. How was Uthari doing that? The dagger was supposed to protect Sorath. Maybe he'd turned the air itself into a weapon that could slip past the dragon steel's protection.

"Have you by chance learned where the entrances are to the druid tunnels since the last time I questioned you?" Uthari asked, impossibly calm as shards of wood rained down around him.

Though Sorath knew the vision had been correct and his death was at hand, he tried to avoid thinking about the tunnel and also Grunk. The last thing he wanted was to lead the mages to the druids.

"I admit I'm having trouble reading your mind right now," Uthari said. "Why don't you drop that dagger before you run out of air? It's tediously difficult to try to read the thoughts of an unconscious man." His voice lowered and turned grim with promise. "Or a *dead* man."

"Do you need help with that?" the woman in bed asked, as calm and unconcerned as Uthari. Whoever she was, she wasn't a servant.

Loathing for them, for *all* mages, flowed into Sorath's muscles, and he almost managed to shift the dresser aside. But Uthari only used his magic to press it down with greater force, smashing him like an ant under someone's boot.

"Not at all," Uthari said, the grip tightening around Sorath's throat.

He couldn't breathe, and crushing pain tore at his windpipe. He managed to shift his arm up to grab the dagger from his mouth. Throwing it might be the last thing he ever did, but he was about to die anyway.

Once more, he flicked his wrist. The dagger sailed point-first toward Uthari, slicing through his protective barrier.

He sprang aside with more alacrity than an old man should have had, but the blade grazed his naked calf. Uthari roared in pain and fury, completely losing his calm.

Sorath bunched his muscles and shoved upward, certain that would have broken Uthari's concentration and that he could escape, but impossibly, his magic remained in place. The weight of the world smashed downward as the hand around his throat tightened, his windpipe creaking along with his ribs, a heartbeat away from being irrevocably crushed.

Another thump came from the foyer.

A shadow whispered past to the side. Magic? A person? A pained shriek came from the bed, and something finally distracted

Uthari. The grip around Sorath's throat disappeared, and the weight on his back lessened.

Sorath heaved the dresser aside and lunged to his feet as Uthari whirled and turned his attention elsewhere. Someone had leaped into bed with the woman. Grunk?

He punched downward—no, *stabbed* downward with a knife.

Another pained shriek came from the woman. Uthari splayed his fingers to cast a spell at Grunk's back. Sorath sprang, intending to knock Uthari off his feet, but he'd already gotten his barrier back up. Sorath bounced off.

Swearing, he scrambled around Uthari and grabbed the dagger. He whirled and slashed it at the barrier. It popped, but Uthari was on the move, jumping onto the bed. Fire roared toward Grunk's back.

Sorath lunged after Uthari, slashing with the dagger. He nicked the wizard in the back of the thigh as flames engulfed Grunk, a scream ripping from the kid's throat. Uthari tore the druid off the woman and spun him toward Sorath, using him as a shield.

Sorath had been about to drive the dagger into Uthari's back, but he halted before striking Grunk. The kid was already scorched, his skin charred by flames.

The doors burst inward, and mage soldiers ran into the room.

"It's about time," Uthari barked. "Get him!"

Sorath threw a pop-bang at their feet, the explosion making them pause for a second, but more men thundered into the foyer behind them. Sorath couldn't face so many.

He hated to leave Grunk, but he sprinted to the window beyond the bed and flung it open. Magical attacks whispered toward him, knocking furniture to the floor, but with the dragon-steel blade in hand once more, they didn't strike him.

Before climbing out, Sorath turned back, hoping he could somehow grab Grunk and get away with him.

The kid met his eyes briefly, then snarled and twisted out of Uthari's grip. He jumped toward the mages flooding into the bedroom. Though horribly injured, he slashed wildly with his two knives, trying to get at them. No, trying to buy time for Sorath to escape.

Uthari hurled more furniture at Sorath. Sorath turned his shoulder as a chest smashed into it. Uthari leaped off the bed toward him, fury blazing in his eyes. The woman he'd been with lay dead, her throat cut.

Sorath pulled himself out the window as more furnishings tumbled toward him. He thought to climb upward so that he could reach the roof and jump in a direction where he might survive the fall—such as the pool—but something heavy slammed into him, knocking him away from the ship.

The pool was too far away. He wouldn't land in it. He shouted in frustration as he fell, certain he would tumble hundreds of feet and die when he hit the ground.

But tree branches battered at him as the waterfall roared nearby. He swung outward with his pickaxe, hoping to hook it on something solid.

Wood snapped as he crashed through leaves and branches, breaking them with his weight. Finally, he reached lower and sturdier branches. His pickaxe caught, and he jerked to a stop, wrenching his shoulder.

He was stuck in the trees on the cliff above the pool, high enough up that he might yet fall to his death if he let go or tried to jump. All he could hope was that Vinjo's device was still working and the mages would struggle to see him.

"He's in the trees," someone yelled from the deck of the yacht fifty feet above. "Get him!"

Cursing, Sorath stuck the dagger between his teeth again and climbed toward the trunk of the tree. So much for the mages struggling to see him. Maybe in the battle, the device had been turned off—or broken.

Orange light burned away the darkness of the night, and a fireball slammed into his tree.

Branches and leaves burst into flame all around him. At first, the magic of the attack left him unscathed, and he kept maneuvering toward the trunk, but more fireballs followed the first. What started as a magical fire turned into a genuine one as more branches burst into flames. All around him, trees caught fire, and heat scorched his face.

Sorath would have to jump and hope for the best. As he peered downward, hoping to find a pile of leaves to land on, more yells came from above. They also came from other ships in the area.

"The portal is activating!" came a clear call.

The fireballs stopped assailing Sorath's tree as the mages shifted their focus. Though images of that deadly flying worm came to mind, and Sorath doubted he was safe, he'd been given a reprieve. Half climbing, and half falling, he reached the solid comfort of the ground and leaped away from the burning trees.

He paused to glance upward, hoping vainly to see Grunk escaping the odds and jumping from Uthari's yacht, but only his screams of agony came from above.

"It's a dragon!" someone on a nearby ship yelled.

Though Sorath knew he should sprint to the druid tunnel and escape before Uthari ordered men after him, he had to see what threat was coming through the portal. Was it truly a dragon this time? And if so, was there any chance it would find and eat Uthari and accomplish what Sorath had failed to do?

He ran to the edge of the cliff in time to see a gray-and-brown dragon fly out of the portal, its great wings flapping so hard that they stirred even distant leaves.

Mages on numerous ships shouted and launched attacks.

Sorath shook his head, knowing this was his chance to escape. The mages could likely deal with a dragon, but they would be busy until they finished.

He ran through the brush toward the tunnel he'd abandoned, almost forgetting about the search party down on the cliff. Voices up ahead made him pause. He turned the stealth device off and on again, hoping it still worked.

But the mages were running to help with the dragon, and he was able to slip by without notice. As he headed for the druid tunnel, Sorath couldn't help but glance back, lamenting that he'd not only failed his mission but he'd lost Grunk. The druids might kill Sorath themselves.

14

THE BLOOD SAMPLE FROM THE DRAGON MALEK HAD KILLED contained the same unicellular flagellate eukaryotes as the sample from the mottled dragon on Vran. Since Jadora had taken the first sample from saliva, she hadn't been certain she would find evidence of it in blood, even in an infested dragon, but it was there.

She leaned back from the microscope and mulled over the ramifications. Since she'd witnessed dragons using the portals, it wasn't that surprising that they might have spread the infestation across all the worlds they visited. It was still possible that the presence of the eukaryotes didn't mean anything significant. Humans had all kinds of bacteria within their bodies, some even symbiotic in nature. Maybe this was simply something that dragons lived with and that didn't affect them much or at all.

But Shikari hadn't had any evidence of it in his saliva. And Jadora shivered to remember the way those magical motes had tried to carry the bacteria from the dead dragon's body to his. Though it wasn't scientific, she couldn't help but feel that this infestation wasn't symbiotic, that it was as she'd believed from the beginning: parasitic. Something they didn't want to let Shikari get.

She eyed the dragon scale leaning against the wall by the hatch. She wanted to examine it too, but getting it under her microscope would be a challenge, and she doubted a perusal with a magnifying glass would be as enlightening.

She removed a scalpel from her tool kit and tried to scrape off a sliver of the scale. But she might as well have been trying to carve a diamond. She wasn't able to get anything but some of the dried skin and blood from where it had been attached to the dragon.

"I would love to see a cross-section of the thing," she murmured. "As well as examine its cells."

Too bad they didn't have anyone with a dragon-steel weapon along on the mission. Tezi's axe would have hacked the scale to pieces without a problem. Maybe, as Jak had suggested, Malek's lesser-dragon-steel weapons could do the job.

Jadora padded warily into the corridor, wanting to check a porthole to see if it was light out yet and she could justify waking Malek, but not wanting to run into anyone unsavory. She had no idea if Tonovan had returned from his night's adventures. She'd lost track of the hour, knowing only that she'd woken early, her legs numb because a dragon had slept on them, and decided to use the quiet time while others slept to do research.

The large porthole in the navigation cabin showed the side of the city's platform. They'd docked facing it, and it wasn't the most inspiring view, but it did seem to be getting light out. She stopped in front of Malek's cabin and lifted a fist, but she hesitated. What would he think about her coming to his cabin in the dark of night? That she wanted to… initiate something?

Jadora snorted and rolled her eyes. He could read her thoughts. He would *know* what she wanted.

Come in, Malek spoke softly into her mind before she knocked.

Apparently, he also knew when people were standing outside of his cabin, torn by indecision.

She eased open the hatch. Though most people had to share cabins in the compact ship, he had the space to himself. Maybe nobody wanted to bunk with the fearsome Malek.

I would chuckle at that idea and say it's only because I'm leading the mission, but Vinjo hyperventilated when I suggested he share the cabin with me. He's been sleeping on the deck, cuddled up to his engine. Malek pushed back his blanket and slung his legs over the side of his bunk.

He wore his trousers but not a shirt or socks, and enough light seeped in from the corridor to highlight his muscular chest and mussed hair. Jadora's mind took her back to the cell under the arena on Vran. Malek in his gladiator loincloth, her naked with only a blanket, and them giving in to their desires to kiss and grope and groan with passion while aching for more…

Jadora swallowed and made herself look at the bland and undecorated wall. "Sorry to disturb you, but I was wondering if I could borrow your dagger."

You want to cut Tonovan's throat?

"No. But is that an option?"

A tempting one. Malek drew his main-gauche and offered it to her hilt-first. *You're going to cut up that scale?*

Since he was reading her thoughts, he'd probably caught her remembering their kisses. Her cheeks warmed, and she muttered a quick *thank you* as she accepted the blade, then hurried back to her ersatz lab in the kitchen.

Do you want help cutting it?

I think I can figure it out. Thanks.

Ah. You're welcome. Did he sound disappointed? Maybe he was curious about what she was doing and wanted to help.

Jadora almost invited him to join her, but the idea of standing close to him in a private and confining space while he was barefoot with his shirt off seemed dangerous. Speaking of scientific things was far safer.

You might be curious, she told him, *to learn that the samples I took from the dragon show that same parasite as the other one had.*

Interesting. What do you hope to find in the scale? Malek appeared in the corridor. He'd donned boots and had his long sword in hand.

I'm not sure yet. I've never examined a dragon scale. As far as I know, few of the records about their kind on our world involve accountings of humans dissecting them.

Dissecting dragons sounds like a dangerous hobby.

I suppose so. She eyed his sword. *Is there trouble?*

Jadora wouldn't be surprised if Tonovan had managed to irk the woman he'd been with, the chief, and the entire city.

Not that I know of—at least not yet. I figured as long as I'm awake, I might as well do some exercises. There's little room on this long, narrow ship, but I might be able to manage a semblance of my blade forms on the deck. Malek nodded toward the ladder leading up to it. *Let me know if you need anything or discover something else of interest.*

I will. Jadora peeked out as he headed toward the ladder, and got a glimpse of his butt as he climbed up.

She rolled her eyes and returned to the scale, telling herself that mature professors in their forties did *not* ogle men's butts. No matter how firm and appealing they were.

"He's a powerful zidarr who works for the king you hate," she reminded herself as she sliced into the scale. "A king who'll cheerfully kill you if you outlive your usefulness."

Malek's main-gauche was far more effective than a scalpel. She cut a chunk off the tip of the scale and also scraped a thin layer from the back and front of it. After making slides, she examined them under the microscope and was disappointed at how unremarkable they were. They were similar to snake scales she'd examined long ago in her biology classes, just much larger. If they oozed magic, she couldn't tell. Maybe she should have asked Malek.

The piece she'd cut off was too large for her microscope, but she examined it all over with a magnifying glass, considering the gray and brown mottling. Both drab colors existed on the scale. She assumed it was a natural camouflage to allow the dragons to blend into their native environment, one of rocks and dirt in a dry climate. There wasn't any green. There was a hint of blue that she hadn't noticed before. Huh.

Her breath caught. That was in the spot that she'd scraped off for her slide. The blue was *under* the brown and gray.

It didn't necessarily mean anything significant, but her fingers shook as she applied the main-gauche again. She scraped away more of the top layer of the scale, hardly caring about the mess she was making, the flakes that dropped to the deck with faint clinks. Her slicing revealed more blue under the surface. A blue that was strikingly similar to Shikari's blue.

Did that mean—

The blade slipped and cut her finger. She cursed and dropped it and the scale, then rushed to the sink, alarmed by the amount of blood flowing from the wound. Those magical weapons were sharp.

Malek, she thought, though she assumed he was busy practicing and wouldn't be monitoring her thoughts. *I found something you should see.*

Noisy clangs sounded on the ladder. Was that Malek? He always moved so quietly.

Jadora turned off the water, aware that they had a limited supply on board, and wrapped a towel around her finger. A thump against the jamb made her turn, the news for Malek on her lips.

But Tonovan leaned against the jamb, his uniform rumpled, that ever-present smirk on his lips. The stink of some fermented beverage lingered about him.

"You missed some good entertainment, Professor. The natives here have some stimulating quirks. *Both* of the ones who attended me did. No wonder Malek likes exploring these other worlds." His eyes focused on her breasts as he spoke. "Oh, but those zidarr are so staid. I'm sure he doesn't care for quirk. He likes scholarly older ladies who bundle themselves from neck to ankle in clothing. I admit there's some appeal to *unwrapping* presents."

Jadora glanced at the main-gauche on the deck, thoughts of her conversation with Malek about using it on Tonovan coming to mind.

His smirk broadened. "I especially like unwrapping *feisty* presents."

"Can't you walk to your cabin without molesting anyone, Tonovan?" came Malek's cold voice from the corridor.

Jadora sagged against the counter in relief. Her finger throbbed under the towel, and she didn't want to deal with perverts.

"I could," Tonovan drawled, turning to face Malek, "but I do so enjoy teasing the woman you're not supposed to lust after but do."

"Because you're a child in a man's body. Go to your cabin."

Tonovan's smirk didn't fade, but maybe the warning in Malek's eyes, or the fact that he was likely still holding his sword, made him decide this wasn't the time to trade insults.

"I *do* need some rest," Tonovan said. "My night was exhausting."

"I don't suppose you gathered any intelligence from the locals while you were bedding them."

"As a matter of fact, I did get the girls out of those ugly skull-caps. Their hair was, alas, too short to grab, and their thoughts weren't enlightening. One of them was praying to some elder dragon god that I wouldn't hurt her. Not Shylezar. I guess they've got their own dragon gods here. She believed he was out there living in the swamp and would swoop in to protect her. Not that such was necessary. I'm not a heathen. I don't give the girls anything they don't want." He winked at Jadora.

As if Tezi or any of the other women he'd forced had *wanted* him. Jadora hoped he hadn't hurt the natives he'd been with, but if they'd been praying to a god out of fear, she wouldn't bet on it. Disgusted, she glanced at the main-gauche again, wishing she dared use it on him.

You won't, Tonovan spoke into her mind. *You're not a killer. You don't break the rules. If you did, you'd have your lips locked to your sturdy zidarr savior. You wouldn't let Uthari's threats keep you from him. But you're a coward. You—*

Tonovan broke off, skittering back from the hatchway and farther down the corridor. The tip of Malek's sword came into view before he did. It was leveled at Tonovan's chest.

"Oh, dear," Tonovan said. "Have I overstayed my welcome? A pity."

A thud sounded, as if he'd drunkenly bumped into a wall, followed by a clang as his hatch shut.

Malek lowered his sword and looked into the kitchen. His eyes widened when he saw the main-gauche on the deck and her at the sink with the bloody towel.

"Did he *hurt* you?" Malek demanded, such fury—and *murder*—in his voice that she would have stepped back if the counter hadn't blocked her.

She knew the fury wasn't directed at her, but seeing him shirtless, every hard muscle tensed, and all that magical power emanating from him made her speechless. A part of her was tempted to nod and unleash all that power on Tonovan, but she made herself shake her head. It wasn't as if he couldn't read the truth in her mind.

"No," she whispered. "Something startled me, and I foolishly did it to myself."

"I will heal your injury." Malek visibly relaxed his muscles, though he still appeared poised to spring into battle—or rush down the corridor and throttle Tonovan—at any second. He took a long slow breath while he sheathed his sword and picked up and cleaned the main-gauche.

"I'm sorry I dropped it," Jadora said, chagrined that he'd walked in to find his prized blade carelessly left on the deck.

"There is no need to apologize. What startled you?"

Jadora hesitated, debating if the information was something she should worry about the others overhearing. If Tonovan had come back, Bakir might have too, and Prolix and more people might be waking up by now. Did it matter if officers in other fleets learned secrets about the dragons? She wasn't sure.

Malek closed the hatch and stepped forward, waving for her to lower her hand so he could look at it. She did so, though having him standing so close was a temptation she shouldn't have allowed. Especially when she felt vulnerable and so very weary when it came to Tonovan and dealing with the machinations of mages in general. She would have liked to lean against someone for support. She would have liked to lean against him.

She locked her knees and stayed upright as he unwrapped the towel and his healing magic flowed into the still-bleeding finger.

"There's blue under the brown-and-gray mottled coloring on top of the scale," she said quietly.

"Blue?"

"Blue like Shikari. I'm forming a hypothesis."

"Tell me," he said gently, holding her hand, the sides of the cut melding back together and transforming from open wound to scar. Soon, even that faded.

"What one scale has revealed isn't conclusive, but I believe the evidence I've gathered is suggestive of the possibility…"

"Do all scientists hem their beliefs so?"

"Yes, it's a rule. I think that organism, what might be a parasitic infection, may have the ability to alter the host, both psychologically and physically."

Malek mulled that over for a moment, but as she'd expected, soon grasped the significance. "You think there aren't younger dragons and elder dragons but simply dragons that have been infested and those that haven't?"

Jadora nodded. "I think it's possible. And if there aren't any elder dragons left around, at least according to the people we've spoken to and what we've seen, the parasite may be *very* effective at spreading and invading hosts." Once again, she remembered those magical motes floating toward Shikari and shivered. If they hadn't reacted quickly enough—if Malek hadn't fried the persistent organisms—Shikari might even now be turning into a crabby brown-and-gray mottled dragon who laid traps for humans and thought eating them was wonderful.

She lifted a hand to her face, more shaken by that thought than any of the rest.

Malek wrapped his arm around her shoulders, and her resolve not to lean on him waned. Her wound had completely healed, but he still held her hand. Was he contemplating the ramifications of what she'd told him? Or thinking that holding her hand was nice?

"I *should* be contemplating the ramifications," he murmured, his mouth not far from her ear. "But I'm smelling your hair and thinking about how I would never forgive myself if Tonovan hurt you because he found a moment when I wasn't around and took advantage."

Her heart had started to lift at his admission of finding her scent appealing, but the rest made her freeze and worry.

"I keep challenging him to duels, and he keeps refusing to accept," Malek admitted, his voice hard, though he kept his touch gentle. "I'm struggling with my honor and the Zidarr Code. Everything I was raised to stand for and believe in makes it hard for me to contemplate forcing an opponent to fight or, even worse, launching a sneak attack. Such as murdering him in his sleep. But I've found myself fantasizing about it. Every time he smirks at you, whispers some cruel taunt in your mind..." His voice lowered to a husky rasp. "I want to kill him."

Another shiver went through Jadora, and it had nothing to do with Shikari and what had befallen the dragons. She ought to find it abhorrent that Malek would contemplate murder to protect her, but she couldn't help but feel that her and Jak's life would be less fraught if Tonovan didn't exist. They would still be stuck walking on eggshells as they navigated the world of these powerful mages, but she wouldn't have to worry about the sadistic bastard raping her or killing her son.

"I know," Malek murmured. "I shouldn't admit this, but if you asked me to do it... I would."

Jadora shook her head, horrified at the idea of having that kind of power. She could never command a man to kill another man. If she truly wanted Tonovan gone from the world, she ought to do it herself. It wasn't as if she didn't know of a thousand substances that could kill a man.

But Tonovan was right; she wasn't a murderer. Her priest father would be horrified if he knew she'd had these thoughts. Even if she didn't follow the god Thanok or even know if gods existed, she couldn't deny that she'd been raised to believe that men could be redeemed and harming others wasn't right. *Murdering* them certainly wasn't. She'd been as formed by her father's teachings as Malek had been by Uthari and the Zidarr Code.

"I should figure out a way to deal with him myself," she made herself say, though she'd been so busy researching a half dozen other things that she hadn't put much brain power toward solving her Tonovan problem. "A nondeadly way. If the tests and my academic results as a student can be believed, I purportedly have above-average intelligence. Finding a way to keep a lout of a man from molesting me ought to be within my realm of competence."

"*Much* is within your realm of competence." Malek still sounded grim, but a hint of humor infused his tone.

Did that mean he believed she could come up with a solution for Tonovan? If so, she appreciated the faith. She'd half expected him to say that Tonovan was too powerful and that she would be a fool to risk irking him.

She almost looked up at his face, wanting to see his eyes and get a hint of what he was thinking, but that might be her undoing. She enjoyed having his arm around her, her hand in his, and leaning against his powerful frame. Resting her head against his chest wasn't much wiser than looking into his eyes, especially when his chest was bare and the longing to run her hand—and maybe her mouth—over it kept sauntering through her mind.

"I'm sure you can come up with a way to get him to leave you alone if you put your mind to it," Malek said. "My only concern is that you'll focus on this dragon mystery and finding the plant instead. I imagine those are more appealing avenues of study for you."

"That is true," she admitted, "but don't contemplate murder on my behalf, please. Especially when you feel compelled to tell Uthari everything. I have no doubt he would punish you for killing his top general, and if he found out I'd asked for it..."

Malek's arm tightened around her shoulders.

"He would probably kill me," she said. "Or order you to do it."

"He would not be foolish enough to give me an order he knows I wouldn't obey."

"Then he would have someone else do it. He's said as much. I can't ask you to go against him, Malek." Jadora looked up, meeting his eyes for the first time.

Frustration marked his face, his desire to protect her warring with his need to be a loyal and trustworthy man, the man his king had raised him and trained him to be.

Jadora wished they could kick everyone except Jak and Shikari off the mageship, take it exploring to other worlds, and never return to Torvil and that loathsome Uthari, who'd punished Malek even though he hadn't deserved it. The thought of Malek on his knees, writhing in pain before that awful old man brought tears to her eyes, and she reached up to touch his face. Why did he endure it? Why didn't he walk away? She would ask him to do that long before she asked him to kill a man, but she sensed he would be far more likely to assassinate Tonovan than walk away from Uthari.

Malek smiled sadly. "Zidarr life is complicated."

"*You're* complicated."

"I know. It touches me that you care."

That smile tugged at her heart, the gentleness in his eyes as he gazed at her making her want nothing more than to kiss him. But that wasn't allowed, and she needed to step away before she—

Malek bent his head and kissed her.

Surprise flashed through her—she hadn't believed he would, not without some drug addling his mind—but any thought of rejecting him and stepping away disappeared as soon as their lips touched. She pressed her chest against his, wrapped both arms around his shoulders, and kissed him like she'd kissed him back in that cell. Having his hard body against hers was the most delicious thing she'd felt in years, and she couldn't keep from molding herself to him, wanting to feel his every muscle.

I want to be with you, Jadora, Malek whispered into her mind, hands stroking her through her shirt, then sliding under the hem to touch his calloused hand to her warm skin. *You never ask me to defy or disobey my king. You're not the threat he thinks you are.*

She knew Uthari wouldn't think that way and that they

couldn't do this. They had to stop. If they didn't, he would be punished and she...

She groaned against his mouth and threaded her fingers through his soft short hair, wishing they could get away with a single night together without anyone finding out. She was falling in love with him, and she'd never thought she would feel like that about a man again, never thought she'd so crave having a man in her bed. Having *this* man in her bed.

A knock sounded at the hatch. Jadora and Malek sprang apart, their chests heaving, curses on their lips. His reaction told her that he feared being caught as much as she, that he might want her, but he also didn't want to risk being punished. No, that wasn't it. He would accept the punishment, she felt certain, whether it horrified her or not. He didn't want to risk Uthari ordering her killed.

Malek nodded sadly at her.

The knock came again.

"Come in, Prolix," Malek called.

The other zidarr? What did *he* want?

Jadora hurried to smooth her clothing and tried not to let any evidence of their kiss show, any evidence that Malek's hand had been under her shirt, touching parts of her that hadn't known a man's touch since her husband died.

The hatch opened, and Prolix walked in carrying a basket of pastries, a couple of the bronze skullcaps, and a rolled-up parchment. Was that the map they'd asked for?

Prolix nodded formally to Malek, didn't acknowledge Jadora's existence, and offered the items to him. Malek accepted them and nodded back. Prolix walked out, closing the hatch behind him.

"He's chatty," Jadora observed, still a little breathless.

"Hence his name."

"Did he offer those to you because you were the closest to the door? Or is he wooing you?" Jadora smiled, hoping to keep the conversation light and also that Malek would leave. That kiss had been a mistake. If her microscope and scale hadn't been in here, *she* would have left.

"Because I'm the team leader. And I believe this is for you. Or Jak." Malek offered her the parchment and seemed willing to go along with her lead on the light conversation. "As for the food, it's for all of us, I suppose. Or maybe this is another offering for Shikari. Does he eat pastries?"

"Maybe if they're made from cricket flour."

Malek eyed the basket dubiously. "Is that… possible?"

"Probably not. I haven't seen any crickets on this world. It would be some other insect."

"Appealing." Malek set the basket on the counter for whoever was brave enough to try the pastries. "Now that we have the map, I'll prepare the ship to leave. Good morning, Professor." He bowed formally to her and walked out.

Jadora stared at the hatch long after he'd disappeared, vowing both to avoid letting herself be in closed cabins with him and to put some thought into finding a way to make Tonovan want to leave her alone.

As soon as Yidar shoved his feet into his boots and grabbed his weapons belt, he hurried for the deck of the *King's Courage*. He'd woken to shouts and immediately sensed the aura of something extremely magical—magical and *powerful*—nearby. Shouts of, "Dragon!" greeted him as he came up on deck.

"Well, that would account for it," Yidar muttered, jogging to the railing to join a number of the mage crew.

They were casting fireballs and lightning bolts at the dragon, a great brown-and-gray creature with a body larger than any of the mageships. When it roared, the deck shivered in response.

Though he was confident in his power and his ability to defend himself, Yidar couldn't help but shrink inside at the pure power that emanated from the huge creature. Ancient instincts implored him to run back to his cabin and hide under the bed.

But he was a zidarr, not a coward. He quashed the notion and joined his fellow mages in attacking the creature.

Far below, the ancient portal remained active, a starry constellation glowing in its center. Yidar hoped that didn't mean that more dragons were on the way.

Did you have a nice nap? Uthari's sarcastic voice sounded in his mind.

Yidar spotted him on the deck of the *Serene Waters*. Uthari wore nothing but pajama pants, suggesting he'd also been sleeping when their enemy arrived. Why the sarcasm?

I was off-shift and sleeping, yes, Your Majesty, Yidar replied.

When I ordered you to find and kill Sorath, I meant for you to apply urgency and alacrity to the task. Uthari waved to several of his bodyguards, then, when the dragon was focused on another ship, leaped to the railing of his yacht and overboard. He plunged a hundred feet before slowing his descent and landing lightly near the portal. As he ran toward it, he added, *I definitely expected you to get him before he sneaked onto my ship, infiltrated my bedchamber, and killed Queen Vorsha.*

Yidar blinked a few times as the reason for Uthari's ire dawned on him. *Vorsha is dead?*

For a confused moment, Yidar thought Sorath had assassinated Vorsha on her yacht before somehow getting over to the *Serene Waters* to attack Uthari. Then he remembered the talk of alliances and making babies. Vorsha must have been *in* Uthari's bed when Sorath attacked.

Yes, she's dead. Sorath had that stealth device—and an ally. Some feral druid leaped at her with a knife. Even though I blasted him with a fireball, he somehow ignored the pain to finish her off while Sorath escaped.

The druid is dead, I assume?

We captured him for questioning and to get the location of the druid headquarters, but he'll be dead soon. You don't need to worry about him. Just do what I asked. Down below, Uthari reached the portal as the constellation inside winked out. He planted his hand on the dragon-steel frame. *Find Sorath, and kill him. And kill the druids he's working with too. I want them all dead. Raze the entire jungle if you need to.*

Yes, Your Majesty. Yidar tensed as the dragon flew toward his ship.

Dozens and dozens of attacks had been launched at it, but a powerful magical barrier protected it. It roared, yellow reptilian eyes locking onto Yidar. If it killed him, he wouldn't get a chance to hunt down Sorath.

No. That wouldn't happen. Yidar lifted his chin and shouted, "Reinforce the barrier around the ship!"

He and his crew ought to have the combined might of a dragon. They could survive this.

Yidar channeled his own energy into the ship's defenses. The dragon flew overhead, talons raking at the barrier, but it held. Instead of turning to attack again, the dragon flew past, heading toward another ship. It raked at their barrier as well, but it seemed a half-hearted attack, and once again, it flew past. As more fireballs targeted the dragon, it flapped its wings and soared higher, indifferent to them. It circled the camp and all of the mageships like a vulture investigating the possibility of a meal.

Red lightning shot out of the portal and targeted the dragon. Uthari. He was commanding the artifact to attack.

For the first time, something penetrated the dragon's defenses. It screeched in pain and wheeled about, sending a wave of power toward the clearing around the portal.

Protected by their own magic, neither Uthari, the ancient artifact, nor the mage bodyguards that had followed him down were affected, but mercenaries flew everywhere as their tents were flattened or ripped from their stakes. Yidar shook his head, wondering why the rulers and fleet commanders had bothered to bring those people.

More red lightning shot toward the dragon. The creature launched another attack, this time ripping up the ground under Uthari and the others. Their barriers didn't keep them from flying backward, and Uthari lost his contact with the portal. It wobbled, threatening to tip over, but then it flashed blue and applied its own magic to right itself.

"Attack!" Yidar ordered his crew, switching his energy from defense to offense. He unleashed a powerful blast at the dragon, but once again, his magic wasn't enough to harm it.

He growled in annoyance.

Uthari ran back to the portal and planted his hand on it again. The artifact sent another branch of lightning out to envelop the dragon and harm the great creature. But it only lasted a couple of seconds before their scaled enemy roared. Instead of a pure animalistic bellow, it almost sounded like a word.

The lightning halted, and the portal dimmed to Yidar's senses. It felt like its magic had gone dormant.

Uthari stared incredulously at it, as if he'd been betrayed.

The dragon roared again—another word? It wasn't the same one.

The portal flared to life, blue light spreading across the clearing and reflecting off the pool. Uthari raised his hands and backed away, and Yidar sensed him strengthening his protective barrier.

The dragon landed atop the portal, talons gripping it as if it were a bird perched on a branch. It peered around, eyeing both Uthari and the nearby mages and mercenaries and also the mageships in the sky. Fireballs rained down upon the dragon, but it didn't bat an eye as its defenses protected it.

Light swirled within the portal, and the same constellation that had been there before re-formed. Yidar didn't think it was one they'd seen before. This was a connection to a world Malek and his team hadn't yet visited. Perhaps a world full of dragons. Based on what he'd seen of this one, Yidar did not want to visit such a place.

The dragon leaped into the air again. It soared lazily over the area, doing a barrel roll in the sky.

Uthari, face twisting in irritation if not outright rage, summoned all of his power and launched one of his own lightning attacks. The dragon roared, its barrier deflecting the assault of even a great wizard.

You'll regret attacking me, a voice thundered into Yidar's mind. Into everyone's mind? *Annoying a dragon scout is never a good idea, especially when you taste delicious.*

The dragon leered at Uthari and his guards, showing its sharp fangs, but instead of attacking again, it flapped its wings and flew back through the portal.

After it disappeared, the constellation vanished, and the artifact went dark.

"A scout?" someone nearby asked. "Does that mean a lot more are going to come through next time?"

Yidar shook his head grimly. He would do as Uthari asked and hunt down Sorath, but he had a feeling the mercenary was the least of their troubles. They should have tried a lot harder to keep that dragon from leaving—and reporting back to its kin.

15

"WHERE ARE CAPTAIN GYARTH AND THE *SKY TALON*?" RIVLEN muttered from the navigation cabin on the *Star Flyer*.

She sensed the druid monument in the jungle below, its magic largely dormant and barely noticeable, and she also sensed Vorsha's ship—it had been lurking about five miles to their port side for the last couple of hours. What she *didn't* sense was the ship she'd asked to meet her here.

"Ma'am?" the helmsman asked.

"I ordered Gyarth to join us here in case we find druids in the vicinity of their monument." Rivlen thought about heading to the private communications cabin but decided it didn't matter if the navigation officer overheard. She activated the dome-jir on the console and envisioned Captain Gyarth.

Long seconds passed as she waited for him to respond. Had she misjudged him? Maybe he was in cahoots with Ular.

"Ma'am?" the helmsman asked again, a different note in his voice. "Vorsha's ship is heading toward us."

Rivlen checked the monument again, wondering if something had changed. Vorsha's captain had spoken of wanting the same prize as she, presumably the other key to the portal. Maybe he'd gathered some new intelligence or sensed activity below that suggested it was down there.

But as far as she could tell, nothing had changed about the monument. Its magic gave off only a faint signature, as if it had been dormant for a long time. Between night's darkness and the canopy, she couldn't see the ancient stones, but they were probably half-buried under vines and fallen leaves.

She also didn't detect any magic users in the area. The druids might be there and underground, hidden by their insulated tunnels, but if so, the other captain wouldn't have sensed them either.

"He's coming fast, ma'am. Straight at us."

"Thank you, Lieutenant. We'll ready our defenses." Rivlen ordered her second-in-command to ready the mages for battle and alert the mercenaries. Why Vorsha's people would want to pick a fight with her, she didn't know, but if they attacked, she would meet them boldly in battle and destroy them.

The dome-jir finally flared to life, Captain Gyarth's frazzled face appearing in the air above it. "We need help, Captain Rivlen," he said before she could speak.

"What's wrong? Why didn't you meet us at the monument?" she asked, though she could guess. He'd been attacked.

But by whom? Captain Ulnar wouldn't have dared attack a vessel in his own fleet just to keep it from helping Rivlen. Maybe Vorsha had more people out here.

"We were on our way when two of Vorsha's ships flew out from behind the mountains. They beelined toward us and attacked. I've called Ular, and he says he's on the way, but—" Gyarth glanced at something beyond her view and cursed.

The dome-jir went dark.

"Prepare to engage that ship in battle," Rivlen barked.

"Yes, ma'am."

They would take care of this enemy, then fly off to help the rest of the fleet. Had she known Vorsha's ships would openly attack them, Rivlen would have gathered her forces together hours earlier.

Growling, she flattened her hand to the dome-jir again, this time commanding it to contact the approaching ship.

But the captain didn't respond. Vorsha's ship kept flying toward them. Thanks to its running lights, it was visible now, dozens of mages at the bow, preparing for battle.

"I'm going out to fight," Rivlen said. "Engage in battle maneuvers, Dragon Wing attack pattern."

"Yes, ma'am."

As Rivlen jogged out to join the mages and mercenaries, a telepathic touch brushed her mind. King Uthari.

Captain Rivlen, he said. *Are you awake?*

Was she awake? Hah.

Yes, Your Majesty. Rivlen realized she should have already reported Vorsha's aggressions to him. Normally, General Tonovan would receive her reports, since he was her commanding officer, but he was gone, and Uthari had personally assigned her this mission. She hurried to explain the situation to him. *Three of Queen Vorsha's ships have emerged from the jungle and engaged our ships in battle. We're at a druid monument and were about to investigate it. They may know about something down there that we don't.*

She hated to admit that, but she had to give him all the information she had so he would know how to respond.

What they know, Uthari said, *is that their queen is dead.*

Rivlen gripped the railing. *What?*

It happened on my ship and in my cabin.

She kept herself from asking if he'd done it, but if he had, that had been ballsy. And she wondered what had prompted the move.

It wasn't by my hand, Uthari said, *but they're blaming me and not listening to the truth.*

A fireball scorched the night air and headed straight toward the *Star Flyer*. Rivlen funneled some of her energy into the barrier already protecting the ship, and it bounced off, but more attacks followed.

To make the night more aggravating, a dragon scout came through the portal.

Do you want us to fly back to help? Rivlen wanted to deal with Vorsha's ships first, but if a dragon was ravaging the fleet back at camp…

It left. It's possible it will return with other dragons, but for now, I want you to deal with Vorsha's ships. Show them that even if I had *killed Vorsha, they would be foolish to strike at us. Destroy them utterly, Captain.*

Rivlen lifted her chin. *Yes, Your Majesty.*

As the helmsman flew them toward their enemy, Rivlen reached out to her second-in-command. *After their next round of attacks, drop our barrier. We're going in, and we're going to obliterate them.*

I look forward to it, Captain.

So did she, but as the *Star Flyer* sailed over the monument, the stones barely visible through the foliage, a faint green glow activated below, and she groaned. Whatever that signaled, it couldn't be good.

As shouts filled the night behind him, Sorath stood where the mouth to the druid tunnel *should* have been.

Positive he'd returned to the right place, he turned slowly in a circle. Yes, there was the bush he'd hit his head on when he and Grunk had climbed out. The druid magic must have collapsed the mouth of the tunnel after they'd left to ensure it wouldn't be found. It had even smoothed the ground, leaving the bushes and undergrowth undisturbed. Either that, or it was a very good illusion.

Sorath prodded around with his feet, then drew the dagger, thinking the dragon steel might be able to pierce magical camouflage. It only poked into solid ground, but on the third stab, a vision swept over Sorath.

It showed him back in the tunnel, alone this time and heading toward the druid meeting area. He kept glancing over his shoulder, the feeling of being pursued raising the hairs on the back of his neck. Could it be Grunk? Having escaped from Uthari's troops and hurrying to catch up with him? No, he didn't think so. Whoever it was felt malevolent. Like someone who wanted to kill Sorath.

He touched the stealth device on his wrist to make sure it was active and ran faster. If he made it back to the druids, they would help him.

But whoever was following him knew he was there, heard the sound of his footfalls as he ran. A man in black leaped out of the shadows and wrapped an arm around Sorath's neck.

Sorath reacted instantly, jabbing an elbow into his assailant's chest and spinning to ram him against the side of the tunnel. But a strong hand gripped his wrist and twisted the dragon-steel dagger free. Before it struck the ground, tremendous magical pain blasted him, stunning him like a blow to the solar plexus. An instant later, a dagger sliced across his throat. Sorath fell backward, hitting the ground hard and seeing his attacker for the first time.

It was one of Uthari's zidarr. One of the three men Sorath had been tasked with killing. Yidar.

You got the wrong target, mercenary, Yidar said coolly, then walked across Sorath's chest and continued deeper into the tunnel. Toward the druid meeting area where he would kill Kywatha and the others.

The vision faded, and Sorath barely stifled a groan as he

knelt back. He was still close to the camp and dared not make any noise. He also dared not curse at the dagger for sharing such an unappealing vision. Was it the future? Or only a possible future?

If he didn't use the tunnel, his death couldn't find him there, right? Of course, it might find him somewhere else.

Sorath looked up at the dark branches, the lights of mageships visible through the leaves. He couldn't stay here. Even if it had been safe, he felt compelled to tell the druids that he'd failed and that Grunk hadn't gotten away. Further, if Grunk had been captured, he might be questioned, and the mages might learn where the druids were hiding. Even though Sorath hated the idea of admitting his failure to them, he had to warn them that trouble was on the way.

But how? If he opened up the tunnel again, he could be leading that trouble right to them.

Maybe he could travel overland and find his way to them. But he hadn't seen the ground or any landmarks above the meeting area and wouldn't know where to look.

Sorath eyed the dagger. *I don't suppose you have any other messages you'd like to share with me? Visions of a better future? Tips on how to find your people?*

He didn't expect a response, but surprisingly, another vision swept over him. In it, he was running off to the south along a faint animal trail. He traveled for miles and miles, his breaths coming in pants, but he knew he had to hurry if he wanted to reach the druids in time.

He crested a rise to run along a ridge, and for a moment, he had a rare view of the surrounding area. Ships were fighting over an ancient druid monument in the distance. Captain Rivlen was on one of the ships, and Captain Ferroki, Rookie Tezi, and the rest of Thorn Company were with her.

Somehow, Sorath sensed that if he ran to reunite with the

mercenaries, he would find the druids. But if Yidar was hunting him, would the zidarr still find him?

The vision faded before Sorath learned the answer to that question or which druids were out there and what would happen when he reached them. The idea of running miles through the jungle at night didn't appeal to him, but it would be better than having his throat cut in a tunnel.

And it was possible that Sorath could, knowing Yidar was coming for him, lay a trap and assassinate *him*. It would be nice to at least partially complete the mission he'd agreed to take on for the druids.

Admittedly, he hadn't managed to defeat a zidarr in any of his encounters with them. It would be arrogant of him to believe the next time would be different.

But maybe Thorn Company could help him. Between Tinder and Tezi, they had two mighty dragon-steel axes. Even a zidarr would be vulnerable to such weapons.

A longing went through him as he thought of Thorn Company, of seeing Ferroki again and perhaps helping them. In his vision, they'd been in a battle. They might *need* his help.

Sorath nodded to himself and headed deeper into the jungle. He would hope the second vision would lead him to the company and that he hadn't imagined it all. After all he'd survived, getting lost in the jungle and dying to some predator would not be an appealing end.

After departing the city early that morning, the ship flew southward for hours, remaining above the trees and following a mountain range that loomed to the west. Normally, Jak would be looking out the porthole or surveying the route from the deck with great interest, but he'd spent the latter half of the night learning about magical wrenches, screwdrivers, and how to feel the *weave of the filaments*, as Vinjo had called it. Now, as he sat in a chair next to the helm officer, assigned the spot in case she needed to consult a cartography expert about the map, he kept dozing off.

A vibration rumbled through the deck, and Jak jerked awake for the third or fourth time that hour.

"Why don't you go to your bunk if you're that exhausted?" Lieutenant Harintha gave him a cross look. Her hair was pulled back in a tight bun, and she might have reminded him of Rivlen, but she was shorter and curvier. She also didn't emanate the kind of power that Rivlen did.

"I'm sorry. I didn't realize my grogginess was disturbing you."

"It's the snoring, smacking your lips, and grunting with surprise as you pitch halfway out of your seat that I object to."

"My bunk has a dragon in it."

"Can't you cuddle up with it?"

"With *him,* and he keeps getting bigger and more, uhm, bed-hoggier."

"That's because he ate all of the pastries that were for us." Harintha scowled at the open hatchway that led to the cabins and the kitchen. "I heard a gift of them had arrived, but by the time I got the ship launched and the chance to investigate, the only things left were crumbs and dragon snot."

"Dragons don't emit snot." At least not that Jak had noticed. "It was probably saliva."

"Yum."

"Are you sure they don't produce mucous?" came his mother's voice as she stepped through the hatchway, lifting her hand to hide a yawn. "Herbivorous iguanid lizards such as the green iguana have nasal salt glands and are capable of producing mucous."

"Have I mentioned, Mother, how wonderful it is that you're still teaching me things, even though I'm a man now?"

"No, but you should. It's polite and respectful to acknowledge that you appreciate your mother's breadth of knowledge." She nodded at the map unrolled on the console, the edges held down by some of Vinjo's tools that Jak had borrowed to study. Hopefully, the engineer wouldn't mind them being temporarily used for paperweights. The wrench that pulsed blue every now and then seemed a touch indignant to be doing nothing more than holding down a corner. "How far are we from the foraging site?"

Whoever had drawn the map had circled a spot near the mouth of a river and labeled it something that meant, according to Zethron, *Moist Cave Porch.* Jak suspected that was a very rough translation.

He could tell from the fresh ink that the map had been made the night before. He hoped that meant someone had copied it from a reliable source, not that they'd drawn up something fanciful intended to lead the ship in circles—or into trouble.

The locals had been civil enough during the team's visit, but the insinuation that the chief believed Jak had kidnapped Shikari disturbed him. So did the way the man had pleaded with the dragon to stay behind. If Shikari had wanted to remain in the city, what would Jak have done? Tried to leash him like a dog and lead him back to the ship? Would Shikari have allowed that? He might be less than two months old and unable to fly yet, but he'd demonstrated more than once that he was intelligent, had some of the memories of his ancestors, and already had the ability to use magic.

"We've got a ways to go," Harintha said, "but we should be getting close to a river that we need to follow upstream. If we stay up here, I'm concerned we'll miss it. The types of trees have changed as we've flown south, and these spread their branches really far and make a nearly impenetrable canopy. There could be a small ocean down there, and we'd miss it."

"Oceans deter the growth of most types of trees due to the high salinity in the nearby soils," Mother said around another yawn. "Salt spray blown into the leaves can also damage them. Of course, there are exceptions, such as our mangroves back home, which thrive in aquatic regions and can endure having their roots submerged in salt water for periods of time."

This time, Harintha's cross look was for Mother. "My point is that I'm going to have to take us below the canopy or risk missing the river. If I miss it, we could keep sailing for hundreds of miles and get lost. I've no knowledge of this world and no frames of reference beyond that map, which may or may not be accurate."

"Do we have a reason to believe it's not accurate?" Mother asked as the lieutenant touched a glowing knob that raised and lowered the ship.

"It depends on how much we trust that those people wanted to help us," Jak said. "I would have felt more confident if I'd seen one of them pull this map out of an atlas and hand it to us. It was freshly drawn last night while we were sleeping."

While they *should* have been sleeping. Jak yawned.

Harintha frowned over at him. Aware that she was a mage, even if she wasn't as powerful as the others, Jak carefully kept his mental bandana wrapped around his thoughts.

"I would be distressed if they'd torn it out of an atlas," Mother said. "What kind of people defile books?"

"You're a strange family." Harintha slowed the ship down, looking for a gap that they could descend through without breaking every branch—and possibly damaging their craft—along the way.

"Quirky," Mother said. "Perhaps we should ask Malek about descending. Zethron said flying under the trees isn't recommended."

"It's either descend or miss the river," Harintha said. "I can't tell from the map how wide the waterway is, but if it's not substantial, the canopy might cover it."

"I understand," Mother said. "My concern is that there's something down there that the natives avoid and that maybe we should as well."

"We came out of the portal under the trees," Harintha said.

"And were promptly attacked by a dragon."

"After six other dragons flew right past us," Jak said.

"I doubt dragons are affected one way or another by tree canopies," Harintha said. "It's not like they're afraid of heights."

"As evinced by Shikari's willingness to climb up into the top bunk," Jak said. "Agreed."

But maybe *dragons* weren't what made the natives uneasy. He looked at his mother, wondering if she knew more.

She wore a conflicted expression. "Zethron wasn't able to articulate a reason, just that the natives build their cities above the trees and only go down below to hunt and gather when necessary."

"Wouldn't that be often?" Jak asked. "We didn't see any farmlands built into their log city."

Mother spread a hand and shrugged. She might be a fount of trivia, but only that which applied to their world.

"I've informed Lord Malek that we're going down." Harintha waved at her temple.

"Thank you," Mother said.

Jak didn't object further, and neither did his mother. She likely wanted to get that plant and return to their world as soon as possible.

So far, this place wasn't as dreadful as Vran, but Jak wasn't that eager to linger either, not when the natives wanted to woo Shikari to stay, someone may or may not have sabotaged the portal, and a flock of dragons was trying to find a way to Torvil. He hoped the team could figure out how to fix the portal when they wanted to leave.

Despite the lieutenant's efforts to find a clear route downward, branches snapped and clawed at the hull as they descended. Above the trees, a warm afternoon sun had been shining in the sky, but it grew much dimmer as they dipped lower. It reminded Jak of the times he'd played at the Sprungtown lake with his father as a boy, and they'd taken turns diving as deep into the water as they could before lack of air had forced them back to the surface. The sun hadn't been able to penetrate the water easily, and it had also grown dark and murky as they descended.

One of the vines draping the tree branches tore off and dropped across their porthole. Jak yelped when it moved and slithered out of sight.

"Was that a snake or an ambulatory vine?" he asked, striving for nonchalance.

Mother opened her mouth but paused. "We haven't explored enough for me to be that familiar with the flora and fauna."

"So, it *could* have been an ambulatory vine." Jak hadn't seen eyes, and whatever its skin had been, it hadn't looked like scales.

"It was a snake." Harintha rolled her eyes at him. "Don't be a pansy. They're hanging from the trees all over the place. I hear they like to munch on brainy scholars."

"I don't think she likes us," Jak whispered to his mother.

"Likely because your dragon ate all the pastries." Mother smiled, though it didn't reach her eyes. She watched the porthole warily as the branches thinned and muddy leaf-littered earth came into view.

The landscape wasn't as swampy as it had been back at the portal, but it was still damp, with pools, puddles, and what looked like quicksand proliferating.

Clangs drifted to their ears, and Jak frowned. Were they coming from outside? They sounded like metal striking metal, not branches scraping at the hull.

Jak swept out with his senses, an ability that had grown more automatic for him, and sensed Malek and Prolix on the deck above. Practicing blade work? While they risked being whacked with branches? Maybe the extra obstacles made the training more fun for a couple of zidarr.

"I'm leveling us off." Harintha stopped their descent about twenty feet above the ground, with trees rising up in all directions. Even though the ship was narrow, navigating through them wouldn't be easy. "I got a little turned around there," she admitted, leaning forward to look up, inasmuch as she could, through the porthole. "The mountains are over there, right?" She pointed in one direction.

Jak adjusted her arm about fifteen degrees.

She scowled at him. "Are you sure?"

He nodded, though it *would* be easy to lose one's way down here. "Head in that direction for a while—" he pointed toward where the map suggested the river would be, "—and if we need to, we can go up again to reorient ourselves."

"Right." The deck vibrated as Harintha pushed the lever that propelled them forward.

An insect larger than a bat landed on the porthole and spread rubbery gray wings, whipping them against the glass.

Harintha shrieked and flung up her arms. Jak sensed her hurl a blast of magical power at the insect. It flew backward and tumbled out of view, only to recover, flap its wings, and fly upward to land in a tree.

She swore, wiped her palms on her uniform pants, and returned her hands to the controls before looking over at Jak and back at Mother. Mother had pulled out a notebook and was drawing something. Probably the moving vine and maybe now also the bat-insect. She wasn't the artist that Jak was, but she could do decent sketches.

Jak offered Harintha an encouraging smile and didn't let it show that he felt better now that someone else had been startled.

A cartographer shouldn't find any types of terrain *creepy*, but he couldn't keep that word from popping into his mind.

Harintha squinted at him, as if searching for mockery on his face, then returned her focus to the controls. "Thanks for not calling me a pansy," she muttered.

"You're welcome. We'll pretend it's because I'm a gentleman, not because my mother is standing behind me and would whap me with her notebook."

Harintha glanced at Mother.

"I would," Mother said without looking up from her drawing. "And Jak *is* a gentleman. I insist."

"Wish all of the men here were," Harintha muttered.

Jak shook his head bleakly, assuming Tonovan had been crude —or worse—to her, but for all he knew, it had been one of the others. He wished he had the power to stop them. Later, he and Malek were supposed to have a training session. He hoped he could stay awake to perform the exercises adequately. Too bad there wasn't a way to absorb all of the necessary knowledge and experience to become a strong mage—as strong as Tonovan —instantly.

Mother lowered her notebook as the terrain outside changed. The land grew less damp and muddy and the trees even denser.

Harintha grumbled under her breath as she was forced to slow down even further to navigate around them. Jak pointed and had her adjust her course a few times, though sometimes, it was more his instincts than certainty that guided him. Could he rely upon them? He was on the verge of suggesting they ascend above the canopy again when Harintha spoke.

"There it is." She tapped the river on the map, then pointed ahead toward a meandering waterway, no hint of sunlight reaching its surface to glint and draw attention. As she'd suggested, the branches stretched over it, tangling with those from trees on the opposite bank, so it was quite possible they would have missed it from above. "It looks like we fly up it about forty miles."

"The greenery growing on the banks is promising," Mother said. "There's much more foliage here than there was on the islands in the swamp."

"Nothing like foliage to get a girl excited," Harintha said.

"Some girls," Mother murmured, then glanced back.

"Is there room for one more in here?" Zethron asked.

Mother stepped into the corridor so he could enter the navigation cabin. There was room, but he tripped, and almost fell into the back of Jak's seat.

"We're under the canopy?" Zethron asked.

"Obviously." Harintha rolled her eyes.

She had to be in her late twenties, but she reminded Jak of the students he'd gone to school with.

"I thought we agreed we weren't going to do that." Zethron tilted his head as more clangs floated down. "Are the mages fighting out in the open? On top of the ship?"

"There's not room in the narrow corridor or the cabins," Mother said.

"But they're much more vulnerable outside." Zethron removed his hat and scraped his fingers through his hair.

"Vulnerable to what?" Jak peered at him.

"Insects and predators." Zethron shrugged. "The natives were never specific, but they always warned me not to spend time down here."

"So far, our mages have been able to handle the things we've encountered. Lieutenant Harintha here blew a bat across the forest." Jak waved at her. "If the natives don't have magic at their disposal, maybe they're less able to deal with the creatures that live down here."

"Maybe," Zethron said, "but I don't think we want to linger. There has to be a good reason why the natives don't."

"I just need a sample of a plant," Mother said.

"*Somebody's* spending time down here." Harintha pointed again.

She was piloting them around a bend in the slow-moving river, and a large paddleboat had come into view. It was turned sideways and snagged on a log or other underwater obstacle. The hull appeared intact, but the big paddle wasn't operating. Projectile weapons similar to harpoon launchers were mounted on the front and rear of the boat. Jak didn't know what the people had been hunting, but a stuffed animal head was mounted above one of the doors. It had a long tooth-filled snout that reminded him of an alligator.

There were also long rectangular cases built into the deck near the railing. They had glass tops—or lids?—and reminded Jak of garden beds protected from frost, though that would be a strange thing to find on a paddleboat.

The door under the stuffed animal head opened, and a man in tattered clothing leaped outside. He spun, slamming the door shut behind him, and yanked a wooden bar down.

To lock someone inside? Jak watched in bewilderment.

The man spotted their ship and waved his arms, a flag gripped in one hand.

Mother pulled her gaze from the cases—she'd also been focused on them—to look at him. "I think he needs help."

"We're not here for humanitarian purposes," Harintha said.

"What if we crash later?" Jak asked. "We'll want someone to come by and help *us*."

"We have a ship full of mages. We won't *need* help from strangers."

"He's not wearing a skullcap." Zethron shifted uneasily.

He was right. After seeing one on every person here, the lack was odd. The man's black hair was matted in places and stuck out in tufts in others. Dried blood on his face suggested a wound.

"Maybe he lost it in the crash," Jak said.

The clang of a hatch came from behind them, and Malek soon joined Mother in the corridor.

"Should I slow down, my lord?" Harintha asked. "Or fly past?"

"Keep going," Zethron said.

Jak blinked, startled by the answer. Zethron didn't seem like a callous person who would leave someone behind who needed assistance.

"We should stop." Mother frowned at Zethron. "That man clearly needs help, and there may be more injured inside. We can drop them off at the city on the way back. It wouldn't be that far out of our way." She looked to Malek. Everyone did.

Malek gestured to Harintha to halt the mageship but asked, "Why don't you want to stop, Zethron?"

"I have a bad feeling about this place and about him." Zethron licked his lips and pushed his fingers through his hair again. "I've been warned before about not coming below the canopy here, especially not without skullcaps."

"The natives gave us two along with the pastries and map," Malek said.

"Well, if you go down there, make sure you wear them," Zethron said. "But don't go down there."

Malek was scrutinizing him—reading his thoughts?—and Jak tried to do the same.

He sensed that Zethron was afraid, but that was obvious without telepathy. Unfortunately, Zethron wasn't thinking about anything concrete that could explain *why* he was afraid. Jak got a sense of night falling and ominous trees and winged and legged predators leaping out of the swamp. Also of the giant insects they'd seen on the way in.

"How would the skullcaps help with predators?" Malek must not have gotten much more than Jak from Zethron's thoughts.

"The natives say they're for protection," Zethron said.

"The magic of the skullcaps is weak," Malek said. "I studied the ones they gave us. They have a minor enchantment at best."

"That's enough to keep you from reading their minds," Jak pointed out.

"Yes." Malek gazed at the man on the paddleboat. "But I can see his thoughts. Some of them. They're scattered and don't make a lot of sense. He's thinking that the crew—his *own* crew—attacked him and that he's barely made it out with his life."

"Are there more people inside?" Mother asked.

"If there are, they're not mages, and I can't sense mundane humans. There's nothing magic about that ship except a couple of faint signatures similar to what those skullcaps emit. Maybe they *are* skullcaps." Malek spread a hand. "I think he might have been out here for a while and lost some of his sanity. Or a *lot* of it."

Malek squinted, noticing the cases for the first time. "What's in those? Fly us closer, Harintha."

As the lieutenant nudged the ship forward, the man stopped waving his arms and lowered the flag. He patted his head, then glanced around. He lunged under a lifeboat upturned on a rack on the deck and pulled out one of the bronze skullcaps. He tugged it over his head, grimacing as it probably rubbed against his injury, then pointed to it and waved again. He dropped to his knees, as if praying to a god—or pleading to them. His lips moved as he shouted an entreaty. It was audible through the ship's walls.

"He's begging us to get him out of there," Zethron translated with a grimace. "Before the crew kills him."

"There's greenery in those cases," Mother said.

They were close enough now to see what might have been plants under the lids. The glass was smudged with dirt and grime, so they couldn't tell if they had leaves or fronds, but the crew either grew its own herbs… or had been collecting native foliage.

Mother and Malek exchanged long looks. If the boat had come

from upriver, might the crew have been gathering Jitaruvak from the foraging site circled on the map?

"I'll go down there, get him, and check out the cases." Malek turned toward the corridor.

"Don't go alone," Mother said. "Please."

Malek hesitated, looking like he'd meant to do just that.

"I'll go." Jak rose from his seat, though it wasn't as if he was as formidable a force as the older mages and could do much. "And Shikari will too," he added. More than once, the young dragon had proven a valuable ally.

His words didn't smooth the concerned expression on Mother's face.

"You better leave him in here. With the hatch closed." She shared a significant look with Malek.

Jak frowned. "Why? What aren't you telling me?"

"After examining that dragon scale, I now believe that there's only one species of dragon, not good and evil kinds, as you call them, or elder and younger, as the Vran people referred to them."

Jak gripped the back of the seat, grasping the ramifications before his mother continued on.

"I believe the brown-and-gray mottled dragons were originally blue dragons that were modified. Their scales—and possibly their personalities—changed when they were infested with that organism."

"*Definitely* their personalities." Jak shuddered, thinking of the threats he'd received from the mottled dragons. Shikari wasn't like that, and neither were the dragons in the visions the portals had shared. Neither were the portals themselves, which Jak believed, thanks to hints he had received from the various peoples he'd interacted with, had been modeled on the personalities of real dragons. It was even possible that the intelligences and souls of dragons had somehow been imbued into the ancient artifacts.

"We surmised that the infestation could make them... grumpy," Mother said.

"If what you're saying is true, it's a lot more than that," Jak said. "They've gone from friendly, willing allies of humans to wanting to eat them. *Grumpily.*"

Mother spread her palm toward the ceiling. "So far, I only know that the parasites exist. I can hypothesize about how they might affect brain chemistry and hormones—things that, at least in humans, could cause significant alterations in personality—but it would be difficult to gain definitive knowledge on the subject without tests. Perhaps those tests were done long ago, and there's documentation somewhere, but I don't believe it exists on our world. Loran, during his extensive studies, would have come across it. But perhaps out here..." Mother waved toward the porthole. "Here, or in another world where dragons frequented, such tests might have been done. It's hard to believe we're the only ones who stumbled onto this knowledge."

Jak noticed the man still waving hopefully, even as he kept glancing back at the barred door. "We need to go help him."

"Yes." Mother nodded. "But leave Shikari."

"He shouldn't be able to catch that parasite from being out in the wilderness here, right?" Jak asked. "The organisms tried to infest him when the other dragons died. They were living in those dragons, not in swamp water or some such."

"We don't know where they originated. Yes, they seem to be able to pass from dragon to dragon, but they may have evolved elsewhere. Such as in water."

Jak eyed the river outside. It wasn't murky and stagnant like the swamp water, but that didn't mean it would be safe.

"I'll take Jak and Zethron to translate." Malek rested a hand on Mother's shoulder, then headed to his cabin to grab his weapons.

Zethron, who might not have had enough mastery of the language yet to catch the nuances of the parasite discussion, understood that. "I don't want to go out there," he blurted to Malek's back.

After buckling on his weapons, Malek returned to the narrow corridor. "Nonetheless, you will come. It won't take long to pick up that man and learn what he knows, if anything."

Tonovan stepped out of his cabin, his own weapons buckled on. "I'll go too."

Jak winced. Of all the people that he didn't want to join them…

He wished he'd known Tonovan's hatch was open and that he was listening to everything. He would have closed the hatch to navigation. Though he wasn't sure what Tonovan could do with the information about the dragons—or that Shikari could hypothetically be infested here—Jak would have preferred he know nothing.

"That's not necessary," Malek said.

"You're not going to explore a ship by yourself and find all the dragon-steel weapons to take back and dump at Uthari's feet for a pat on the head. *I* will also go and receive credit."

"It's unlikely there will be anything valuable on a fishing boat," Malek said, though Jak had no doubt he meant to look in those plant cases.

"We'll see."

Malek climbed the ladder to the hatch. Jak waved for Tonovan to follow him first, though he was hesitant to go at all now that the general was going. But someone had to watch Malek's back in case Tonovan found another opportunity to *accidentally* attack him while *helping* in a battle.

Tonovan smiled cruelly at Jak as he climbed up the ladder.

"I don't like that man," Zethron whispered.

"Nobody does," Jak said. "Trust me."

16

As fireballs smashed into the *Star Flyer's* defensive barrier, Lieutenant Sasko eyed Sergeant Tinder's dragon-steel axe with envy. The *Star Flyer* was battling a big green-hulled warship and holding its own thus far, but Sasko wished *she* had a weapon that provided protection from magic. Every time the mages lowered the barrier to attack, the *Star Flyer* and Thorn Company were vulnerable. A few of Vinjo's defensive bulwarks were erected on the deck, but they weren't large enough to shelter everyone.

"I wonder if we're going to get close enough to be of some use," Captain Ferroki said from Sasko's side, gripping her magelock rifle and eyeing the enemy ship.

The *Star Flyer* was faster and kept circling it but hadn't yet closed to melee range. They'd only once been ordered to open fire, and the enemy had raised their barrier quickly enough that the company's magelock blasts had all ricocheted off.

"*I* wonder if we're going to be boarded, overwhelmed, and utterly destroyed," Dr. Fret said from where she crouched behind one of the bulwarks. As she often did in battle, she kneaded her medical kit with worried hands.

"Just hide behind me, and you'll be safe." Tinder leaned over and patted her on the shoulder. "I bet if you put a hand on my ass, the axe will extend its influence over you so magic can't hurt you."

"It prefers that I touch your *ass* for that?" Fret asked.

"No, but *I* prefer that." Tinder winked at her as fireballs slammed into the barrier not twenty feet away.

Prepare to drop the barrier and return fire, a telepathic command came from Captain Rivlen.

She stood on the forecastle with several of her mage officers at her side. Surprisingly, Tezi was up there too. Earlier, Rivlen had taken her aside. Maybe she wanted the other dragon-steel axe within reach. If they were overwhelmed by enemy fire, Tezi might get a butt grab too.

The *Star Flyer* maneuvered low over the jungle so that some of the taller trees blocked the enemy's view of them. Sasko crept closer to the railing with Ferroki and knelt down, bracing her rifle on it.

Lower the barrier, Rivlen ordered. *And fire!*

Sasko, Ferroki, and the rest of Thorn Company opened up with their firearms as the mage crew blasted magical attacks at the enemy ship. A wall of fire roared upward from Rivlen's fingers. As always, Sasko felt useless next to such power.

Several of their attacks struck the enemy ship before its crew halted its own assault so they could raise their barrier. Sasko had the satisfaction of watching her first shot get through and peg an officer in the shoulder, knocking him to the deck. Rivlen's flames charred the hull of the ship and started fires up and down its length. Then the enemy crew got their barrier up, and the mercenaries' magelock blasts bounced off.

Sasko sighed and stopped firing. With limited charges, there was no point in wasting them.

"Press the attack!" Rivlen yelled as she unleashed another wall of fire.

"I think our people are close to breaking through." Ferroki pointed her rifle toward one of the enemy mages as the man gripped his head and dropped to one knee. She tried firing, but however weak, their barrier was still up.

Her charge bounced off and into the jungle below. A green flash near the ground surprised Sasko, and she peered through the railing.

The shot had struck the ancient druid monument, a monument that now had a green glowing barrier around it.

Unlike the ones the mages created, the barrier was visible and provided enough illumination to highlight four rectangular slabs inside it. As with other monuments Sasko had seen, they were tipped inward to lean against each other. *Unlike* others she'd seen, there was a flat square slab resting at the apex with a concave copper indention in the top. Vines were draped over the slabs, and moss grew up the sides, as if the structure had been abandoned for ages. But the magical barrier suggested otherwise. Someone or something was still protecting that monument.

Sasko pointed at it. "That wasn't glowing like that before, right?"

Had Ferroki's shot woken it somehow? Or had someone been down there all along, watching the battle?

"Congratulations, Captain," Tinder said. "I think you rang the druids' doorbell."

"Our goal *was* to find them," Ferroki murmured, though she cast a worried look at the monument.

"Their barrier is down," a mage shouted. "Fire with everything you've got!"

Sasko wrenched her gaze back to the enemy ship. They could worry about the druids later.

Or so she thought. Sasko only got one shot off before a green beam of energy shot out of the top of the monument. It slammed into the bottom of the enemy ship, blowing a huge crater in the hull. The deck quaked, and mages toppled, some tumbling over the railing.

The beam shifted, blowing away wood and more. An explosion ripped through the night as fiery orange light burst from the vessel, so bright that Sasko had to close her eyes. That beam must have struck one of the magical power supplies.

Sasko thought Rivlen would take advantage and launch more fire at the enemy ship, but she shouted, "Raise our barrier!" Before the words were out of her mouth, she sprang down from the forecastle and sprinted for the navigation cabin. "Lieutenant, steer us away from that thing."

"Should we fire at it?" a mage asked, then gasped, as if he'd been struck.

Another beam had shot out of the monument, this one targeting the *Star Flyer*. Green light surrounded them from all sides as the beam tried to blast away the ship's defenses. The mages had raised their barrier in time, but more gasps escaped their lips, and their faces twisted as they struggled to conjure enough magic to *keep* it raised.

A crash sounded as the enemy ship—what *remained* of the enemy ship—struck the trees. Many of the surviving crew members leaped overboard. Others *fell* overboard, tumbling to their deaths.

The *Star Flyer* wheeled away from the monument. The beam kept striking them, bending to follow them as they pulled away.

"Can't keep the barrier up," a nearby mage panted.

Rivlen ran back out of the navigation cabin and to the railing so she could see the monument. Green light bathed her sweaty face. Only the flagging barrier kept the beam from striking her.

"Mages, mercenaries, come help me." Rivlen waved them forward. "We're going to attack it. All together. I want to blow those stones to pieces."

Sasko grimaced, but Ferroki waved for Thorn Company to

obey, and they joined Rivlen. A mage pitched to the deck, the heels of his hands pressed to his temples.

"Barrier down," Rivlen barked. She must have given the helmsman another order, for the ship abruptly dipped lower, branches scraping at the hull. The maneuver kept the beam from striking them. As it sailed over their heads and into the night sky, Rivlen shouted, "Attack now!"

She led the way, hurling not a wall of fire but an invisible blast of energy. The air wavered as it passed. Thorn Company and the mages joined her, opening fire not at enemies but at an ancient mass of stone. An ancient mass of stone that managed to keep a protective barrier around itself as it kept firing at them.

The monument was intelligent enough to retarget, and that beam crept lower, inching closer to the *Star Flyer*. Already hugging the trees, the ship couldn't descend farther without crashing.

"Fly us out of here," Rivlen yelled over her shoulder.

The helmsman was trying, but the branches came alive. They gripped the ship and kept it from escaping. The monument couldn't be doing that, could it? There had to be druids down there as well.

"Tezi, Tinder." Rivlen glanced at them. "We need your axes."

The beam crept closer to the ship. Tezi sprinted toward Rivlen, but Sasko doubted one of them could get down there in time to attack the monument and save the ship. The dragon steel might not even be enough against the ancient druid magic.

"It's been good serving with you, Captain," Sasko said, in case this was the end.

Ferroki nodded an acknowledgment. "I wish I'd gone with Sorath. I wish all of Thorn Company had gone."

"I don't think Vinjo's device could have camouflaged everyone." Sasko refrained from saying that she wished she'd kept the device for herself and that *she'd* been the one to disappear into the jungle. She couldn't truly imagine abandoning the company, but then again…

"Alas. The farm dogs suffer the farmer's wrath after the stray makes off with eggs from the coop."

Sasko shook her head bleakly.

The beam struck the ship. The hull blew open right below Sasko, and the deck exploded upward, hurling her into the air.

She flew from the ship and into the trees, not able to keep from screaming. Branches battered her as she plummeted downward. One struck her wrist with an agonizing smack, and her rifle flew out of her grip.

She twisted with a notion that she might be able to roll as she landed and keep from breaking every bone in her body, but the tumble had stolen her sense of up and down. She smashed into the ground on her back, pain erupting as her air whooshed out of her lungs.

A wrenching noise thundered through the jungle. The ship was crashing too.

Sasko lay on her back, with every nerve shooting pain through her body, amazed that she hadn't passed out. She almost wished she would, but a sense of duty told her she should stand up and try to make her way back to the ship and the company. Just because the *Star Flyer* had crashed didn't mean the battle was over. It certainly didn't mean the company was safe.

That idea was reinforced when movement stirred leaves off to the side. A faint groan escaped her lips as she turned her head, certain some wolf or panther was ambling out of the jungle to eat her.

But two men appeared instead, men with green hair, tattooed faces, and staffs. And Sasko had lost her weapon.

One of the druids pointed his staff at her. The last thought that came to mind was that she wished she had kissed Vinjo before he left, and that she was with him, wherever he was, instead of here in this hell. Then green light flashed, another jolt of pain blasted her, and she knew no more.

When Jak and Zethron climbed out onto the deck, Malek was waiting for them while Tonovan stood nearby, glowering down at the man on the paddleboat. He'd stopped waving his flag, and he wasn't looking up at them. A thump came from the door that he'd barred. He darted behind an upturned lifeboat mounted near the railing and started untying it. It was far too large for him to maneuver into the water by himself.

"I'm ready," Jak said.

Malek pulled out the two bronze skullcaps the natives had given them. They'd looked like metal on people's heads, but they were surprisingly malleable. He handed one to Jak and one to Zethron, who breathed a sigh of relief and tugged it on over his hair.

Jak didn't know if Zethron was superstitious and had adopted the natives' beliefs about their importance without having seen any evidence that they did anything, or if he had a better idea of how they protected people than he'd let on. But Malek, who had presumably been checking his thoughts, didn't indicate that he'd learned any great secrets.

Jak removed his father's hat and affixed the cap underneath it. Just in case.

"Those protect against magic or some such?" Tonovan asked. "And you're giving them to our most expendable people?"

Jak rolled his eyes, positive that if it were put to a vote, everyone on the ship would unanimously agree that Tonovan was the most expendable person.

"You and I ought to be able to protect ourselves from any threats that appear." Malek leaped over the railing, dropped thirty feet, and landed in a crouch on the deck of the paddleboat.

The man whirled toward him, his eyes wide, and whipped out a dagger. Jak sensed Malek raising a barrier around himself, but the man only crouched defensively. He didn't rush forward to attack. With his clothing ripped and bloody gashes visible, he barely looked like he could stand.

Malek twitched a finger, and Zethron levitated into the air, gasping a protest and flailing his arms. Tonovan snorted and sprang over the railing, falling past him, though he used his magic to slow his descent and soften his landing. He might be nearly as powerful as Malek, but he didn't have the zidarr enhancements that made his body stronger and more resilient than a normal human's.

The hatch clanged open behind Jak, and he turned with a frown. He'd shut it so nothing could get out of—or *into*—the ship.

Shikari's head appeared. He shouldn't have been able to climb a ladder, but he kept proving that he could. His talons scraped on the metal hatch frame as he pulled himself out and plopped down on the deck. Wings flexing and tail swishing, he trotted toward Jak.

"You can't come this time." Jak held up his hands. "Mother said it's too dangerous for you."

Shikari looked up at a cloud of insects buzzing nearby, each one as large as Jak's fist. This world didn't seem to enjoy any *normal*-sized bugs.

"If you're hungry, I'll bring you something later. This shouldn't take long." Jak pointed Shikari toward the hatch and tried to turn him around, but he'd gotten too large to easily pick up and carry. With hollow bones like an eagle's, he wasn't that heavy, but he was big and awkward and tended to slash things, whether intentionally or not, with his razor-sharp talons.

Before Jak could get him to go below, a burst of wind blew up under him, and he floated into the air. Malek.

"Wait," Jak blurted. "I'm trying to convince Shikari not to follow us."

"He can't fly yet, right?" Malek asked as he levitated Jak toward the deck of the paddleboat.

Judging by the man's bulging eyes, he wasn't used to seeing people float down from the sky.

"No," Jak said, "but—"

A splash sounded, and water spattered Jak in the back as he landed.

"He fell!" Zethron blurted.

"Damn it," Jak cursed, whirling.

Shikari came up, tail splashing and forearms churning as he navigated toward the paddleboat. But the deck was too high for him to reach.

"Malek, pull him out," Jak blurted.

"*Lord* Malek," Tonovan corrected with a growl. "Pull him out, *please*, Lord Malek, so I won't be robbed of the only being in the universe willing to warm my bed at night."

"Captain Rivlen said you were able to levitate people now." Malek looked at Jak and ignored Tonovan. "This can be a lesson."

Jak, worried about the leeches that had affixed themselves to Vinjo's legs, glared in exasperation at both of them. This wasn't the time for *lessons*, and panic made it hard for him to remember what he'd done the time he'd levitated Rivlen.

Shikari scratched at the hull, tail flailing in the water as he tried to find a way up. Terrified that he would drown, Jak almost dove over the side to rescue him physically. Just because Shikari had managed to swim once in the pool by the waterfall didn't mean he'd mastered it and would be fine in a river. What if predators down there yanked him under?

The image of a geyser popped into his mind. That was what he'd envisioned when he'd levitated Rivlen.

While he attempted to gather his power to apply the magic,

Shikari's head disappeared under the surface, as if he were diving for something—or as if something had grabbed his snout and pulled him down.

"Geyser, geyser, geyser," Jak whispered, struggling to concentrate. He envisioned a map, his favorite tool for summoning magic, and the geyser fields in the Misty Mountains back home. His power erupted under Shikari and thrust him high out of the water.

Though he was relieved it had worked, Jak feared it had worked too well, for Shikari shot up twenty feet. Jak willed the magic to lessen and directed his mental geyser to arc its stream and bring the young dragon down on the paddleboat deck.

Belatedly, as Shikari settled beside him, Jak realized he could have used his magic to levitate him back up to the mageship. But Shikari might not have stayed. Jak didn't have the ability to magically force a dragon through a hatchway and lock the hatch behind him.

Malek snorted softly. "I don't think that *fall* was as accidental as we believed."

Shikari had landed with a speckled brown fish in his mouth, the prize flapping its tail and trying to free itself. But he didn't let go. He strutted around the deck, showing off his catch, before settling down like a hound to chomp down his meal.

Jak rubbed a shaky hand down his face, relieved there weren't any leeches sticking to the dragon's blue scales. Maybe the fresh running water of the river was safer. Though the parasites that afflicted the dragons were microscopic, so he couldn't truly know if Shikari was safe anywhere here.

Zethron asked a question in the local language.

The man had recovered from his shock of people floating down to the deck, but he kept glancing at Shikari and pointing up at the mageship, his meaning clear. He thought they should leave and leave now.

Zethron nodded and turned to Malek to translate, but a wrenching noise came from the nearby door. The bar the man had used to block it snapped. Hinges creaked as the door was forced open.

Two shirtless men with red streaks on their chests ran out with axes raised. The weapons were for cutting wood, not going into battle, but the men bellowed war cries and sprinted at Malek and Tonovan.

Even though he wasn't the target, Jak sprang to Shikari's side and raised a barrier around them. Zethron dove behind the lifeboat with the native. Malek and Tonovan faced the attackers, Malek's face as calm as always and Tonovan's face twisted with a bored sneer.

Neither of the axemen wore skullcaps. Their short hair stuck out in matted clumps, the red streaks on their chests looked like blood they'd applied with their fingers, and their eyes had a savage craziness to them that chilled Jak.

A snap sounded, and one man jerked to a halt as his neck twisted impossibly to one side. He pitched over backward, falling dead to the deck.

Tonovan yawned. "They're not mages and have nothing to protect them."

Jak shivered. Tonovan had broken the man's neck with a thought.

The second attacker reached Malek's barrier, smacked into it face-first, and roared in rage. He swung the axe, but the blade bounced off as if he were striking a metal wall.

"Are you saving that one for later?" Tonovan quirked an eyebrow.

"Reading his thoughts," Malek said quietly. "They're a jumbled mess. All I'm getting is intense hatred and aggression."

Jak shivered again, thinking of their discussion about the dragons and how the parasites might have been what affected their minds. As the man roared and swung again and again at Malek's barrier, determined to break through and slay him, Jak shook his head slowly. The men couldn't be affected by the same parasite that had changed the dragons, could they?

Mother had surmised that it could only take dragons as hosts. No, she'd surmised that it *preferred* dragons. She hadn't believed that human and dragon physiology were similar enough that they could both appeal to such an organism, but she'd been guessing. She couldn't truly know. This was a different world from theirs, possibly with different rules, and the parasites had either been magical or had possessed access to magic, for they had flown over on twinkling motes to try to infest Shikari.

Jak glanced down at his charge, double-checking to make sure his barrier protected both of them. But would a magical barrier be enough to keep a microscopic organism from getting through?

"Oh, just end it, already." Tonovan lifted a hand to the side of his head. "That screaming is obnoxious. You can't possibly be getting anything from that mind."

"A few flashes," Malek said, "but he's not very coherent."

"Can we subdue him and take him up to the ship?" Jak questioned the words as soon as they came out—if the man was afflicted with a parasite, the last thing they wanted was for him to spread it among everyone on board—but his mother wouldn't want helpless humans murdered. *He* didn't want that either. Maybe if they knocked the man unconscious, they could examine his blood and learn—

Bone snapped, and the man's swings halted.

"No," Tonovan said firmly as the dead man pitched backward, the axe clattering to the deck as it fell from his fingers. "No crazy people allowed on the ship." He gave Jak a flat look. "You're lucky we allow you and your fisher-dragon aboard."

Malek sighed, but if he was irritated with Tonovan, he didn't show it beyond a quick cool glance. He'd probably still been trying to dig useful nuggets of information out of the man's mind.

"Uhm," Zethron said from where he crouched behind the lifeboat. "The one we came to help fainted. I think." He looked warily at Tonovan.

"I didn't touch him," Tonovan said. "That one's desperate, not crazy. I wanted to ask him about dragon-steel weapons."

"He might have passed out from blood loss." Malek levitated the unconscious man up to the deck of the mageship. "I'm telling Professor Freedar that he's up there. She can examine him and determine if it's safe to let him ride with us."

"He's probably full of mange and lice," Tonovan muttered.

If only they were worried about such benign pests.

A clank came from within the interior of the paddleboat. The door remained open. Were more injured people inside? Or were more *crazy people* inside?

"Are we exploring?" Jak asked uncertainly.

He wasn't surprised when Malek strode to one of the cases with the glass lids to look inside, since it was possible the natives could have been collecting the very Jitaruvak the team sought, but Tonovan walked around the deck, poking into chests and barrels like a looter.

"Just enough to see if there's anything valuable here." Tonovan strode through the doorway.

Jak couldn't tell how many people were inside, but the interior soon lit with flame as Tonovan cast a fireball. A man's terrified scream sounded before being cut off.

"Wait!" Jak called, torn between running in to try to stop Tonovan and focusing on keeping his barrier up. He didn't want to risk removing his protection from Shikari, and he still struggled to do two things at once. "There could be more innocent people in there."

"There could be more innocent people, *General*," Tonovan's

cool voice floated out as the paddleboat interior caught fire and flames danced around him. Feet thundered as people ran away from him. "And I'm only killing the crazy ones."

"It could be possible to cure them."

"Malek, shut up your idiot boy. We're not a traveling medical ship doing good deeds for the poor."

Jak clenched his jaw. He walked slowly toward the door, carefully moving the barrier along with him and waving for Shikari to stay at his side. What he could do to stop Tonovan, he didn't know, but he couldn't stand aside while the general murdered people.

I told him to stop, Malek spoke into his mind. *But it sounds like most of the people in there are already dead.*

A creak came from the side as Malek opened one of the cases. Jak glimpsed green fronds inside.

A splash came from the water, and Jak jumped. He glanced over but wasn't quick enough to see more than a ripple. A *large* ripple.

Using his senses, he tried to detect magical creatures under the surface, but whatever lived in the river didn't have an aura that he could detect.

"Probably just a fish," he whispered.

Shikari's head was cocked as he also peered toward the water. He'd already chomped down the fish he'd caught.

"Guess this means your tastes have broadened from bugs," Jak said as he joined Malek at the case.

"Bugs aren't that appealing." Malek pulled out several plants that someone had extracted from the forest and potted. The dirt was still loose, so it had been done recently. They were all different, one dark green, one gray-green, and one green with purple stems, but they all had familiar fern-like fronds.

"Is one the Jitaruvak?"

"Your mother will know." Malek lifted his arms, and the pots floated up to the mageship.

"That's a quirky collection of items you're leaving on the deck for her."

"She likes quirky." Malek smiled faintly, but it diminished at the sound of wood snapping inside. The fire Tonovan had started was spreading. "We'll check for more survivors."

Jak nodded, relieved, though he feared Tonovan had already killed everyone he'd found, whether they'd attacked him or not.

Thumps and clanks floated out of the interior. That was probably Tonovan searching every cabinet, trunk, and drawer for dragon-steel weapons, as if an entire collection of them would be squirreled away on a fishing boat.

Jak shook his head. Even on Vran, where they had been much more commonplace, they'd always been on someone's person. One didn't leave such powerful weapons jammed in a dresser drawer.

An angry buzz sounded overhead as Jak and Malek neared the doorway. A cloud of insects hovered above the paddleboat. Malek eyed them but continued inside. His barrier was up, and Jak was also keeping his up. Nothing would be able to sting, bite, or otherwise assail them.

Zethron, who was sticking with them, scooted as close as he could before bouncing off Jak's barrier.

Are you protecting Zethron? Jak asked silently, not sure if he could extend his barrier to include someone else. Walking and protecting Shikari was already taxing his abilities.

Yes, Malek replied.

Inside, flames climbed up the curtains and crackled from beams and walls that Tonovan had assaulted with his incendiary magic. The fire provided enough light to see all the upturned chairs and tables in what had been the dining hall. Several bodies were strewn among the mess, and Jak's stomach churned at the terror frozen in the eyes of the dead.

Unlike the men who'd attacked them, the dead wore their

skullcaps. Jak reached up to make sure his was still affixed. Most of the men had been killed by blades—maybe those axes—with deep cuts and gashes visible. The blood on the deck underneath them was still wet.

A man without a skullcap lay in Malek's path, his charred body still twitching. That had to be the one Tonovan had taken down.

Malek looked into more cases with glass lids. Different plants, these with leaves instead of fronds, were preserved inside. A chest with an opaque lid held trays of mushrooms.

"Your mother will lament that she didn't join us down here," Malek murmured.

"If you bring her samples of everything, she'll probably kiss you."

Malek's eyebrows rose. "You think so?"

Jak blinked. He'd been joking and hadn't expected genuine hope to appear in Malek's eyes.

Malek's expression quickly grew masked again. Maybe Jak had misread it.

"She'd at least kiss the samples," Jak offered.

Pots clanged in an adjacent kitchen.

Malek looked at the closed door that led to it. "That's not Tonovan. He went that way." He pointed toward a corridor on the opposite end of the dining hall.

"I'll wait here." Zethron hadn't moved far from the door, and, judging by the way he set his feet, he didn't plan to. He reached up and rubbed his skullcap, like he was trying to scratch an itch through it. "Nothing good will come of exploring this place further. We should go."

"What we came to this world looking for may be here." Malek paused before opening the door to the kitchen. "I won't be able to protect you from another room."

"I'll risk it," Zethron said. "If you need me to translate, bring the person here."

Malek opened the door and walked into the kitchen. Though Tonovan might not fear any threats here, Malek was warier and had his main-gauche in hand.

Jak stayed in the dining hall and stepped closer to Zethron, so he could practice extending his barrier around him, but Shikari was moving around and snuffling things. That made it more difficult to keep him within his sphere of influence, so Jak had to trail after him. He didn't want Zethron to be hurt, but he felt even more responsible for keeping Shikari safe. Shikari was his charge and might be the only dragon alive in the universe right now who hadn't been turned evil by that parasite. Jak had to keep him that way.

A clatter came from the kitchen.

"Everything all right?" Jak called.

"Yes," came Malek's dry reply.

A moment later, a furry animal resembling a giant badger charged out the door with a rat in its mouth. It raced toward the exit, tiny claws scraping on the wood deck, but it saw Zethron and veered toward the corridor.

Shikari squealed and crouched, as if he might pounce on it.

"Don't attack anything as big as you are," Jak warned.

Shikari rustled his wings and swished his tail, but he didn't give chase when the animal ran past and down the corridor. Jak hoped it found Tonovan and bit him in the butt.

"The people who were murdered all have skullcaps on." Zethron was looking at the bodies and had barely noticed the animal racing through the hall. He rubbed his head through the cap again. "The crazy ones didn't."

Jak's own scalp itched in sympathy. The skullcaps were hot, fit too tightly, and he could feel a headache coming on.

The kitchen door swung open, and Malek walked out with

another potted plant, its fronds larger than the others and more gray than green. Little purple berries hung in clumps among them.

"Fancy," Jak said. "Definitely worth a kiss."

"From you or your mother?" Malek asked.

"Uh, her. Plants don't get me that excited."

"Just maps?" Malek produced a scroll and flicked his wrist to open it, revealing a navigation chart of the river.

"Oh, yes." Jak stepped forward, his fingers twitching, but paused.

He didn't truly have to kiss Malek for it, did he?

"That's not necessary, no." Malek lowered his barrier long enough to give the map to Jak. "It was in the navigation cabin past the kitchen. It's of this river all the way up into the mountains. We can compare it to the other map and find out if the chief gave us something genuine or not."

Before Jak could take a look, a buzzing came from outside the door. The same insects that had hovered overhead earlier?

No. He frowned as he sensed magic for the first time.

"Stay here." Malek must have sensed it as well. He set the pot down and strode for the door.

But Shikari charged for it ahead of him, as if that magic was calling him like a cook ringing the dinner bell.

"No," Jak blurted, funneling more energy into his barrier, both to protect Shikari and to keep him from running outside.

Shikari ran right through the barrier, bursting it. The whiplash snapped at Jak's mind like a rubber band between the eyes, and he stumbled back, ramming against the case holding the mushrooms.

Malek charged for the open hatch, but he was a few steps behind Shikari. The dragon disappeared from Jak's view.

"Stop him!" he yelled as he recovered and ran after them.

But Malek sprang back inside, raising his hands, and Jak halted abruptly.

Glowing green bugs zipped into the dining hall, an entire swarm of them. They were smaller than the fist-sized insects Jak had seen earlier, but they had stingers more than an inch long and made wasps look like the friendly, cuddly bugs of the insect world.

Malek's barrier was up, but the bugs pierced it as easily as Shikari had slipped through Jak's.

That startled Malek, but he reacted instantly, creating a curtain of fire all around him. Heat roiled away from it, as if he'd opened a furnace door.

Zethron yelped and sprang back. Even Jak stumbled away as the heat blasted his face. He managed to raise his barrier again, but he didn't know if there was a point. Not if the bugs could cut through it.

Tiny charred husks of insects fell to the deck all around Malek, but more of the glowing green bugs flew through the doorway. They avoided his flames and veered toward Zethron and Jak.

Jak groaned, wishing he'd learned to create fire when Rivlen had tried to teach him. He'd been too horrified at the idea of incinerating people to get past his mental blocks. He *could* create wind, so he released his barrier and blew the flying bugs away from him.

Fear gave him more power, and his blasts struck them hard enough to knock them into a wall. Some stuck, their stingers embedded in the wood, and others bounced off, undamaged.

They recovered and flew at Zethron. With no magic of his own, he could only swat at the air, batting at insects with his arms.

Malek extended his flames, incinerating the bugs attacking him. Zethron cried out in alarm at the closeness of the fire and dropped to the deck and rolled away.

"Get up," Malek barked, grabbing him. "We're going back to our ship."

Jak sensed even more of the magical bugs outside. Terrified for Shikari, he ran around Malek and toward the door. But he skidded to a halt as a giant version of the bugs flew in, its stinger twice as long as the others. It had to be the leader or queen.

Malek pushed Zethron toward the door as he yelled, "We're leaving, Tonovan!"

He was looking toward the corridor, not the giant bug.

"Look out!" Jak cried as it flew straight toward Zethron.

Malek spun Zethron away from it, putting his back to the giant bug. It sailed for his neck. No, it was angling its stinger toward the back of his *head*.

Too discombobulated to call upon his magic, Jak smacked it with the map.

As he made contact, the giant bug burst into flame. Malek's doing. Jak yelped and yanked the map back, afraid it would catch fire.

Malek's aim, however, had been pinpoint, and the map wasn't damaged. More of the bugs swept toward him. *Many* more. They'd been enraged by him killing the queen.

Malek gripped Jak and propelled him outside as he dragged Zethron with him, all the while incinerating hundreds of bugs. Unfortunately, there were hundreds more. Maybe *thousands*.

One pelted Jak in the back of the head, and with a sickening lurch of realization, he knew exactly what the skullcaps were for. And he prayed to Shylezar that his had saved him.

But Malek didn't have one. Neither did Shikari. He was out in the open on the deck and had been for many long seconds.

Jak squeezed past Malek to lunge for Shikari. Hundreds of insects were diving at the young dragon, their stingers leading.

Jak swore and for the first time, genuinely and with all of his heart, he wanted to make fire. He envisioned a roaring inferno sweeping down the forested slopes of the map in his mind and springing up to incinerate all of the bugs around Shikari. His flames were clumsy compared to Malek's pinpoint strikes, but they leaped to life around the dragon, catching many of the insects.

Belatedly, Jak noticed that the bugs and their stingers had been bouncing off Shikari's scales. They weren't getting through, and they didn't seem to be bothering him at all. Even more, he was springing about, snapping his jaws and catching them. He chomped into them, biting off the stingers and leaving them scattered on the deck around him as he devoured their bodies.

Between Jak and Malek—and the ravenous Shikari—they thinned out the swarm. Soon, hundreds and hundreds of blackened husks of insects lay all over the deck. Their remaining attackers gave up and flew off into the forest.

Malek made a disgusted noise. "I'd rather fight a dragon than those things."

"No kidding." Jak rubbed the back of his head.

Fortunately, the skullcap remained firmly in place. He'd felt no fewer than five insects hit him during the skirmish and resolved to have his mother examine his head later. He didn't *think* any of those stingers had pierced the cap, but he wanted to be sure.

Shikari rolled onto his back with his legs in the air and made contented lip-smacking sounds.

"You're a *lot* of work to raise," Jak told him.

The tail flapped, and Shikari's head lolled farther back, jaw dangling slack and fangs on display.

"Mother dragons must be very patient," Malek said.

Tonovan walked out of the mess hall carrying a bag of who knew what that he'd pilfered from inside. Gewgaws for King Uthari, no doubt.

"What'd I miss?" he asked.

Jak would have rolled his eyes, but when Malek turned to look at Tonovan, Jak noticed blood trickling down the back of his neck from his hairline. One of the insects had stung him.

17

THE GREEN LIGHT WASHING OVER THE MANGLED DECK OF THE crashed ship went out. Tezi shoved aside a piece of the railing—or was that a structural *beam*?—that had fallen on her. Warm blood ran from a cut above her forehead, trickling down through her brows and into her eyes. She dashed it away with her sleeve and gripped the haft of her axe, glad she hadn't let the weapon fall free. Who knew where it would have ended up? Who knew where *she* had ended up?

She gingerly touched a knot swelling on the side of her head. The last thing she remembered was Rivlen yelling at her and Tinder to bring their axes to help, then that beam of energy hitting the ship and something cracking her in the head. She hadn't even felt the crash.

Mages and mercenaries groaned nearby, some caught in wreckage on the deck like Tezi, others having tumbled through the broken railing to the jungle floor. Tezi pushed herself to her feet, wobbling and groping for balance on the slanted deck.

Orange light came from a fire in the distance—the other crashed ship. The druid monument was just visible through the trees, no longer emitting beams or a green barrier. Once again, it appeared dormant in the jungle.

Tezi glimpsed movement between the ship and the monument, someone darting between the trees. Whoever it was disappeared into the shadows before she got a good look.

"Thorn Company," came a shaky call from across the deck—Captain Ferroki. "Form up."

As Tezi headed in that direction, moving wreckage off her fellow mercenaries groaning on the deck, green light blazed once more. Another green beam shot out of the top of the monument. Tezi hefted her axe, hoping it would protect her if the beam struck the ship again.

But it lanced through the trees toward the night sky.

"Damn it." Captain Rivlen had been thrown from the ship and was climbing over one of the intact railings, but she paused to glare at the monument. "It's firing at the *Moon Spear.* They're trying to fly close to help." She lowered her voice to a mutter that Tezi almost missed. "Or so Ular says."

"Where's Lieutenant Sasko?" Ferroki asked from the spot where the mercenaries were assembling in a ragged formation. "And Corporal Basher. Words?"

"I'm here, Captain," Basher said, climbing over the railing to get back aboard, just as Rivlen had. She hissed, gripping her hip as she limped toward the unit.

Tezi headed over to join them, but Rivlen strode up, stopping her with an upraised hand. "I need your help." She waved at the axe rather than Tezi, then pointed at Sergeant Tinder in the back of the formation. "And you too. We're going to knock out that beam before it can blow up any more ships." Rivlen cast a baleful glare toward the monument. "Or any more of *us.*"

Did that mean some of her crew had been killed? Tezi hoped all of Thorn Company had made it. Even as Ferroki counted heads and formed up the unit, she kept glancing into the jungle and looking for missing people.

Tezi thought of the movement she'd glimpsed out there. It might have been Lieutenant Sasko or one of the other mercenaries, but it also could have been druids.

Rivlen snapped her fingers. "Pay attention. We're taking out that monument, and then you two are on a druid-hunting team with me. I sense them out there, and we're going to deal with them."

Grimacing, Tinder hobbled over, her uniform top in tatters. She wasn't in much better shape than Corporal Basher.

"I'm ready, ma'am," Tezi said. "Maybe Sergeant Tinder can stay."

Rivlen's baleful glare turned to Tinder, even though she hadn't been the one to speak. "Her axe is coming. It's up to her if she wants to join it."

"I'll come," Tinder said. "The chance to fling myself in front of magical attacks always fills me with glee."

"I'll bet." Rivlen barked orders for her lieutenant and Captain Ferroki to find everyone, arrange healing for the injured, and get the ship repaired as soon as possible.

Fireballs streaked through the trees toward the druid monument, but its barrier popped up again, and the attacks deflected into the jungle. One soared alarmingly close to the *Star Flyer*. Nearby trees burst into flames.

"That won't work!" Rivlen yelled, then lowered her voice. "Those idiots will hit *us* while we're taking care of the problem. I better send him to help Captain Gyarth. Right now, he's just a target for that monument." She held up a finger while she presumably relayed the message telepathically to the captain of the other ship.

Tezi exchanged a worried look with Tinder. She didn't know if it would be more dangerous to go with Rivlen or stay behind. Not that they had a choice.

"Come." Rivlen sprang over the railing, falling ten feet, then turning her landing into a roll.

Tinder and Tezi, bodies battered after the crash, climbed more gingerly to the ground. They joined Rivlen and six other mages who'd floated themselves down with their power.

"I tried to levitate you down before I remembered magic wouldn't work on you," Rivlen told Tinder and Tezi.

"Darn," Tinder said. "I love it when mages send me flying."

Rivlen squinted at her but was too busy to remark on her irreverence. She waved for everyone to follow as she strode toward the monument.

The fireballs had halted, but the green beam continued to shoot into the night. Tezi couldn't see its target through the trees but imagined a mageship with a barrier up around it. If the beam was as powerful as it had been when it struck the *Star Flyer,* the crew wouldn't be able to keep that barrier up for long.

"At least Ular is getting some of what he deserves," Rivlen growled.

She reached the monument first, the green light illuminating the sweaty faces of her and all the mages. Tezi and Tinder were the only mercenaries Rivlen had brought along.

As she stared at the magical beam, its power tangible even to her, Tezi wished she'd said goodbye to Ferroki and given her a hug. Just in case.

"Do we all attack together, ma'am?" one of the mages asked.

"No." Rivlen pointed at Tezi. "Climb up to the top and bash it with that axe."

"Bash *it,* ma'am?" Tezi didn't know what *it* was. The beam? Would that do anything?

"Whatever is emitting that beam. There's a concave metal plate up there. Hit that." Rivlen twitched a finger, then glowered.

"Give me your axe, and I'll levitate you to the top, then throw it up."

Tezi eyed the glowing barrier around the monument and the powerful beam that had crashed the ship and was on the verge of crashing another one. She didn't want to get anywhere near the druid magic without her anti-magic axe. Even *with* the axe, she could think of other places she wanted to be.

"We don't have all night." Rivlen held out her hand for the weapon.

"I'll try to climb, ma'am." Tezi tucked the axe into the sling on her back.

Rivlen sighed. "Just get up there as quickly as possible."

The vines hanging from the stone slabs helped with the climb, as did the tilt that kept them from standing vertical, but Tezi progressed slowly up the side. The mages below sighed and shifted their feet. A distant shout of desperation floated to them from the other ship.

Tezi winced and tried to climb faster. It didn't help that the slabs tingled with power that she felt even through the axe's protection.

You're doing fine, Rivlen spoke into her mind. *I apologize for being short with you. I don't want to lose that other ship. Uthari put me in command of the fleet, and I need to excel. At the least, I can't fail miserably.*

I understand, ma'am.

Tezi pulled herself onto the top of a square slab perched on the tall rectangular stones. As Rivlen had said, the beam came out of a hole in a concave copper indention. Whatever magic or mechanism powered it was hidden within the stone.

"Smash it, Tezi," Rivlen called up, her voice ringing with power. "The *Moon Spear* is trying to fly away, but that beam has a long range. The ship doesn't have much time."

If Tezi hadn't had her axe, the magic in those words might have compelled her to act immediately. Maybe that would have been for the best. As it was, she hesitated, worried the beam would react by turning to target *her*. Would the axe be enough to protect her against such raw power?

Swallowing, Tezi lifted the haft, bracing herself to bring the blade down on that hole. Even with the magic of the dragon steel, striking a metal plate in a stone slab would be jarring.

Another beam shot out, this one angling off nearly horizontally. Tezi dodged to the side, but not before it brushed her. She expected a blast of pain—or to die instantly—but her axe brightened with a blue glow and its magic protected her.

"Thank Thanok," she whispered.

"Careful up there, Tezi," Rivlen called. "And stop that beam. It's hitting the *Star Flyer* again!"

She was right. The beam sliced through trees to pour its power into a fresh barrier that the weary mages had erected around the downed *Star Flyer*. Sweat streamed from their reddened faces, their tortured expressions making it clear they wouldn't be able to defend against it for long.

Afraid it would blow up Thorn Company right along with the rest of the ship, Tezi smashed the axe down onto the hole. The magical blade bit into metal and stone, hurling broken pieces everywhere, but the beam kept shooting out. This close, it nearly blinded Tezi with its brilliance.

She struck another blow, smashing the big axe down again and again. With a great snapping of stone, the slab under her feet split. Finally, the beam halted. But the half of the slab Tezi stood on tilted and slid off the top of the monument.

Tezi cried out as she pitched backward. She threw the axe free so she wouldn't land on the head and impale herself.

Rivlen's magic caught her before she hit the ground. It held her in the air as the broken slab hammered down scant feet away, hurling dust and shards of stone into the air. Tezi covered her face for protection as she hung above the ground. Finally, the dust settled, and Rivlen lowered her down beside her axe. Tezi plucked it up again, afraid the monument might have some magic left and strike out at her in vengeance.

"Good work." Rivlen thumped her on the shoulder.

Tezi coughed and wiped rock dust out of her eyes. "Thanks."

All she'd done was bash a stone into pieces, but it was better to be appreciated than not.

"I don't sense any tunnels or a hideout of any kind under us, ma'am," one of the mages said, "but earlier, I sensed druids out here."

"So did I. They must have a warren of tunnels down there, magically insulated so we can't sense them." Rivlen shifted her hand to grip the mage's shoulder. "You're our earth mover. Find the most likely spot and tear into it. I'll add my power to yours. We all will." She tilted her head toward the other mages.

"Yes, ma'am."

Her power must have flowed into the man, because he gasped and arched his back. Not in pain, Tezi thought. He smiled, appearing energized and even pleased. He spread a hand toward the ground beside the monument.

Tinder couldn't have had much more of an idea what was going on than Tezi, but she took several large steps backward to get out of their way. Tezi scooted toward a tree and rested a hand on it for support while keeping a tight grip on her axe, well aware that it had saved her life. Again.

The ground rumbled under their feet. Leaves rained down on Tezi. Just as she was rethinking the spot she'd chosen, a tremendous sinkhole opened up near the monument, right where the mage was pointing. Clatters sounded as the ancient stones shifted and bumped together. Tezi expected them to topple, but it was a tree that pitched over, roots tearing free from the ground.

"Found a tunnel," the mage blurted as his sinkhole expanded. "And made an entrance."

"Good job. Let's capture some druids." Rivlen jogged toward the sinkhole but must have sensed an enemy off to the side.

She whirled, launching a wall of fire toward the trees. The orange light drove back shadows, and Tezi caught movement to her side. She spun in time to see a green blob of energy hurtling toward her.

"Look out," Tezi barked as she ducked behind a tree, holding the axe out like a shield.

The blob shifted its trajectory to follow her around the tree and washed over her, green light flashing, but once again, the axe kept her from being hurt.

Before she could feel relief, four druids ran out of the jungle. Three of them sent magical attacks toward the mages, but one gripped a knife, his eyes locked onto Tezi and her axe as he sprinted toward her.

She resisted the urge to run, instead stepping away from the tree while keeping it at her back. She lowered into a fighting crouch to face her enemy. He kept glancing at the axe, even as he sprang over a log to land right in front of her. He was either wary of it, or he wanted it as a prize.

Tezi slashed toward his stomach to drive him back. He sucked in his belly to avoid the blade, then stabbed toward her hand. Someone trying to kill her should have gone for her gut or her throat, but maybe he only wanted the weapon.

Tezi wasn't giving it up, not to him, not to anyone.

She growled and slashed at the attacking blade, meeting it in the air. Her axe sliced through the dagger, parting its blade from its hilt. The druid stumbled back, throwing a magical attack to buy time as he drew another weapon. But the attack did nothing to her, and Tezi lunged in, slicing into his forearm.

Her attacker screamed and stumbled, falling backward. A fireball blasted past Tezi, engulfing the druid, and the scream grew even louder before it cut off abruptly, the smell of charred meat turning her stomach.

She glanced back to catch Rivlen looking at her before she had to turn to defend against an attack from another opponent.

A grunt came from behind Tezi. Another druid was squaring off with Tinder, slashing and stabbing with a lesser-dragon-steel sword. The magical weapon met her axe with decisive clangs instead of breaking in his grip. Between parries, Tinder managed to slip a hand into her ammo pouch and throw an explosive at his feet.

It roared, hurling dirt and smoke into the air, but the druid's magic protected him. Barely fazed, he lunged in, feinting, then stabbing. Tinder deflected the attacks with her axe and countered, but he recovered quickly, sweeping his sword up to block her in time. Another clang rang out over the sounds of other nearby skirmishes.

Tinder had more experience than Tezi and matched the druid's skill with blades, but the ground was uneven and treacherous. Her heel caught, and she pitched back, the axe tumbling from her fingers.

The druid's eyes widened in triumph, and he raised his hand to blast her with a magical attack.

Tezi shouted and ran for him. He spun, reflexively hurling his attack at her. But she still had her axe, and it whooshed past without stopping her. She swung the weapon at him, and this time, he was the one to stumble as he tried to spring away. Her blade cut into his side with a meaty thud.

One of the mages appeared behind him and slammed a glowing hammer onto the top of his head. The druid had been in the middle of a scream, but it cut off as his eyes rolled back in his head. Tezi yanked her axe free as he toppled.

"Not bad, kid," the mage told her.

Kid? She'd fought two druids, destroyed an ancient monument, and had dried blood all over the side of her face, and people were still calling her *kid*?

Rivlen stepped up to her side and put a hand on her shoulder. "This is Rookie Tezi, not kid."

She nodded at Tezi, as if she'd read her mind, though she shouldn't have been able to through the protection of the axe. Maybe Tezi's indignation had been stamped on her face.

"And you should talk to your superiors about getting a promotion," Rivlen told Tezi, as if it were up to her. "Aren't you a corporal by now?"

"I'm not even officially in the company." Tezi bent to grab Tinder's axe, hand it to her, and help her to her feet.

"You are if I have anything to say about it," Tinder said.

"Do you?" Tezi asked curiously.

"Well, no. But I can show you how to kiss the captain's ass."

"A useful skill."

"I've found it to be so."

"There are more druids out here, ma'am," a mage reported to Rivlen, squinting into the trees. It was starting to get light out, but there were still a lot of deep shadows to hide in. "Shall we try to get them?"

Rivlen followed his gaze, then looked toward the tunnel. "I want to find their leaders, and I'm betting they're down there somewhere."

"Yes, ma'am."

"Mind if I stay with the ship, Captain?" Tinder pointed her axe toward the *Star Flyer*. "To help the company in case the druids you're leaving behind attack?"

Tezi thought Rivlen would object, since she'd made it clear she wanted both dragon-steel axes with her, but she looked at the ship and nodded. The mage crew and mercenaries were both out in the jungle now, looking for people they'd lost in the crash. They would be vulnerable to attacks.

"Go ahead," Rivlen said. "Tezi will come with the rest of us. We're heading into the tunnel to do as King Uthari wants. Get rid of the druid opposition, one way or another."

Tezi wished she could stay behind as well. She didn't want to hunt druids. Even though their people had attacked first, back when the *Star Flyer* had first been sailing inland from the coast, Tezi couldn't help but think that she and the company were doing the wrong thing by assisting mages against the natives. She hadn't forgotten that a druid—the healer Gelira—had saved her life when she'd jumped to what she'd believed would be her death. If not for her, Tezi wouldn't be alive today. She wouldn't have found the battle-axe, and she wouldn't now have the power to make a difference.

But what kind of difference was she making? She was helping the mages that she hated.

As far as she knew, the druids were doing what they felt they had to do to defend their homeland and protect their people. And the mages... All they were trying to do was find snazzy resources on other worlds to empower their already overpowered people.

Tezi wished she'd talked to Captain Ferroki more on the flight. Maybe she could have assuaged Tezi's doubts. Or maybe Ferroki had doubts of her own.

"Gift for you, Professor," Vinjo said as he and Prolix levitated the man who'd been on the paddleboat into the kitchen.

"Uh." Jadora didn't know if it was an appropriate place for the sick and injured, but Vinjo hadn't built an infirmary into the ship, and she *had* been using it as a laboratory. "Maybe one of the bunks would be better."

The poor man drooped unconscious in the air between them, his face pale, his clothing torn, deep slashes visible. He'd lost a lot of blood and was still dribbling it onto the deck.

"Malek doesn't have a roommate," Vinjo said cheerfully. "Maybe he'd like to share."

Prolix gave him a cool look, as if to suggest zidarr were above having roommates.

"Are there any cots? Maybe I can treat him in here." Jadora ducked into her cabin to pull out the first-aid kit she'd brought along.

It wasn't as comprehensive as Fret's medical kit, and she lamented that Malek hadn't requested the Thorn Company doctor for this mission. Given the way their adventures went, this wouldn't be the first person who needed medical treatment.

Vinjo brought two collapsible cots into the kitchen, flourishing them with a smile. He pressed a button on the end of each one, and they sprang from a bundle of sticks and canvas into a fully formed bed. Jadora didn't know if they were magical, but his proud smile suggested he'd built them.

Prolix and Vinjo helped her spread her patient on one cot, and she grabbed her canteen of water so she could wash off who knew what infectious grime he'd picked up down there. She removed his shirt to examine his wounds and wondered if she should throw away the tattered fabric instead of saving it, but she didn't know if anyone had spare clothing to share.

As she started washing the numerous wounds—they had been caused by blades, not animal claws or fangs—he twitched and jerked awake. His eyes grew round with fear and horror.

"It's all right." Jadora showed him the rag she was using and the bandages she would apply. "My name is Jadora. I'm going to treat your wounds."

He wouldn't be able to understand her words, but hopefully, her soothing tone would put him at ease.

If anything, he grew more agitated. He sat up, tugged off his skullcap, and grabbed the back of his head with both hands.

"Headache?" she guessed. "I have some herbs that are strong analgesics. Give me a moment."

As she dug into her first-aid kit, he moved his hands around, shoving his fingers through his hair and probing his scalp all over. Maybe a headache wasn't his problem.

After her discussions with the others on parasites, Jadora couldn't help but worry something like that had him concerned.

"An insect like ticks?" she guessed. "Does your world have ticks?"

Or unicellular flagellate eukaryotes? Jadora grimaced and told herself he wouldn't be checking his scalp for microscopic organisms. It had to be something else.

His face contorted with distress. He pointed at her, then turned the back of his head toward her, and pointed at it.

"You want me to check? All right."

Though she didn't know what she was looking for, she did her best to investigate his scalp for cuts or something like ticks. His hair was short but thick, and it took a few minutes before she was convinced that nothing had disturbed his scalp.

"You're fine." Jadora patted his shoulder. "At least your head is. The rest of you is a mess." She pointed at a long gash on his torso that was weeping blood and gestured for him to lie down.

He hesitated, then nodded and complied, emitting a deep shuddering breath as he finally relaxed an iota.

"When our translator returns," Jadora said as she cleaned his wounds, "I hope you'll be able to tell me what happened."

A knock came from the open hatch, and Lieutenant Harintha poked her head into the kitchen. "You might have some more patients coming."

Fear for Jak and Malek punched Jadora in the stomach. "What happened?"

"Some people attacked them on the ship, which didn't seem like anything for powerful mages to worry about. I didn't even get out of my seat." Harintha tilted her thumb toward the navigation cabin. "They handled it and went inside. But then huge swarms of big glowing insects swept onto the boat like green clouds. Malek incinerated tons of them. Everyone was still standing in the end, but it looked like their barriers were down for some reason. They might have gotten bitten or stung. Whatever the bugs here do."

Jadora looked from the lieutenant to her patient's head, the fear in her belly tightening into a ball and growing stronger.

"I didn't know how to help. I'm not that good at fire, especially not at a distance." Harintha shrugged. "It's why I'm a navigation officer, not a combat mage. But they were just battling bugs, not anything really dangerous."

Jadora couldn't croak out a word of agreement.

"Oh, and Lord Malek sent these up for you." Harintha ducked back into the corridor, picked up something, and returned to the hatchway. She set what looked like a potted fern down inside, then grabbed a few more plants in pots.

Was one of them the Jitaruvak? Jadora would check them later, but she couldn't muster any excitement for the finds. She was too worried.

Harintha tilted her head, her eyes growing unfocused. "They're on their way back. Good. We can get out of this creepy place. Another snake flung itself onto my porthole while we were waiting. They're almost as disturbing as the bugs."

"No doubt," Jadora murmured.

She made herself return to her patient. Assuming Malek could magically heal the man's wounds when he arrived, she didn't attempt to suture them and simply bandaged the cuts.

Clangs on the ladder rungs announced the return of the team. Jak was the first to peek into the kitchen.

"Mother?" he asked, a worried note in his voice. "We may have a problem."

"Did people get bitten?"

"Stabbed by huge stingers." Jak held up his hands, indicating a size that had to be an exaggeration. "All right, more like this." He closed his fingers to show a measurement of an inch or two. "But Zethron got stung in the arm, and Malek…" Jak glanced back into the corridor.

"What?" Jadora asked, imagining Malek perforated all over with sting wounds. She rose to her feet, half-climbing over her patient to reach the corridor.

"He's all right." Jak lifted a hand to stop her. "But one of them stung him in the back of the head. Right here." He turned, pointing to his neck at the base of the skull. Thanks to the skullcap he wore, the spot was protected. On him.

"Was Malek wearing one of those?" Jadora whispered.

Jak shook his head. "He gave the two we got from the natives to Zethron and me."

"Tell them both to come in here, please," Jadora said, trying to keep her voice calm, though she heard a tremor in it.

In the corridor, Malek was giving Lieutenant Harintha orders to continue up the river, but he must have known Jadora would want to see him—or he wanted to see *her*—for he stepped into the kitchen afterward.

"I don't know if any of those plants are the Jitaruvak," Malek said, spotting the pots and pointing to them, "but I need you to examine them and let me know. If one is, our mission is complete, and we can return to the portal."

Jak opened his mouth, as if to protest that there was more he wanted to do here, but his gaze landed on the back of Malek's neck and stuck.

"I will." Jadora took Malek's hand and led him to the vacant cot. "Though you forgot to say please."

"My apologies." He bowed to her. "The skirmish below left me…" He trailed off, noticing her patient was awake.

"More zidarry than usual?" Jadora asked.

When they'd first met, he'd never used pleasantries like *please* and *thank you*. He'd been getting better about it, at least with her, but sometimes he forgot.

"The typical amount, I'd think." Malek sat on the empty cot.

Zethron appeared, squeezing past Jak. His sleeve was hiked up, and he pointed Jadora to a welt rising on his forearm with a puncture in the middle. It was oozing serous fluid.

"Is yours like that?" Jadora asked Malek.

He touched the back of his head. "Likely. It's under my hair. But you should attend him first. If necessary, I can meditate and use my regenerative powers to break down toxins and heal my wound."

Jadora hesitated, not sure if that would be enough, and worried that the neck wound might have more of a deleterious effect than the arm wound, especially if the stinger had been long enough to reach the spinal cord. It was unlikely it had been sturdy enough to pass through muscle, and only luck would have carried it between his protective vertebrae, but the fact that the natives wore skullcaps and the bug had attacked him in such a precise spot made her uneasy.

Her first patient had been watching warily as people came in and didn't speak until Malek lowered his hand from his head. Then a rapid chain of concerned words came out, along with a lot of pointing. He pointed at Malek, then at Jadora, Zethron, and Jak, finally slicing a finger across his neck in an unmistakable gesture.

"I was afraid it would be something like that," Zethron whispered.

"Translate for us," Jadora said when Malek—surprisingly—didn't order him to. "Please."

She grabbed a bug-bite antiseptic she kept in her kit,

lamenting that it might be woefully inadequate for the insects on this world, and dabbed the paste on Zethron's wound. A hint of green was visible at the center of his welt, and she realized the stinger had broken off inside his arm. She pulled out her tweezers and fished for it.

Zethron grunted, flinching but not pulling his arm away.

"Sorry," she said.

"Do you want me to incinerate it?" Malek asked absently. He was prodding the back of his neck again, probably trying to figure out if the stinger had broken off inside his wound as well. "There's a faint magical signature about it. The *insects* were magical. Not vastly so, but they managed to unexpectedly break through our barriers. I've never had anything like that happen to me. The closest I've seen was Shikari sauntering through Tonovan's barrier when he was only a few days old."

"We don't have magical animals on our world, do we?" Jak asked. "Not like dragons. Or those bugs. Maybe it's their inherent magic that gives them the power to thwart ours."

"Perhaps," Malek murmured.

Jadora caught the broken end of the stinger with her tweezers. Good. She wanted to examine it under her microscope. That would be difficult if Malek incinerated it.

"Some people believe dragons evolved here," Zethron said, his gaze locked on the extraction. "It is not the world with the most dragons or the one the elder dragons once called their home, but it is what the people here believe, as well as others I've encountered on different worlds. There is some fossil evidence to support the notion. There used to be many, many dragons here, but most were slain, and dragons aren't as frequent here now. I was surprised when we encountered them right after arriving."

"They were slain by the mundane bird riders with spears?" Malek asked skeptically.

"No. There are others here with magic."

The stranger spoke again, gesturing urgently at Zethron.

"You haven't told us what he said." Jadora slowly pulled out the stinger, eliciting winces from Zethron. Maybe she should have yanked it out swiftly, but she hadn't wanted it to break off inside his arm.

"I know. I'm hesitant to do so when…" Zethron glanced at Malek, then bit his lip.

"I'm getting the gist from the man." Malek nodded to the patient, then reached over and removed Zethron's skullcap.

Zethron's fingers twitched upward toward it, but he seemed to realize he didn't need it in here—and that there was little point in denying Malek the ability to read his mind when their patient wasn't wearing a skullcap either.

"His name is Wharan," Malek said. "And he and the other boatmen were selected from their village to brave the wilderness to replenish their people's medicinal herbs and attempt to catch a type of fish with eggs that are sacred and believed to impart vitality and longevity upon their people."

Jadora might have snorted at the idea, but wasn't she looking for a plant that reputedly did the same? She glanced at the potted ferns.

"They all wore skullcaps and stayed indoors as much as possible, because they're aware of the *death darters*. That's their name for the bugs."

Jadora held up the stinger. It was an inch and a half long, its length glistening with Zethron's blood. When she dropped it on a metal tray to examine later, it clinked, as if it were also metal. Zethron was lucky it hadn't struck a bone.

She couldn't keep from glancing at Malek and hoping the bug that had stung him hadn't left its stinger behind. That thing was long enough and hard enough that it could indeed have pierced muscle and maybe even bone. The memory of the *kerzor,* with its vile needle, came to mind, but she banished the thought immediately, lest Malek catch her dwelling on it.

But he was focused on Zethron and Wharan—on reading their thoughts.

"They were successful in their hunting, fishing, and gathering, and figured they could relax on the trip back down the river," Malek said. "They hadn't seen the death darters or any of the prey the insects regularly lurk around, so they felt confident that they would escape unscathed. They drank and celebrated, but a few people had picked up rashes from interacting with some of the stinging plants. Their scalps were irritated so they risked removing the caps. That's when the death darters attacked, using their magic to slip through closed doors—Wharan isn't sure if that's what happened or if someone accidentally left one open and lied about it. The crew was attacked. Most got their skullcaps on quickly enough, but some didn't."

Jadora finished cleaning Zethron's wound and knelt beside Malek. If he had one of those stingers in his neck, she wanted to remove it as quickly as possible. It could be oozing some venom or some other substance into him. She shuddered at the thought.

"They had a hard time driving the bugs away, since none among them were mages." Malek bent his head so Jadora could examine his wound. "And all of the crew suffered multiple stings. Those without caps were stung in the spinal cord, right below the skull and the brain stem. That is the favorite target of the death darters."

"Because it's so close to the brain?" Jak asked softly.

Malek didn't reply.

Jadora was trying to examine Malek's wound through his hair. "Can I shave this? I can't tell if the stinger is in there."

"I believe it is. I feel…" Malek lifted a hand to his head and closed his eyes.

"There's a substance that oozes out of the stingers," Zethron said, taking up the story. "Like venom but different. All of the crew were sick, but if the sting isn't close to the skull, the substance doesn't usually get into the brain. Those who were stung elsewhere didn't go insane."

"Insane?" Jadora lifted her tweezers to the back of Malek's head.

"It's there." He twitched his fingers. "I'm attempting to incinerate it, but since it's magical, it's defying me, and—" His words broke off with a growl.

"Trying to burn things inside of your own body hurts?" Jadora guessed.

"It does. Pull it out." Malek bent his head forward again, then quietly added, "Please."

Jadora found a razor and shaved the hair around the wound. The skin was red and swollen, so she had to be careful. What would Uthari think if his mighty zidarr and representative of his kingly authority came back with a huge canyon shaved in the back of his head?

That is not my largest concern right now. Malek thought into her mind.

I know. I see the end of the stinger. It's broken off in here, the same as Zethron's.

"Doesn't the brain protect itself from things getting into it?" Jak was watching the extraction with wide eyes. "Like *venom*?"

"Most of it is protected by the blood-brain barrier, which keeps out circulating toxins and pathogens, yes." Jadora had no idea if the brain could protect itself from *magical venom*. Humans hadn't even evolved on this world. As far as she knew, they'd all come from Torvil, taken by the dragons long ago. "It doesn't protect the circumventricular organs, since they secrete hormones into circulation."

You know a lot about brains for a chemist. Malek smiled, though he was looking downward.

Lucky you. Jadora didn't know if her knowledge would be useful in this matter, but she rested a hand on his shoulder to reassure him.

"Should I get Shikari to help remove the stinger?" Jak asked. "The way he did with the *kerzor* brain surgery?"

"I can get it." Jadora had successfully extracted the other stinger and was confident she could do it again. Whether removing it would be enough, she didn't know. "Zethron, what did you mean by *insane*?"

Wharan continued on without prompting.

"Those people on the ship went crazy and killed each other," Zethron translated. "Specifically, those who were stung in the back of the head did. The venom does something that makes them incredibly aggressive and turns them into killers who can't be reasoned with. The crew knew it would happen, and they argued. The first officer wanted to shoot the affected men before it could happen. He said there was no hope and that they would become too dangerous."

Jadora made herself focus on getting a good grip on the stinger and tried not to let the ramifications of the story make her hand shake.

"The captain couldn't bring himself to give that order," Zethron continued to translate. "He said to lock them up and maybe when they got home, their medicine woman could do something. But the insanity made them strong. They broke out and attacked the others. Three men took down twelve. Wharan was the last one alive, and when we arrived, they were still trying to get him. The captain had died right before that, and Wharan is sorry we didn't get there in time to save him. But maybe the captain wouldn't have wanted to be saved."

Jadora pulled the stinger farther and farther out, its length and how deep it had been horrifying her. Malek didn't flinch, didn't move a muscle.

"The captain's dying words were to apologize," Zethron continued. "He'd known better and should have given the order to kill those who'd been stung in the head."

"*We* won't be foolish enough to make that mistake," Tonovan said from the corridor.

Jadora cursed in surprise and dropped the stinger on the deck. When had that bastard slunk close enough to listen?

Tonovan smirked at her, his arms folded across his chest as he leaned against the far wall. Admiral Bakir and Prolix were out there too, their faces grave.

"Hilarious, General," Malek said. "I'm not some weak mundane with only a primitive immune system to rely upon. I can destroy this venom and command my body to heal any damage that was done."

Jadora didn't chide him for his zidarr arrogance. She hoped it was true.

"Is that possible?" Tonovan asked Zethron. "Are the mages of this world able to heal themselves if they get stung? Because I'd *happily* shoot Malek. For the good of the ship."

"I'd cut my own throat before I gave you the satisfaction of shooting me," Malek said.

"Promise? I've got a dagger you can use."

"Nobody's shooting or stabbing anyone," Bakir said. "Or themselves. I trust Malek will be able to heal himself and recover without trouble."

Jadora exhaled slowly, though she didn't fully relax, not with Tonovan's eyes gleaming and that stupid smirk on his face.

"Shikari will heal him if he can't heal himself," Jak said, his eyes as stricken as Jadora knew her own were.

She didn't know what was worse. The idea of Malek going crazy and killing them all or the thought of him being fine but Tonovan sneaking into his cabin and murdering him in his sleep.

And proudly telling Uthari that he'd done it for the good of the ship.

"I'll let you know if that's necessary," Malek told Jak. "You know I enjoy it when your baby dragon performs surgery on me."

"Last time, you had a seizure." Jadora bent and carefully picked up the stinger, using the tweezers instead of touching it.

"I did?" Malek blinked in surprise, the earlier arrogance disappearing under a hint of vulnerability.

"It might have only been involuntary muscle spasms. I used a sedative to knock you out so the surgery would go more smoothly."

"Handy," Tonovan said. "She can knock you out again to make it easier for the rest of us to shoot you."

"Find another pastime, General," Malek said coolly.

"Maybe I'll take up tinkering with our engineer. I understand he enjoys teaching people." Tonovan gave Jak a significant look before returning his focus to Malek. "Your young mentee has taken a sudden interest in learning how to make magical devices. Did you know that, Malek?"

Jak's face grew ashen. Jadora didn't know what he'd been up to, but she emptied her mind of thoughts and hoped Jak was protecting his own.

Malek sighed. "Go away, Tonovan. You're giving me a headache that has nothing to do with the stinger that was embedded in my head."

Tonovan opened his mouth, no doubt to torment them with more of his repartee, but the hatch clanged shut in his face. Jadora squeezed Malek's shoulder, trusting he'd done it.

Malek glanced at Jak, but he thankfully didn't ask what Tonovan had meant. Jadora cleaned his wound and dabbed the bug-bite cream on it, hoping it would do some good.

Wharan spoke a few more words.

"He says I can expect to get sick and should lie down," Zethron said.

Wharan avoided looking at Malek or giving him advice.

"He also wants to know if we'll let him off the ship. He would rather take his chances in the bug-infested wilds and walk home than…" Zethron glanced at Malek but didn't finish.

Malek stood up. "Once I meditate, I'll be fine. There's nothing to worry about from me. Tell him we'll finish our mission and let him off in his village on the way out." He bowed to Jadora. "Thank you for your assistance, Professor. Please examine those ferns and let me know if any of them are what we seek."

Jadora longed to tell him to stay here on a cot where she could keep an eye on him, but she nodded and said, "I will."

She knew he had the power to heal great wounds—she'd watched him save Jak's life with his magic. She had to trust that he knew himself and his abilities and limitations. If he believed he could destroy the venom before it did anything to him, she had faith in him.

Thank you, Jadora, Malek spoke into her mind and gave her a gentle smile before walking out.

She would have felt better if Wharan hadn't watched him go like a man who'd escaped a deadly tsunami with his life only to be thrown into an active volcano.

18

Daylight brought chaos to the mageships in the air above the portal. In addition to the uproar caused by the appearance and disappearance of the dragon *scout,* the news of Vorsha's death had all the fleets on edge. More than that. Many of the ships had backed away and had their weapons pointed toward Uthari's fleet. The fact that Vorsha had died on his yacht had people believing he'd been responsible or at least complicit.

Yidar doubted that was true, but he couldn't help but think this might be an opportunity for him. If war broke out, maybe he could take advantage.

Oh, he planned to do as Uthari wished by finding and killing Sorath, but what if Uthari were to die in the fighting? Or be assassinated by a zidarr? Yidar had envisioned carving out or taking over his own kingdom, but if Uthari's kingdom abruptly became available, that one would do quite well. After all, he'd grown up there and had a fondness for it.

Had Uthari been smart, he would have kept Yidar at his back to protect him, but he was too arrogant to believe someone could strike at him. He wasn't even on his yacht. Instead, he was nestled up to the portal, sitting casually with his back against it, letting everyone know that he would use it to lash out if they took action against him.

That was fine with Yidar since it left him unmonitored as he stepped into the corridor below decks on General Tonovan's *Dread Arrow*. Uthari wasn't paying attention to him, and with Tonovan away with Malek on another world, nobody on board dared question Yidar's right to be there.

"I've been sent to question the prisoner," Yidar told the two mage soldiers guarding the druid that Uthari had captured the night before.

The king's yacht didn't have a brig, so the prisoner had been transferred over here. Tonovan's *Dread Arrow* had an expansive brig, complete with numerous magical torture instruments hanging on the walls. Yidar didn't need those to question someone.

"Of course, my lord." The guards nodded to him, and one touched a panel to slide open a gate made from magical bars that had been newly installed. Only one cell had them.

The prisoner wasn't shackled, but extensive burns on his back kept him curled on his side in the corner. At first, Yidar thought he was unconscious, but when he stepped inside, the druid lifted his head and growled at him.

With greasy green hair, dirty bare feet, and dried blood on his tattooed face, he looked more like a wild animal than a human being. Under the grime, he was younger than Yidar would have guessed. Nineteen? Twenty?

Yidar scoffed that the druids had sent someone so young and inexperienced. A true assassin would have done the deed and escaped. Like Sorath had. Maybe he'd used the kid as a distraction to ensure *he* could escape. Yidar nodded to himself. That seemed likely.

"You'll tell me where Sorath went," Yidar said.

That earned him another growl.

"How delightful it'll be to question a hound."

Said hound showed more life than he should have had and lunged toward Yidar's calf.

Yidar raised a barrier to keep him from reaching it and quirked an eyebrow. "What would you do if you got me? Drag me into your lair and eat me?"

The prisoner bared his teeth. Several were sharpened to points.

Yidar clasped his hands behind his back, stood in the center of the cell, and drilled into the druid's mental defenses. They weren't great or refined in the least. It was as if the boy had taught himself to use his magic. What a strange choice Sorath had made for his assistant, even if he had been meant as a sacrifice. Maybe the druid was better with weapons than magic.

The growls turned into hisses of pain as Yidar tore away the prisoner's defenses and searched for information on the mercenary colonel. It didn't take long for him to locate the druid's memories of the night's events, of his hatred for Vorsha—he'd wanted her all along and had been largely indifferent to Uthari—and his surprise and then delight when they'd stumbled across her in Uthari's bedroom.

Yidar snorted. They hadn't even expected to find her. What bumbling assassins.

Though if Vorsha hadn't been in Uthari's bed, was it possible they would have succeeded in killing him? That shouldn't have been possible, but it appeared Sorath now possessed a dragonsteel weapon *and* one of Lieutenant Vinjo's stealth devices. Yidar couldn't believe Uthari had let that traitor of an engineer live and continue building tools that could hurt his own kind. After that mistake, Uthari would have *deserved* to die.

Interestingly, the druid had made a deliberate choice to distract the others while Sorath escaped. He'd been willing to trade his life to ensure Vorsha's death, and once that mission had been completed, he hadn't cared if he lived or died. He didn't care *now* if he died.

Yidar supposed he shouldn't oblige that feeling.

Show me where your tunnel entrance is, Yidar thought, digging deeper. *Did Sorath go back there?*

The druid didn't know. They hadn't formed a plan to meet back there ahead of time, but Yidar did locate the entrance in his mind. It was practically on top of the waterfall, created by some magic that might have hidden it again once Sorath had returned through it.

Yidar would find it, regardless.

He took a step back, intending to search for the tunnel immediately, but he paused, wondering if the prisoner knew where that druid woman Kywatha was. The druid woman who'd been pivotal in attacking the camp and trying to steal the portal. The druid woman who had the only other key to operate that portal.

Maybe Yidar could find it while he was hunting down Sorath. It had grated when Uthari sent Captain *Rivlen* after the druids. Yidar was far more capable and a more obvious choice for special missions. Yet Uthari was barely using him down here.

Because Yidar still had to prove himself trustworthy again. He sneered. If he found that key, he wouldn't need Uthari's help to establish a kingdom for himself. With the way things were going for the old king, he might not be alive much longer anyway.

Yidar smiled as he dug deeper into the prisoner's mind, searching for memories of Kywatha and where she resided.

After their instruction session ended and Vinjo left with his toolkit and his gizmos, doohickeys, and doodads—all terms Vinjo had forbidden Jak to use—Jak dimmed the mage lamp and lay on his bunk. Mother was still working in the laboratory, but that wasn't surprising. She would probably be there all night.

The ship was flying slowly up the winding river, Lieutenant Harintha having to halt it frequently while she cleared branches that blocked their way. She'd come in three times to get Vinjo's help. Apparently, admirals and zidarr were too powerful to bother with requests to torch wayward foliage. Jak had suggested flying up over the canopy again, so there would be fewer obstacles, but when she'd pointed at the layers upon layers of branches blocking the sky, he'd admitted they would struggle to see and follow the river from above.

Jak was worried about Malek and wanted to get the mission over with as soon as possible. Since Mother hadn't suggested leaving immediately, he assumed none of the potted plants they'd found were the Jitaruvak.

Jak closed his eyes and tried to sleep, but he kept thinking of Malek, who was in his cabin and possibly turning into an insane beast that would kill them all. Whenever he forced his mind away from that topic, he started worrying about what Tonovan had been implying when he'd pointed out Jak's new interest in learning Vinjo's craft.

How had he found out? The instruction had been behind closed hatches, Jak had been careful to keep his thoughts locked down, and Vinjo was a practiced mage of many years, so his thoughts also shouldn't have given them away. Had Tonovan simply sensed them spending time together in engineering? Maybe that was all it was. Maybe he only had suspicions that they were up to something, and for all Tonovan knew, Vinjo could be Jak's new best friend.

Given the abrasive options for friendship on the ship, that wasn't that hard to believe, was it?

Jak yawned, but sleep was elusive. For him, at least. Shikari was snoring on the bottom half of the bunk, sleeping on his back with his wings folded under him and all four legs crooked in the air. A wrench, pliers, and two glowing tools that Jak had already forgotten the names of stuck out from underneath him. Vinjo had started to retrieve them before thinking better of disturbing a sleeping dragon.

Meanwhile, Jak had to lie with his legs scrunched to his chest to fit on the mattress. He supposed he could sleep in his mother's bunk until she returned. She hadn't left her lab since everyone had returned to the ship. Her patients were all back in their cabins, with their reluctant passenger bunking with Zethron. But Mother... Jak doubted she'd even paused in her research to eat dinner.

He didn't know if she was studying the plants they'd brought back, the venom from those stingers, or the dragon blood and scale. Or all of those things.

Since he couldn't sleep, he slid out of his bunk to check on her. When he stepped into the narrow corridor, he almost crashed into the two servants Admiral Bakir had brought along. One carried what smelled like alcoholic drinks and the other had a tray of sweets pilfered from some secret stash in the kitchen that Jak didn't know about.

"Sorry," he said, stepping back into the hatchway so they could pass. Idora and Yira, he remembered. He hadn't interacted with them often, but he'd asked their names when they'd all boarded.

"Thank you, my lord," Idora said, inclining her head toward him.

"You can call me Jak. I'm not a lord or an anything. I *was* a cartography student, though that's on hold now." A silly twinge of sadness came over him at the realization that his autumn classes had started and he wasn't there to attend them. That was the *least* of his worries right now.

"Thank you, Jak," she said in a wooden voice and continued

toward an open hatch. Bakir's cabin. Male laughter came out of it. Tonovan's?

Jak grimaced at the thought of those two becoming friends, especially since Tonovan was now fantasizing about murdering Malek *for the good of the ship*.

Yira watched Idora go into the cabin, though she hadn't moved yet. She took a deep breath, as if visibly bracing herself. Her silver slaveband pulsed as it magically shared a sensation of pleasure with her, something to take the edge off what were likely unpleasant duties. Her shoulders relaxed slightly, but she still didn't appear overjoyed to serve.

"I'm sorry," Jak whispered, touching her forearm, wishing he could free her from her life.

With what he was learning from Vinjo, he might eventually have the knowledge of how to remove the slavebands without harming the wearer, but would that solve anything?

Yira stirred. "Do you wish a cookie, my lord? Or something else?" She looked toward his face, though she didn't meet his eyes.

Jak jerked his hand back, hoping he hadn't inadvertently given her a signal that he wanted her to come to his cabin. Even if he'd been dumb enough to want to lure Bakir's servant away from him, the dragon taking up half the bunk would have precluded much in the way of a sexual encounter. And for some reason, Rivlen's stern face popped into his mind. He imagined her having scathing words for any man who couldn't woo a woman without a slaveband compelling her into his arms.

"No, thank you," Jak said. "I shouldn't have interrupted you."

Not unless he could somehow free her forever. He smiled sadly, barely keeping himself from fantasizing about what he would do if he learned to make those *kerzor*. Unfortunately, Vinjo had implied the components were difficult to manufacture and wouldn't be found in a remote swamp. Once they returned to

Torvil, Jak would have to make friends with a mage blacksmith who didn't ask many questions.

"Are you sure, my lord?" Yira whispered. "You seem... not like them. Like you wouldn't be cruel."

"Jak, please," he said. "And I'm sure." He hated the thought that they were cruel to her. He hated *Tonovan.* And if Bakir tormented his servants, Jak hated him too.

"Girl," came Tonovan's stern voice. "*Come.*"

"Yes, my lord."

Hands off, boy, Tonovan growled into Jak's mind.

Yira scurried into the cabin, and the hatch clanged shut.

Jak clenched both fists, wanting nothing more than to rush in there, defeat the mages, and save both girls from further torment. But *the mages* were wizards and so much more powerful and well trained than Jak that they would squash him under their boots like a bug.

And if Jak got himself in trouble, Malek might not be able to help him right now. Jak sensed him sleeping in his cabin. Or still meditating? Hours had passed since the insect incident. The thought that Malek, who'd healed Jak of what had almost been a fatal wound in less than an hour, might be stumped by whatever that stinger had done to him was chilling.

"I'm going to choose to believe he's just sleeping," Jak whispered and stepped into the kitchen.

As he'd suspected, his mother was inside, bent over her microscope. All manner of slides, vials, and tools sprawled across the counter, a strange juxtaposition to the nearby pitcher of lemonade. The dragon scale leaned against the wall beside her.

Tempted by the drink, Jak walked in to hunt for a cup. A tiny tinted bottle of liquid next to the pitcher made him pause. It looked like something out of his mother's collection rather than a kitchen staple.

"Don't drink that," she said, glancing at him.

"The bottle or the lemonade?"

"Either." She took the bottle and tucked it into one of the numerous pockets in her backpack.

Jak leaned back to close the hatch, then whispered, "Did you do something to the lemonade?"

"The girls prepared it and turned their backs on it while they were looking for the cookies."

"You didn't *poison* it, did you?" Jak couldn't believe his mother would do such a thing, but a part of him hoped she had.

"No." She scowled at him. "I would never contemplate murder." She turned back to the microscope and muttered, "Not when there's a chance the girls would sip from it too." She recorded something in an open notebook beside the microscope, then straightened and rubbed the back of her neck.

"What *does* it do?"

"Substantially diminishes one's libido."

"Permanently?" Jak asked hopefully.

"No, only for a day or so."

"Damn."

Mother glanced toward the hatch. "It was an impulsive thing to do—I only had a few seconds to contemplate the lemonade and act if I was going to—and they might figure out it was me, especially if I can't avoid thinking about it. I'll do my best. I have a lot of other things to think about right now." Her distraught expression ensured him that Malek was on her mind, not Tonovan or Bakir.

"Yeah," Jak said. "Do you want help with anything?"

"I'm not sure what you could do. Or what *I* can do for that matter." She leaned her hip against the counter and fidgeted with the end of her braid. "Those stingers inject more than venom."

"What?" Jak whispered, horrified.

Mother nodded toward her microscope. "I've isolated bacteria that were swimming around in the sample I obtained from the tips of the stingers. It's not the same organism that came out of the dead dragons, which is good, but it's nothing I've seen before, so I have no knowledge of it. I gave Malek and Zethron doses of the antibiotic I have along, but since these bacteria aren't from Torvil, I don't know how effective my medicine will be on them."

"Won't Malek be able to point his immune system to the bacteria and magic them out of his body?" Jak knew Zethron wouldn't have that option, but their visitor had said someone who'd been stung in the arm would just get sick, not go crazy.

"I hope so. Assuming Wharan's story was true, I believe these bacteria may be what were responsible for the changes to the personalities of the affected boatmen. The venom itself is a simple mixture of proteins, similar to what bees on our world issue, and causes inflammation, pain, and is a mild anticoagulant. Presumably, the insects use their stings to defend the swarm and their hives. I do wonder what evolutionary reason there would be for the addition of the bacteria and the instinct to sting the victim in a spot where they could more easily travel to the brain."

Jak winced at the application of the word *victim* to Malek. It seemed too inappropriate for someone so powerful. Could microscopic bacteria truly affect a powerful zidarr? The *kerzor* had.

He rubbed his eyes. They were moist and gritty. From lack of sleep, he told himself, not because he was worried about Malek and on the verge of tears. Malek, who kept putting himself into danger to protect others. He didn't even *like* Zethron. Why had he risked his own body to protect the man?

"I suppose it could be part of their defense mechanism," Mother mused. "If you're an insect, and animals try to raid your home and your stash of honey, or whatever it is you create, if you inject something that prompts the potential invaders to fight amongst themselves, they will forget they were originally looking for your hive. This is all wild speculation, of course. I would have to gather more samples, observe the insects in the wild, and spend much more time analyzing my data to create a feasible hypothesis."

Jak tried to tell if his mother looked wistful, like she longed to do that. He couldn't imagine wanting to stay in this bug-filled world longer than it took to get to the bottom of the dragon mystery. And, he reminded himself, find Uthari's plant. Not that he cared about the Jitaruvak beyond getting the king to leave them alone.

"Did you have a chance to look at the fronds yet?" Jak pointed to the potted fern-like plants that Malek had brought back.

"Yes." Mother waved to an open notebook on the counter, one with a sketch of the Jitaruvak and columns of information describing it and its benefits. "They're not the same."

"That's disappointing."

"Maybe, maybe not. It would have been convenient if we found pots of Jitaruvak floating downriver on a boat, but we wouldn't have known where it originated and where to locate more, so that would have been of limited use. I *have* however determined from these samples and their similarity to Jitaruvak that we came to the right place. It's highly likely it grows on this world."

"That's good, I guess."

"It may be worth doing some phytochemical screening of these plants to determine if they have medicinal benefits. Those people had to be collecting them for a reason."

Jak nodded, trying to muster a smile for his mother. If not for the rest of their problems, she would have been delighted by the chance to more closely examine and experiment with new plants.

"It crossed my mind," Mother said, "that extracts might be used in treatments for the death darter venom or bacteria. The natives, who travel through these forests and swamps to forage and hunt, would naturally know a lot more than we do about the local flora."

"If they had a cure, wouldn't they have been carrying it along with them and used it as soon as people were bitten?"

"Probably." Mother smiled sadly. "Nonetheless, I've started bacteria cultures in a couple of containers so I can experiment and gauge how they react to having phytochemicals from the various plants inserted into their growth medium." She paused, as if debating whether she should admit more. "I've also started a couple of containers growing the organism from the dragon blood."

Jak stared at her.

"I thought it would be useful to experiment on ways to destroy it," she added.

"But it can spread by itself." Jak shuddered, remembering the floating motes that had tried to carry the stuff to Shikari to infect him. Or *infest* him. Whatever the proper term was, he didn't care. He wanted to make sure the parasite stayed far away from Shikari. "It doesn't need to be injected on some sword of a bug stinger."

"That's not necessarily true. The organism was catching a ride on those motes. Whether they created them from material within the dragon's body or found them already made, I don't know. Once you add the element of magic, all of the scientific laws and certainties become less reliable."

"It's not a good idea to grow more of them here, Mother. I appreciate that you like to research everything and want to help, but it's too dangerous. It's too dangerous for Shikari, and it might be too dangerous for *us*." Jak thumped his chest. "We don't even know for sure that humans can't be affected."

"That's something else I plan to determine."

"Mother… this is a bad idea."

"I'm being careful. And I'm not doing this solely out of scientific curiosity. If all of the dragons that are living today, aside from the freshly hatched Shikari, have been infested with that parasite, then there's only one solution to our problem. *Their* problem."

Jak leaned back. "Finding a way to destroy the parasite?"

"In case Shikari *does* get infected, wouldn't you like to be able to do that?"

"To keep him from being turned into a horrible demonic dragon who eats people? Dear Shylezar, yes."

"I also would like to know how to effectively treat people who are infected with the insect bacteria." Mother looked in the direction of Malek's cabin.

"Why does everything on this world want to turn people and dragons into crazy evil bastards? That's not *normal*, is it?"

"Perhaps on this world it is. I wouldn't be surprised if we learned these new bacteria are close on the phylogenetic tree to the dragon organism. Maybe if I can learn what works to kill one species, I'll gain insight into what would work against the other."

"Do you think destroying the parasite would return the dragons to their old selves? Could what I've been thinking of as the evil dragons revert back and become fun, frolicking dragons again?" Jak couldn't keep the hope out of his voice as he gazed intently at his mother. If she could do that, they might actually have a chance of finding the allies they needed to help oust the wizard rulers back home.

Mother sighed. "It's probably more complicated than that."

"You *like* complicated."

"First off, it's possible that the parasite and host over time become irrevocably entwined. If you were able to destroy an infestation early on, it would likely be possible to return the patient to normal, but after a while, if the parasite became ingrained in every tissue within the host, it might be impossible to remove the former without killing the latter."

"Oh." Jak slumped, that stark possibility throwing cold water on his hopes.

"Further, we know that the dragons are—or were—not only powerful magic users but intelligent and advanced as a species. If they'd realized their kind were being infected by a mind-altering parasite, I can only imagine they would have done everything in their power to destroy it themselves. If they weren't able to figure it out, and if the parasite is resistant even to dragon magic, I fear there may be little I can do."

Jak thought of Malek, meditating in his cabin and trying to heal himself—eradicate the infestation—with magic. Magic that might not work on the equally magical bacteria.

"You'll try to figure out a way anyway, right?" Jak asked quietly.

"Yes. Of course." Mother smiled and waved to her work, indicating she already *was.*

Maybe he shouldn't have come in and disturbed her. "Good. Thanks."

He started for the hatch, wanting to check in on Malek. While he was deep in his meditation, he might be vulnerable to a vengeful wizard lunging in and sticking a dagger in his chest.

"Jak?"

"Yes?"

"What did Tonovan mean earlier when he said you were being instructed by Vinjo?"

Jak hesitated. "Vinjo said he wouldn't make the *kerzor*, that he couldn't risk being found out and his family being punished—or killed. But he said he would teach me the basics of crafting magical devices so that maybe *I* would be able to figure out how to do it."

"Oh, Jak," she breathed.

"We couldn't ask Vinjo to take the risk of creating them without being willing to take that risk ourselves."

"I… don't disagree. But you're my son. And this goes far beyond wishful thinking about finding dragon allies out there. This is a very real and concrete way that we could potentially hurt mages. Uthari wouldn't forgive us for trying to do that. Neither would Malek."

Jak winced, well aware of that. "I know. Just protect your thoughts around them. Don't think about it. I'm getting better at protecting mine. As long as they don't know…"

"They're going to know as soon as mages start showing up with those discs inserted into their skulls."

"We'll worry about that if it turns out I can actually make them. Besides, maybe we can hand them to other mages—or druids—and convince them to use them on each other. And nobody would think to wonder too much about how they came to be."

Her eyebrows rose. "Malek and Uthari both know we brought one back from Vran."

"And Malek destroyed it. They don't know about the schematic, right?"

"I don't think so, but be careful. Tonovan is already suspicious."

"I'm well aware. But I have to do something." Jak looked down at the deck. "Everyone's been saying I have a lot of potential to learn magic and become powerful and turn into a real mage. I could be welcomed into Uthari's sky city and bring you with me and probably Grandfather too. I could become one of them and have an easy life."

"Are you tempted by that?"

"No. I mean, I don't know. I hate Uthari and everything he and the other rulers stand for, but what if once I actually have the power to fight him and possibly do something, I don't act? What if I have the ability to change the world, to really make a difference, but I'm too afraid to risk myself and that comfortable life to do it?"

"My greater fear is that you *won't* have the power to change things but that you'll try to do it anyway and get yourself killed."

"Gee, thanks, Mother."

She smiled at him, but her eyes were haunted, and he could tell that was a genuine fear of hers. Jak thought of the two servant women and how badly he'd wanted to spring into Bakir's cabin and punch him and Tonovan in their noses. And how easily they would have killed him.

"I'll be careful, Mother." Because she didn't look convinced, Jak walked over and hugged her. Maybe that would help. And maybe he wasn't too old to need a hug himself.

"I hope so." She squeezed him hard.

"What do we do if Malek goes crazy—or gets killed here—and we're left alone with Tonovan and Bakir in charge?"

She sighed and looked toward the lemonade pitcher. "Be resourceful."

Jak followed her gaze and bleakly wondered what Tonovan would do if he figured out she'd been responsible for that. With her inability to hide her thoughts from him, it seemed inevitable. And if Malek wasn't around to protect her...

Damn it. Jak wiped moisture from his eyes as he left the cabin, worried Mother was even more likely to get herself killed than he was.

19

MALEK WOKE HOT AND SWEATING, HIS MOUTH DRY AND HIS BLANKET tossed on the deck. For hours after the attack, he'd meditated, successfully breaking down the venom the insect had injected, but something else had lingered. He wasn't sure what, other than that it was magical and that its magic clashed with his own as it swam through his bloodstream. And into his brain?

He couldn't help but think of the squiggly-tailed, one-celled organisms that Jadora had shown him under the microscope back on Torvil. The parasite that had infected the dragons. He envisioned his skin turning brown and gray as he slowly lost his mind and turned into an animal. Worse than an animal. Someone who preyed on his own kind.

Malek groaned and sat up. Though he felt far from refreshed, he sensed others about on the ship and knew a new day had arrived. He wanted to talk to Jadora and see if she'd learned anything during the night. Uthari wanted the Jitaruvak prioritized, and what Uthari wanted Malek wanted, but he hoped she'd studied those stingers as well as the plants. With more information, he might have a better chance of successfully applying his magic to destroy the foreign *thing* that had invaded him.

He'd no sooner dressed than shouts sounded in the corridor.

"That's our prisoner," a woman yelled. Lieutenant Harintha?

Malek stuck his head out as she ran past. A whisper of muggy swamp air floated down from the open hatch at the top of the ladder. She raced up it, but a distant splash sounded before she reached the deck.

With his thoughts still muzzy from sleep—from *more* than sleep—Malek climbed up to the deck. He found Harintha standing at the rear of the ship, lifting her arms as she scowled at something below.

Malek reached her side in time to see a man swimming in the river. Due to the bronze skullcap covering his hair, it took Malek a moment to identify the person. Wharan.

"I've got him, my lord."

Harintha might have struggled to keep Wharan from jumping overboard, thanks to the skullcap, but it only protected the wearer from mind magic. Her power wrapped around Wharan, keeping him from making further progress with his swimming. She wasn't a strong mage, and sweat broke out on her forehead as she slowly levitated him out of the water.

"This isn't the prisoner I was sent to keep an eye on," Harintha growled, "but I won't let him go."

A few seconds passed before Malek realized she referred to Zethron—Queen Vorsha's prisoner. His mind truly was working slowly this morning. Once he recovered from the sting, he would mull over a way to make sure Zethron needn't return to a cell on one of Vorsha's ships. Jadora would appreciate that, even if it meant sending Zethron back to Vran.

Wharan flailed, trying to paddle away from them as he floated up toward the ship. His eyes bulged when he spotted Malek, and he screamed.

Though Malek didn't understand the words and couldn't read Wharan's mind, he knew without a doubt what the man was saying. He feared Malek and what he believed Malek would become. And he didn't want to live through that experience again.

Malek had a hard time believing he would succumb to madness and start killing people, but he couldn't blame Wharan for believing that. And it chilled Malek to think about how much damage a man with zidarr power could do if he went crazy. Even with Tonovan, Prolix, and Bakir here, it was possible he could kill everyone on the ship. At the least, those without power would be most vulnerable.

His heart ached as he thought of Jadora. No, he wouldn't hurt her. That wouldn't happen. One way or another, he would *ensure* it didn't.

"Let him go," Malek said quietly.

"Sir?" Harintha had almost reeled Wharan in but paused to give Malek a puzzled look.

"He was never a prisoner. If he wants to leave..." Malek spread a hand toward the dense vine- and moss-draped trees rising to either side of the river, their canopies blocking the sun and keeping the waterway in perpetual twilight. Something that sounded like a lion roared in the distance, and large predatory birds screeched. Insects droned, insects that were a far greater threat than those back on Torvil.

"He'll get himself killed out there alone." Harintha glanced at a wolf-like creature watching from the bank of the river, long fangs on display as its tongue lolled out.

"He must believe his odds are better out there than aboard our ship."

Her puzzlement only increased, her eyebrows drawing together in a V. "I don't understand, my lord. Aren't we just following a map to a plant-picking place?"

Ah, nobody had briefed their helm officer yet on his malady.

Not wanting to be the one to do so, and still hoping nothing would come to pass, Malek waved toward the hatch. "Let's hope."

With palpable reluctance, Harintha lowered the man back into the water. His arms flailed as he swam as quickly as possible to the nearest bank. The wolf-creature eyed Wharan intently and lowered into a crouch. Malek used a flick of power to scare it away. Wharan ran off into the trees without looking back.

Malek skimmed past the auras of the people aboard the ship and picked out Jak's. It had grown stronger of late, and though he was no Tonovan or Prolix, his vibrant power was easy to sense now.

Jak, meet me in navigation, Malek spoke telepathically.

Are you all right? Came the prompt reply.

Malek did his best to ignore his fevered skin and dry mouth but couldn't ignore that the symptoms existed and didn't foretell anything good. *For now. I want to see the new map. I trust you've taken a look at it?*

Since Jadora hadn't pounded on his hatch during the night, Malek assumed none of the potted plants were a match for the Jitaruvak. She would have told him immediately if they were, and they could have abandoned their trek up the river and returned home, home where powerful healers might be able to cure Malek. Assuming the portal let the ship leave this world. Malek sighed, realizing he *shouldn't* assume that.

Yes, Jak replied. *There weren't any discrepancies.*

Malek paused, looking toward the route ahead as Harintha climbed down the ladder. The dense trees made it hard to see far, but the river was rushing past more quickly than before, the terrain rising steeply. They'd reached the mountains that had been in the distance before.

I'd like to take another look anyway, Malek said.

Of course. I'll spread out both maps.

The angry buzz of insects came from one bank. Malek hurried

below, shutting the hatch behind him. He would rather face a dragon than more of those death darters.

As he stepped into navigation, Malek pushed a hand through his short hair. It was damp with sweat, and he suspected it stuck up in all directions.

Jak, who'd arrived in navigation first, looked at it before peering into Malek's eyes with concern. Harintha sat in her seat, so Malek didn't say anything. He didn't yet believe there was a threat to those aboard, and it would be better not to alarm the crew. They would be in a tough position if Vinjo and Harintha also jumped overboard.

Did your meditation... not work? Jak asked telepathically.

I detoxified the venom.

And the, uhm, bacteria?

They're still there. They have a magic that makes it hard to target them, but I sense them. I haven't given up. I'll mull over other ways to deal with them.

Jak licked his lips. *I had a chat with Shikari during the night.*

Oh? Malek hadn't been pleased at the thought of Jak's baby dragon performing brain surgery on him again, but if Shikari could heal him, he'd be willing to try. *Is he becoming a better conversationalist?*

Not really. He thinks we should go hunting together. He shared images of the two of us climbing cliffs and devouring tarantulas nesting in the rocks. I was somewhat disturbed by his vision of me with hairy spider legs sticking out of my mouth as I noshed happily.

Insects do seem to be a staple on this world.

Yeah. I wasn't able to get a clear answer from him on whether he could or couldn't help with your problem. He was a little distracted.

By tarantulas?

I'm not sure. He kept glancing at the hull of the ship and running up to navigation to peer out the porthole. At one point, he was more *than distracted. He was agitated.*

Maybe he knows something about what lies ahead. Malek found that ominous. He couldn't imagine a dragon being agitated by plants growing in the jungle. There had to be something else up there.

"Let's see the maps," Malek said aloud.

Harintha had glanced at him a couple of times during his silent conversation with Jak. She had to be wondering what they were discussing.

"Here's our original map from the bird riders." Jak spread it on the console and then unrolled the second. "The one you found is mostly of this river. It covers this specific area on the larger map."

Malek studied both and pointed to what looked like the mouth of the river. "That's where our plant is supposed to be. In the mountains, near the headwaters of this river. It looks like there's a cave, and those tufts presumably represent what we seek."

"Hopefully. They were added by another artist, the person who copied the map, rather than the original cartographer."

"How can you tell?"

"A different artistic style and a lack of ferns in the legend."

"Are ferns *usually* put in the legends?" Malek didn't recall ever seeing such on maps.

"Any symbols that aren't widely regarded as universal usually are. At least on Torvil." Jak's shrug acknowledged that map-making could be handled differently on other worlds. "I confess that the squiggly lines that represented that dragon-steel-altering vapor on Vran also weren't in a legend. They were mystery squiggles."

"As these are mystery ferns."

"Yeah. They're not on the new map. There's just a cave in that spot, or maybe that's a canyon? It's hard to tell. It's also not defined on a legend. There isn't a legend at *all* on the new map." Jak's voice oozed disapproval.

"Wouldn't it make sense," Harintha asked, "that the natives, when you asked them about your plant and where it was, would have marked the map specifically for you?"

Jak nodded. "That's what I suspect happened. We won't know until we get there and see plants. Or don't."

Malek remembered the illusion of a greenhouse in the fortress on the frozen world and how the Jitaruvak had already been used once to lure them into a trap. He couldn't help but believe that it could be happening again. Unlike on Vran, the natives here had let them leave their city, but that didn't mean they'd had nothing but goodwill toward them.

"The best I can tell," Harintha said, "we're twenty or thirty miles from that point."

Jak nodded his agreement.

"So, an hour?" Malek asked.

A scrape came from the side of the hull, low-hanging branches clawing at the ship.

"Maybe two or three," Harintha said. "It's slow going flying over the river. As soon as it got light out this morning, I took us above the canopy, but it was too easy to lose the river when flying above the trees. I got several miles off course and had to come back down."

Malek stifled the urge to snap that she'd wasted time and made himself say, "Understood."

Normally, he wouldn't be in a hurry, but the fear that something was growing inside of his body and that he could get worse made him impatient. He hoped that was the *only* thing making him impatient. He couldn't help but remember the madmen on the paddleboat hacking at his barrier with their axes and little comprehension in their wild eyes.

He sensed Tonovan walking up the corridor and turned so his back wouldn't be to him.

"Malek, you look like something a dragon chewed up and spat

out." Tonovan smiled half-heartedly at him, though he was also rumpled and appeared irritated by something this morning.

"The venom had a kick," Malek said. "I'm sure Zethron had a rough night too."

"Uh huh. You make sure to let me know if you start going crazy. I've got a knife right here for your throat." Tonovan patted the dagger at his hip.

"For the good of the ship?"

"Naturally. A quality fleet commander cares about his crew."

Jak's face turned flinty as he regarded Tonovan, but he managed to keep his thoughts guarded. Good boy.

Malek hoped he could find time for a few more lessons for Jak on this trip. During the skirmish with the insects, Malek had been too distracted to say anything, but he'd noticed Jak had managed to conjure fire for the first time.

He sensed Shikari in the corridor behind Tonovan and wondered if the young dragon would take a bite out of his calf. Maybe Tonovan wondered the same thing, for he flattened his back to the wall so Shikari could pass by. He scowled, as if he were thinking of kicking him in the back, but he refrained.

Shikari ambled past Malek, swatted Jak in the leg with his tail, and hopped into the empty seat beside the lieutenant. He sniffed the map, then nibbled at the corner.

"Not for eating." Jak extracted both maps and rolled them up.

"You'd think he would have sufficiently gorged himself on the bugs yesterday," Malek said, trying to decide if Shikari appeared agitated, as Jak had suggested.

"He's a growing dragon," Jak said. "He needs regular gorging."

"I hope Uthari gets some use out of him," Tonovan said. "It seems a waste feeding him when he's essentially a decorative pet."

Shikari looked over the seatback, his tail whacking Harintha as he turned, and hissed at Tonovan like a snake.

"A pet who's either learning our language quickly," Jak said, "or can read the irreverence in your thoughts."

"One doesn't need to be *reverent* to flying lizards." Tonovan scowled at Shikari. "It's idiotic enough that half the population of our world prays to one. How embarrassing for them."

Shikari showed off his fangs, but then he turned in the seat again, tilting his head and peering up the river. Had he detected some threat?

Malek reached out with his own senses. He picked up a couple of faint magical signatures that might represent swarms of those bugs or some other creatures in the area with magic, but nothing had as significant of an aura as the mages onboard.

Shikari emitted a keening noise that prompted everyone to cover their ears. Malek had never heard him make that sound before, and he didn't like it. Irritation rose up in him again, and he clenched his jaw to keep himself from lashing out.

"Uhm." Jak patted Shikari on the back. "What is it?"

Shikari shifted from foot to foot in the seat, talons ripping holes in the covering. He moaned, then keened again.

"He must sense something," Jak said.

"No kidding," Tonovan said. "Get him to shut up, or I'm turning him into dragon-scale luggage for the trip home."

"I doubt that would go well for you if you tried," Jak said, though he patted Shikari again and issued soothing sounds.

Shikari hopped down from the seat and charged out of navigation, knocking Tonovan into the wall before darting through the open hatch of Jak and Jadora's cabin. Tonovan snarled, yanked out his dagger, and lifted it, as if he did indeed mean to kill the dragon.

"Knock it off, you foul-tempered jackass," Malek snarled, blasting Tonovan with a disgruntled surge of power.

Tonovan had been protecting himself with a minimal barrier, and Malek's magic ripped it away and blew the dagger out of his grip. It flew down the corridor, clattering to a stop under the ladder. Uncharacteristic smug satisfaction surged through Malek along with the desire to knock Tonovan's head off and send it bouncing after the weapon.

Tonovan spun back toward him, reinforcing his barrier as he snarled, his single eye lighting with rage. "You *dare* belittle me in front of these *peons*?" he roared.

Anger erupted within Malek, spawned by years of disgust and loathing from having to work with this pompous ass. He snarled and raked his power across Tonovan's barrier, tearing it away again and hurling him down the corridor. Tonovan flew away as if a hurricane gale had blasted through the ship.

Malek's own defenses were down, but he didn't care. He wanted to channel all of his power into destroying Tonovan.

Ah, what are you doing, Lord Zidarr? Prolix spoke into his mind.

Malek had stomped out of navigation after Tonovan, but he halted at the words—and the realization that Bakir and Prolix had rushed out of their cabins. Bakir helped Tonovan to his feet as Prolix peered down the corridor at Malek, wariness in his eyes and his hands on his weapons.

Tonovan spun, seething with indignation, but it was the other two who made Malek pause. They hadn't attacked yet, but he sensed that they would. If they believed he'd been afflicted with some illness that would turn him into an unbalanced and dangerous monster...

Malek smoothed his shirt as he wrapped a defensive barrier around himself. He wished he could smooth his mind as easily.

Losing my temper, he told Prolix.

He refused to sound apologetic, but he had better sound coherent and like himself. If all three of them attacked him, he couldn't defend against that. He would end up curled on his side at Jak and Jadora's feet. The idea of appearing anything but powerful and capable in front of them was even more repulsive than thinking of the smug smirk that would ride Tonovan's lips.

Perhaps this is not the time for that, Prolix suggested.

You're correct. Malek nodded to them and glanced back, aware of Jak and Harintha gaping through the hatchway at him. "Check on your hatchling, Jak."

Jak swallowed. "Yes, my lord."

My lord. It was the proper way for Jak to address Malek but also something he rarely used unless Uthari was in the area. When Jak darted past, he glanced at Malek with fear in his eyes.

Malek frowned, troubled. It was right for Jak to respect him, but he didn't want Jak to *fear* him.

"He's all right," Jak called from his cabin. "But, uhm, he's hiding under my bunk."

"Isn't his normal place *in* your bunk?" Malek asked, trying to make a joke, to ease Jak's fear. To prove that he was still normal. But damn it, why was his mouth so dry?

Aware of sweat beading on his forehead, Malek resisted the urge to dash it away. Tonovan, Prolix, and Bakir were watching him intently. He couldn't hear the telepathic words they were exchanging, but from their glances to each other, he knew a conversation was ongoing.

"Yes," Jak said. "At least *he* thinks so. Something has him spooked."

"We'll proceed with caution." Malek thought about hunkering in his cabin until they arrived at their destination, but if they were about to run into trouble, he wanted to face it. Besides, it would be easier for the others to conspire if he disappeared.

He walked back into navigation and sat beside Harintha. Her wary glance suggested she wasn't pleased to have a possibly unbalanced zidarr three feet away from her.

"Focus on the route ahead," he snapped, annoyed with everyone's reactions. "The dragon alarm went off. There must be threats ahead."

Not inside, he wanted to add but didn't. He merely clenched his jaw, determined that he would *not* be a threat.

A faint green glow came from the sides of the tunnel, enough to brighten the way. *Most* of the time. Every now and then, it dimmed, and the earth rumbled, as if with displeasure. Maybe it was Tezi's imagination, but she couldn't help but believe the underground passageways, passageways that had been carved out of the earth by druids, were unhappy that invaders who wanted to hurt their makers were walking through them.

No, not hurt. Tezi was fairly certain that Rivlen had orders to *destroy* them. To make sure they couldn't make another attempt at stealing the portal.

Enrobed in glum thoughts, Tezi barely spoke as she walked beside Rivlen, the two of them leading the squad of mages that Rivlen had chosen for the infiltration. Tezi was the only mercenary along and couldn't help but wish she were back on the ship with Captain Ferroki and the others. She didn't even know if everyone had been accounted for after the crash. Maybe she should have lent the axe to Rivlen and stayed behind. The weapon was the reason Rivlen had brought her along, not any great combat skill that Tezi possessed.

Rivlen stopped and held up a hand. "There's more magic up ahead."

"Just a slight amount more," one of her men said. "There's been some natural variation in the tunnel. It's not surprising, given that they're carved out with crystals." The man wrinkled his nose, as if this represented a substandard form of magic.

Since Tezi couldn't tell druid magic from mage magic or dragon magic, she had no idea.

Rivlen squinted ahead. "It's different."

To Tezi, the route ahead appeared the same as the tunnel they'd been walking through all along.

"There might be a trap," Rivlen added.

The mage sighed. "I'm sure it's nothing we can't handle, ma'am. Our barriers are up, and the girl has the axe for protection." This time, he wrinkled his nose at Tezi. "Assuming you're worried about her and she's not disposable."

"She's *not* disposable." Rivlen glowered over her shoulder at the man.

"Thank you, ma'am," Tezi murmured.

"I do want you to walk through there first though." Rivlen pointed ahead of them.

"Uh?"

"The dragon steel will protect you from magical traps."

"Our *barriers* will protect us," her mage said, rolling his eyes. "Ma'am, we shouldn't delay. The druids will know we're coming after all that chaos at their monument. I'm sure the ones we fought there have warned the rest of their kin."

Rivlen ignored him and pointed for Tezi to walk ahead of her. "I'll help if you get into trouble."

Tezi frowned, now feeling *very* disposable, and hoped Rivlen was wrong about traps. As Tezi well knew, the magic of the axe wouldn't protect her from *non-magical* harm. Like a ceiling caving in on her.

But it wasn't as if she could say no. The mages could doubtless find a way around the axe's protection to force her to go ahead.

Tezi took a deep breath and walked slowly forward. Five steps. Ten. Twenty. Nothing happened.

Just as she started to believe she was safe, yellow light flashed. Tezi stumbled and squinted her eyes shut against the brilliance. Air whooshed past her, but it barely stirred her hair. Swearing came from behind her in the tunnel, followed by a thud and a thump. Several groans filled the air as the light faded.

Nothing had hurt Tezi, but two of the mages who'd lingered several paces behind her were crumpled on the ground. The one who'd doubted Rivlen was gripping his head and glowering at Tezi, as if *she'd* done it. She was still blinking dots out of her vision as her eyes watered.

"It's possible your barrier isn't as protective as you thought, Lieutenant Viggert," Rivlen said mildly.

She offered him a hand up. He glowered at it for a moment before accepting her assistance.

"I stand corrected, ma'am," he said stiffly. "There *are* booby traps. Powerful ones."

"Yes." Rivlen nodded for Tezi to continue on.

Though this seemed like a good reason to turn around and go back, Tezi continued reluctantly forward.

A hundred yards down the tunnel, another flash of light tried to blind her as magic whooshed past. This time, the mages were more prepared. They must have combined forces to reinforce each other's barriers, for nobody went flying.

Tezi rounded a sharp bend, and the tunnel widened. She hoped that meant they were getting to the end.

The ground didn't change, the packed earth appearing the same as it had all along, but on the first step after the bend, it shifted as her foot came down. Tezi braced herself for another blinding flash, but the ground trembled, as if she'd triggered an earthquake. Or a rockfall?

She turned and sprinted back toward the group. Rivlen jogged forward, reaching out to her, but the ground gave way first. Tezi cried out, envisioning a bottomless pit, and her axe did nothing to keep her from falling.

A hand clasped around her wrist. Rivlen.

But the ground under Rivlen crumbled too.

"Captain!" a female mage blurted.

Tezi and Rivlen tumbled several feet, falling below the level of the tunnel, then halted abruptly. Tezi hung lower than Rivlen, nothing but Rivlen's grip around her wrist keeping her from falling farther, but what had caught her?

Tezi peered up, but dirt kept raining down as what had been the ground pelted her in the head and shoulders. She barely glimpsed a glowing yellow rope that Rivlen gripped with one hand. As if it were attached to a winch, it slowly pulled them up, Tezi's belly scraping against the dirt wall. She could feel the dampness of Rivlen's palm around her wrist and didn't move a muscle, barely even breathed, fearing Rivlen would lose her grip on her.

But Rivlen made it to the top, and other mages helped her out of the newly formed pit.

"Sorry, ma'am," one said. "We weren't able to levitate you while you were holding her and she was holding that axe."

"I know." Once Rivlen knelt on solid ground again, she helped Tezi up. "Getting her across is going to be fun."

Tezi let out a long relieved breath as her butt landed on firm earth. The yellow rope had been made entirely of magic and disappeared as she peered at what was now a hole in the tunnel floor twenty feet across. She peeked over the edge. Enough of the green glow emanating from the walls reached the bottom for her to see a bed of sharp metal spikes jutting out of the ground.

"Old-fashioned." Rivlen sniffed.

"It would have been effective." A piece of the edge crumbled, and Tezi scrambled backward. "Are we, uh, continuing on?"

Hopefully, they would wait for her heart to slow down from its current five hundred beats per minute. She closed her eyes, memories of sparring with Sergeant Tinder and the others flashing into her mind. Even the early mornings of exercise and hazing that she'd once hated were fond memories in comparison to this.

"Yes." Rivlen stood up, pulled Tezi to her feet, and brushed dirt off her uniform. "Aren't you glad you aren't disposable?"

"Oh, yes. *So* glad." Tezi clamped her mouth shut on the sarcasm. If she seemed unappreciative, Rivlen might let her fall the next time.

But Rivlen only smirked. "Can you throw your axe to the other side?"

"Uh?"

"Mercenaries are articulate, aren't they?" the lieutenant muttered to his comrades.

"More articulate than you were when you hit the wall," came the reply. "Your exact words were *ooph, blergah,* and *owp.*"

"I didn't know you would record them for posterity."

"For the annals of great mage heroes."

With some bemusement, Tezi realized the mages were as likely to haze each other as mercenaries were.

"So I can levitate you over," Rivlen explained.

Tezi had assumed that was the reason, but she grimaced. What if she missed the throw—the low roof and narrowness of the tunnel would make it challenging—and lost her axe into the spikes? The mages wouldn't be able to levitate *it*. She would have to climb down while the others watched and sniggered at her ineptitude.

She was tempted to ask Rivlen to make the throw, but she hated the idea of admitting she couldn't handle such a simple task. She'd been training with the axe for weeks now, and she was improving as a soldier and a fighter. Maybe she just needed to have faith in herself.

"Yes, ma'am," she made herself say, hoping she wasn't about to look like an idiot.

Tezi hefted the weapon, planning to throw it more like a javelin than an axe but paused to give it a few silent words. Jak had recommended she communicate with it, after all. He'd even had the portal teach her a command she could use to cause it to flare with more power. A command in the roaring-screeching language of the dragons, admittedly.

She wouldn't attempt to make the noise here, not with all these mages watching on, but she thought to it: *Thanks for the assistance with the booby traps. Will you help me get you to the other side safely, please?* She envisioned what she wanted to do.

The axe flared blue, the way it often did when she took it into battle. Hoping that was promising, Tezi lined up her aim and threw the weapon.

It flared brighter blue and sailed over the hole without tumbling in the air or clinking off one of the walls. As soon as it reached the far side, Tezi exhaled in relief. Then it thudded into something where nothing appeared to be.

An animalistic yelp sounded as the axe lodged into an invisible foe. Some panther? Or wolf?

Whatever it was shook itself and batted at the axe until it fell free. The weapon landed on the ground, blood darkening one of the edges. Growls and whines followed as the invisible creature spun and ran back the way it had come.

"Stop it," Rivlen barked and hurled a fireball across the hole.

More fireballs, as well as branches of lightning, flew forth from mage fingers. The air heated with flames and crackled with electricity, and Tezi's neck hair stood on end. She hunkered down, wrapping her arms over her head for protection, and hoped none of them forgot she was without protection and scorched her by accident.

The dying cries of the creature floated down the tunnel. It was hard not to think about how that could be her fate, too, if she irked these people when she didn't have her axe in hand.

"Let's hope that keeps the guard hound or whatever it was from reporting back," Rivlen said as their attacks dwindled. "Good throw, Tezi."

"Lucky throw," someone muttered.

"If you'd thrown it, you would have cleaved off your own dong. I've seen your weapons skill."

"Hilarious."

"Ready?" Rivlen touched Tezi's shoulder and pointed across the hole. "I'll levitate you over now."

"I get to go first again?" If there were more guard animals over there, Tezi hoped she could get her axe before they got *her*.

"If I let these knuckleheads go first, one of them might grab your weapon and not give it back."

Tezi sighed and drew a dagger, the ordinary weapon probably useless against invisible druid animals.

You'll be fine. Rivlen hefted her off her feet and levitated her over the edge. *I have plenty more fire if anything else is lurking over there. Lieutenant Viggert was lusting after the axe earlier, so you truly do need to keep an eye on him. If he attempts to take it while I'm watching, I'll roast him, but it's more likely he'll try to get you alone.*

I used to only have to worry about men wanting me alone so they could grope my boobs. What did it say that Tezi almost missed those simpler days? The axe wasn't more trouble than it was worth, but… it was a lot.

Even so, she wouldn't give it up if she didn't have to. It was worth fighting for just to keep mages from being able to read her mind.

Well, I'm sure he'd gladly do that too, Rivlen said. *If he tries either, you have my permission to lop his hand off. Or his penis.*

Tezi thought she heard a noise in the tunnel ahead and didn't reply. A few more feet, and she would reach the far side of the hole, and her axe wasn't far from the edge. She kept herself from glancing down at the spikes and thinking about how Rivlen held her life in her hands.

When she landed, she resisted the urge to drop to her knees and kiss the ground. Mostly because more noises were audible ahead, the sound of something running.

Afraid another invisible creature was about to pounce, Tezi dove for her axe. She snatched it up and sprang to her feet, but she forgot that an invisible creature was lying dead in the tunnel. It came into view as she stumbled over it, a large scaled lizard the size and shape of a lion. Cursing, she caught herself on the wall and dropped into a ready stance beside it.

But the running sounds were retreating, not coming closer. There was another bend in the tunnel ahead, and the fast-moving creature sounded like it was close to it.

"Another one is getting away," Tezi yelled.

If she'd been able to see it, she might have thrown her axe, but she didn't want to risk letting it go when the mages might—

Fireballs roared down the tunnel, orange light overpowering the green glow. Tezi flattened herself to the earthen wall while keeping both hands firmly on her weapon. An inferno of multiple fireballs filled the tunnel, and long seconds passed as she saw nothing but flames. She closed her eyes against the brightness, well aware that she would be incinerated without the axe's protection.

No cries of pain came from the tunnel ahead, and she suspected the creature had escaped. Escaped to warn the druids of intruders?

Tezi couldn't help but feel she'd failed. If she'd been quicker to react and hadn't forgotten a body was in the tunnel and tripped over it...

The flames disappeared, and Rivlen and the other mages landed beside Tezi.

"Sorry, ma'am," Tezi said. "I think the other one got away."

"We'll be wary and ready to deal with whatever comes as a result. If not for your first throw, we wouldn't have known they were there at all." Rivlen patted her on the shoulder.

Even though Rivlen wasn't her commander and wasn't exactly a friend, Tezi appreciated that she'd started treating her decently.

She was slowly coming to accept that not *all* mages were abhorrent human beings. She still didn't want to work for them anymore and hoped Thorn Company escaped all this alive, returned to the Southern Desert, and found contracts that didn't ally them with or pit them against magic users.

One of the mages drew a sword and used it to prod a collar around the dead lizard's neck. It was made from heavy canvas and looked like something a dog in any city in the world might wear.

"This is magical." He tapped a gem attached to the collar. "Maybe it's what grants the animal invisibility."

If it did, Tezi wondered if they would object to her taking it. She would happily wear a dog collar if it could make her invisible.

Using the sword, the mage sliced off the collar. It tumbled to the ground, the gem landing in the dirt, and the animal remained invisible to those more than a few feet away.

"Or maybe it does something else," Rivlen said.

"Apparently."

Rivlen waved for Tezi to continue forward. It seemed she was still the leader.

Tezi picked up the gem. It was warm in her palm, but that might have been from the fireballs.

"Whatever it does," Rivlen said, "I doubt it'll work on you while you're holding that axe."

"Good point," Tezi said, but a tingle ran up her arm from it, and she had the urge to continue down the tunnel, as well as the certainty that it would lead her home.

Her axe flashed blue. A warning that the gem was a threat? Tezi was about to toss it onto the ground, but her weapon flashed again and imparted a quick vision of her standing at a crossroads and the gem leading her in the right direction.

"I'll keep it," Tezi said and strode down the tunnel, hoping the mages wouldn't object.

Rivlen shrugged and didn't stop her.

Can you allow magic to affect me when it's beneficial? Tezi asked the axe. *Or in line with what I want?* She wasn't sure a magical homing pigeon was beneficial to her, especially since it was likely pointing her to the druids.

The axe never answered in words, and it didn't this time, but it conveyed a sense of smugness. As if it was pleased with its abilities.

Tezi arched her eyebrows. So long as it protected her from further booby traps.

20

Jadora rubbed her gritty eyes, fantasizing about a long nap, but she couldn't shake the feeling that she didn't have time for sleep, didn't have time for anything. She willed the bacteria in her experiment containers to multiply faster. Not that she had more substances she could test on them. She'd already made extracts from the three potted plants that Malek had brought back and tried them on the bacteria. On the bug bacteria at least. She hadn't yet dared open the containers to experiment on the dragon organism. She worried she was being reckless by growing a population of that one. If it could magically float through the air and infect Shikari... Jak would never forgive her if she lost control and allowed that to happen.

The hatch opened, and Jak walked into the kitchen laboratory.

"Have we reached the foraging spot yet?" Jadora asked.

She hoped they found the Jitaruvak for more reasons than appeasing Uthari. It had occurred to her that a plant that could promote longevity in humans might work, at least in part, by boosting the immune system so much that it was able to quash everything from cancerous cells to infections to viruses to all the other varied things that could impact human health. Maybe *it* could drive the magical bacteria out of Malek and Zethron.

"We're getting close," Jak said. "The river has gotten narrower as we've climbed into the mountains. It would be hard to get to this place without a mageship. Or a bird mount, I suppose. Though I wonder how many people actually visit it. Shikari is still hiding under the bunk. Malek and Bakir say they don't sense anything major yet, but there's got to be something out there. The deck under the bunk isn't *that* appealing."

"I wouldn't think so." Jadora lowered her voice. "How's Malek?"

Jak hesitated. "Kind of grumpy."

"I heard he hurled Tonovan down the corridor." Was it wrong of her to wish she'd seen that?

"Yeah. Grumpily. Maybe you should check on him."

"Me?" Jadora wanted to help him, but the thought of Malek's personality changing before her eyes made her cringe. She wanted to spend time with the Malek who'd hugged her—and kissed her—and who she was falling in love with, not someone she had to fear.

Still, she'd gone in to check on Zethron, bringing him water and speaking with him for a time about the Ancient Zeruvians on Torvil. It wasn't right of her to avoid Malek because she was afraid of watching him descend into madness—of her own discomfort.

Jak shrugged. "You know medical things. And Tonovan, Bakir, and Prolix are back in a cabin, plotting together. Debating how they'll relieve Malek of command—or worse—if they need to. Maybe if you check him out and say he's fine, they'll believe you."

"What if he's not fine?"

"He *is*. Tonovan is trying to convince the others that because Malek lost his temper with him, he's not fit to command this mission, but I wanted to smack Tonovan too. He's a bastard. I just don't have the power to do it. I wish I did."

"All right. I'll make some tea."

Jak blinked. "Tea?"

"*Soothing* tea. For Malek. And anyone else who needs to be soothed." Jadora would take some to Zethron too. He might not be in as much danger as Malek, at least according to the departed Wharan, but he had a fever and hadn't wanted her to leave his side. She'd felt bad about doing so, but the need to keep researching had driven her back to her lab.

"Oh," Jak said. "You think that will counteract the bug stuff?"

"Maybe it'll help a little."

"Can it also help Tonovan be less of a bastard?"

Jadora smiled faintly. "Maybe it'll help a little."

"Just be careful so he doesn't start associating you with drugs in beverages." Jak glanced at the counter where the lemonade pitcher had been the night before.

"I will be."

He nodded and left her to brew the tea, heading to their cabin to comfort his dragon.

Jadora had taken a risk putting powder from the zithzara herb in the lemonade the night before, but it had been more calculated than she'd admitted. Oh, she'd made the decision quickly when the opportunity had presented itself, but it had been as much an experiment as petty revenge. Zithzara was a relatively innocuous compound, so she'd assumed that if Tonovan somehow sensed it, his retaliation would have been minimal. Or at least survivable. If he had detected a poison, a genuine attempt to kill him, he would have lashed out and killed *her*. And it would have been a justifiable action, though she liked to think that if Tonovan did kill her, Malek would kill *him*. That wouldn't do anything to bring her back to life, but at least one vile mage would be taken out of the universe.

But as far as she knew, Tonovan *hadn't* discovered her tinkering. That suggested she might be able to get away with putting something stronger into a beverage he was consuming. If she tried, she would have to be careful, lest he catch the scheme in her thoughts and make her drink it. It would be an act of last resort. Jak's question about what they would do if something happened to Malek had been on her mind.

After brewing the tea, she took a mug to Zethron, who'd fallen into a restless sleep, then carried two more to the navigation cabin. Surprisingly, their helm officer wasn't there. Malek sat in the lieutenant's seat, though his hands weren't on the controls. He merely gazed through the porthole.

The ship was flying twenty feet above rocky ground that sloped upward. As Jak had noted, what had been a wide river in the lowlands had narrowed, tumbling around boulders and over cliffs as it flowed down the mountainside.

"Are you capable of piloting a mageship?" Jadora asked.

"Of course I'm capable," Malek surprised her by snapping. "This is a simple task of pushing buttons and levers. A monkey could do it."

Jadora stared at the back of his head, his mussed hair damp with sweat. He never snapped at her. She feared it indicated the infection was progressing and that his meditation hadn't been able to thwart the bacteria.

Malek looked back, and she tried to wipe the worry off her face.

"I'm sorry." He waved her to the other chair. "Sit. Please."

"It's all right," she made herself say, though it wasn't. Not by a long shot.

Malek gazed at her for a moment before looking back to the route ahead and nudging a lever to increase their altitude.

"I agree," he said quietly. "It's not."

"Can you feel yourself, ah, changing?"

He didn't look well. There were bags under his eyes, sweat gleamed on his brow, and his lips were dry and cracked with dehydration. She wanted to tuck him into his bunk and sponge off his forehead for him.

Malek glanced back at the open hatch and used his magic to close it. "I feel myself unable to control my temper. There's this sense of irritation growing inside of me. Like ants crawling all over my skin." His mouth twisted. "Or giant bugs with stingers like swords."

"Maybe this will help a little." Jadora set the tea beside him and sat, her hands wrapped around her own warm mug.

"Is it drugged?"

"What? No." Since she'd drugged *Tonovan's* drink and had just been thinking about doing it again, guilt surged up within her. She struggled to tamp it down, afraid Malek would sense it and believe the guilt was because she'd done something to his drink. "It *is* supposed to be soothing. It's a blend of herbs that increases cerebrospinal fluid concentrations of neurotransmitters known to improve mood."

"I thought they might have talked you into throwing something in there to leave me drooling on my bunk while visions of fuzzy pink bears cavorted through my mind."

"I didn't bring any bear-vision-inspiring substances along."

"Short-sighted."

"Well, there are only so many things you can pack."

"Even with a magical bag with enhanced volume?" He managed a smile for her.

Emotion welled up in her, making her throat tighten.

"Even with," she whispered and blinked at moisture forming in her eyes. She sipped from her mug, hoping to hide her emotions—her worry—from him, though that was pointless. He would sense it.

"Yes," he said softly and reached over to rest a hand on her arm.

That only made *more* emotion well up. She wiped her eyes.

He patted her arm and drank from his mug. After his first sip, he eyed it contemplatively, then drained it.

Either his dehydration was prompting him to guzzle water, or he hoped it truly would do something to help.

Jadora looked out the porthole, eyeing the vegetation growing along the banks, hoping to see the distinct fronds.

"Do you have a substance that could knock a person out?" Malek asked, still eyeing his mug.

"I suppose I could come up with something. Why?"

"I would prefer being knocked unconscious to having Tonovan or one of the others drive a dagger into my heart."

Jadora stared at him, realizing what he was suggesting. "Do you think that's going to be necessary?"

"I don't know. Right now, I'm just fevered and irritable. It doesn't bode well that the one person who could have told me if those were the first symptoms on the way to much worse symptoms leaped off the ship to his possible death to avoid me."

Jadora licked her lips. "I heard about that."

"If I was unconscious, I couldn't hurt you. Or anyone." Malek looked over. "But especially you."

"It would be distressing to have you try," she admitted.

She didn't know why she'd used the word *try*. If he lost his mind and attacked any of them, he would succeed in hurting them. In *killing* them. She'd seen him take down whole crews of enemy mages and knew his capabilities.

Malek sighed. "The problem is that Tonovan might take advantage of me being unconscious and vulnerable and slit my throat."

And Jadora and Jak wouldn't be capable of stopping him. Not unless they drugged *him* too. And Bakir and Prolix. She highly doubted she could manage that, not with them all constantly sifting through her mind. Also, neither of the two sedatives she had along would be fast-acting or as effective if they had to be digested first. The ideal delivery method was to insert them directly into the bloodstream. There was no way Tonovan would let her stick a needle in one of his veins.

Besides, if all of their powerful mages were unconscious, what would they do if a dragon showed up? Or something *worse* than a dragon? Whatever Shikari feared, it couldn't be anything innocuous.

"No," Malek agreed. "Just knocking me out would have to do."

"Let's keep that as a last resort."

"It would have to be before I… got to the point where I wouldn't allow it."

"I understand. But even if I sedated you, how would we *keep* you sedated? I've been experimenting on the magical bacteria in my lab, but I haven't yet found anything effective against them. I wasn't even able to kill them when I applied heat. They're either naturally thermophilic, or their magic makes them so."

"I appreciate you doing the research to help me."

"Of course. Unfortunately, I'm limited by what I can accomplish working out of a backpack and a kitchen." Jadora almost said that if she had access to a full lab back home, she would have better luck, but would she? Or would it turn out that she needed something that grew here to thwart the bacteria? "I could render you unconscious quickly if I delivered an anesthetic directly into your bloodstream, but it would be dangerous to keep sedating you for an extended time period."

"More dangerous than Tonovan's dagger?"

"Well, it's possible it could have the same end result if things went badly. I would prefer to find another solution."

"As would I." Malek frowned out the porthole. "But keep it in mind." He held up a finger. "I sense something. A powerful source of magic."

"A dragon?"

"I don't think it's a living thing."

"Is it something a dragon would fear?" Jadora wondered if Shikari had come out from under Jak's bunk yet.

"I don't know. I haven't observed that mature dragons fear much." His forehead creased. "But it *is* strong."

The hatch opened, and Tonovan walked in, not bothering to knock.

"I thought I might catch you two in here fornicating," he said, though he also frowned and looked at the route ahead.

"Something intelligent to do while flying a mageship," Malek said.

"I've done it." Tonovan smirked at him.

Jadora carefully kept her thoughts away from their discussion, especially when Tonovan looked at her and scowled.

Maybe it was her imagination, but she thought she sensed him raking through her mind.

"Stop it, Tonovan," Malek said.

"Or what? You'll hurl me down the corridor again? Do it one more time, and Bakir and Prolix will agree that you're too unbalanced to lead this expedition."

"What do you think is out there?" Malek pointed up the slope ahead. "I trust your meager abilities are sufficient to sense it."

"My meager abilities can sense that you're about to get your ass kicked. I—" Tonovan scowled and focused on the porthole again. "What *is* out there? It's making me want to turn this ship around and go in the opposite direction."

A moan came from the corridor, and Vinjo stumbled in with a hand pressed to the side of his head. Had he been injured?

"Who made that *barrier*?" Vinjo groaned. "It's so powerful it's giving me a headache."

Malek and Tonovan looked sharply at him.

"You can tell it's a barrier?" Malek asked.

"Yes. A headache-inducing barrier." Vinjo frowned at him. "Can't you tell?"

"I can tell it's *something*," Malek said.

"Articulate, zidarr," Tonovan growled.

Jadora, as mundane as always, couldn't sense a thing. Judging by Vinjo's winces and groans, maybe that was a blessing, at least this one time.

Up ahead, a dark area grew visible through the branches. A cave? It was right above the stream. Or did the stream flow out of it? That would make more sense.

"That's the source," Tonovan said.

"Definitely a barrier," Vinjo said.

"I think so too," Malek said. "It's blocking that cave entrance. Too bad. The ship is small enough that we could have flown into it. I wonder how far back it goes."

"Do we *want* to fly into it?" Tonovan asked. "I thought we were looking for a plant."

"We are, but the map says to follow the river, and we won't be able to follow it if it disappears underground. Although... the plant is supposed to be at the mouth of the waterway. This might be the place."

Jadora leaned forward, gripping the edge of the console as she studied the foliage to either side of the stream. "I see some fronds. There. Growing behind those mossy boulders. It could be the Jitaruvak."

"It had better be." Vinjo slumped against the back of Malek's seat. "I can't stay here for long, or my head will explode."

Jadora expected Tonovan to mock him, but he and Malek only nodded in agreement, painful expressions on their faces. Malek tapped a control to bring the ship to a stop.

"That's as close as we're getting?" Jadora didn't see trails alongside the stream, and the steep vegetation- and boulder-filled slope would be hard to navigate on foot.

"That's as close as we *can* get. Unless we can force down that barrier out there." Malek scowled back at Vinjo. "Quit breathing all over the back of my neck."

Vinjo stumbled back, lifting his hands. "Sorry."

Malek only glared at him for a moment before catching himself, turning around, and taking a deep breath. He looked sadly over at Jadora. *The tea didn't work.*

I'm sorry. Out loud, she said, "If someone can lower me down to the ground, I'll get samples of the plant."

"You won't be able to get through that barrier," Vinjo said. "It's extremely strong. I'm surprised it doesn't affect the plants. How could anything grow with all that magic pummeling it all the time?"

"I don't feel anything," Jadora said.

"Must be nice," Malek grumbled, then stood up. "Unfortunately, we didn't bring anyone with a dragon-steel weapon along. I'll see if I can poke a hole through the barrier with lesser dragon steel." He touched his main-gauche.

There was a time when Jadora wouldn't have been uneasy about Malek touching his weapons, but now...

He turned the sad look at her again and lowered his hand. *I know. After we figure out how to get you a plant sample, you had better prepare that knockout potion.*

Malek...

He didn't respond, only pushing past Tonovan and Vinjo to leave navigation. "If this doesn't work, we'll have to try Shikari. He walks through powerful barriers with ease."

"Tell me about it," Tonovan grumbled.

"He doesn't want to go out there," Jak said, his voice floating out of his cabin's open hatch. "He's not only hiding under the bunk and trembling, but he's sharing images with me of dragons being chained in caves for all of eternity."

"We may not have a choice." Malek climbed up the ladder.

"This is what we came for. If it's the last thing I accomplish, I'm getting that plant for Uthari."

Jadora rose to grab her specimen-gathering tools and follow him.

Tonovan lifted a hand. "It may not be safe for you with him."

As if it was safe for her here with Tonovan.

He squinted at her, his eyes boring into her skull. She blanked her thoughts, save for reciting rhymes from *The Mind Way*.

Why is the boy suddenly learning to craft magical devices? Tonovan demanded.

Like a hound that had caught an enticing scent, he refused to back away from that.

"He likes to learn." Jadora tried to duck under Tonovan's arm to slip out of navigation—Malek had already gone outside and jumped to the ground.

Tonovan clamped his hand on her shoulder, his grip hard. *He's trying to learn to make something specific. What?*

Jadora shook her head, lowering her hand to a pocket. She hadn't stopped carrying vials of acid around, not on this ship filled with mages.

And tell me, Tonovan continued, his eyes boring into her, *why the lemonade tasted funny last night.* His grip tightened painfully. *And why my cock has been limper than Malek's wit ever since I drank it.*

I don't know what you're talking about. Damn it, she hadn't been thinking about that. How had he known?

I'm not a dullard, and I know those two mindless girls wouldn't have done it. Tonovan pulled her close, a snarl on his lips. *After your crazy zidarr is dead, you're going to spend the night in my cabin. Without lemonade.*

Just as she wrapped her fingers around a vial, Vinjo stumbled into them. He bumped her in the back and jostled her free of Tonovan's grip while making it appear accidental.

"You idiot," Tonovan snapped.

"Sorry," Vinjo groaned, clipping Tonovan in the chest with his elbow as he grabbed his head. "Isn't that magic bothering you as much as it is me?"

"*You're* bothering me."

Jadora took advantage and darted away, grabbing her tools from the lab as quickly as possible.

"Thanks," she whispered to Vinjo as she passed. She was beginning to like him.

I'm glad. He winked at her, though pain tightened his mouth and eyes. *When we get back, make sure to let Sasko know how noble and sexy I was on this mission.*

Sexy? Jadora climbed up the ladder and onto the deck, hurrying to escape any further wrath Tonovan wanted to unleash on her.

Surely, you noticed how sexily I banged Tonovan in the chest.

Ah, of course. Jadora went along with Vinjo's joke since he'd helped her. Humor was far from her mind. *It was quite a lovely gesture.*

A sexy gesture.

As soon as Jadora reached the railing, her feet lifted from the deck. Her stomach flip-flopped, both because of the sensation of being levitated into the air and because she was going down there to be alone with a man who might be losing his mind.

"Nothing to worry about," she whispered.

She landed on a mossy boulder slick with spray from the river. From below, the mouth of the cave appeared much larger. It was taller and wider than the center of the portals and appeared to travel far underground, but with little sunlight filtering through the leaves, it was too dark inside to see much.

Malek crouched between her and the plants, with his main-gauche in hand. As she navigated toward him, he thrust the weapon into the air—or what *appeared* to be nothing but air—in front of him.

Light flashed, and he flew backward, sailing over her head.

"Malek!" Jadora blurted, spinning to watch him arc toward the boulders.

Her foot slipped, and she flailed before catching her balance. Malek managed to twist in the air like a cat. He came down lightly on one of the boulders, his weapon still in hand, a glower on his face as he once again faced the cave—and whatever barrier blocked it from them.

Usually, Jadora admired his athleticism, but now she worried about defending against it if he snapped. Would the onset continue to be gradual? Or would he lose his temper—and his mind—all at once?

His glare shifted to her, and she emptied her mind, the same way she had with Tonovan. Maybe her doubt in him was irritating him.

"I'm going to tell Jak to bring Shikari down," was all Malek said.

"I'll see if I can find any of the plant growing outside of the barrier," Jadora said, though she couldn't know exactly where its boundaries were. Hopefully, she wouldn't accidentally brush it and end up flying through the air. *She* would land on her back and crack her head open on a rock.

"Be careful." Malek looked toward the ship and switched to telepathy to speak to Jak.

Jadora clambered over the rocks and logs, and through numerous types of vegetation, but the only plants with fronds were beyond the area where Malek had encountered the barrier.

"Oh," she said, halting.

Of course. If this was the Jitaruvak, a plant that had been valued by humans and likely the dragons who'd given it to them, it made sense that it would be protected. Maybe some of the dragons of eld had lived in that cave and cultivated the plant in this very spot.

"Could this barrier be ten thousand years old?" she wondered.

"Magic usually fades over time." Malek lifted a hand to Jak, who'd come up to the deck, but Shikari wasn't with him. "I said bring the dragon!" Malek roared, jerking his hand down.

"He won't come," Jak called, appearing uneasy in the face of Malek's anger. Jadora couldn't blame him. "If that's something to keep dragons away, it's not likely that a dragon could puncture the barrier."

"Not if he's busy cowering in your cabin."

Jak spread his hands helplessly.

"Don't worry about it," Jadora said, not wanting Malek to lose his temper and hurt Jak—and knowing Malek wouldn't forgive himself for that either. "I'll keep looking. Hold on. I think I see a plant growing outside of the barrier."

Jadora didn't know what shape the barrier had but envisioned it as concave around the mouth of the cave. She crept farther away from the water before angling toward a cliff. There *were* plants with fronds growing near it.

"Jadora, stop," Malek called.

She halted so quickly she pitched forward and almost fell.

Malek swore. "Are you all right?"

"Yes." She straightened and looked around warily. "Why?"

A long moment passed, and it was Jak who spoke first.

"You went through the barrier, Mother."

"Are you sure?"

"Yes," Malek and Jak answered together.

"Nothing happened, as far as I can tell. I'll see if I can get to the plants."

Malek hesitated. "Be careful."

"I'll just take a sample and get out." But as Jadora pulled out her tools, the musical notes of a flute or something like it wafted out of the cave. It had a pleasant and almost hypnotic quality to it, but she feared whoever was making the noise was far from an ally.

She hurried to cut pieces of the fronds and pull up roots of the plant, stuffing everything into her backpack. She could examine the samples more carefully later.

Malek drew both of his weapons and faced the cave. "Get out of there, Jadora!"

"Mother, look out!"

From her position, Jadora couldn't see into the cave and didn't know if someone—or something—was coming, but the flute song played again.

Not bothering to secure the lid on her pack, she scrambled back toward Malek. The air shimmered in front of her, and a man appeared out of nowhere.

Jadora squawked and stumbled back, almost falling into the plants she'd been gathering. Another man appeared beside the first. They wore something similar to moccasins and buckskin trousers, with their chests bare except for ornate bone flutes that hung diagonally across them on straps. Each man also had a large tattoo of a blue dragon across their pectorals and bore a mace and short sword on their belts. A *dragon-steel* mace and short sword.

If she could grab one and throw it, might it bring down the barrier so Malek could reach her to help?

Maybe, but the men had the same dangerous miens as zidarr and the muscular builds of warriors. Further, they were scowling intently at her, not distracted in the least by Jak and Malek.

You came to steal the Jitaruvak, one man thundered into her mind, the words in another language but their meaning clear.

To harvest some of it, Jadora thought. *I assumed it grew wild and that anyone could gather it.*

You assumed it grew wild behind a magical barrier?

I can't sense the barrier. Never mind that everyone else had.

"Jadora!" Malek called. "Are you all right? Are they hurting you? If they do, I'll kill the bastards." Rage seethed in his voice.

Most people would have quailed at the presence of an angry

zidarr. These men didn't even glance back. They faced Jadora, their backs to Malek and Jak and the ship, and they weren't worried in the least.

"I'm not sure yet," Jadora said, not taking her focus from them.

Not only are you a thief, but you carry the young of a dragon with you. One of the young that was stolen from the secret place where the Eggs of Hope have been hidden for millennia.

"We didn't steal it. The portal asked my son to take it." As soon as she blurted the words, she wished she hadn't. She didn't want to bring their attention to Jak.

One man looked balefully over his shoulder at him. The other focused on Jadora, lifting a hand toward her face.

Powerful magic scraped through her mind. Painfully. She gasped and arched her back.

Panting, she dug out one of her vials and threw it at her assailant. It burst into flame in the air and never reached him.

Her memories of the previous weeks flashed into her mind. Of unearthing the artifact and having it taken by Uthari's people. Of the battle in his sky city and escaping to Zewnath with the portal. Of returning it to the pool in the jungle and using it to find the frozen world. Of fighting the dragon, carrying the injured Malek back to the glacier, and discovering the portal inside. Of finding the eggs. Of Jak smiling as he walked out with one of them.

But did the man see that the portal had directed Jak to that egg? That it had *told* him to help Shikari?

Agony pulsed in her mind as her tormentor tore through her every thought. Her limbs grew weak, and blackness threatened to overcome her. She was aware of Malek shouting threats in the distance, but he was as powerless to affect these people as he had been against the rulers in Vran.

As Jadora's legs gave out and the darkness pressed in closer, her last thought was that the chief and his wife had sent them here because they'd known about these people, known she and Jak and Malek would be punished for having taken a dragon egg.

Sasko hadn't expected to ever wake again, but when she did, with her head throbbing in sync with her heartbeat, she thought she would find herself in an underground druid dungeon with roots growing out of the ceiling and binding her like shackles. Instead, she sat propped up with her back against a tree. A stony-faced, white-haired druid woman with a staff gazed down at her.

She didn't look like someone who would leap into battle, but a swollen lump marked her temple, and a bloody gash stood out on her hand. Had she joined her people in fighting Thorn Company and the crew of the *Star Flyer* after the ship crashed? The tip of her staff glowed green, so Sasko had no doubt she had magical power.

The stabbing behind Sasko's eyes intensified when she slowly turned her head left and right, trying to figure out where they were and if the others had survived. Dawn had come, and all around her, the jungle was torn up with leaves and branches littering the ground.

The druid monument was visible through the trees, the stones pitted with age and unremarkable in the daylight. Someone had blasted the slab on top, leaving rock scattered around the base, but whoever had done it wasn't in the area now. Sasko couldn't see either of the mageships. What if the *Star Flyer* hadn't crashed, after all, but they'd left her here in the jungle with the druids?

She spotted a few bodies lying amid the debris. Druid bodies. Those who'd survived wouldn't be pleased.

Sasko reluctantly turned her gaze back to the woman—to her captor.

I ordered the warriors to spare your life, the woman spoke into her mind. *Darmok was going to kill you, as your mages killed our people, but I sensed that you are a reluctant warrior here.*

"You've got that right," Sasko muttered.

Her lip must have split during the fall, for speaking caused it to bleed, tainting her mouth with the taste of iron. She dabbed her sleeve to it and decided to stick with thinking her responses. The druid would be able to understand them.

You work for the mages because being a soldier is what you trained for and it is all you know.

Yeah.

Sasko wasn't thinking about her past or her career. How was the woman dredging the information from her mind?

You are the second in charge of your mercenary unit and have sway over your commander.

Uh. I am second in command, Sasko replied. There seemed little point in denying it when the woman was certain. *My sway over the captain is limited. Usually, when I try to talk her into something she doesn't agree with, she tells me fables.*

About animals?

Often.

She is not unappreciative of nature then?

Sasko stared at the woman. This was a strange conversation, not the kind of interrogation she would have expected.

I guess.

If I let you return to your people, will you give a message to your captain?

A message? I can probably do that. As long as the druid woman didn't command her to slit her captain's throat or something equally vile.

No. Your Colonel Sorath wishes our people to help your mercenary company escape the jungle and the mages. It is difficult for us to help *you when you attack us. Tell your captain to cease all hostilities toward the druids, leave the mageship and the mages, and wait for us in the jungle. Only then will we fulfill our part of the bargain.*

Sorath was bargaining on our behalf? Sasko couldn't help but feel wistful about the idea of leaving the mages and this hot, humid place. She longed for the dry air of the Southern Desert, for simple work that pitted her against other soldiers instead of ridiculously powerful mages. A part of her wouldn't mind retiring from even that work, but she didn't know what else she would do.

He was.

What did he promise you in exchange for helping us? Sasko felt certain there had been a deal. If she was going to deliver messages to the captain, she had better get all of the details.

The druid hesitated before saying, *It is best that you do not know. Otherwise, the mages will read your thoughts and pass on warnings. He has not completed the task yet.*

Ah. Sasko wanted more information, but she wasn't in a position to demand it.

As a gesture of good faith, I will give you the gift of a magical future stone. I suggest you use it, take it to the other soldiers, and also have them use it.

Does that mean my people are nearby? Sasko looked around again.

They are repairing the crashed ships beyond the meeting stones. We kept them from finding you when they searched. Take my message to your leader, and take this. The druid stepped forward, her legs oddly wreathed in mist. Sasko wondered if she was dreaming and would wake up in shackles after all.

The woman drew something from a pocket, what looked like a dark blue egg. She tossed it into the air, but instead of falling, it floated slowly toward Sasko.

Sasko didn't know if she wanted it, but she felt compelled to hold out her hand. The egg landed in her palm, lighter than she expected. It emanated warmth, and she wondered if it was partially made from dragon steel.

Sometimes, the stones show you the past, the druid said, *to remind you of the dreams you once held, so that you may determine if you are still on the path to achieving them. Other times, they show you possible futures. I have no sway over what that one will show you, but I have found the stones useful in helping me follow a path that leads toward good instead of toward evil. Magic and power are as much of a temptation for our kind as for mages. Perhaps if they had such stones, they would make different choices.*

"I'm sure," Sasko muttered, dabbing her bleeding lip again.

The druid stepped back, and the mist thickened as the shadows merged and swallowed her. Before, it had been silent in the jungle, but now, Sasko grew aware of insects buzzing and the screeches of a hunting bird. If not for the warmth of the stone in her hand, she would have believed she'd dreamed the exchange. Or hallucinated it.

She leaned her head back against the rough bark of the tree, wishing the druid had given her painkillers instead of an egg. It warmed in her hand, and Sasko barely resisted the urge to throw it into the jungle. But if the woman *had* saved her life—and given what Sasko remembered from when she'd lost consciousness, she believed that claim—maybe Sasko owed it to her to let its magic ooze over her.

The mist thickened, and she dozed off. Dreams swept in as the egg pulsed warmth into her hand.

Brilliant sunlight replaced the hazy jungle morning, and she was on the deck of a black-hulled mageship, fighting with Thorn Company soldiers. Captain Ferroki and Sergeant Words were there, as well as Dr. Fret with her medical kit. She knelt over Tezi, who was sprawled on her back, blood staining the deck underneath her. She'd lost her battle-axe and appeared to be near death.

The ship tilted wildly, as if struck by a tidal wave, and Sasko saw the sea far below. They weren't flying over the Zewnath jungle any longer. Why had they left? A forced retreat? A mission to address a threat elsewhere?

Two brown-and-gray mottled dragons swept down, hurling magic at the ship. Nearby mages struggled to keep a barrier up, but it shredded under the assault of their powerful enemies. One dragon flew in close, knocked mages and mercenaries over the railing, and landed on the deck. The ship tilted again, and the crew struggled to cast fireballs while keeping their balance.

Captain Ferroki threw a grenade, angling it into the dragon's maw. It blew up, but the explosive only angered the great creature. It roared and lunged for her, jaws full of sword-like fangs snapping for her. Ferroki rolled away, but she wasn't quick enough, and the dragon plucked her up and bit her in half.

"No!" Sasko cried.

Almost carelessly, the dragon flicked its tail. Sasko tried to leap away, but it was too fast. The tail struck her like a battering ram and knocked her over the railing. She flailed as she tumbled hundreds of feet toward the deep blue sea. Sharks swam below, already devouring the bodies of those who'd fallen before her.

Sasko woke with a gasp.

She was back in the jungle, her back still against the tree. Growling, she raised her hand, again thinking of hurling the egg into the trees. But her head throbbed, and pain blasted her shoulder. She dropped the egg and jerked her arm in close, cradling it and wishing for Dr. Fret.

If the druid had spoken the truth, the others were still alive, and the crashed ship might be nearby.

Sasko groaned as she used the tree for support and levered herself to her feet. The mist had faded, but there was enough foliage scattered on the ground that it took her a moment to find the egg. She thought about kicking dirt over it and leaving it there.

The druid had given it to her to manipulate her. It wasn't a *gift*. Not in the least.

But it *was* magical, and it doubtless had some value. Maybe she could talk some mages into holding it, and they would have dreams that prompted them to give Thorn Company severance pay and break off their occupation of Zewnath.

"Wishful thinking," Sasko muttered, but she bent and picked up the egg.

If nothing else, Vinjo might enjoy playing with it.

As she shambled toward the monument, Sasko wondered where he was and how his trip was going. Better than hers, she hoped.

Though as she walked through the jungle, searching for the ship, another dream swept over her. She stumbled, surprised that could happen while she was standing.

Thankfully, the new dream was different. Sasko was in one of the adobe homes that were typical back in Perchver along the desert coast. She was monitoring a couple of toddlers wrestling on a rug. That confused Sasko until she realized they were *her* toddlers. Children she'd never had. Children she… *could* have?

That wasn't anything she'd thought she wanted. After the man she'd fallen for and married at a young age had sold her into slavery, she hadn't ever wanted another serious relationship, hadn't wanted to risk being vulnerable like that again. And as a mercenary, she certainly hadn't planned to have children.

A flashing toy with wheels rolled past the toddlers, and they stopped wrestling with each other to chase after it. It zigzagged, sped under a sofa, and effectively eluded its pursuers, though the children giggled mightily at its antics. They chased it into an adjoining room, and Sasko followed, only to come face to face with its maker. Vinjo.

He was fully clothed and free of bruises, wearing simple

civilian garments favored in the desert, not one of Zaruk's uniforms. When he saw her, he smiled and kissed her.

Sasko jolted out of the second dream as she almost ran into a tree. She stopped herself, the coarse bark under her fingers helping bring her back to reality.

She scowled sourly down at the egg. "If you think I'd have kids with that big goof, you don't know a thing. Magical future stone, my left tit."

"Lieutenant Sasko?" a familiar voice called out uncertainly. "We've been looking for you."

Sasko had walked farther as she'd dreamed, and the hull of the *Star Flyer* was now visible ahead, half-hidden among the trees. The bangs and sawing noises of repairs reached her ears. Either by accident, or through the egg's guidance, she'd found the company.

"Captain Ferroki? Is Dr. Fret with you?" Sasko headed for the ship. "I need some of her potions."

"Yes," Ferroki said. "The only one not here is Tezi."

Sasko halted. "Did she… not make it?"

"She's all right. Or she was a few hours ago. Captain Rivlen grabbed her for an incursion team, and they haven't returned yet."

"Rivlen took Tezi? Why? To be a sacrifice?"

"Because of her axe."

"Did she take Tinder too?"

"No, Tinder was injured."

"I hope that doesn't mean Dr. Fret has used up all of her potions." Sasko found a place where she could gingerly climb up to the deck. The pain in her shoulder made her wish she could levitate herself like a mage.

Ferroki pulled her over the railing. Thorn Company had been put to work nailing wood over holes in the deck while the engineers used their magic to fix the devices that powered the ship.

While Sasko relayed the druid's message to Ferroki, she rubbed the egg and debated whether to give it to the captain.

"What is that?" Ferroki noticed her looking at it.

"A druid manipulation stone."

"A what?"

Sasko snorted. "The woman called it a *future* stone, but judging by the dreams it gave me, dreams meant to guide me away from continuing my life as a mercenary working for mages, it's meant to manipulate me. Do you want to hold it?"

"You want *me* to be manipulated?"

"I guess not, but I thought I should give you the option. One of the dreams showed me with my children I'm not planning to have."

"Children? You're not the most maternal woman in the company."

"Please, there aren't *any* maternal women in the company. Except maybe Fret."

"True."

Ferroki eyed the egg. "Perhaps you should give it to the mages. Or Captain Rivlen when she returns."

"Good idea. She might die of shock if it showed her having children."

"Did someone call for a doctor?" Fret headed toward them, her medical kit in hand.

"I don't think anything is broken," Sasko said, "but I'm hoping you have painkillers."

"Naturally. Why don't you let me examine you first?"

"How about concurrently? My head is throbbing."

"Maybe that's understandable if you dreamed of children," Ferroki murmured. "I hear they can be trying."

"More trying than commanding sixty squabbling women?"

"Perhaps not."

Sasko sank down so Fret could fix her up and thought about

telling Ferroki that the first dream had been much worse. The memory of the dragon snapping the captain in half would haunt her.

Sasko hoped it had been a dream—a nightmare—and nothing more. Not truly some prophecy of the future. If it had been... how could she keep it from coming true?

21

YIDAR LOCATED THE TUNNEL THAT SORATH AND THE DRUID HAD used to sneak into the camp. Not easily. Some druid magic had filled in the mouth of the tunnel, as well as the first hundred yards of it, and smoothed over all evidence that it had ever existed, replanting the plants and shrubs that must have been uprooted in its creation.

But Yidar had magic of his own. Once he knew the location of it, courtesy of the prisoner he'd left in the brig, he dug into the ground above it and excavated a vertical shaft. He smiled in triumph when that shaft intersected with the tunnel.

Before he'd dug the hole, he hadn't sensed any magic in the ground, no evidence of the secret passageway twenty feet below him, but now he could feel it as well as see it. Unfortunately, his magic couldn't tell him if Sorath had gone that way.

He scratched his jaw, debating if he should hop down and follow it. It might spit him out in the middle of a horde of druids. It could also be full of booby traps. If Yidar had a secret underground base with a tunnel leading to it, *he* would booby-trap it. Copiously.

Yidar gazed up at the canopy, stretching out with his senses to see if any of the mageships had changed position since last he'd looked. Not noticeably. Most of Uthari's ships were circled together, poised to fire at the enemy fleets if needed, while continuing to protect their treasured dragon artifact.

Uthari was still snuggled up to the portal. The ships closest to his fleet, some closing to within firing range, belonged to Vorsha's people, King Dy, and Zaruk. The same rulers who'd originally allied to try to steal the portal from Uthari.

Farther out lurked the ships of the other kings. Yidar believed they'd only shown up because they were opportunistic and hoped to acquire the portal, or at least some of the resources found in other worlds, while the other fleets squabbled and were too distracted to notice them sneaking in.

Might Yidar find allies among them? Beyond his own *King's Courage*, he had few resources to call upon. Uthari seemed to want him to handle Sorath single-handedly, but if the colonel was back in the collective bosom of the druids, it would be hard to pull him out.

Not that Yidar *had* to crawl through their tunnel and into their laps. During the interrogation, he'd gotten the location of an underground druid village from the prisoner, the place where he believed Kywatha lived when she wasn't plotting to get the portal. It might be easier to strike there than at the druid headquarters. Perhaps he could find people close to Kywatha, grab them, and use them as bait to lure her out. Her *and* the key.

In case Yidar ended up facing all of the druids, it wouldn't be a bad idea to have some backup. Rivlen was out there, but Yidar was reluctant to reach out to her. It still rankled him that Uthari had sent *her* out in command of a fleet and wanted *her* to get the key. Yidar would love to accomplish that task before she could, to show Uthari that he'd made a mistake.

Yidar knew a few zidarr among the other fleets. Might he offer to share the key with one of them in exchange for assistance? Though zidarr from rival powers rarely worked together, they tended to respect each other. One could be a contact for him, a possible way in.

King Jutuk's fleet was on the fringes, neither an aggressor nor a firm ally to Uthari, but since they'd sent men along with Malek, Yidar had to assume they were putatively working together. Jutuk's zidarr might tattle on Yidar if he reached out to them. Besides, Prolix was the only one he knew, and he'd also gone with Malek.

He spotted a zidarr called Moon Stabber from King Darekar's fleet and reached out to him.

Lord Yidar? came the surprised reply. *What do you want?*

I have information that your commander may be interested in.

In exchange for what?

Help defeating the druids.

Doesn't your king have people out trying to do that already? Thus proving that Darekar's commander and likely all of the mageships out there knew that Rivlen was hunting for the druids. Not surprising.

I wish to beat them to it and earn the honor of destroying them myself. Once the druids are no longer a threat, our people can more easily make a deal and operate the portal and gain resources from the other worlds. If you bring a few ships and join me, I'll share that honor with you.

I have no need for further honor, and you're known to have betrayed your king recently. I do not trust you. Contact me no more.

Yidar snorted. So much for that idea.

He scanned the ships lingering in the distance again, looking for someone who might be more amenable to striking a deal. He might have to hint of the key and promise more than *honor*.

Maybe his mistake was in reaching out to those too cowardly to take a stance. Zaruk's fleet was nudging closer to Uthari's ships. Zaruk had ordered them into Uthari's territory before to brazenly attempt to acquire the portal. Maybe he was the one to reach out to. Except that he wasn't here in person. Yidar would have to use a dome-jir to contact him, and he doubted a king who was irritated with Uthari would accept a communication from one of Uthari's supposedly loyal zidarr. He would have to reach out to Zaruk's fleet commander and hope for the best.

Or… was Zaruk's zidarr Night Wrath still skulking in the area? He and Yidar had worked together, however accidentally, against Kywatha already. If Sorath hadn't bumbled into their ambush, they would already have her.

No. Yidar narrowed his eyes. Sorath had *pretended* to bumble. Belatedly, Yidar realized the mercenary colonel must have been deliberately helping the druid woman get away.

Night Wrath might be happy to join forces with Yidar to get Sorath and Kywatha. Yidar might not even need to mention the key.

He crouched in the brush and carefully combed Zaruk's ships for the familiar aura of Night Wrath. Picking out people among crews of hundreds wasn't easy, but at least zidarr had powerful signatures. Even so, Yidar didn't find him on any of the ships. Was he still down in the jungle, lurking around the camp and trying to find his brother?

Yidar directed his senses lower and jumped up, startled. He sensed Night Wrath far closer than he'd expected, standing near the top of the waterfall and looking down on the camp, though his aura was barely detectable. Maybe he was doing something to camouflage himself. If Yidar hadn't been looking for him specifically, he wouldn't have noticed him.

Good morning, Night Wrath, he spoke telepathically.

He sensed Night Wrath's surprise, the zidarr perhaps believing his camouflage had been sufficient to keep normal mages from noticing him. Normal mages, yes. But not someone with Yidar's abilities.

What do you want? Night Wrath asked.

To kill Sorath and all of the druids he's been working with even as he lied to our leaders and said he was working for them.

Yes, my king is irked with the man. With all of those Thorn Company mercenaries. They abandoned their contract to him, just because the captain they reported to was killed.

Sorath can't be trusted. You heard about Vorsha?

Oh, yes, Night Wrath said. *Everybody has heard about that. I wouldn't be surprised if war broke out soon. You and I could end up battling each other within the hour.*

We've worked together before. Why not do so again? I've learned from Vorsha's assassin where Sorath and the druid leader who brought those animals back from the other world are. At the least, he'd learned where they *might* be.

The druid leader who has the only other known key to the portal? Night Wrath asked.

Yidar hesitated. Maybe he'd been naive to believe he could collect allies without mentioning that.

The key to the portal that rightfully belongs to my king? Night Wrath added.

If Zaruk believes that, he would be pleased if you acquired it for him.

You know where it is?

I do. Bring three ships, and we'll slip away while the rest are posturing with each other. We'll find the key and destroy the druid threat. Your king will be pleased.

And your *king will be furious if you act against him and help Zaruk.*

You may have heard that Uthari and I had a bit of a falling out.

Yes, because you betrayed him. That tends to irk rulers.

Yidar clenched his jaw. *I want my own kingdom, not to obey him for the rest of my life.*

A zidarr with such ambitions? The Code doesn't encourage that.

The Code can fondle my sweaty balls.

What do you want, Yidar? The key for yourself? And to use me and our ships to get it?

Obviously, but we can share it. You can give it to your king and curry his favor, as a loyal zidarr should. But first, I will use it to find a world that I can claim for my own and rule over. That wasn't what Yidar wanted, but there was no need to mention his true goals to Night Wrath. If Night Wrath believed Yidar would be out of the story on another world, thus leaving the key to him...

Interesting.

I'll allow you to visit me on my world once I'm established.

How delightful. Will there be eager voluptuous women?

Of course. Yidar rolled his eyes. From what he'd heard of Malek's reports, the worlds they'd visited so far had been more inclined toward eager man-eating dragons. *Bring the three ships, and I'll give you a gift that you can grant to your fleet commander, a sign of good will.*

And that would be?

The back door that leads to the druids' headquarters. Yidar mentally shared the shaft into the tunnel at his feet. *Perhaps your people can attack through this passage while we find the woman and the key.*

Let Zaruk's fleet deal with the booby traps.

Interesting, Night Wrath repeated. *I'll see what I can arrange.*

Good.

Jak gripped the railing of the mageship, his voice hoarse as he screamed. His head ached as he tried to hurl power at the barrier that kept Malek from reaching his mother, that kept *any* of them from reaching her.

He couldn't see who was attacking her, but he sensed that two beings with magical auras had come out of the cave and now stood above her. She'd crumpled into the ferns she'd been gathering minutes earlier.

Malek slashed at the barrier, as if he could cut through, but even his lesser-dragon-steel blades couldn't manage it. He roared, his frustration as great as Jak's.

A white flash filled the air, and a great charge of power unleashed, like lightning in a storm. It hurled Malek backward twenty feet.

He twisted in the air and came down in a crouch, water splashing as he landed in the stream. Once more, he roared in frustration—and fear for Mother.

Shikari, Jak called telepathically. The dragon was the only one who might be able to help, but he'd been too afraid to leave the cabin. *Please, we need you. My mother is in trouble. And I— I can't lose her.*

Jak feared the scared dragon would ignore his plea. When the hatch opened behind him, he thought it would only be Tonovan and the others, coming up to gloat or say there was nothing that could be done.

But Shikari popped through the hatchway and crept to the railing.

"Can you force that barrier down?" Jak whispered, his gaze locked on to his mother. She wasn't moving, but the invisible beings stood over her, as if contemplating her death. "*Please*?"

The air shimmered next to Mother, and two bare-chested men appeared. Two *powerful* bare-chested men. They had auras like zidarr, if not even greater. Were they the ones who'd created the barrier? And were they what Shikari feared?

As the men's gazes locked onto Shikari, Jak rested a protective hand on his head, even though there was nothing he could do against such foes.

You are the boy, one of the men boomed into his mind.

Uh, I'm a man, thanks. Jak decided this wasn't the time to mention his chest hair. Neither of them looked like the types to appreciate humor, and he had no idea what they'd done to Mother. Dear Shylezar, what if they'd killed her for trespassing and taking a plant sample? *Is my mother all right? What did you do to her?*

Malek made his way back to the barrier, his gaze roaming the ground above the cave and to the left and right, seeking a way past the obstacle.

Your power is nascent and negligible, the man said. *Why did the portal speak to you?*

Probably because it had been buried for ten thousand years and was lonely. There weren't that many options. My mother? Is she all right?

The man who was communicating with him looked at Malek. *That one would have been a more logical choice. He has the power of a guardian.*

Yes, he does, Jak replied though he had no idea what a guardian was.

Shikari cheeped uncertainly, sounding more like a baby chicken than the predator he was growing into. The other man hadn't taken his gaze from him and tilted his head. Was he trying to communicate with Shikari? Could he? Jak had never managed to do more than exchange images with him.

We see from the woman's thoughts that you do not believe you stole the dragon egg. The dragonling has no ill intent toward you and does not seem to be a prisoner.

That's right. Jak allowed himself a hint of hope that these people could be reasoned with.

The one who'd been speaking to him turned back toward Mother and spread his palm above her.

Jak tensed with worry. *Malek, can you tell what they're doing?*

The growl that echoed in Jak's mind as a response was atypical for Malek. He prowled back and forth in front of the barrier, springing from boulder to boulder, his grip tight on his weapons. He was more like a caged animal than a man. Than a zidarr.

Can you levitate Mother through the barrier and back up here? Jak asked hopefully.

For that matter, could *Jak*? He'd levitated people before. Not with barriers involved, but maybe...

He took a steadying breath and reached out toward her, but he couldn't locate her with his mind. He *saw* her without trouble, but the barrier obfuscated what was beyond it to his magical senses. All he could detect were the auras of the men, but even they were hazy and indistinct, and without his eyes, he wouldn't have known for certain that they *were* men.

Mother stirred. Jak was positive he'd had nothing to do with it.

She peered blearily up at the men. Her eyes were wary but not bulging with fear. Jak hoped that was a good sign.

Mother? he asked telepathically. *Can you hear me?*

It was hard to target someone that his senses didn't think was there, but she nodded, and he heard the whisper of her thoughts.

Yes.

Are you injured? What did they do to you? Jak gripped the railing more tightly. *We can't get through the barrier to you.*

I think they read my mind and got all of my memories—and then some. Mother looked bleakly toward him. *If they didn't know about the dragon eggs and where they were before, they do now.*

I think they already knew.

Mother pushed herself to her feet, wobbling and spreading her arms for balance. The men watched impassively, not reaching out to help. Instead, they bent their heads together, as if to trade whispers, but they conferred telepathically.

You may not take the sacred plant of our ancestors, one said when they broke apart. He looked at Mother rather than Jak or the ship, but the words were for all of them.

Jak sensed Tonovan and the other mages inside the navigation cabin below, watching but doing nothing to help. Jak ground his teeth. Why had Uthari bothered to send them along?

Not until we've determined that you may be worthy of it. We would not even consider it, but we do not wish to act against the desires of a mighty dragon. The man looked up at Shikari.

Shikari plopped down on his butt, lifted a wing, and scraped one taloned foot against his side to scratch an itch. He looked far more like a dog than a mighty dragon.

I am Rathidor. The man who'd been doing all the speaking pointed at himself. *And this is my brother Ramidor. You will follow us up the stream to our home and see our chief. She will determine the full truth and what to do about the hatched dragonling.*

"Do about?" Jak whispered.

He hoped the dragons tattooed on their chests meant they revered dragons, not something more ominous, such as that they liked to hunt them down and roast them over a spit.

Return to your flying boat. The journey is one of many hours.

The brother—Ramidor—tapped his arm and pointed at Mother's backpack in the dirt at her feet.

Yes. I see. Rathidor nodded toward it, and the lid opened.

The plant specimens floated out, raining dirt down onto the pack. Mother's fingers twitched toward them, as if she would try to stop the theft, but her shoulders slumped in defeat. Like Jak, she was powerless against these people.

Jak assumed they would stop at removing her samples, but flames burst from the foliage all around them. Mother stumbled away from the burning bushes—the burning Jitaruvak.

If the plants were so valuable, why would the men *destroy* them? Simply to keep strangers from gathering them?

Jak shook his head. They had to know where more were. Or maybe the plant grew back quickly.

"That wasn't necessary," Mother said. "If you'd said it was

forbidden to take it, I would have accepted that." She glanced toward the still-seething Malek.

Mother couldn't know if *he* would have accepted it, or if he would have felt compelled by Uthari's orders to defy the locals. Right now, he didn't look like he was thinking about the plant at all, simply that he wanted to attack the men who'd knocked down Mother.

Jak wouldn't have minded seeing that, but now that she was on her feet and didn't seem badly injured, he could calm down. He felt even better when the men levitated her and her backpack into the air, floating her over the stream and back onto the deck of the ship. Jak sprang over and hugged her.

"I'm all right," she whispered, patting his back.

You will follow us, Rathidor repeated. *Do not attempt to deviate from the river. There are dangers in the side tunnels, and predators swim in the waters. Few are invited into our home. Those who attempt to sneak in without an invitation never leave.*

"Do we have to go at all?" Jak muttered.

He cared little about that stupid plant. What he wanted was to find a way to fix Malek and destroy that dragon parasite so he could keep Shikari from being turned into a mottled monster.

"The chief they spoke of may have useful knowledge," Mother said. "And I doubt Malek would want us to give up on the Jitaruvak."

"*Malek* isn't in his right mind now." Jak shivered as he remembered that growl.

Malek was still on the ground, glaring at the men as they discussed something else, and eyeing the barrier, as if he meant to attack as soon as they lowered it.

"I'll figure out a way to help him," Mother said firmly.

In the water at the mouth of the cave, two skiffs floated into view. Somehow, they held their position against the current. The men sprang into them, landing as lightly and agilely as Malek might have. Whoever these guardians were, Jak guessed they were this world's equivalent of the zidarr.

A startled squeak came from Shikari. He rose into the air.

Jak gaped, at first believing he was using his innate dragon power to levitate himself, but why would he? The men had to be responsible.

"You can't take him!" Jak lunged to grab his charge.

But a barrier appeared around Shikari, and electricity shocked Jak as he tried to grab him.

He will come with us, Rathidor said, *until the chief makes her decision in regard to you and your suitability as a protector. It is likely she will decide that he will be safer with us.*

"You can't *take* him," Jak yelled, barely keeping himself from grabbing for Shikari again as he floated over the railing. Mother had seen him be shocked, and she gripped his shoulder to keep him from doing it to himself again. "He's my friend. I get insects for him, and I'm trying to teach him how to fly. I'm a good protector."

The two brothers answered only with condescending looks as Shikari floated toward them.

"You don't have the right to take him from me," Jak tried again. "Or the right to judge whether or not I'm *suitable*. Who *are* you people?"

We are the guardians of the dragon legacy.

Jak shook his head, unable to believe their magic was working on Shikari. He could waltz through Tonovan's barrier, was impervious to deadly bugs, and already had magical power of his own. Why was he letting them take him? Why couldn't he stop them?

Shikari swished his tail as he floated toward the skiffs. He looked back at Jak, his yellow eyes always more expressive than one would expect from a scaled creature. Jak read the sorrow in them, the sadness that he was being taken from him. Unless that was all in Jak's mind. It was certainly what *he* felt.

"Soar to the stars, my friend," he whispered, afraid he was about to lose Shikari forever.

"We're being invited to go along," Mother reminded him. "Maybe we'll be able to get him back."

"Or maybe they'll never let me see him again."

"If it's possible this place is safer for him, that these people would be strong protectors, maybe that wouldn't be the worst thing," she said softly.

"Yes, it would be. I found him, and he's *my* friend. One day, we're supposed to fly together and save our world and be heroes." Jak stopped himself from saying more. He sounded like a child, and he knew it. But in a short time, he'd come to care for Shikari, and it was hard to imagine never seeing him again. He pushed his hands through his hair in frustration.

The hatch opened, and Prolix stuck his head out.

Malek sprang up from below, startling Jak and Jadora as he flew over the railing and landed in a crouch next to them. He hadn't put his weapons away, and they eyed him warily. The wildness that cloaked him was alarming.

But he didn't growl. He sheathed his weapons and spoke like a man, though there was an uncharacteristic rasp to his voice. "They lowered the barrier. We will follow them."

Jak nodded. "We have to get Shikari back."

"And find help for you," Jadora told Malek.

He held her gaze, and Jak thought they might have shared words telepathically. Mother dabbed at her eyes.

"Go below and rest," Malek said. "I will remain up here and watch for threats as we follow them."

"I can stay up here too," Jak said.

The skiffs were disappearing into the shadows of the cave, and he was reluctant to lose sight of Shikari.

"It would be better for me to be alone," Malek said quietly. "Safer."

Mother blinked away the moisture in her eyes, hugged him, and headed for the hatch.

Prolix had been standing on the ladder as he waited for them. Now he climbed all the way out and said, "Wait. We've got a problem with your guide."

He reached out to Mother, touching her arm to keep her from climbing down.

Malek snarled, his gaze locking on to that touch. Before Jak knew what was happening, he leaped all the way to the hatch.

"Do not touch her." Malek shoved Prolix away and drew his weapons, his face twisting with anger.

Prolix, with zidarr reflexes as honed at Malek's, drew his own weapons and faced him in a crouch. Malek sprang for him, his weapons blurring as they slashed toward Prolix's neck and chest. Prolix's eyes widened in surprise, but he parried instinctively.

"Malek!" Mother called. "Stop. He didn't do anything."

Malek snarled as he and Prolix fought. He didn't seem to hear Mother at all.

As the men lunged and parried, moving in and out in a furious and potentially deadly sparring match, Jak worried one of them would accidentally mow over his mother. He ran in and pulled her back to the railing. Even there, he didn't feel they were safe.

"Malek," Mother shouted again, barely acknowledging Jak. "You have to stop. Both of you."

"If you get killed, Tonovan will be in charge," Jak called, trying his own reasoning.

But weapons rang and clashed, the men fighting as if they were sworn enemies. At first, Prolix had acted only defensively, doubtless realizing Malek was affected by the bacteria and not himself, but as soon as Malek drew blood, slashing his longsword across Prolix's cheek, the other zidarr went on the offensive.

Jak could only watch, mesmerized by their skill but horrified at what they were trying to accomplish.

What if Tonovan or Bakir came up here to help? To gang up on Malek and ensure he didn't survive?

Jak used his senses to check on them. Only Harintha and Vinjo remained in the navigation cabin. Tonovan and Bakir were in the corridor. On their way to the ladder? Jak couldn't tell, but they had to hear the ruckus. They would come up soon.

A shadow fell across the ship, and Jak glanced up. He hadn't realized they'd started moving, but they'd flown through the former barrier and into the wide mouth of the cave. The river was louder now, the gurgle of water echoing from the walls.

The clashes of swords striking were also louder, and the frenzied sounds of the battle had to be carrying to the skiffs up ahead. Jak peered toward the two guardians, wishing he could get Shikari back, certain that the young dragon could somehow put a stop to this.

A grunt of pain and a thud came from the fight, and Mother gasped.

Jak spun back, lifting his hands and readying a gust of wind to hurl at Prolix if he'd come out on top and meant to kill Malek. But Prolix was the one on his back on the deck, bleeding from a half-dozen wounds, his mace still in hand but his short sword out of reach several feet away. Malek, chest heaving and eyes wild, had his own sword tip pressed to Prolix's throat.

"Malek." Mother crept toward him, her hands patting the air in placation. "Malek, he's not an enemy. He didn't mean anything when he touched me. Please put down your weapons. Let him up."

Malek didn't glance at her. Jak wrapped a protective barrier around her, not certain how Malek would react to her approach and afraid for her. He didn't want to believe Malek would hurt her, but...

Prolix didn't say a word and didn't move an inch, but he summoned a magical attack and tried to knock Malek away.

Malek still had the presence of mind to keep a barrier around himself, a diamond-hard barrier. The attack didn't so much as stir his hair, but Malek sensed it and growled a warning deep in his throat.

"Malek, please." Mother didn't risk touching him, but she stepped around until she stood in his peripheral vision. "Don't do this. Find the calm and rational man deep inside of you. Please. I need more time. I'll find a solution, and we'll destroy the bacteria." She swallowed. "I promise."

For the first time, Malek looked over at her. "Destroy the bacteria," he rasped.

Was it a question? Did he remember what had happened? Jak couldn't tell.

"Yes." Mother nodded. "It's affecting you, remember? This isn't you. You don't try to kill your allies." She tried a smile. "Even the ones I wish you would."

"I don't try to kill my allies," Malek repeated, then peered down at Prolix. "Correct." He pulled his sword from Prolix's throat, blood dribbling from the puncture it left. "We were sparring."

Jak managed to keep from blurting an incredulous, "*Sparring?*" He was impressed that Prolix did as well.

"A good match," Malek told Prolix, saluting him with his sword, his bloody sword.

As soon as he stepped back, Prolix rolled to the side, plucked up his fallen weapon, and sprang to his feet facing Malek.

Jak prepared a gust of wind in case he attacked when Malek wasn't ready—or what if he took out his irritation on Mother?

After a long moment, Prolix straightened. "It is always an honor to test myself against another zidarr."

He inclined his head toward Malek and cleaned his blades, going along with the charade. He did not, however, take his gaze from Malek.

A clang came from below, and Prolix seemed to remember

what had brought him out of the ship. "Professor, your guide has gone crazy."

Mother blinked. "Zethron?"

"Yes."

Her brow furrowed. "But Wharan said a sting in the arm wouldn't drive him mad."

"He attacked the helm officer and tried to take control of the ship. I sense that they got him out of navigation, but now he's between the admiral and the general. It is possible they will kill him."

"What?" Mother swore and lunged through the hatchway.

Jak hurried after her, afraid she would be caught in the middle of another fight.

But she halted at the bottom of the ladder, and he almost crashed into her. She peered into the corridor, first one way and then the other.

"Just kill the crazy bastard," came Tonovan's voice from the left.

"He's the only one who speaks the language here," Bakir said from the right.

"I'll take care of him," Mother told them. "Please let him go."

"Oh, no," Tonovan said. "We're not letting him go. He tried to destroy the navigation orb, and he almost knocked our helm officer through the porthole. Look at his eyes. He's as crazy as the savages that killed everyone on the paddleboat."

Mother eased into the corridor, putting her back to the wall so she could look in both directions, and Jak jumped to the bottom of the ladder. He peeked out of the alcove, and his heart sank. Zethron *did* look crazy.

Bakir had him in his grip, Zethron's back to his chest and a dagger to his throat. Bakir used his magic to lock him down even further. Zethron could barely move enough to breathe, but hostility and a desire to kill everyone roiled off him like body odor.

Jak wasn't trying to read his thoughts, but he caught glimpses of them anyway. They were dominated by fear and anger and a certainty that everyone wanted to kill him. Unless he killed them first.

Zethron had always been a mild-mannered man. How could he have changed so drastically?

Mother stared at the bandage on his forearm. It covered the spot where he'd been stung, but angry red lines indicating an infection crept out from under it.

"I don't understand," she whispered. "Wharan said only those who suffered stings to the back of the neck developed the mental imbalances. It was Malek he feared, not Zethron."

Malek, who'd lost control of himself not minutes before.

Jak shook his head, feeling utterly helpless. What could they do?

"We can speak telepathically with the natives," Tonovan said. "We don't need a guide. Just kill him."

"No," Mother croaked. "We can lock him up until I figure out a cure. I'm working on that."

Jak didn't think she'd made any progress, but he didn't say anything. What could he say?

Wait, the natives. Maybe those pompous brothers knew how to heal this. Unlike everyone else in this world, they weren't wearing skullcaps. Maybe they weren't worried about the threat from these bugs because they had a cure.

Tonovan rolled his eyes. "Lock him up where? This tube of a ship doesn't have a brig."

"Vinjo could make something," Bakir said.

Now that they were all inside the barrier, Jak had no trouble sensing the two powerful mages riding the skiffs ahead of them. He selected the one who'd deigned to speak with them—Rathidor—and reached out.

Our friends were stung by venomous bugs that pass on bacteria that affect their minds. Do your people know anything about them?

We are well aware of the threat the death darters pose.

Do you know how to cure people who've been stung? Two of our crew are afflicted.

I'd wondered if that was why your mage was so feral.

Feral. What a strange word to describe the usually even-tempered Malek. But Jak couldn't reject it now. *Yes, he and another are suffering because of the stings.*

You must kill them or abandon them to the predators in the waters. Otherwise, they will be a threat to you.

No kidding. *You must know a way to treat the bacteria. Otherwise, you'd wear skullcaps too, right?*

Our barriers keep our home protected and safe from bug infestations.

But not predators in the waters?

Those predators were bred by our people. They help protect our home and what we guard.

"What a waste of time," Tonovan said. "Just *kill* him. He's a useless terrene human. It's not worth worrying about saving him."

"Yes, it is." Mother raised her hands. "Any one of you could be stung if more of those bugs show up. If I can find a way to save these two men, I'll know how to treat anyone who's afflicted."

She glanced upward, though Malek hadn't left the deck. Jak sensed him up there, looking into the cave.

"You think you can experiment on this one?" Bakir asked. "And find a cure for Malek?"

"I thought we were going to kill Malek as soon as he lost it," Tonovan told him.

Bakir twitched a shoulder. "I'll do so if we must, but a cure would be better. We shouldn't sacrifice our own kind unnecessarily."

Tonovan's mouth twisted in disagreement.

Are you sure there's no cure? Jak asked Rathidor.

It is possible the ancient one knows, but she has not woken for many years. And we cannot wake her for something as trivial as that.

Why not?

Her years remaining are few. Each wakening shortens her life further.

Jak slumped against the ladder. He wasn't getting anywhere with them. Shikari would be more likely to help—if Jak could get him to focus on magically destroying the bacteria. And if he could get Shikari back.

"How are you going to lock him up?" Tonovan asked. "Chain him to his bunk?"

Zethron snarled, the tendons in his neck bulging as he strained against Bakir's magical grip.

"I have something that can knock him unconscious," Mother said. "Put him in a coma of sorts until such time as I can figure out a cure."

"All right. Do it." Bakir turned his head to bellow into navigation. "Vinjo. Come make some shackles. We're locking the savage up until the professor can knock him out."

The savage. The crazy bastard. How quick these people were to steal someone's humanity and classify him as an animal. Or worse.

"Thank you, Admiral," Mother said.

Bakir only grunted and maneuvered past her, dragging the wild-eyed Zethron to his cabin.

"You know it'll be a lot more difficult to subdue Malek," Tonovan told Bakir.

"I know."

"But if a sedative works on the guide, it should work on Malek too." Tonovan's gaze shifted to Mother, and his vile smirk curved the corners of his mouth. "Right, Professor?"

Mother didn't answer. She didn't need to. They knew.

"He would be a lot easier to deal with if he was unconscious," Bakir said wistfully.

"Yes," Tonovan said. "He would."

They held each other's gazes and exchanged nods. Jak was certain they'd already discussed subduing Malek. Permanently.

Jak realized Prolix was above him on the ladder, waiting for him to move so that he could come down. His face was in shadow, blood drying on his jaw and neck.

After Malek had attacked him, Prolix would doubtless help Tonovan and Bakir too.

Jak found his mother looking at him and could only shake his head slowly. This mission kept getting worse and worse, and he had no idea how to change that.

22

Rivlen was tired of traipsing through the druid tunnels and aware that they were getting farther and farther from her ship, a ship that might be in danger of further attacks. She'd left behind capable mages to defend it, but she would feel derelict of duty if she wasn't there herself during a battle.

They came to a three-way intersection, the fifth such intersection they'd passed. After the sinkhole trap, they'd become a regular feature of what had turned into a large subterranean tunnel system.

Tezi paused, then pointed right and walked that way. At the first intersection, she'd explained that the gem she'd taken from the fallen lizard was guiding her. Rivlen could sense its magic, so she didn't doubt it, but she had no idea if it was taking them in the direction they wanted to go or trying to divert them from finding the druids. Since they'd passed three more booby traps, with Tezi and her axe triggering them, it was clear the natives didn't like visitors.

Was it possible they were close to the druid headquarters? The place where all the troublesome schemers had been plotting before attacking the camp? Rivlen hoped so. She'd wanted the opportunity to prove herself on this mission, and having her ship crashed by a pile of rocks wasn't an effective way to do that.

The yeasty scent of something baking reached their noses.

Tezi paused. "Are the druids making bread?"

Rivlen shrugged as she stopped beside her. "Smells like it. Or something similar."

They followed their noses through the tunnel, and the walls grew brighter, the magic stronger. Rivlen rested her hand on her sword hilt, though she didn't sense the auras of anyone powerful ahead. She picked out a few magical tools, weapons, or other devices and suspected they were reaching their destination, but wouldn't there be druids guarding the entrance of their headquarters? Especially if the second lizard had made it back and let them know that intruders were in the tunnels? Rivlen glanced back, telepathically telling the other mages to be ready.

As the group crept forward, rounding another bend, the smooth dirt walls that had been formed by magic grew rougher and rockier. The tunnel broadened as it shifted into a natural cave, and up ahead, a cavern came into view, with stalactites dangling from the high stone roof. What sounded like the clanks of a blacksmith's hammer echoed from the rock.

Two men in hide tunics and woven grass trousers stood guard at the entrance to the cavern. Neither had the auras of mages, but as soon as they spotted Rivlen and her group, they drew swords. She wrapped her power around them, holding them in place and keeping them from crying out.

"Strange," Rivlen murmured, as she easily levitated them toward her group.

It didn't surprise her that there were terrene humans among the druids, but it disappointed her. Their presence suggested that whatever this place was, it wasn't the headquarters she sought.

The men struggled against her magical bonds, and their eyes grew round with fear as she reeled them in.

"Hold them while I interrogate them," Rivlen told Lieutenant Viggert.

She could likely do the two tasks at once, but she didn't want to risk one of the captives managing to cry out a warning. The camp or settlement or whatever was in the cavern wasn't far away.

"Yes, ma'am."

As soon as she sensed Viggert's power wrapped around them, Rivlen poked into one man's mind, shifting past his fear to gather information about the settlement. Or maybe it was more of a camp. She saw a lot of tents and temporary houses in his thoughts and learned that the people had recently moved there from a village near the waterfall. The druids had facilitated the move and hidden them in this place so they would be safe from the foreign mages invading the area.

Rivlen frowned to think of herself as a cruel invader who would blast through terrene humans who might have been in the way, but… she couldn't deny that this wasn't the Uth Kingdom and this land didn't belong to Uthari or any of the other rulers who'd sent fleets. It just happened to be where the portal could operate.

"I don't think we've found the druid headquarters." Rivlen leaned against the rock wall. "After all that walking and triggering of traps, we've found a refugee camp. What a waste of time."

"Are you sure, ma'am?" Lieutenant Viggert asked. "They could be tricking you."

"They're too simple to trick a sloth."

Tezi frowned, probably taking slight at an insult to a terrene human. Rivlen didn't care. She was too frustrated to worry about being political with her words.

She checked the other man's mind and found similar thoughts, though he was also dwelling on the group of druids who'd brought his people here. Rivlen glimpsed Kywatha's face among them. That made her straighten with interest.

If her team captured these people, could they use them to lure Kywatha and the other druids to this place? It wasn't an appealing idea, or an honorable one—for some reason, Jak's face floated in her thoughts—but if she failed Uthari, he wouldn't be pleased with her. She might already be in trouble when he learned she'd let the ship crash. He—

Captain Rivlen, Uthari spoke into her mind, as if she'd summoned him with her thoughts.

Rivlen swallowed, surprised he'd been able to contact her in the druid tunnels. She wished she had far better news to report. *Yes, Your Majesty?*

What is the status of your mission?

Rivlen took a deep breath. *One of Vorsha's ships crashed, but the* Star Flyer *is also down. We were engaged in a battle that her people instigated when a druid monument turned into a weapon and took both of our ships down. It also fired on the* Moon Spear, *but we helped them get away by destroying the monument. The* Star Flyer *is being repaired, and I'm hunting down the druids who were responsible.* She thought about mentioning that Ular might know more about the monument and the druids since he'd set her up for that attack, but Uthari wouldn't appreciate excuses.

I see.

As she'd feared, he didn't sound pleased.

Unless you're on the verge of capturing the druid leaders, I need you to get the Star Flyer *in the air as soon as possible. Return with it and your other ships to the camp.* Uthari shared an image of the dragon he'd mentioned the night before, followed by one of numerous ships from other fleets, all pointing their weapons toward his yacht. That was a new development.

Yes, Your Majesty. I'm underground in a druid tunnel, but I'll be on the way as soon as possible.

Rivlen winced, hoping her crew and those mercenaries were making excellent progress on the repairs. The thought of the *Star Flyer* listing into the camp two days after the fighting was over grated. She would make sure the repairs didn't take that long.

"We have to go back," Rivlen said. "Uthari just spoke to me. There's trouble back at the camp."

Relief flashed in Tezi's eyes. At first, that made Rivlen indignant—did the mercenary *want* Uthari to be in trouble?—until she realized Tezi probably didn't want to be commanded to charge into a refugee camp swinging her axe. She hadn't been privy to the men's thoughts, but she must have gotten the gist.

The earth shivered, and Rivlen gripped the stone wall, afraid another hole would open up in the ground. A tremendous boom came from the cavern, and tremors coursed through the cave. Several of her mages fell to the ground. Tezi stumbled and caught herself on her axe.

The two refugees escaped, charging back toward the cavern, but the ground heaved and buckled, and they tumbled against each other. Stalactites fell from above, plunging into the tents and other temporary structures before shattering. Men and women and children screamed.

Confusion gripped Rivlen, and she didn't know what to do beyond reflexively raising her barrier. She tried to protect Tezi as well, especially when rocks plummeted down from the roof, but with Tezi's grip on the axe, the barrier failed to wrap around her.

Rivlen sensed magical attacks, not from the cavern but above it. A thunderous crash sounded, and the entire roof collapsed. Trees and bushes fell through along with dirt and rocks, half-burying the encampment below. More screams of pain and fear erupted from the people within.

Rivlen waited until the ground steadied to creep closer. She sensed mageships hovering over the destroyed cavern, what had been the roof now open to the day. Sunlight slashed through the jungle to highlight the rubble of the camp—and three blue-hulled mageships floating over it. The uniformed crew stood at the railings and sent fireballs and lightning down to strike at the refugees.

Refugees without magic of their own, people who couldn't put up a fight. Rivlen gaped in confusion.

A familiar zidarr in black stood among the blue-uniformed mages. That was Yidar. What was he doing riding with Zaruk's forces? Had he betrayed Uthari? *Again?*

But if so, why were they here attacking this encampment instead of fighting for the portal or whatever it was Yidar thought he was going to get out of this betrayal?

Rivlen clenched her jaw, tempted to launch a fireball straight at him. He was scanning the wreckage of the encampment, and she didn't think he'd seen her yet. Her team was still hidden in the shadows of the tunnel. But if she attacked, she could end up with three ships full of mages attacking back. And her priority was to obey Uthari and find her way back without delay. She would, however, be sure to report this to him.

"What's going on?" Tezi whispered.

Her words were barely audible over the moans and cries from the camp. The mages had stopped hurling fireballs, but many of the refugees lay injured or dead under the rubble.

Yidar's roving gaze traveled toward their tunnel. Rivlen reached over and gripped Tezi's axe, knowing it would camouflage her strong aura, and stepped farther back into the shadows.

Yidar sprang down from the ship, dropping more than thirty feet to land in a crouch amid the rubble. He rose with his weapons in his hands and grabbed the nearest person, a woman without a hint of magic about her. He gripped her with his power, and she screamed.

Tezi stepped forward and hefted her axe, as if she meant to charge out and attack Yidar, but Rivlen tightened her grip, keeping Tezi in place. Confronting a zidarr would only get her killed. Tezi was no match for Yidar, whether she had protection from magic or not. Yidar had the weapons skills to decapitate her with a flick of his wrist.

He's probably just questioning her and trying to find out where the real druids are, Rivlen told her.

Tezi scowled at her, not reassured.

Yidar snarled and flung the woman aside. Her head struck a boulder as she fell, and she didn't stir.

"Where is the woman Kywatha?" Yidar yelled, as if those people understood their language.

What I don't understand is why he appears to be here with Zaruk's forces, Rivlen added.

What I *don't understand is why he's hurting these people.* Tezi tugged her axe free from Rivlen's grip. *We should stop him.*

You're no match for him one-on-one and certainly not with dozens of mages up there ready to open fire. They have cannons as well as magic, and your axe won't help with that. Besides, Yidar could be here because Uthari ordered it. He's supposed to be getting a second chance.

Yidar snarled and, with a surge of magic, flung one of the men twenty feet.

A second chance for what? Tezi demanded. *To prove himself a villain*?

Rivlen sighed. She didn't know. If Zaruk's ships hadn't been there, she would have confronted Yidar and asked him what he was doing. As it was, she worried that someone would notice the auras of her team and open fire on them. The shadows under the overhang of the tunnel protected them from view, but one didn't need vision to sense auras.

As Yidar hefted another woman to question—if that was truly what he was doing as he shook and tormented these people—a soft shifting of rubble sounded behind him. That was peculiar, since the rockfall had ended, and Rivlen hadn't seen more debris tumble down.

Yidar must have heard it and thought so too, for he shoved his prisoner away and spun toward the noise. It didn't repeat.

Rivlen scanned the area, trying to detect other magic users among the moaning refugees, but she could only sense Yidar and the mages on the ships above. They were leaning against the railings, but most appeared bored with the show and were talking to each other instead of watching intently.

Something hit Yidar's barrier and clattered to the ground. A pebble?

Rivlen doubted any of the mages dared flick debris at a zidarr, but *someone* had thrown it. A mundane human who needed to physically test a barrier to determine if it was there?

Yidar prowled in the direction the pebble had come from, squinting into the debris, but Rivlen didn't see anyone crouched amid the broken stalactites. Even if there was, she doubted these people would be foolish enough to pick an attack with a grumpy zidarr.

Someone's out there with them, Rivlen told Tezi and glanced back, silently ordering her men to stay back and not use any magic that would draw the attention of the other mages. *Someone who's either very good at hiding among the wreckage... or who's invisible.*

Tezi sucked in a breath.

Yidar threw a wide wave of power in the direction the pebble had originated. It caught two injured refugees, who cried out in pain as they flew backward.

I know who it might be, Tezi thought. *And* he'll *stop Yidar from hurting those people.*

Something dark spun through the air at Yidar. He must have expected it to bounce off his barrier, for he didn't try to dodge, instead sprinting toward the source. But the dark projectile turned out to be a dagger—a dragon-steel dagger—and it popped his barrier and continued on.

He jerked aside, trying to deflect it with his sword, but even he wasn't fast enough to compensate for such a late reaction. He moved enough that the dagger gashed the outside of his shoulder instead of sinking into his chest, but he grunted with pain nonetheless.

The weapon clattered to the ground. Yidar re-formed his barrier within a second and bent to grab the dagger, but something exploded on top of it. He reeled back and launched another magical attack.

But whoever had thrown the dagger must have moved. There was no sound of anyone thudding to the ground, only a few rocks stirred by the magic.

Yidar spun in a circle, throwing attacks in all directions. Rivlen crouched, pulling Tezi down beside her when one came toward their hiding spot. She had a barrier up across the tunnel, so it didn't harm them, but the magic slammed into the earth, and the walls and roof rained dirt and rocks down upon them.

Yidar must have caught their movement, for he paused and squinted at the tunnel.

Rivlen was about to say something when the dagger near his feet was snatched up. Yidar spun toward the invisible thief and roared, lunging and slashing with his sword. Steel clanged as his target parried. Rivlen couldn't see anyone—the dagger had disappeared from view—but Yidar must have been close enough to see through whatever camouflage hid his attacker. Or *had* hidden him.

A masculine grunt sounded, and whoever it was retreated under the rapid-fire blows, the superior training of a zidarr warrior.

"It's Sorath," Tezi said with certainty. "I have to help him."

She sprinted out of the tunnel so quickly that, when Rivlen lunged to grab her, she caught only air.

Stay out of it, Rivlen barked into her mind.

If it *was* Colonel Sorath, he'd chosen to work against Uthari, to turn sides. He was even more likely to be an enemy than Yidar.

But Tezi didn't glance back. She raised her axe and ran toward Yidar's back with determination in her stride.

Afraid Tezi would get herself killed, Rivlen tried to wrap a magical grip around her before remembering the dragon-steel axe would prevent that.

"Someone else is going to attack him!" a mage on one of the ships cried.

Rivlen groaned, afraid her prediction of all three vessels opening up with magic and cannons would prove true.

Yidar glanced back, spotting Tezi as she rushed toward him, and without slowing his attacks against Sorath, he flicked a fireball at her. Belatedly, when it whistled past her without singeing so much as a hair, he realized she also had a dragon-steel weapon. Cursing, he drew a throwing knife and launched that at her.

Look out, Rivlen barked and used a pinpoint burst of power to knock the spinning blade aside.

She didn't want to pick sides, especially when she feared she was choosing the *wrong* side, but after all she'd been through on Vran with Tezi, she hated to watch the girl get killed. Besides, Jak would be disappointed if he learned that Tezi had died when Rivlen could have stopped it.

But maybe Rivlen needn't have done anything. Tezi's double-bladed axe had flared blue, and she'd turned the weapon at such an angle that it would have deflected the knife.

A boom came from the ground next to Yidar's feet. Sorath throwing another of his small explosives. They seemed designed more to distract than harm, but with two people with such deadly weapons now attacking Yidar, a distraction might be deadly for him.

When Tezi reached him, she tried to maneuver behind him so she could swing her axe at his back, but he used his enhanced zidarr muscles to spring twenty feet. When he came down, he faced both of his opponents—or at least Rivlen thought he did. She still couldn't see Sorath.

Lightning streaked down from one of the ships. It targeted Tezi, and she flinched as it branched and tried to envelop her, but the electricity never touched her skin. Her axe flared blue again.

Yidar turned toward the other threat and started defending, weapons clanging. The mages on the ship couldn't see Sorath any more than Rivlen could, so they focused on Tezi. Her axe continued to nullify their attacks, but someone realized the problem and appeared with a flintlock rifle. As Tezi ran toward Yidar, again trying to flank him, another crewman used magic to heft a head-sized boulder to hurl at her.

Tezi saw the huge rock flying toward her and dropped to her belly. It tumbled past her head, but the other mages had also realized that physical attacks could hurt her. One of them pummeled her with a broken stalactite.

"Damn it," Rivlen growled and created a barrier above Tezi. Rivlen couldn't enrobe her while she held that axe, but she could create obstacles between Tezi and her attackers.

Mages started firing at Yidar's invisible opponent, or where they believed him to be based on Yidar's slashes and parries. When the one with the flintlock rifle took aim at Sorath, Rivlen growled and shifted and expanded her barrier. She created a dome that covered all three fighters.

Lightning and fire struck it, as well as flintlock bullets and magelock charges, but everything ricocheted off.

"There's someone else down there!" one of the geniuses called. "A druid!"

Rivlen would have rolled her eyes, but she was too busy gritting her teeth and concentrating as more and more mages unloaded on her barrier, trying to wear it down. As if a druid would have protected Sorath, Yidar, *or* Tezi.

Help me, Rivlen told the rest of her mage team.

Had they had a clear foe, she suspected they already would have, but they recognized Yidar as surely as she did and had to be wondering about her decision. They hesitated even after she ordered their assistance.

Fury rose up in Rivlen, but she couldn't spare the concentration to glare back at them. Dozens of attacks were striking her barrier now, and it was as if she were defending an entire mage-ship in a battle by herself.

Those are Zaruk's mages up there, she added, forcing herself to be rational instead of threatening her officers. *Yidar has turned on Uthari.*

A few officers continued to hesitate, but two others crept forward and added their energy to hers, reinforcing the barrier.

Meanwhile, Sorath and Tezi worked together. Yidar was faster than either of them and, as a zidarr, had received the best training in the world, but their weapons nullified his magic, leaving him with only his blades for protection. That helped even the odds.

He might still have won against two opponents, but Sorath had more tricks up his sleeves than a crooked gambler. Explosives rained down at Yidar's feet, and Tezi sprang in to pop his barrier every time he got it back up. To further harry Yidar, some of the less-injured refugees threw rocks at him whenever they had an opening.

Rivlen glanced up at the ships to make sure none of the mages were preparing to enact some plan that would circumvent her barrier, and her breath caught when she spotted a dark figure at one of the railings. Another zidarr. That was Zaruk's Night Wrath.

She groaned. He would have the power to rip away her barrier, and if he leaped down to help Yidar, Sorath and Tezi would be outmatched. Even with those weapons, they couldn't defeat *two* zidarr.

Surprisingly, Night Wrath only watched the fight, his face cold and calculating. After a moment, he turned his back and walked out of view.

Did he *want* Yidar to die? Or not care enough to help him?

A furious clanging of blades drew Rivlen's attention back to the battle in time to see Yidar shove Sorath back, then whirl on Tezi. He clearly wanted to get rid of one of his opponents. With blinding speed, he feinted toward her face, then stabbed for her heart.

With the mages still casting attacks at her barrier, Rivlen didn't dare divert her attention to help Tezi further. But the axe pulsed blue again, and she deflected the sword, the big weapon whipping about faster than Rivlen would have thought possible. Was its magic guiding her arms? Rivlen had sparred with Tezi and knew she wasn't *that* skilled.

Tezi not only deflected the rapid chain of stabs and slashes, but she pressed in, taking a swing at Yidar's head.

He jerked out of the axe's path, his back bending impossibly to avoid the big blade. As soon as he recovered, he started to spring for Tezi, but he must have realized he'd taken his focus from Sorath for too long. He turned back but didn't maneuver his blades into place fast enough. The colonel's dragon-steel dagger plunged into his chest.

Yidar screamed and lunged for Sorath, barely acknowledging the weapon sticking out of his torso. That left his back to Tezi, and she leaped in. With a mighty swing, she sank the axe between his shoulder blades and into his spine. Sorath tugged his dagger out of Yidar's chest and finished him off with a slash to the throat.

After Yidar tumbled to the ground dead, Rivlen expected the mages on the ships above to stop hurling their magic, to realize there was no one left to defend, but the attacks grew more numerous and stronger, almost frenzied.

"Druids!" one yelled.

Rivlen almost shouted that she wasn't a druid, but what would it matter? Zaruk and Uthari weren't allies, and those mages would cheerfully take her down.

A green ball of energy spun out of the jungle and struck one of the ships.

Since all of Zaruk's mages had been attacking, they hadn't had their defenses up, and the blast blew a huge hole in the hull. More attacks followed, the green balls streaking toward the ships from several directions. From below, Rivlen couldn't see the people throwing them, but she recognized druid magic when she saw it.

The casters weren't refugees; they were the powerful enemies who had vexed the mageships ever since they'd come to Zewnath. They'd slipped out of the jungle and positioned themselves all around the collapsed cavern.

Zaruk's mages managed to get barriers up to protect their ships from the whirling balls of energy, but tendrils of power came next. They rose up like green snakes, wrapped around the barriers, and squeezed them. Several mages on the decks groaned and cursed at the effort required to keep their defenses up.

"Retreat!" someone bellowed as more and more druids arrived. "This isn't worth it."

Defending Yidar's corpse? No, Rivlen agreed. It wasn't worth it.

The mageships flew out of view, and she slumped against the wall. She was tempted to keep her barrier up since these were the druids she'd been sent to hunt. They were *not* allies. But she sensed dozens of them up there in the jungle, many with powerful auras. She might have held off a few of them, but if they attacked collectively, her barrier would drop as certainly as if Tezi swung her axe through it.

You better get back here, Rivlen told Tezi, who was talking to what looked like empty air. *The druids aren't going to think of you as a friend.*

Unfortunately, Rivlen doubted her team would be safe going back through the tunnels. It was also likely the druids knew about her wrecked ship. What if they'd already visited it and defeated her crew?

Tezi started toward the tunnel, but no fewer than twelve druids appeared at the edge and gazed down at her.

"Show yourself, Colonel Sorath!" a woman called in Dhoran.

Rivlen had only heard about Kywatha and hadn't yet encountered her, but from the descriptions of a voluptuous woman with green eyes who spoke their language, Rivlen was certain this was she. Would Sorath obey? Was he working with them? If so, Rivlen should do her best to kill him and drag his severed head back to Uthari. But if he'd just killed Yidar, and if it turned out that Yidar had switched sides and betrayed Uthari, would Uthari still want Sorath dead?

"I have a headache," Rivlen mumbled.

"I'm here." Sorath appeared as if he'd pressed a button. Maybe he had.

His dark wiry hair stuck out everywhere, as if he'd been struck by lightning, but from what Rivlen remembered, he *usually* looked like that. The cuts dribbling blood down his arms and staining his shirt were less typical.

He stood with his pickaxe appendage hanging at one side and the dragon-steel dagger at the other. Rivlen had forgotten about his missing hand and wondered how he'd wielded the dagger while throwing explosives. She envisioned him sticking the weapon between his teeth every time he delved into his pocket and wondered if ancient dragon steel could be affronted by having saliva spattered on it.

"Mage from Uthari's fleet," Kywatha called. "You will also step forth."

"I don't take orders from druids," Rivlen called. Besides, she preferred the semi protection of the tunnel.

"You came here to slay druids. You cannot escape, especially not from within our passageways. You are now our prisoner."

"You can *try* to capture me," Rivlen growled, reestablishing her barrier around herself, "but I wouldn't advise it."

Tezi was only about twenty feet away. Rivlen thought about running out and wrapping a hand around her axe for extra protection. But that would leave her troops behind her vulnerable.

Sorath sheathed the dagger—where had he gotten that blade, anyway?—and raised his pick. "I've partially completed what you wanted. With Rookie Tezi's help, I've killed Yidar."

"We are not taking *you* prisoner, Colonel." Kywatha only glanced at him before locking a glower on Rivlen.

"I appreciate that, but Captain Rivlen over there is the only reason we were able to succeed. She protected us from Zaruk's mages while we fought."

"We are aware, but it must only be because Yidar betrayed Uthari." Kywatha lowered her voice to mutter, "And because he's an ass."

Rivlen clenched her jaw as she eyed Yidar's body, almost expecting him to spring back to life to defend himself. The legends made zidarr out to be nearly immortal, after all. Nearly impossible to kill. But he'd received three fatal blows from dragon-steel weapons. He didn't stir, and he never would again.

"If you're not aware," Sorath called up, turning slowly to look each druid in the eyes, even though it was possible only Kywatha understood their language, "a dragon came through the portal last night. A self-identified dragon *scout*. There could be more returning at any time. I don't know what they want from our world, but it can't be anything good. Not for mages, not for druids, and not for terrene human beings. We need to form a truce, however temporary, to deal with the threat."

"Dragons would not be threatening us if we'd succeeded in removing the portal and ensuring it can't be used again."

"Uthari won't allow that," Sorath said.

"*Uthari* has new problems to worry about." Kywatha sounded smug.

Rivlen wanted to launch a fireball at her face. If she hadn't been certain it would be a futile attack, one that would result in her and her team being obliterated by the rest of the druids, she might have tried.

"He also has the druid boy, Grunk," Sorath said. "He was captured when we sneaked in and things went wrong."

Tezi stirred. "The druid boy? The wild one who likes his knives?"

"Yes." Sorath nodded to her.

"He helped me. When the druids came to get their prisoner back, he attacked the mercenaries who were attacking *me*. I think he was supposed to kill me—kill all of the mercenaries who might have interfered with their mission—but he didn't. I don't know why, but I owe him."

You don't owe someone for not *killing you,* Rivlen snapped into her mind.

But Tezi didn't acknowledge her. She was staring bleakly at Sorath.

Rivlen realized that even though the colonel had gone rogue, Tezi still considered him a commanding officer, someone she should defer to or help if he requested it.

"We will attempt to retrieve him," Kywatha said, "when we go to destroy the portal."

"*Destroy* it?" Rivlen asked.

"We attempted to take it so we could bury it again, but that didn't work. It is too dangerous to leave standing. The arrival of this dragon only proves that. It must be destroyed so it can never again allow powerful enemies to invade this world and kill our people." Kywatha gazed around sadly at the fallen refugees and lowered her voice. "We have enemies enough already to deal with here."

She waved a finger, and several of her people levitated into the cavern and started sifting through rubble, pulling out those who'd only been injured and could yet be helped.

"We have a team out there," Rivlen said. "We can't destroy their only way home."

Kywatha snorted. "Yes, it would be awful if we kept Zidarr Malek from coming back with more dragon steel to hand over to his ruler to be made into weapons." She frowned at Rivlen. "Do you truly wish that? You just witnessed how powerful those weapons are. They are a threat to your kind as much as to us."

Rivlen eyed Yidar's body. It was true that without the stealth device and the two dragon-steel weapons, he never would have fallen, not to two mundane mercenaries.

"That's no reason to keep *Malek* from returning," Rivlen said. "And Jadora and Jak. They haven't done anything to you druids."

"They *started* all of this." Kywatha flung up her hands. "They're the reason the portal is here now. If they hadn't dug it out of the ground—"

"Someone else would have," Rivlen said.

"Not in our lifetimes."

"You don't know that. Tezi, come on. Your mercenary company is working for Uthari. We need to get back."

"Working for that monster?" Kywatha shook her head. "Do you want to be like his zidarr? And kill people like this for no reason?" Kywatha spread her arm to indicate the injured being pulled out of the rubble. "Innocent people with no means of defending themselves against mages?"

The question might have been for Tezi, who stood between Sorath and Rivlen, appearing torn about who she was supposed to follow, but Kywatha was staring at Rivlen.

"I'm not the one who killed the innocent people," Rivlen said. Just because she'd been hunting them down, believing this was the druid headquarters—the *enemy* headquarters—didn't mean she would have attacked the refugees.

"And what if your ruler one day orders you to do so?" Kywatha asked.

"He won't. He's not a monster."

"They're *all* monsters. They've invaded our world, killed our people, and let out horrible predators. You either choose to be one of them or not."

"I'm not walking away from my career, my family, and what my father—" Rivlen cut herself off, tamping down the emotion that wanted to well up. She didn't have to defend herself to this woman. The druids had killed mages. They were guilty of everything that Uthari and the others were.

Sorath cleared his throat and lifted his hand and pick. "Let's focus on the immediate threat. As I said, we need to work together."

"I won't work with them." Rivlen pointed at the druids and then into the tunnel, reminded that Uthari had ordered her to return before all this started. "Tezi, come with me."

"I..." Tezi looked at her and then at Sorath. "I need to stay, ma'am, and help them get that druid boy back. I owe him."

"That *druid boy* was captured because he was attacking Uthari on his yacht," Rivlen snapped.

She hadn't heard all of the details yet, but she was positive she knew the gist. And the way Sorath looked away confirmed it for her.

"If that one wishes to stay, we won't allow you to take her." Kywatha pointed at Tezi and lifted her chin. "You'd have a hard time forcing her anyway when she's got that weapon."

"It wouldn't keep me from lifting her up and throwing her over my shoulder," Rivlen growled.

Tezi shook her head, her loyalties torn.

"Go, if you want to suckle at the bosom of a monster, mage,"

Kywatha said to Rivlen, "but we won't let you take someone with you who doesn't want to do the same."

Rivlen growled, but she didn't argue further. A part of her was relieved and not only because Kywatha had stopped talking about taking her prisoner. If Rivlen returned with Tezi and reported to Uthari what had happened, and Uthari revealed that Yidar *hadn't* betrayed him, that Uthari had sent him with Zaruk's mages as a double-agent, Uthari would be furious to learn of his death and Tezi's involvement. Rivlen's *own* involvement made her uneasy. If she hadn't kept Zaruk's mages from striking Sorath and Tezi, Yidar might still be alive.

Tezi announced her final decision by going to stand beside Sorath. *I'm sorry, ma'am.*

Rivlen didn't reply. She walked into the tunnel, gathered her mages, and headed back toward the ship. She would report in to Uthari and hope this fiasco wouldn't end her career. What would her father say then?

23

In the kitchen laboratory, Jadora stared at the formula she'd put together, the liquid form of a long-lasting sedative. She pulled out syringes she'd brought along in case she needed to take blood samples to test for the dragon parasite. She hadn't expected to inject anything *into* people, certainly not her teammates.

As she measured out doses, guessing at Zethron's weight, she tried to focus on her preparations, not all of her fears. Her fears for Zethron and Malek but also for Jak and herself and what would happen to them if Tonovan ended up in charge.

Jadora hoped the chief these guardians were leading them to might be able to help them, but the way the brothers had treated her thus far didn't suggest they made a habit of assisting strangers. Her head still ached from their mental invasion. Their chief might also condemn her for trying to take samples of the Jitaruvak and do the same to Jak for having taken Shikari's egg. Even though the guardians must have seen the truth in her mind, they'd seemed skeptical of it, not believing Jak would have been chosen by the portals.

A knock sounded at the hatch, and she turned. "Yes?"

She hoped it was Malek but was also afraid it was Malek. He'd lost it with Prolix, turning into a rage-filled beast who attacked his allies, and nobody had believed his ruse about having challenged Prolix to a sparring match. He'd been trying to kill the other zidarr, and he'd almost succeeded. Right now, Prolix might be plotting his revenge.

She'd prepared enough of the sedative to knock out Malek as well as Zethron, but the idea of using it on him scared her almost as much as the idea of *not* using it. If she knocked out Malek, he wouldn't be able to defend himself. Tonovan could amble into his cabin at any time and slit his throat.

Jadora could sedate Malek in her laboratory so she could keep an eye on him, but how would that help? If Tonovan showed up with a knife, she would be powerless to stop him. He would kill Malek, and then he would do Shylezar and Thanok knew what to her.

The hatch hadn't opened yet.

"Come in," she called, willing steadiness into her voice.

Maybe someone had bumped the hatch on the way past. No, at her second call, it opened.

But nobody stood there. She scowled, slipping a hand into her pocket for a vial of acid. The ring Malek had given her caught on the edge of her pocket, reminding her that it had magic and was a possible weapon too. Still, she trusted her chemicals more and wrapped her fingers around a vial.

The hatch shut, leaving her alone in the lab. *Seemingly* alone. Was that breathing she heard?

She hefted the vial as an indistinct blur appeared in front of her.

"It's me, Professor," came Vinjo's voice from the blur. "Don't shoot. Er, throw."

He took another step closer, and the blur solidified into his distinct shape, his palms raised toward her. A clunky device was attached to a band on his wrist.

"What are you *doing*?" Jadora scowled. This wasn't the time for pranks or whatever he had in mind. "Wait, is that one of those stealth devices?"

"A clandestineness creeper, yes." Vinjo beamed a smile at her. "Women love them. I think. I made one for Lieutenant Sasko, and she was so grateful that she kissed me, but then she gave it to Colonel Sorath, which seemed a bit of a mixed message. Do you have an opinion on what that means? Jak didn't when I told him."

Jadora shook her head and returned her vial to her pocket.

"At least she didn't kiss *Sorath*," Vinjo said. "I don't think. I heard Captain Ferroki did though."

Jadora tamped down impatience and fought the urge to order him to get to the point. If he could turn invisible and wouldn't mind doing so to avoid the other mages, maybe he would be willing to help her by… she wasn't sure.

Vinjo lowered his hands and unfastened the wristband. "Actually, I came to give it to you."

"You did? I would appreciate having such a device, but why?"

Vinjo glanced toward the closed hatch. He'd already been whispering, but he lowered his voice even further. "I believe you and Jak are in danger."

She snorted. "Tell me something I don't know."

His brows rose. "Uhm, such as that steel is an alloy of iron and carbon, in which the carbon can compose up to two percent?"

"I did know that."

"Ah, right. You *are* a professor, after all." Vinjo handed her the stealth device and pulled a second one out of his pocket. "I made one for you and one for Jak. I don't want them to hurt you."

"Them?" Jadora asked, though she had little doubt which *them* he meant. She accepted the devices without hesitation, relieved for any extra advantage she could gain.

"Tonovan and Bakir. I heard them talking about how they would have to combine forces and kill Malek before he went wild. I see that such may be necessary, if you can't turn around his affliction, but not the rest of what they were plotting." Vinjo shook his head firmly.

Jadora wanted to deny that Malek's death would be necessary under any circumstances, but she made herself ask, "What rest?"

"They were talking about jointly leading the ship after Malek is gone and visiting all of the worlds where valuable resources can be found. They would collect enough to make them wealthy and give them vast power, more than even the kings on our world have. They talked about not going back to our world at all, instead finding a place like this where they could easily rule over the populace, turn them into slaves to serve them, and maybe each rule an entire world or half of one world." Vinjo shook his head. "Tonovan said he liked the sexual practices of the women in that city, so he wouldn't mind ruling *it*. They both agreed it was stupid that Malek insisted they walk on eggshells around such puny humans. They figured if they never took the ship back to Torvil, nobody would know that they hadn't been killed by a dragon or something. They couldn't get in trouble, because Uthari and the other kings and queens don't have keys. Only the druids do, and they wouldn't share theirs."

"No," Jadora murmured numbly.

"It was all... brainstorming, I guess. The only thing they solidified is that Malek would be dead and that they'd run the ship the way they wanted. I don't think they realized I could hear them blathering from engineering. Or maybe they didn't care that I could hear."

"Probably not. They don't seem to see you as threatening."

"Few do." Vinjo's mouth twisted wryly but only briefly. "There's more you should know. Bakir asked if Jak is a wild one and why Malek is teaching him. Tonovan said yes and that the first thing he would do once he's in command would be to kill him."

Jadora stepped back, bumping into the counter. She shouldn't have been surprised, but she was horrified nonetheless.

"And, uhm, he wants to put you in your place sucking his—er, it was quite foul. He has loathsome bedroom plans for you because you've irked him. He wants you to watch your son die and then..." Vinjo spread his hand, the words too vile for him to speak.

She appreciated that *someone* found them so. If Bakir had listened to all those awful plans without objecting, she would file him in the same cabinet of detestability as Tonovan.

"Bakir isn't quite as cruel, at least from what I could tell," Vinjo said, "but he's perfectly content to let Tonovan be cruel and do nothing to stop it. Their kind are all like that. They believe they're superior and that terrene humans should serve them however they wish."

Yes, even Malek had refused to act against Tonovan.

No, that wasn't true. He had in the past, but the other day, he'd offered to kill Tonovan to protect her. That had been before he'd been stung. In his normal state of mind, he'd said he would if she'd asked, and she... she'd said she would figure out a solution on her own. As if she'd had time to mull over such things. There was too much else to worry about.

Oh, why hadn't she said yes to Malek's offer? She could have joined her father in praying for forgiveness *after* Tonovan was gone from this world. From *all* the worlds.

"Why don't you feel that way, Vinjo?" Jadora asked.

"Well, they think *I* should serve them however they wish too. Just because I make things instead of throwing fireballs around." His expression was more disgusted than wry this time. "Engineers made the sky cities that they all spend their lavish existences in. They ought to revere us." Vinjo shook his head. "But that's a problem for another time. I can't stand against them. I'm sorry, but I'm not strong enough, and if I openly defy them, they can kill my entire family, everyone I care about. My parents have had an honored position in Zaruk's city because my brother is a zidarr, but after I've let myself be captured and forced to work for enemies, I'm afraid of what will happen. But..." He gestured toward the devices. "Maybe these can at least save you and Jak. If the others find out, I'll say you stole them. Is that all right? You'll be gone, so it won't matter."

"Gone?"

"Yes. I think that's the only thing that would work. This ship had to be so small—so narrow—to fit through the portal that there aren't many places in it to hide. As you saw, the devices work well—they hide you from sight and magical senses—but not if others are close. If someone gets within five or six feet of you, they'll see through the illusion. Oh, and I haven't yet been able to figure out how to camouflage *noise*, so you have to be quiet when you're wearing them."

Jadora remembered hearing his breathing and nodded.

"The safest thing would be to leave," Vinjo said. "Take some supplies and weapons and skullcaps, and sneak off the ship. This would be the ideal place since we're flying low because of the roof of the cave. We're just a few feet above the water. We could jump down without a problem."

"We?"

Vinjo smiled lopsidedly and withdrew another stealth device. "I've been contemplating going with you. Tonovan already jammed me up against the wall earlier and asked me why I was teaching Jak about engineering. I'm not sure if he has any idea about your devices, but this ship is so small that it's hard to keep secrets. Another reason you two should leave. And I'm afraid they'd see through my lie about you stealing the devices, so I think joining you is my best option."

She couldn't imagine tramping through that swamp for… "How far are we from the portal? It must be hundreds of miles."

Vinjo nodded. "It is. It would be a long walk, and I'm sure dangerous, but do you think anything out there is as dangerous as the mages in here with us?"

Jadora thought of the dragon they'd battled. Would Vinjo's devices fool such a powerful magical creature? She doubted it. Even so, she wasn't sure Vinjo was wrong. When it came to her and her son's safety, Tonovan might be more of a threat.

"We don't have the key to the portal," she said. "Even if we survived the trek and reached it, we couldn't activate it."

Even *with* the key, they might not be able to activate it. She hoped that whatever had kept the portal from operating had been temporary and worn off by now.

"Malek has the key, doesn't he?" Vinjo asked.

"I think so."

"He trusts you. You could get it from him."

Could she? He would surely wonder why she wanted it.

"Especially if you sedate him like you said you would," Vinjo added. "Though you'd have to hurry and grab it before the others thought to take it from him. You'd have to leave right away."

"I couldn't leave without him. *Especially* if he was unconscious. Tonovan would kill him. He'd have no defense."

"We couldn't take him with us. Not when he's losing his mind. He'd kill all of us, the same way those crazy people killed their whole crew on that ship."

"I could keep him sedated."

"For a trek of hundreds of miles?"

"You're a mage. Can't you levitate him?"

"Not for that long. I'd—"

Footsteps sounded in the corridor, along with a faint clang as someone brushed the hatch. Fear flashed in Vinjo's eyes as he spun toward it and jammed his stealth device back in his pocket.

Jadora's heart pounded in her chest as she quickly hid the two he'd given to her.

The hatch opened, and Bakir leaned in.

Jadora wiped her thoughts from her mind.

"You need to sedate your guide," he told her. "We've got him tied to his bunk, but he's moaning and thrashing. Tonovan's cabin is across the corridor, and the noise is bothering him."

Though she tried her best to keep her mind empty, she couldn't keep from snapping, "I'm terribly sorry that another human being's plight is disturbing his rest."

Bakir's bushy eyebrows drew together. "I see why you irk Tonovan. For a terrene woman, you do *not* know your place. Why hasn't anyone slavebanded you?"

"Maybe they believe my brain would be less valuable if mind-altering magic was being pumped into it."

"Uh huh. Sedate the man, or Tonovan is going to kill him."

"I will." Jadora waved toward the syringes she'd prepared and kept herself from fantasizing about jabbing one into Tonovan's neck. And this bastard's as well.

Bakir's gaze shifted from them to her. Damn it, maybe she *hadn't* kept herself from the fantasy.

He only snorted. "It would be the last thing you ever did, Professor. Don't make me kill you. Tonovan has plans for you." He eyed Vinjo. "Don't you have an engineering orb and tools to fondle?"

"Yes, Admiral. And I enjoy doing so very much." Vinjo squeezed past him and into the corridor, then retreated to the engine room.

Thankfully, Bakir also left, closing the hatch behind him. Jadora hoped she'd at least kept from letting him know about the stealth devices. Maybe Vinjo's scheme wasn't the worst one they could have come up with. It sounded dangerous, but it did give them an option, when options were few.

She needed to talk to Jak. Was there any way he would agree to leave Shikari behind? For that matter, if they tried to leave the ship while they were in this cave, would the stealth devices keep them safe from the predators the brothers had promised lived in the water?

She groaned, another realization smacking her. What of Zethron? They couldn't leave him alone here. Tonovan was *already* threatening to kill him.

"There's no way we can run," she muttered.

As she finished preparing the syringes, she realized there was only one logical course of action. Somehow, she and Jak had to sedate Tonovan, Prolix, and Bakir and throw *them* off the ship.

The idea of trying to sneak up on two powerful mages and a zidarr made her shudder. With the stealth device, maybe she could get close, but even if she somehow succeeded in sticking needles in their veins, her substance would take a minute or two to act. That would be *plenty* of time for them to break her neck.

Jadora groaned and clunked her forehead against the counter. How were she and Jak and the innocents aboard going to get out of this?

After Captain Rivlen left, Sorath watched Kywatha levitate down into the destroyed camp. The rest of the druids continued unburying people, healing injuries, and floating the refugees up to the surface for transport elsewhere.

Tezi warily watched Kywatha approach. Sorath rested a hand on Tezi's shoulder, both to reassure her and to let Kywatha know that she was an ally. He was encouraged that Kywatha had been willing to help Tezi stay with him, to keep Rivlen from marching her back to her ship and ultimately Uthari, but Sorath didn't know if Kywatha would consider Tezi an ally or how she felt about

Thorn Company. Sorath didn't even know how Kywatha and the druids felt about *him*. Not only had he failed to assassinate Uthari, but he'd escaped while Grunk had been captured.

As Kywatha was about to speak, a new druid appeared, levitating down from above, and ran up to speak with her. It was Tovorka, the druid Grunk had helped rescue from the camp.

Kywatha nodded and murmured something back to him. They spoke rapidly in their own tongue amid several gestures toward the sky. They might have been discussing the dragon threat or perhaps that mageships were coming. Sorath had no idea how far away Zaruk's ships had flown and if they would return. He didn't even know why they'd been here, helping Yidar.

Tovorka trotted away, and Kywatha faced Sorath again.

"My people are pleased with your progress so far," she said.

"Oh?"

"Grunk's detainment wasn't ideal, but we hadn't originally wanted him to go along at all. He's a fighter, but he's not the calmest head in a crisis."

Sorath lifted his chin. "He helped me. And he was the one to slit Vorsha's throat. I know she wasn't on the list of people you wanted assassinated, but Grunk had a grudge against her."

Tezi stirred in surprise but didn't interrupt. Sorath doubted she would judge him for agreeing to help the druids, but he couldn't help but wonder if Ferroki would.

"We're aware of his past with her," Kywatha said. "And what a vile monster she is. *Was*."

"Then you know more than I do," Sorath said, though Grunk had hinted at some of that.

"You couldn't have guessed? They're *all* vile. All of the rulers."

"Sounds like a good reason for you to use your powers to overthrow them." He smiled wistfully. "Though I think the dragon is the larger concern now. As I said, I got the impression it would be back."

"We may not *have* to overthrow them—such wouldn't be within our power anyway, as there are only scant numbers of druids in the world compared with mages. Because of your actions, they've started fighting each other." Kywatha smiled tightly and gazed toward the trees in the direction of the mages' camp.

Thanks to having run all the way here, Sorath knew it was more than fifteen miles away, but it was possible she could sense magical happenings from that distance. He didn't know.

"Vorsha's people blame Uthari for their queen's death, and they're convincing the others that he'll kill their fleet commanders and rulers one at a time so that he can keep the portal for himself." Kywatha nodded firmly. "With luck, they'll decimate each other. While they're doing that, *we'll* go in, recover Grunk, and destroy the portal."

Sorath grimaced. He didn't care if the mages killed each other, though he feared Thorn Company wouldn't be able to avoid getting caught up in that, but the thought of the portal being destroyed when Jak and Jadora were out there didn't sit well with him. Why couldn't the druids wait a week? Sorath wouldn't care if Malek or that General Tonovan ever came back, but Jak and Jadora didn't deserve to be stranded.

"Do you know how?" Sorath asked. "You're aware of how resilient dragon steel is, I'm sure." He tapped the hilt of his borrowed dagger.

"I am aware. Thanks to our spies in the jungle—" Kywatha waved to a large black bird perched on a rock overlooking the cavern; it was watching the goings on with unnatural intensity, "—we've learned that Malek's team brought back an interesting acid as well as a chest of dragon steel. The rumors say the acid can alter the nearly impervious substance. If we can get ahold of some of it, we can destroy the portal. Or at least burn off the symbols to keep it from working ever again."

Sorath had left the camp before Malek's team returned from their last mission, and he had no idea if that was true, but Kywatha appeared to believe it.

Tezi shifted from foot to foot and glanced toward the tunnel that Rivlen had left through. She might have been having second thoughts about staying with Sorath and the druids. As a lover of history and archeology, Sorath couldn't keep from cringing at the idea of destroying an ancient artifact crafted by dragons. There had to be another solution.

"I just stayed to help the druid—Grunk," Tezi whispered.

Kywatha squinted at her and eyed Sorath. "My people can worry about the artifact. If you two are willing to attempt to retrieve Grunk, I'll send Tovorka to help you. He knows their ships well and can fly a skyboard up there. I'd send a larger party along, but..." She gestured toward the stealth device on Sorath's wrist. "Do you know how many people you can camouflage with that?"

"Grunk and I were both able to use it as long as we stayed in contact. It made climbing difficult."

"Sending a whole party along wouldn't be feasible then. But you two with those weapons took out a zidarr. You can handle a rescue attempt, I assume?"

Sorath almost said that he would go without Tezi—he didn't want to risk her—but if not for her help with Yidar, he wouldn't have survived that battle. He didn't know how much her improvement in fighting was due to the axe guiding her hands, but some of it had to have come from simple determination and willingness to practice. Useful characteristics in a soldier.

"If we can get on board, yes." Sorath nodded.

Tezi hesitated, then also nodded.

"Get some rest. You'll go tonight."

Kywatha walked off to check on the other druids. A worried expression lingered on Tezi's face as she watched.

"Thanks for the help with the zidarr, killer." Sorath thumped her on the shoulder.

"You're welcome. He was killing those poor people. They weren't even druids."

"I know."

That was what had prompted Sorath to jump down into the destroyed village and try to kill Yidar right under the noses of all those mages. It had been impulsive, and he knew it, but when Yidar had dropped the ceiling on the natives, he'd murdered a bunch of innocent civilians without the power to defend themselves.

"Is that why you attacked him?" Tezi peered up at the jungle, roots dangling over the edge of the caved-in roof. "How did you find us?"

Sorath hesitated, reluctant to speak of something as goofy as a *vision* propelling him in this direction, but since Tezi also carried a dragon-steel weapon, maybe she had experienced similar things.

"The dagger guided me here." Sorath tapped its hilt.

"To help us?"

"To find Thorn Company and help if you needed it, yes. The other option was to be killed by Yidar in a dark tunnel."

Tezi's forehead wrinkled. Maybe she hadn't experienced the visions yet. Or maybe he'd simply been in too many battles and had hit his head one too many times.

"I didn't know you specifically would be here," Sorath added. "Is the rest of the company nearby?"

"I was afraid to mention them," Tezi whispered, "but I think the druids must already know about them. We were on the *Star Flyer* when different druids and a monument attacked the ship and forced it down. It's back that way, I think." She pointed, then hesitated, and pointed in a different direction. "I'm not sure. We traveled through twisting tunnels for hours to get here."

"What was your—their—mission?"

Tezi hesitated. "To kill the druids."

"Well. That would explain why Rivlen was reluctant to come with us to help a druid."

"Among other reasons." Tezi eyed him. "King Uthari wants you dead. I think Rivlen would have tried to kill you if you hadn't been fighting Yidar and he hadn't been tormenting helpless refugees."

"Does Rivlen actually care about these people?" Sorath hadn't interacted often with the captain but had received the impression of a frosty, rigid mage who obeyed her king without question.

"I think she was bothered by what he was doing. And she wasn't sure if he was doing his job—working for Uthari—or had betrayed him." Tezi spread her arms.

"I wouldn't be surprised either way."

"I want to get Grunk," Tezi said, "but I'm worried that we'll make trouble for Thorn Company if we're seen attacking Uthari's people. If we… kill any of them." She glanced at Yidar's body. "Any *more* of them."

"I know. That's why I disappeared without telling Thorn Company my plans. Maybe it was a vain hope, but I didn't want them to get in trouble for my choices."

"Why is this all so complicated, sir? I just want to do what's right."

"Unfortunately, when we become soldiers and agree to fight for coin, we don't get to choose between right and wrong. We serve those who give us contracts and pay our salaries."

"But you get to choose which contracts to take, don't you?"

He shook his head bleakly. "We didn't this time. With mages, there's often not a choice. If you wanted to lead a righteous life, this wasn't the best line of work for you to get into." He smiled sadly at Tezi, wishing he had more reassuring words for her. In truth, the same things were bothering him right now. "After we get Grunk, I'll make sure you're reunited with Thorn Company. Then you can talk it out with them. Maybe Ferroki is ready to turn her back on her contract—the one we were forced into, mind you—and leave the jungle. If so, the druids promised me they would help the company get out of here."

And maybe he would yet get his chance to kill Uthari. If he did, one evil would be removed from the world, and—even better—Thorn Company wouldn't be under contract anymore. There would be nothing to keep them from walking away from this crazy war.

24

JAK'S PALMS WERE MOIST AS HE CLIMBED THE RUNGS TO THE HATCH. He sensed Malek on the deck—he'd been up there for the last two hours—and needed to talk to him, but he was afraid of what he would find. What if Malek had crossed the point of no return? What if he whirled and attacked the first person to pop out of the hatchway behind him?

Jak took a deep breath and opened the hatch anyway. He peered around before climbing out, though his senses told him exactly where Malek was.

He sat cross-legged up front, his back rigid, his palms on his thighs. Meditating? His weapons belt lay next to him within easy reach.

Malek? Jak asked telepathically, not wanting to startle him. *I'm coming to see you. All right?*

Malek neither answered nor stirred. Maybe he *was* meditating.

As long as he wasn't setting a trap, luring Jak close with his silence, only so he could pounce and kill him.

Jak snorted. As if Malek needed to use a trap to kill him.

He climbed out, surprised by how bright this section of the

cave was. Greenish-blue light filtered down from the rocky roof. He glanced up, expecting to find mage lamps mounted up there, but long, fat snakes or maybe worms crawled over the damp, lumpy surface. They were the source of the glow. Jak didn't sense magic from them, so maybe their bioluminescence was natural.

Ahead of the ship, the two skiffs were visible in the low light. The two brothers stood, neither of them using paddles or anything but magic to propel their slender vessels forward.

Shikari was curled up on the back of one skiff, the tip of his tail dangling in the water. His head was down, but his eyes were toward the mageship. Did he miss being aboard it with Jak? Or was he glad to be away from the chaos of the ship?

Though fish or other creatures occasionally jumped in what had once again become a wide slow-moving waterway, none of them disturbed Shikari. Jak tried to swallow the lump in his throat. At least that was something.

As Jak walked slowly toward Malek, one of the brothers looked back, but he didn't say anything. His face was indifferent. Or was that condescending and judgmental? Jak didn't think these people would help them. He also worried they wouldn't give Shikari back to him.

"Malek?"

Malek didn't stir. Sweat gleamed on his forehead, and his lips were dryer than ever. Whatever those bacteria were, they didn't seem to care about keeping their host healthy.

Jak sat down beside Malek.

I will not hurt you, Malek spoke into his mind without opening his eyes.

I'm glad.

I've been meditating to marshal my willpower and attempt to force calm into my mind. To hold on to rational thought and sublimate the urge to let animal instincts take control. Malek's cheek twitched, as if his efforts to sublimate those instincts were an ongoing struggle.

Good. Mother is in Zethron's cabin. She's going to—

Malek's head jerked around, his eyes opening. Some of that animalistic rage flashed in them, and Jak leaned back. Maybe he should have *leaped* back.

"Sedate him," he blurted, not sure what Malek had thought he would say.

Malek faced forward again, took a deep breath, and visibly struggled to get control of himself.

"His sting turned him crazy too. It wasn't supposed to, but Mother thinks maybe it's because he's not a native of this world. It's possible that those humans who've spent countless generations here have evolved more immunity to the local viruses and bacteria. Zethron is as much a stranger as we are, though. He's even more far gone than..." Jak waved a hand, realizing Malek might be offended if he finished the thought.

He cannot meditate or use magic to slow the process, Malek said, switching back to telepathy. *Unfortunately, I haven't been able to do more than that. The bacteria are magical.*

I know. That's why Mother is sedating Zethron. Tonovan and Bakir —especially Tonovan—were going to kill him, but she convinced them she might be able to come up with a solution if she had more time. She asked me to come get you.

Actually, Jak had volunteered. He'd wanted to make sure Shikari was doing all right and also to see Malek one more time before he... before he wasn't himself anymore. Just in case Mother couldn't find a solution.

Malek looked sadly at him. Reading his thoughts? Jak thought he'd been keeping them to himself, but who knew with Malek?

She wants to sedate me as well, he guessed.

I think so. That's what she told the others. Jak shrugged. He wasn't sure. When he'd left, Mother had been wearing a thoughtful and calculating expression rather than an utterly defeated one.

Indefinitely, Malek said.

Only until she finds a solution.

Which she may never find. The people who live *here haven't, and they've had millennia to search.*

They're not my mother. She'll figure it out. You know she's smart, and look around this place. Jak gestured at the cave walls, though he meant to indicate the entire world. *Have you seen any libraries here? Any vast repositories of knowledge? I don't think they have the resources that we have back home. If she can't figure something out here, we'll take you back, and we'll find a solution there.*

While I am sedated? For weeks? Months? Malek looked bleakly up at the glowworms. *Years?*

Hopefully, it won't come to that.

Anger darkened Malek's eyes, and his hand jerked toward his main-gauche.

Jak tensed and leaned back again. Malek gripped the hilt but paused. Once more, he smoothed his face and pulled himself together. He drew the weapon, flipped it in his hand, and extended the hilt toward Jak.

I don't want to be a mind-dead log sleeping forever and requiring a nurse to water and piss me.

"Uh." Jak stared at the blade, not wanting to grasp what Malek was asking but certain he knew.

Cut my throat. I won't stop you.

I can't do that.

I would rather you do it than Tonovan.

Jak shook his head. *I can't. You're my... friend. You're my mentor. I...* With tears pricking at his eyes, Jak leaned forward and hugged Malek.

Given how slim Malek's control was, it might not have been the wisest choice, but it was all he could think to do, all that made sense. He couldn't cut Malek's throat.

I won't do it, Jak told him, *and I won't let Tonovan do it either.*

Malek sighed. *The Zidarr Code forbids taking one's own life unless it is to prevent enemies from torturing one and stealing secret information. I suppose these bacteria are* like *an enemy.*

Don't do anything rash, Malek. Give my mother a chance to figure this out. Trust her. Please.

Another sigh escaped Malek, and his head drooped. He patted Jak on the back. *You have also come to mean much to me. Like a son. I wish there had been more time for me to teach you.*

There will be. Jak looked away and wiped moisture out of his eyes. *Put that away, and go to my mother. She'll figure this out. If she can't, I'll find a way to get Shikari back, and we'll work together to fix you. Just like last time.*

More hatchling brain surgery? A ghost of a smile flickered across Malek's face.

I know you love it.

Malek rose to his feet, rested a hand on Jak's head for a moment, then buckled on his weapons belt and descended into the ship.

Jak watched him go, afraid the next time he saw Malek, he would be unconscious on a bed. Jak and Mother would have to figure out how to protect him from Tonovan. He wished he had Shikari back on the ship to help. Mother had given him one of Vinjo's stealth devices, and Jak touched the lump in his pocket, glad to have it, but he didn't know how it could help him with their problems.

Up ahead, the cave grew even brighter with more of the large glowing worms wriggling across the roof. Nearby, one plopped into the water. Something that looked like a giant eel surged up and grabbed it in its maw, then slipped below the surface with its prize. For a few seconds, the glow was visible under the water. Then it disappeared, extinguished like the worm's life.

Jak caught one of the men looking back again, his face unreadable. The fear that they were traveling into even greater trouble crept over Jak. If so, they would have to deal with it without Malek.

Images formed in his mind, images of Shikari alone in a cave with enemy dragons wheeling and flying overhead, their talons outstretched as they prepared to dive at him. They seemed to come from Shikari himself. A view into the future? Or a manifestation of Shikari's fear of the unknown?

Either way, Jak wasn't reassured.

Thumps and pounding noises came from belowdecks as the mage crew worked on repairs. Earlier, Sasko had helped, but it had been a long night, and around noon, she settled down on the deck next to Ferroki to rest. Several other mercenaries were doing the same, some lounging against the magical bulwarks they'd used during the earlier battle.

Vinjo, Sasko decided, would be pleased to know Ferroki was making use of the devices he'd built. As unimpressive looking as they were, they *did* effectively divert magical attacks. The frames were also sturdy enough to act as a backrest for a napping mercenary. When one might be called into battle at any moment, one had to rest when one could.

Birds screeched in the jungle, and an animal roared. A *large* animal. It didn't sound that far away. One of the birds soared past overhead, shrieking like a dying woman, as it peered down at them. Sasko didn't know what it was, but it was much larger than an eagle.

"Even in the middle of the day," she said, "this place is creepy."

She didn't think the sun was out above the canopy. Down below, it felt like twilight, regardless.

"Is that your professional assessment of the area?" Ferroki asked. "Creepy?"

"And the animals living in it, yes." Sasko nodded firmly. "But since we have powerful mages with us, we shouldn't have to worry about the wildlife getting assertive with us, right?"

"Likely not." Ferroki nodded toward two red-uniformed mages standing guard near the railings, one aft and one in the forecastle. "But druids could be controlling the animals around here, so I wouldn't get complacent."

"So, a nap is out?"

"Unless you pull down that barrier and sleep under the tarp."

Sasko prodded the center of the collapsible frame. It looked like canvas, but it was as stiff as a board and oddly oily to the touch. "I could think of more comfortable things to sleep under."

"Like a sexy man?" Sergeant Words asked. She and Tinder were leaning against the railing and facing them while they cleaned their weapons. "A muscular, athletic one with piercing eyes and a roguish smile?"

"Muscles aren't that comfortable to sleep under either. Or so I'm told." Tinder winked and flexed a biceps.

"Better to be on top for maximum comfort," Words said. "Though that mage engineer that Sasko favors isn't overly muscled. He might be all right to sleep under."

Sasko was used to being razzed by the mercenaries and didn't so much as blush, though the vision that future stone had given her came to mind, and she wondered if Vinjo was doing all right, wherever he was. She'd given the druid's gift to Ferroki, but if it had shared any insights with her, she hadn't mentioned it.

A screech sounded as another large bird swept through, flexing its talons as it seemed to debate if it could snatch up a mercenary to snack on. This time, one of the mages lifted a rifle and fired at it. The magical charge struck it in the chest, and it shrieked and flapped off at top speed, leaving feathers behind, along with the faint scent of singed meat. Leaves rattled and branches snapped as the bird crashed into the underbrush.

Sasko appreciated the proof that the wildlife was mortal.

Uthari had killed the jaguar that the druid woman had brought for the attack on the portal, but that didn't mean the creatures under their magical sway were easy to bring down.

Tinder yawned and lay down on the deck. "I'd take a blanket from Fret right now. If she weren't busy tending the wounded down below, I'd ask her to knit me one."

"She must be running out of yarn by now," Ferroki said. "We've been out here a long time."

"She can *always* get yarn. She has a knack for procurement."

A fog was creeping in from the jungle, and Sasko wondered how much time had passed since Rivlen, Tezi, and the others had left.

Leaves stirred, and chewing sounds wafted up from the undergrowth, from the place where the bird had gone down. Sasko grimaced, realizing they were listening to a scavenger eat dinner.

"I'm ready to return to our headquarters back home," she said. "I miss my bed. Walls. Peace and quiet."

Tinder started snoring. At least that drowned out the eating sounds. Words slumped down beside her, using her as a pillow. Most of the other mercenaries were lying down now too, everyone weary after being up all night. Even the sounds of repairs from belowdecks had faded.

"The company could use some leave," Ferroki said, then lowered her voice. "And less ambiguous duties. And loyalties."

"Tell me about it."

"The knowledge that winter is coming drives the bear to forage and feast with single-minded determination to see himself through to the spring."

Sasko slanted Ferroki a long look, well aware of her love for morals from fables, but she wasn't sure how to interpret that one. "Are you saying that winter is coming, and we're going to starve because we're not foraging?"

"Just that not having a clearly defined goal makes everything harder. I've heard grumblings from the women, as I'm sure you have. Even though they're getting paid regularly, they don't like that we were forced into a contract with Uthari against our wishes or that our enemies change from week to week."

"I'm not sure most mercenaries care that much who they point their rifles at or if the target changes. I'd guess the grumblings are more about the lack of amenities out here. We get paid, but to what end? There's nowhere to *spend* our coin. Sergeant Words can't amble into town and find a pretty man to satisfy her urges, Tinder can't get pastries from a bakery, and I…" Sasko paused.

"Don't you know what you want?" Ferroki smiled at her. The gesture was barely visible in the thickening fog.

"Well, I do like pastries. The layered honey ones in Perchver are some of my favorites. The best you can do out here is chew on a piece of sugar cane to satisfy your sweet tooth." Sasko glanced at Ferroki, wondering if her talk of grumblings was more a reflection of her own feelings than discontent in the company. Ferroki was always so even-keeled and hard to ruffle, taking the blows the mages delivered literally and figuratively without flinching. It was hard to imagine her being frustrated with the situation, but Sasko had caught her gazing sadly off into the jungle from time to time. Especially since Sorath left. "You ever think of retiring, Captain?"

"Yes," came the prompt reply.

"That was a fast answer."

"I'm fifty now. The body doesn't recover as quickly from being pummeled as it used to."

"True." Sasko woke up stiff just from sleeping on the ground, and she was fifteen years younger than the captain.

"And it gets harder to lose people after a while," Ferroki added softly. "You'd think it would get easier, that you'd become inured to it, but when you're in charge of these soldiers, each loss is like a weight that drops into a bag hanging around your neck. They accumulate, and you can't ever remove them. For some reason, you remember the failures more than the victories, more than the good times. The brain seems made for that. Having stronger feelings and memories about loss than gain."

Sasko nodded. "I like training the women and getting the satisfaction of seeing them progress, but it's depressing to lose someone after you go through all the effort to turn them into a decent soldier." Sasko wrinkled her nose, catching an unfamiliar odor wafting in on the fog. It had a slightly acidic scent. Was someone burning something in a campfire nearby? "I could see myself retiring if I knew what else to do with myself."

Their nearest mage guard was still standing, his rifle in his arms, but his chin had drooped to his chest. Almost everyone was snoring now.

"You're not allowed to retire," Ferroki said. "You're my replacement. You get to lead the company to great victories after I step down."

"I've forgotten what a great victory looks like." Sasko didn't comment on the rest. Several years earlier, when she'd stepped up to take the position as second-in-command, she'd known it had been with the understanding that she would take over the company if anything happened to Ferroki. That was the duty, after all. She'd been proud to be chosen, even if it had been because the *previous* second-in-command had fallen. These past weeks had drummed her down though, made it all seem like a slog. She told herself that she would feel better once this fiasco with the mages was over and they all had a chance for some leave and rest. If she didn't... Well, she would have to have another conversation with the captain and consider stepping down in favor of someone else becoming Ferroki's successor.

Sasko would feel like a failure and a poor friend if she backed out, but she would also hate to see the company disbanded after the captain passed or retired. Ferroki would want Thorn Company to continue on. She'd spent nearly thirty years building it up, establishing a reputation, and making contacts with the wealthy people who could afford to hire mercenaries.

"What's *in* that fog?" Ferroki pointed to the mage guard.

Not only was his chin to his chest, but now he slumped against the railing, sleeping on his feet. Sasko craned her neck to check all around the ship and didn't see anyone awake around them.

Sasko swore. "Magic?"

Some sort of magical sleep gas? If so, why weren't she and Ferroki being affected?

Hushed voices came from behind them, and Sasko started to relax, thinking she'd overreacted, but the speakers didn't sound like they were on the ship. Someone was out in the jungle. It might be Rivlen, Tezi, and the others returning, but it might not.

Ferroki pushed up to her knees and peered over the top of the bulwark. She jerked her head back down and grabbed her rifle.

"There are two people out there," Ferroki whispered. "Druids, I think. They're in those grass tunics with hoods up."

Sasko picked up her rifle and crawled over to Tinder and Words, staying low so the druids wouldn't see her from below. She shook both women, but other than a slight alteration in Tinder's snores, neither moved. She shook them harder. Nothing.

Whatever that fog was, it had knocked them out. Up in the forecastle, the mage sleeping against the railing slumped all the way to the deck, his rifle tumbling from his grip with a clank.

The murmuring voices stopped, but Sasko doubted the druids would go away.

Ferroki crawled toward the railing with her rifle in her grip. Sasko started after her, but Ferroki pointed her toward the other side of the ship. Right, they had better make sure they weren't surrounded.

As Sasko maneuvered around sleeping mercenaries, an animal leaped from branch to branch in a nearby tree, chattering and screaming as it went. A distant screech promised there were more large and deadly birds out there. Before, with everyone awake, Sasko hadn't been that worried about the wildlife, but with the arrival of druids who might be *controlling* that wildlife, she was more concerned.

The first yawn came over her as she approached the railing. It was so wide that her jaw cracked. Sasko frowned back at Ferroki. She'd reached the railing on the other side and was using a post for cover while she took aim at the intruders.

Would a magelock charge stop druids? Only if they weren't expecting it and didn't have their barriers up.

Sasko flattened herself to her belly and also used a post for cover as she peered through the gaps in the railing. She didn't hear any voices or sounds to indicate anyone creeping up from this side, but as she fought off another yawn, she spotted movement.

Two dark figures were creeping toward the ship, dressed similarly to the description Ferroki had given. One carried a staff and the other a sword. They levitated up from the ground, removing any question about whether they possessed magic or not.

One pointed the sword at the red-uniformed crewman slumped against the railing in the forecastle, then drew a magelock pistol. Neither intruder had seen Sasko yet—or if they had, they might not have realized she was awake, since she was prone. Only as she took aim did it occur to her that a magelock pistol was an odd weapon for a druid. She hadn't yet seen one of the magical firearms in their hands.

That was something she could contemplate later. She fired a second before the intruder could shoot the crewman.

He wasn't protected by a barrier, and she had the satisfaction of watching her charge blast into his shoulder. He spun in the air, and she fired again, this time taking him in the chest. His levitation spell disappeared, and he fell ten feet to the ground below.

Unfortunately, the second intruder got a barrier up, and it

deflected Sasko's next shot into the branches. An animal squeaked a protest.

The druid pointed his staff at her, and the tip brightened with an orange glow.

Sasko rolled away from the railing an instant before fire enveloped it. She scrambled toward the bulwarks, knowing they would help protect her. At the other railing, Ferroki was also shooting.

A fireball whizzed over Sasko's head as she rushed across the deck as fast as she could. The flames were close enough and hot enough to scorch her neck hair. She urged her limbs to greater speed, but they were surprisingly lethargic, given the situation. Another yawn threatened.

Who *yawned* when people were trying to kill her?

Sasko reached the barrier, scrambled around it, and peeked back. The intruder landed on the deck behind her, with all the slumbering mercenaries vulnerable at his feet.

Cursing, Sasko rose up on her knees and fired at him over the bulwark. Once again, her charge bounced off his barrier, but at least she had him distracted, and he didn't attack the mercenaries.

Ferroki skidded behind the bulwark beside her as a fireball streaked over her head, clipped the top of the frame, and deflected into the trees.

"Are we the only ones *awake*?" Ferroki demanded, grabbing another bulwark and turning it so she and Sasko were sandwiched between them.

One of the druids from her side of the ship soared over the railing and landed on the deck. Ferroki must also have only been able to take down one intruder before the other got his defenses up.

"I'm pretty sure *they're* awake." Ferroki ducked as a wave of magic blasted toward them, knocking sleeping people aside on its way to strike Vinjo's bulwark.

It was incredible that the flimsy, collapsible thing could deflect any kind of attack, but it didn't skid even an inch under the assault. Meanwhile, poor Sergeant Tinder rolled fifteen feet and smashed into a hatch. She groaned and swatted at the air sleepily. Sasko willed her to wake up as she fired at the intruder. Then she realized Tinder had been sleeping on her axe—and left it behind when she'd been knocked away. The haft was visible under her rumpled blanket.

Sasko kept firing, aware that she was almost out of charges, but wanting to keep the druid too distracted to hurt anyone—or sense that axe and claim it for himself.

But he frowned right at it, as if the dragon steel were calling to him.

"Cover me, Captain," Sasko barked.

She hefted the bulwark, thankful that it was light, and charged at the druid. He was beelining for the axe, but he spotted her and paused, preparing another attack.

Her yawns had disappeared, and fear charged through her as she rushed at him. A fireball spun toward her, and she crouched and lowered her head to make sure the bulwark completely covered her.

Flames crackled all around it, heat blasting her exposed skin, but she kept running until she smacked into her target. The bulwark wasn't a weapon and didn't force the druid's barrier down, but she'd surprised him enough that he hadn't fully braced himself. He stumbled backward a few steps. It gave Sasko the time she needed to dive out from behind the bulwark and wrap a hand around the axe.

The intruder snarled and launched another fireball. Without the bulwark to protect her, Sasko worried she'd made a huge mistake. But everything she'd heard and seen of the dragon-steel axes proved true, and this time, when the fireball swept past her, she didn't even feel the heat.

As it faded, Sasko hefted the axe, hoping it would bust through the intruder's barrier, and hurled it. The second it left her fingers, she regretted it, afraid he would be able to use his magic to catch it and that Tinder and Thorn Company would lose the powerful weapon forever.

Sasko sprang back toward the bulwark, in case her throw failed and she needed protection again, but the axe flared blue as it sped through the air. The intruder lifted his hands and muttered to himself, as if he planned to knock it away with his power. But the axe flew through his barrier and lodged in his chest. Pain and shock spasmed on his face as he tipped backward, tripped over the sleeping Corporal Basher, and landed on his side.

Though awed by the axe's effectiveness, Sasko didn't have time to admire it. The *thwomps* of Ferroki's magelock firing mingled with her curses as she tried to deal with the other intruder.

As Sasko yanked the axe out of the man's chest, she spotted a red uniform under the druid tunic, but there wasn't time to contemplate what that meant. She ran to Ferroki's side, then past her, confident now that the dragon steel would protect her even better than the bulwark.

The druid was in the middle of casting lightning bolts at Ferroki as she crouched behind cover, but when he saw Sasko with the axe, he whirled toward her and drew a sword. The blue metal of the long blade gleamed, and doubt made Sasko pause. His blade was *lesser* dragon steel, not dragon steel, but it would still be a formidable weapon.

Just as she was bracing herself to engage the man in a battle of blades, someone shouted, "What in all the cursed magic is going on on my ship?"

Captain Rivlen appeared, levitating over the railing and landing behind the intruder. He spun toward her, not saying a word, but his weapon and his presence—and the unconscious mercenaries all over the deck—said plenty.

Rage burned in Rivlen's eyes, and she launched a wall of fire at the man.

It was far greater and more impressive magic than the fireballs the intruders had cast, and Sasko hunkered down, holding the axe up like a shield. Rationally, she understood that it would protect her, but her instincts yelled at her to run far and run fast.

The intruder got a barrier up, but it was only strong enough to deflect Rivlen's angry power for a few seconds.

Sasko couldn't sense magic, but she knew when his defenses went down, for he screamed and collapsed. Within seconds, all that remained of the intruder was a blackened lump on the deck.

The rest of the mages in Rivlen's party landed on the deck beside her. "What happened?"

"Search the jungle for more attackers," Rivlen barked at them, "and find out what's causing that damn fog, and destroy it."

Ferroki came to stand beside Sasko, her hand singed and her cheek reddened. Otherwise, she appeared unarmed, and she still carried her rifle, though it was out of charges.

Sasko, realizing she was crouching and hiding behind the axe, straightened with as much dignity as she could manage. "How much do you think Tinder would charge me for this?"

"A million gold oroni," Ferroki sad.

"Worth it."

"Do you have that much?"

"Not quite, but if she would set up an installment plan, I'm sure I could pay it off."

"By your four hundredth birthday?"

"That sounds about right."

Rivlen strode up to them, still glowering in irritation. Not with *them*, Sasko hoped. She and the captain were the only reason everyone hadn't been killed. Sasko didn't know *why* they hadn't been knocked out, but Rivlen and the *Star Flyer* were lucky the fog hadn't affected them.

"I apologize, Captain." Ferroki sounded more chagrined than triumphant as she faced Rivlen. "I didn't realize people were *magically* falling asleep until your mage guard tipped over."

"Why weren't you two affected?"

"Good question," Sasko murmured, hoping they wouldn't somehow get in trouble—or be suspected of collusion.

"I believe we may have the engineering lieutenant Vinjo to thank for that." Ferroki pointed her rifle toward the bulwarks.

Sasko blinked. "You think those protected us from *fog*?"

"It's all I can think of, especially since you weren't holding Tinder's axe at the time." Ferroki faced Rivlen. "When next we see Vinjo, perhaps my lieutenant will reward him with a kiss."

Sasko scoffed, though if it turned out that the bulwarks had been responsible, she *would* kiss Vinjo. They'd saved their lives.

Ferroki considered the axe. "I'm surprised that didn't protect Sergeant Tinder from the fog."

"I think she was sleeping next to it instead of *with* it," Sasko said. "If she sells it to me, I'll be sure to wrap my arms around it every night like an enthusiastic lover."

Rivlen was frowning at the man Sasko had killed as one of her officers searched him, but she arched her eyebrows at the words. "Is the axe for sale?"

"I'm hoping to persuade the sergeant that it should be," Sasko said. "I have an installment-plan scheme that should entice the secret capitalist within her."

"This man isn't a druid," the officer said.

"Oh." Sasko turned, realizing she'd forgotten an important detail. She pointed with the axe. "That's right. He has a red uniform on underneath the tunic. I didn't see it until after the axe struck."

Ferroki nodded. "When they were whispering in the woods and thought everyone on board was sleeping, I heard a few of their words. They spoke Dhoran, not the druid tongue."

Rivlen strode over to the dead man.

"I don't understand," Sasko whispered to Ferroki. "Are these our own people? Er, Rivlen's own people?" Uthari's coffers might be paying her wages that week, but Sasko didn't want to claim any allegiance to him.

"Perhaps the ones who sent the location of the monument," Ferroki said, "a monument brimming with druidic power ready to take us down."

Two of Rivlen's mages alighted on the deck with a prisoner between them, one of the hooded intruders. But his hood had fallen back, and his grass tunic was ripped open, revealing another red uniform underneath.

"Captain Ular sent you to attack us?" Rivlen demanded, the fury returning to her eyes as she clenched a fist.

The prisoner clamped his mouth shut and said nothing.

"To kill soldiers in your own army?" Rivlen added.

His eyebrows flew up. "No, ma'am. We had special charges in our pistols that were only supposed to make sure the crew didn't wake up prematurely from the fog." He pointed to a pistol in the hand of one of his captors. "We were only supposed to sabotage the power supply, not kill anyone."

Sasko frowned at his pistol, but if he spoke the truth, there had been no way for her to tell.

"Are we going to get in trouble for having killed some of Uthari's people?" she whispered to Ferroki. "I thought they were going to kill the crew and all of our mercenaries."

Ferroki shook her head. "We defended the ship to the best of our abilities. If Uthari's troops decide to play war games in the jungle without letting us know, we can't be blamed for a deadly outcome."

Sasko hoped Rivlen agreed. And that *Uthari*, when he found out about this, would also agree. She'd helped him at the battle for the portal a few weeks back, and he'd seemed appreciative, in his cold and aloof wizard way, but she had no idea if he remembered her and would be lenient about a mistake.

"*Why* did your captain want to sabotage our ship?" Rivlen asked.

"To keep you from getting back first. Uthari ordered us to return to the camp, but we were still making repairs, and I think the captain was worried you'd report in about..." He glanced in the direction of the monument.

"If he hadn't played immature games and tried to get us *killed*, he wouldn't have to worry about what I report."

"I know, ma'am." The soldier shrank under Rivlen's glower and studied her boots.

"And it's not as if I don't have a dome-jir. Maybe I've already reported everything to him."

"Yes, ma'am."

"Throw him in the brig," Rivlen told her men.

As they marched the prisoner away, Sasko realized she hadn't seen Tezi yet. She jogged to the railing, expecting to find her on the ground and that the mages hadn't bothered to levitate her up to the ship. But the only people down there were the soldiers Rivlen had ordered to find the source of the fog. They must have succeeded, for it no longer blanketed the area, and Sasko had stopped yawning.

But unease crept into her, much like the fog, as she looked for and didn't find Tezi.

Rivlen had started toward the navigation cabin, but Sasko called, "Ma'am?" to stop her.

"What?" Rivlen asked.

"Didn't Rookie Tezi come back with you?"

Ferroki lifted her head, also glancing toward the jungle.

Rivlen's scowl wasn't reassuring, and Sasko slumped, certain something bad had happened. Would she have to add Tezi to the list of all the troops she'd trained and lost over the years?

"Rookie *Tezi* joined Colonel Sorath and went off to help the druids," Rivlen said.

"Help the druids?" Sasko mouthed.

"Sorath?" Ferroki asked, her tone wistful.

"Yes, the druids who are our enemies and who we were supposed to flush out and destroy." Rivlen stalked into navigation and slammed the hatch shut behind her.

Sasko joined Ferroki by the bulwarks. The other mercenaries were starting to stir as the effects of the magical fog wore off. They might have been better off continuing to sleep.

"Are we *sure* we aren't going to get in trouble?" Sasko asked. "Because if we are, I object vehemently. *We* just kept the ship from being sabotaged."

"You don't need to object vehemently to me." Ferroki sighed. "I agree."

"Well, Rivlen is crabby. If I get vehement with her, she might incinerate me." Sasko glanced at the charred lump that had been a man but quickly looked away.

Ferroki waved at the axe. "You better talk to Tinder about that installment plan then."

Sasko shook her head, the vision of herself as a mother—and married to *Vinjo?*—returning to her mind. She'd never thought she wanted children or to marry again, but after the chaos and craziness of working for these mages, who couldn't even be relied upon to be loyal to *their own side*, she couldn't help but wonder about other possibilities. Still, could she truly see raising children in this world? One where those responsible for the chaos and craziness ruled?

She didn't know.

25

MALEK STOOD IN THE CORRIDOR OUTSIDE OF THE KITCHEN laboratory. He'd already checked Zethron's cabin, but he wasn't there. He assumed Jadora had taken him to her laboratory, to one of the two cots set up in there. The second one was likely reserved for Malek. For sedation.

He grimaced, his hand straying to his main-gauche, but when it came to asking someone to end his life, he doubted he would have any more luck with Jadora than Jak. Malek could ask Tonovan to do it.

No. He pulled his hand away from the weapon. As soon as he was dead, Tonovan would be in charge, and he might hurt Jadora and Jak. Malek was sure he *would* hurt them. The idea of not being there to protect them filled him with rage.

Too much rage. It welled up in him, threatening to take over his mind, to take back the control he'd so assiduously worked to regain through his meditation.

He planted his hands on either side of the hatch and sucked in deep breaths, willing his magic to tamp down the furious urges coursing through him. Vinjo's and Harintha's voices floated out of navigation, an ongoing debate about how long the cave could be and what they would find at the end. He could also hear the muffled voices of Tonovan and Bakir in one of their cabins, plotting who knew what.

Long seconds passed as Malek struggled for control. Sweat dripped from his hairline and slithered down his spine. Slowly and with great difficulty, he pushed away the fury, locking it up once more. For now.

He knocked softly.

"Come," came Jadora's response, equally soft.

Malek stepped inside and closed the hatch. As he'd suspected, Zethron lay on one of the cots, his eyes closed, his lips as dry and cracked as Malek's. He was still, his chest barely rising and falling. Soon, if Malek allowed this, he would lie in an identical state on the cot next to him.

Jadora stood with her back to her counter, leaning on it as she gazed at the wall, four syringes of a yellow liquid in her grip. She was as still as Zethron, but her mind was whirling.

"You don't want to sedate me," Malek realized, catching a hint of her thoughts even though his ability to read minds was fading along with his humanity. Even if he hadn't gotten anything from her, the presence of four syringes instead of one would have told him something.

"I do—reluctantly—but I need you to do something first." Jadora met his eyes, her own eyes full of determination. "I refuse to render you unconscious and leave Tonovan in command of this ship. I don't want Bakir or Prolix stepping up to take charge either. I don't know what we're going to find when we reach wherever those people are taking us, but those three *cannot* be in charge." Concern replaced her determination. "I'm also not sure they would let us live more than two minutes after you were sedated. Vinjo heard them talking."

Her thoughts escaped in a jumble of conflict and emotions.

This time, Malek caught everything from what Vinjo had shared to all the threats Tonovan had made to her aboard the ship and before. He also saw her fear warring with her desire to handle her own problems, her need to protect her son warring with her desire to let him stand as his own man.

Malek focused on her thoughts of Tonovan and how he'd threatened her, and his rage came roaring back to the forefront. He shook with fury.

"I'll *kill* him now." He spun toward the hatch.

"Wait, Malek." Jadora rushed over and gripped his shoulders. "I have a plan. Listen, please. I need—"

He whirled back around, the fury threatening to explode. Someone had touched him, tried to restrain him. He snarled. The animal within him couldn't allow that.

Jadora stumbled back from him with terror in her eyes. Her heel clipped one of the cots, and she flailed and started to fall.

He lunged and gripped her arms. Jadora wasn't an enemy. She was someone to be protected. By him. He was her protector.

He drew shuddering breaths, once again sublimating the animal. The monster.

"Malek?" she whispered, the fear still rolling off her.

Fear of him.

"He's still here," Malek whispered hoarsely. "*I'm* still here."

"Good." Even though she was afraid, she didn't try to pull away from him.

"Yes." He stroked her hair. It was smooth and soft and cool under his touch. It soothed the monster the way his deep breaths hadn't.

"I want to sedate those three," Jadora whispered, showing him the syringes. "Until we deal with the people out there. Until I find a cure for you. Ideally, until we get back to Torvil and can dump them in a pile at your king's feet. I can't work with them threatening me."

"No," he agreed, still stroking her hair. "I will use the dagger instead of your needles. I'll make sure they never threaten you again."

Jadora shook her head.

Malek bent forward so he could lean his forehead against her soft cool hair. "You *can't* care if Tonovan lives, not after all he's done to you, to so many. You must want him dead."

He sensed that she was tempted to agree, to nod yes, to unleash him.

But what she said was, "I think that we should refrain from killing our powerful wizards until we see where these people are taking us and what they plan to do with us. I tried to steal their plant, and they're not happy about Jak having taken Shikari's egg. As much as I hate to admit it, we may need Tonovan and the other two to have a shot at escaping. If I need to, I can wake them up again. Maybe not instantly but with time. Once I sedate you..." She stared at his chest. "I can't risk waking you up again until I've figured out how to cure you."

He growled, wanting to deny her logic, but he'd forgotten about the men on the skiff—the powerful mages on the skiff. He hadn't tried to attack them since the barrier had come down, but he sensed the strength of their auras and knew a battle with them would be dicey. Like many of the mages on Vran, they carried dragon-steel weapons and emanated great power. Vinjo and Harintha would be no match for them. Neither would Jak.

Malek struggled to gather his scattered thoughts and remember what Jadora wanted. What she'd asked. The scent of her hair tickled his nose, a faint floral essence lingering from the last time she'd bathed. He noticed where her body was pressed against his, her feminine curves. She rested a hand on his chest and looked up at him, her lips parting as she searched his eyes for a response. That she dared stand this close to him when he was like this, that she was willing to touch him...

For a moment, the monster stirred again, not with the desire to hurt but with the desire to take. To take *her*. Another growl rumbled in his chest, and he started to kiss her, to pull her harder against himself, but...

He halted and released her. He couldn't allow the animal to take control in this any more than he could in killing.

There was a mission. Jadora had a mission for him, and he was zidarr. Missions were what he'd trained his whole life for.

"They will sense me coming," Malek said, forcing his mind to consider how he could sedate three mages as powerful as he. Had it been night with everyone sleeping, he could have done it, but they were all awake. And Tonovan and Bakir were together.

"Yes." Her gaze had been locked on his mouth, but she pulled it away and reached into her pocket. "I have something that might help."

When she withdrew a blocky device attached to a wristband, Malek sensed that it was magical, but he didn't know what it was until he saw the explanation in her mind. One of Vinjo's stealth devices. She wanted him to use it to get close to the others, close enough to surprise them and jab the needles into the arteries in their necks before they could pull away.

The honorable part of him shied away from the idea of sneaking up to dispatch enemies like an assassin in the night. But if he failed to defeat those three honorably, and they got the best of him, Jadora would be in danger. They would kill her. Tonovan would do *more* than kill her.

"I will do as you wish." Malek fastened the device around his wrist.

"Thank you. Here." Jadora handed him the syringes. "It'll take a minute or two for the sedative to kick in. They'll have that long to strike back."

"I understand."

He started to turn, but she rested a hand on his chest again.

Didn't she know how dangerous that was? How close he was to losing control?

"Be careful, please. I... I love you." Jadora looked like she wanted to kiss him, but maybe she did realize how close he was to the edge. Instead, she nodded to him and stepped back.

He wrestled with the beast again, with the urge to spring for her and take her to the cot. He had a mission.

"I am your protector," he growled, then activated the device and stalked out.

Jadora resisted the urge to creep out after the invisible Malek to track his progress. If she stuck her head into Prolix's cabin, he would know something was going on. All she could do was wait and hope the stealth device made Malek's imposing task more feasible.

A few hours earlier, she'd watched him sword fight like a legendary hero out of eld, outmaneuvering a fellow zidarr with all the same training and experience he had, so she had faith that his physical abilities weren't overly diminished by the infection. His mind was what was questionable. Could he hold it together long enough to knock out all three mages?

The whole time he'd been in the laboratory with her, he'd been on edge, visibly fighting for control over himself. At times, he'd seemed on the verge of lashing out at her, his eyes wild and unseeing, as if he hadn't known a friend stood in front of him. Other times, when they'd been standing close, his body had been taut with dangerous sexual energy, and she'd thought he would drag her over to the cot—or shove her up against the wall.

For a brief moment, she'd almost encouraged that, almost kissed him, her mind flirting with thoughts that she might lose him and that this would be the only chance they got to be together. But she wanted Malek as he'd been two days ago, not Malek in the throes of a mind-destroying disease.

Not that she would have tried to stop him if he'd lost that wrestling match with himself. She snorted softly and shook her head.

While she waited, she checked on Zethron to make sure he was resting easily and that his biological needs were taken care of.

A shout and a thud came from the back of the ship. It had started.

"Where's Malek?" someone roared. Tonovan.

Well, he was still conscious. Unfortunately.

Had all three of the mages realized Malek was missing and gone looking for him? Before he could sedate any of them?

Jadora grimaced. If those three realized something was up, they would come looking for her.

She heard them speaking but couldn't make out further words through the closed hatch. She fought with the urge to hide in a cabinet and the desire to listen in and find out what was going on. Since she couldn't fit in a cabinet, she eased closer to the hatch. She pulled out one of her vials of acid as she opened it a couple of inches, then flattened herself against the wall.

"...happened to him?" Tonovan demanded.

It sounded like he was in the corridor, down toward engineering.

"He's not dead," Bakir said.

"I can sense that, you idiot, but he's lying on the floor and won't wake up."

"Watch your tone with me, General," Bakir said.

Jadora clenched a fist. Malek had gotten one of them. Too bad the others were together. That would make his second strike harder. Maybe they would lose their tempers and fight with each other.

"It's that sedative," Tonovan barked.

Uh oh.

Footsteps thundered down the corridor. Jadora closed the hatch, but it blew open, slamming against the wall.

She sprang into the farthest corner of the kitchen, but there was nowhere to run. Tonovan charged inside with Bakir right behind him.

"Don't disturb my patient," she blurted, envisioning them knocking Zethron out of his cot, but the raw fury in Tonovan's eyes promised she had a lot more to worry about than her patient's welfare.

"You *bitch*," Tonovan snarled, stalking toward her. "You knocked out Prolix! What were you *thinking*?"

A wall of power slammed into Jadora, locking her into the corner. She couldn't move and could barely breathe. She still held her vial, but she couldn't lift her arm to throw it. The ring Malek had given her was on her finger, but she couldn't lift a hand to tap it twice against Tonovan's flesh.

Further, Bakir stood just inside the hatchway, blocking her escape. If Malek was in the corridor and wanted to sneak in, Bakir was blocking that too.

"I didn't do it." Jadora glanced toward the counter, emptying her mind of thoughts. "Someone took some of my syringes though."

Tonovan stalked up and wrapped his hand around her throat. "You've crossed the wrong wizard. I'm going to teach you a lesson, but first, I'm going to kill your boy and make you watch." He glanced toward Bakir. "Go get Malek. Make sure that crazy wild monster isn't going to interfere."

"I still can't sense him. And don't give me orders. You're not in charge."

"I'm about to be." Tonovan smiled, focusing on Jadora again.

Bakir gasped, his back arching and his body going rigid.

Jadora was too far away to see Malek, but she trusted he was there, hopefully with the needle jammed in Bakir's neck. She couldn't feel any triumph, not when Tonovan's hand was tightening around her neck and his magic had her crushed against the wall so hard that her ribs creaked.

Tonovan glanced back, swore, and tugged Jadora away from the wall. He spun, put his own back to the corner, and wrapped an arm around her. He smashed her to his chest to use her as a shield.

A tremendous wrenching filled the lab as the hatch was torn off and wood snapped. Bakir was fighting Malek, launching magic at him even as Malek had the admiral trapped in his grip. Lab equipment flew off the counter, and slides shattered. Bakir roared, jerking his body and trying to escape.

"Help me, you bastard," Bakir shouted at Tonovan, though his eyes were growing glassy.

Without releasing his grip on Jadora, Tonovan launched a blast of power that hurled Bakir into the corridor—and likely Malek along with him. He cast fire next, heat and light exploding in the lab as his spinning ball of flames flew over the unconscious Zethron and through the hatchway.

From the corner, Jadora couldn't see into the corridor and didn't know what was happening, but she feared Malek would be hit. Her vial was still in her sweaty grip. She didn't have the right angle to throw it and break it in Tonovan's face, not with him using her as a shield, his snarling mouth right behind her head. Instead, she eased her hand downward, trying not to think about anything and hoping his focus was locked on the battle in the corridor.

A body flew through the hatchway and landed on the deck. Admiral Bakir. He groaned but didn't rise again.

Jadora's hand brushed against Tonovan's trousers pocket. No, that was his fly.

"Malek!" Tonovan bellowed in her ear. "Show yourself. Quit being a coward, or I'll kill your woman."

Guided only by touch, Jadora tried to find a gap between Tonovan's buttons that she could slide her vial through.

"Did you ever get to screw her?" Tonovan demanded. "Or were you too proper? Too *zidarr*?"

He launched a blast of energy that knocked more equipment off the counter, and Jadora winced as her microscope smashed to the deck. Fury of her own built up within her. How was she supposed to find a cure if these damn mages broke all of her equipment?

Tonovan snarled and cast a fireball. It hit the wall, charred wood exploding and bursting into flame. Thunderous snaps came from the deck, and pieces of wood flew everywhere, thudding off the walls. A broken board sped into the corridor and struck the far wall hard enough to lodge in it.

If any of the pieces hit the invisible Malek, or his protective barrier, Jadora couldn't tell. She found the gap she was looking for and slid the vial into Tonovan's trousers.

"What are you—" His grip tightened on her, but then his head snapped back, as if he'd been punched. His physical and magical grip loosened.

Jadora crouched low enough to ram her elbow into Tonovan's crotch, hoping to catch the vial before it slipped down his trouser leg to the deck. Glass crunched as he grunted in pain.

Whatever Malek was doing to Tonovan, it kept him too busy to retaliate. His grip loosened enough for Jadora to pull away. To further distract him, she twice tapped the ring against his exposed wrist. Tonovan stiffened, but she couldn't tell if it hurt him more than Malek's attack.

As she darted to the side, Malek stepped to within the stealth device's five-foot range of visibility and came into view. He sprang onto Tonovan, jammed the syringe needle into his throat, and pressed the plunger.

Tonovan screamed and grabbed Malek, trying to headbutt

him. But Malek had emptied the syringe, and he leaped back in time, avoiding the blow.

Tonovan crouched, as if to lunge after him, but he looked down instead. "Why is my cock *burning*?"

He shook his leg, and pieces of glass tinkled to the deck. He glowered at Jadora, but he knew Malek was the true threat and tried to leap for him. But he stumbled, his legs leaden from the sedative kicking in.

"What did you *do* to me?" Tonovan stretched his arms toward Malek, fingers grasping at the air.

Malek wasn't far out of his reach, but he didn't bother dodging the feeble attack. He merely held the empty syringe and watched as Tonovan pitched to the deck. The warped and buckled deck that now had a three-foot-wide hole in it between them and the hatchway. The empty cot had been knocked on its side. Somewhat miraculously, Zethron hadn't been disturbed.

"That's all of them," Malek said.

"Thank you." Jadora rushed over and hugged him.

He returned the hug but only briefly before stepping back. He removed the stealth device and handed it to her, then held a fourth syringe up between them, this one still full of her sedative.

"Now you have to finish the task," he said.

Jadora slumped, though she knew he was right. She wished she could keep him awake and at her side, to help her and Jak if they needed it wherever they were going.

Malek shook his head. "I want nothing more than to stand at your side, but I almost lost it with Bakir. I found my main-gauche in my hand before I knew how it got there and had to fight down an intense urge to slit his throat instead of jamming the needle into it. I don't even dislike him." He glanced at the supine Tonovan, as if such urges would have been understandable against him.

"If it helps, I'm not that fond of him." Jadora guided Malek to the empty cot and set it upright.

As Malek settled onto it, as stiff and tense as his sword, Vinjo appeared in the hatchway.

"Uh, what happened to my ship?" He peered around, gaping not at the unconscious Tonovan or Bakir—whom he'd stepped over to reach the hatchway—but at the charred walls and the hole in the deck.

"Not now, Vinjo." Jadora readied the syringe but paused. "If we have to fly back while you're still unconscious..." She swallowed, nervous about finishing the sentence, since Vinjo had voiced that plan about them stealing the key, abandoning the ship and crew, and trekking back to the portal. Even if they'd ended up doing that, she wouldn't have left without Malek. He had to know that, but would he think it suspicious that she wanted the key?

Wordlessly, he unbuttoned his pocket and held it out to her.

"Thank you," she whispered.

"There's a huge hole in the deck." Vinjo stared at it. "It goes all the way through to the hull. Did you see this?"

Jadora tucked the dragon-headed medallion into her pocket and turned over Malek's wrist. While she couldn't fault him for going straight for the carotid artery when he'd attacked the others, a vein in the arm would do fine. She couldn't imagine herself stabbing Malek in the neck.

"I can see the *river*," Vinjo moaned.

"Not *now*," Jadora repeated, glaring at him.

Vinjo finally seemed to realize the magnitude of what she was doing and *harumphed* and stepped outside. "I'll lock these other mages up. How long will they be out?"

"A few hours. I'll have to reapply the sedative regularly until... until we find a solution."

"Rolling them through the hole and leaving them to be eaten by eels comes to mind," Vinjo muttered.

Jadora sighed and turned back to Malek. As she pressed the needle to the skin, his lean body mass making the vein easy to see, he gripped her wrist with his other hand. His eyes grew wild, and she worried she'd dawdled too long, that he would fling her away —or worse.

"I have to do this," she whispered to him, forcing herself to meet those wild eyes, though they were so different from the eyes of the Malek she'd come to know and care about. It was hard to see the honorable man in there when there was a growl on his lips and his grip hurt.

Though she worried he would attack, she slid the needle in and pressed the plunger. He hissed and jerked upright on the cot. The syringe fell away and clattered to the deck.

"You stabbed me," he rasped.

"You know why." She winced, his grip painful, but if that was all he did, she could endure it. A few more seconds, and the sedative should kick in.

His brow furrowed. "I forgot."

"It would take too long to explain. You'll have to trust me."

He gazed at her, confusion mingling with the wildness, but he released the painful grip. He touched her cheek gently and said, "Yes," then lay back down.

A tremor went through her, the fear that his trust was misplaced, that she wouldn't find a solution and that they wouldn't be able to wake him up again.

As his eyes closed, Jadora stroked the side of his head, trying to smooth the wild sweat-dampened hair. If this somehow worked out, she wondered if he would remember that she'd said she loved him. And she wondered what would happen if Uthari found out.

"Focus on the here and now," she murmured to herself, glancing back as Tonovan floated out of her laboratory.

Vinjo was tidying up.

"We've reached a cavern," Harintha called back from navigation. "There are a bunch of people in it, a big bonfire, and uhm, something with a very powerful aura in the shadows back there."

Jadora grimaced. She'd hoped to have time to do more research on the bacteria before they reached… wherever they were.

Jak rushed in, flailing to keep from falling through the hole.

"I'll have to find a board for that," Jadora said, resting her hand on Malek's chest before rising to face her son.

"We're here, and Shikari is afraid," Jak blurted.

"He's not the only one."

"I think he wants us to rescue him."

"He communicated that with you?"

"The way he does. With images. He's been scared since we were separated. Since *before* then." Jak ran to the navigation cabin.

Jadora was reluctant to leave her patients, but she followed him. They were here because she'd sneaked through a barrier to pick a plant. Whatever was about to befall them, she had to face it along with the others.

"I sense a dragon back there." Jak pointed toward the shadowy rear of a large cavern that opened to one side of the river. "But I can't tell if it's a good dragon or an evil dragon. So far, all of the ones we've encountered have been affected by that parasite."

"I know," Jadora said grimly.

Harintha brought the ship to a stop, the mageship hovering over the water. Braziers burned around the front half of the cavern, though it had to be for warmth or ceremonial purposes, not light. Numerous glowworms meandered along on the roof and sides of the cavern, providing enough light for Jadora to count more than twenty men and women watching their arrival. Like the brothers, many of the men were shirtless with dragon tattoos on their muscled chests. The women wore dresses, their arms bare, save for bracelets. If their chests were tattooed, their clothing hid it.

Shikari hunkered in front of a woman seated on a litter that had been brought out and set before a bonfire.

"They're all mages," Jak whispered. "*Powerful* mages."

"Too bad someone knocked out all of *our* powerful mages," Harintha grumbled.

"I can rouse them with a stimulant if needed." Not that Jadora wanted to do that, not after fighting so hard to render them unconscious. Besides, if each of those people was the equivalent of a zidarr, it wouldn't have mattered if Tonovan and the others were awake. And Malek...

She couldn't rouse him under any circumstances.

"I don't think you want Tonovan in charge for this," Jak said.

Harintha frowned at him but didn't argue that, other than to say, "Who *is* in charge now?"

The thief of the plant and the thief of the dragon egg will come forth, a woman's voice boomed in their minds. It had to be the lady in the chair—the chief the brothers had spoken of?

"I think *she's* in charge." Jak looked at Jadora. "Do we go out? Do we take weapons? Gifts?"

"I have some vials of acid left," she said.

"I'm not sure which category that falls into."

You will come now. We are a patient people, but thieves try even the most tolerant.

"Do you want us to come with you?" Vinjo waved at himself and Harintha.

Harintha turned her frown on him, and Jadora was confident she wouldn't have volunteered.

"No," Jadora said. "Stay here, and keep an eye on everything. On *everyone*. If anyone starts stirring before I get back, there are more syringes full of my sedative in the drawer under the microscope. Ah, under where the microscope was before a mage blew it to the deck."

"All right." Vinjo looked relieved as he nodded.

Nobody wanted to go out and face these people. Jadora couldn't blame him. She was tempted to tell Jak to stay behind, since she'd been the one to snip the plant leaves, but he wanted to rescue Shikari.

With a determined nod, Jak grabbed a magelock pistol out of his cabin, then squeezed past Jadora to climb the ladder first. He probably had some notion of protecting her. She shook her head and followed him.

As soon as they reached the deck, a powerful magical grip wrapped around them and floated them over the railing. Eels and fanged fish stirred in the river, jumping and creating ripples at the surface. Jaws snapped. Jadora tried not to think about being dropped.

They were levitated all the way to the chief's litter. A brawny man stepped forward and removed Jak's pistol. Another man eyed Jadora, but she wasn't wearing any obvious weapons, and he didn't search her and find her vials. The two brothers stood to the side, their arms folded over their chests.

Shikari bounded over and butted his head against Jak's hip. He sat beside him and curled his tail around Jak's ankle. It was the most overt expression of attachment that Jadora had seen from the young dragon.

The chief, a lean woman in her seventies or eighties, propped her elbow on the armrest of her litter, gripped her chin, and considered them.

I will have your thoughts, she said into their minds.

Jadora grimaced, hoping that it wouldn't hurt as much as the last time and that she wouldn't pass out again.

And I will assess your suitability as a protector of a young dragon, the woman added, focusing solely on Jak.

He lifted his chin. "I'm good at helping him catch food, and I take him on adventures. And I always make sure he has a bed. Specifically *my* bed."

Power is what you must have to save him from the tainted dragons.

"Tainted?" Jadora asked.

It was the first she'd heard the term. Given what she'd learned, it made more sense than referring to the dragons as elder and younger varieties. But she'd wondered if the dragons themselves understood what had happened to them.

They seek to spread their dreadful disease at every opportunity, and they have unfortunately been very successful. Until this hatchling was born, only one dragon still lived that remained untainted.

Jak peered toward the shadows at the back of the cavern.

One dragon that our ancestors swore to protect, the chief continued. *For a hundred generations, our people have done that. We've not only protected her, but we've ensured the hope for the future could not be found and destroyed.*

"The eggs," Jak guessed.

The eggs. You were wrong to take one to raise.

"The portal told me to."

It was wrong to do so.

"Shikari would have died if I hadn't."

Better for him to die than be turned into one of those vile monsters.

Shikari peeped unhappily and lowered his chin to the ground. Would they kill him out of some deluded notion of saving him from that fate?

"That's *not* going to happen," Jak said.

The chief stretched her palm toward him. Though Jadora couldn't see anything, an invisible beam seemed to strike Jak. He gasped and stumbled. As Jadora grabbed his arm to steady him, his head fell back. Her palm tingled with pain where she gripped him, but she didn't let go.

"What are you doing to my son?"

Assessing his power. The chief had no trouble understanding them even when they spoke in their own tongue.

Jadora gritted her teeth. It looked more like they were torturing Jak, but what could she do? As always, she was powerless around mages.

The chief lowered her hand, and Jak slumped, wobbling on his feet. Shikari peered uncertainly up at him, and Jadora wrapped an arm around his waist.

"I'm all right," he whispered, locking his knees so he could face the chief.

You are not without potential, but it is not enough. Your powers haven't been developed yet, and you are no match for a tainted dragon.

"Is anyone?" Jak muttered.

We will keep the hatchling here and protect him as we have the ancient one, until such time as one is born who can cure the taint. The chief shook her head. *I do not know why the portal believed you could do anything.*

"Keep him?" Jak rested a hand on Shikari's head. "But what if he doesn't want to stay? And who's the ancient one? Can we talk to him?"

To her, and she sleeps. She must sleep a great deal, spending centuries in hibernation, to extend her life. It is important that she live until the taint has been cured. She must survive so that she can pass along that which is not in the hereditary memory to the new generation. Only when the taint is gone will we allow them to be born. The chief frowned at Shikari.

He squeaked at her.

Perhaps it would be safest for him to sleep, as well, until one is able to raise him properly in the dragon ways.

Shikari hid behind Jak's leg. Was *that* what he was terrified of? Being put to sleep indefinitely?

Malek had wanted to choose death over that possibility. Jadora couldn't blame Shikari for fearing such a fate as well.

"My mother might be able to cure the dragon taint," Jak offered. "She's a scientist. A chemist and an herbalist. She knows all about synthesizing drugs from natural substances, drugs that help people. Maybe she could cure the tainted dragons."

Jadora shook her head as not only the chief but all the men and women in the cavern looked at her.

Then the sensation of ants crawling around between her brain and her skull came over her. She groaned, bent forward, and gripped her head, not sure if it was an attack or a mind reading. Or both. These people did *not* have a gentle touch.

"Mother?" Jak touched her shoulder.

She felt it but couldn't react, could only clench her jaw as mages pawed through her mind, stirring up memories of her years of school and research, especially what she'd done before putting her career aside to finish her husband's quest for the portal. Would her work mean anything to people who lived in these simple caves? If they had universities or libraries on this world, Jadora hadn't seen evidence of it yet.

We are not uneducated, the chief's dry voice spoke into her mind. *But perhaps your people have studied more in this area. Interesting. We'd always assumed that the savior would have great power and use magic to remove the taint.*

I don't know if I can remove it, Jadora felt compelled to point out. She would research the possibility if they wished it, especially since she had to research the planet's bacteria to find a cure for Malek and Zethron, but she wouldn't mind if these people simply sent them all home. Admittedly, Uthari might send them right back here with more weapons and warriors if they didn't manage to get some Jitaruvak.

That plant is for our people. We train a great deal to become worthy protectors and fight off the tainted ones when needed. It is important that our lives are not short.

Right, she'd said they'd been protecting the dragon for a hundred generations, not the five hundred that Jadora would have expected to have passed in more than ten thousand years.

Any chance you'd be willing to share? she asked, though she cared little about Uthari's desires at the moment.

If you can heal the dragons of the taint, we would give you anything you wished.

Jadora sighed. *I can try, but I don't know if that's possible.*

I don't know either.

The crawling sensation disappeared, and Jadora drew in a shaky breath and straightened. The chief still gripped her narrow chin as she considered them.

One of the nearby warriors asked her something in their tongue.

I believe it is worth waking her. Let the ancient one decide. Come. The chief gestured to several of her people. *You remember the ceremony?*

If they replied, Jadora didn't hear it, but three men and three women came to her litter and linked hands with each other and with her.

"What's going on?" Jak must not have received all of their words.

"I think they're waking the dragon."

26

The skyboard wobbled and sagged under the weight of three people. Tezi balanced on the edge, with the druid—Tovorka—on the other edge, each of them gripping one of Sorath's shoulders so that his stealth device would include them. It would have worked fine if they had been walking, but the skyboards weren't meant to hold more than two people, if that. Sweat bathed Tovorka's face as he struggled to keep it aloft, and they brushed the treetops frequently.

If they succeeded with their mission, Tezi had no idea how they would add a fourth person. They would have to grab another skyboard off the ship.

"The camp is ahead," Sorath murmured.

Night had fallen, and the glow from lamps on the mageships on the outskirts came into view. Tezi squinted. That glow came from *more* than lamps. Magical attacks ranging from beams of energy to lightning to fire flew back and forth between the ships. She and the others were flying into a battle zone.

When Tezi had woken from a nap that afternoon, she'd heard that a conflict had broken out between Uthari's fleet and the fleets that had considered themselves allies of Queen Vorsha, but she hadn't realized it had continued throughout the day and into the night.

Maybe this would help them, as the mages would be distracted, and it might be easier to sneak in. But if the ships were protected by barriers, gaining access might be impossible.

"Slow us down." Sorath glanced back at Tovorka. "We'll have to be careful. A stray lightning bolt could fry us. They wouldn't even see us until they found our charred bodies on the ground later."

I will be wary, Tovorka replied in their minds. He didn't seem to speak Dhoran but must have gotten the gist. *When I was a prisoner, after the torture in the tent, they put me in a cell in the brig of the* Dread Arrow. *Is it likely Grunk will have been taken to the same place?*

"Yes," Sorath said. "He was captured on Uthari's yacht, but there isn't a brig there. The *Dread Arrow* is also where they kept Vinjo when he was being questioned and tortured."

"They like taking prisoners and torturing them," Tezi said.

"Tell me about it."

"Do you know for sure that Grunk is alive, sir?" Tezi had only learned the druid's name that day and hoped he had another one. Even though he was by all accounts somewhat crazy, it didn't seem to fit him.

Sorath hesitated. "No. Unfortunately, it's possible he's not. He was badly burned. But they may have kept him alive to question him about the druids. Someone must have given Yidar information on where to find their people."

"Except that he found the *wrong* people."

"He wasn't far from their headquarters. He might have seen someone running into a tunnel to that settlement or some other evidence of people living there and assumed anyone out in the jungle was a druid." Sorath shook his head. "He also might not have cared that those people weren't druids."

Tovorka nodded, as if perfectly willing to accept that the zidarr had knowingly made a vile choice. After what Tezi had seen, she would have had a hard time arguing.

As they flew closer, Tovorka sticking to the shadows in case their skyboard was visible, Tezi could see the colors of the mage-ship hulls more easily. Uthari's black vessels had formed a circle above the camp and the portal, and they were firing toward ships of several other colors, though a few red-hulled craft seemed to be helping Uthari by weaving among the enemies and launching attacks at them. And were those yellow-hulled ships working with Uthari's fleet too? It was chaotic, and night made it hard to truly tell what was happening.

"I can't believe they're fighting when there's a possibility of more dragons coming at any time," Sorath said. "Why doesn't anyone realize we need to work together right now?"

One of their rulers was killed, Tovorka pointed out. *That's the ultimate crime among their kind, is it not?*

"Yes," Sorath said, "but I'm surprised Uthari didn't blame me for that."

"Maybe he tried," Tezi said, "and they didn't believe him."

She didn't pretend to understand mages or their politics, but even those who were allied seemed mistrustful of each other. If a dragon appeared and ate them all, she wouldn't weep, but she hoped her team could get Grunk first.

Abruptly, red lightning shot up from the ground by the waterfall. From the portal.

It branched out in four directions, avoiding the black-hulled ships as it sizzled through the air to strike at more distant targets. Tovorka sucked in a startled breath, and the skyboard tilted alarmingly as he flew it lower to avoid a branch streaking in their direction.

Tezi crouched down, banging one knee on the board before

catching her balance. Her axe was in a sling on her back, but she grabbed the strap to make sure it wouldn't fly anywhere.

The weapon flashed an angry blue, surprising her, and she planted a hand on Sorath's boot to make sure she was still in contact with him. For a second, she'd forgotten about that, and she peered around, hoping nobody had seen her.

But with all the magic flying from ship to ship, her axe's flash shouldn't have been that noticeable. Why had it done that when she hadn't been in battle? Because of the proximity of the lightning?

Tezi peered through the trees toward the portal. King Uthari stood by it, a circle of his red-uniformed mages standing guard and watching the skies. The portal flashed, much as her axe had, its blue light reflecting in the pool. The red lightning that shot out from its frame seemed disconnected from the blue magic.

A sense of disgruntlement emanated from Tezi's axe. That surprised her. *She* hadn't done anything that should have offended it. Was it linked somehow to the portal? She remembered how Jak had consulted the portal on Vran to ask it about her axe. Maybe all dragon-steel weapons, tools, and artifacts were linked by their inherent magic.

He takes a great risk, Tovorka told them as he steadied the skyboard. *I am not well versed on dragon steel or that artifact, but even I can sense that the portal is not pleased to be forced to attack others on his behalf.* He sneered. *Nobody would want to be a tool for a power-hungry ruler.*

"No kidding," Sorath muttered. "I'm surprised he got it to work on his behalf at all. I remember seeing him at the camp one night with some book that was probably a thousand years old, dredging up commands until he got the portal to respond to him."

Quiet, Tovorka warned as they drew close enough to see mages on the decks of Uthari's ships. *Or speak only telepathically. We grow close.*

Sorath gave him a sour look. The druid could read their thoughts, but since neither Sorath nor Tezi could speak telepathically to each other, it would be hard for them to communicate.

Tezi took a deep breath, resolving to follow their lead, but she had one last question. "If we have to, do we kill people?"

She was well aware that Thorn Company was currently employed by Uthari and on Rivlen's ship. If Tezi killed some of Uthari's troops, would Ferroki and the others be punished? She scowled at herself, acknowledging that it was a question she should have asked *before* volunteering for this. Yes, Grunk had saved her life, but he was a crazy druid who licked blood off his daggers. Was it worth risking the company for him?

Officially, Tezi wasn't on the Thorn Company roster at the moment, but she didn't know if Uthari would care about that bookkeeping annotation if Tezi killed his people. And the wicked double-headed axe wasn't the best weapon for knocking someone out of a fight without doing serious damage.

A long moment passed before Sorath answered. "Try not to," he finally said. "If we're forced to fight, I'll make any killing blows if we must. I'll try to keep them from knowing you're there. In fact…" He considered her over his shoulder, then unfastened the wrist strap for the stealth device and handed it to her. "Tovorka, we'll have to keep in contact with Tezi now."

Tezi accepted it but didn't put it on. "Sir, are you sure? Uthari *hates* you."

No matter how hard they tried to remain in contact and invisible to the mages, it seemed inevitable that they would be knocked apart at some point or walk too close to someone. Her fight with Yidar had shown her the device's range of effectiveness. At times, she hadn't been able to see Sorath on the zidarr's other side. At other times, he'd been fully visible.

"Yes," Sorath said, "but I'd prefer he not hate *you* as well."

He nodded once and faced the ships again, making it clear the conversation was over.

There wasn't time for further discussion anyway. They were flying toward the *Dread Arrow*, coming in at a lower level as Tovorka tried to avoid the attacks lancing through the night at Uthari's fleet.

Tezi strapped on the device while keeping hold of Sorath. Tovorka reached over and gripped her shoulder, though he continued to watch the route ahead.

They slowed down as they approached until they hovered in the air about twenty feet below the hull. Tovorka gazed intently up at it.

The barrier that wraps around the ship is a few feet above Sorath's head, he spoke into their minds. *I believe your weapons could break it, but the mages would know an enemy with dragon steel approached. Let's see if they drop it to return fire. That would be the easiest way for us to slip in.*

Tezi didn't respond, not wanting to speak aloud when they were this close.

Another round of red lightning streaked out from the portal. More powerful than attacks from the mages, it ripped through the barriers around the ships of Uthari's enemies. Many of them backed farther away, though they returned fire. Magic of all kinds streaked toward Uthari and the portal as well as his ships.

Tezi thought of Kywatha's desire to destroy the ancient artifact, but every lightning bolt or beam of energy that struck it was deflected. It didn't seem to be protecting Uthari, but his own barrier, and perhaps those that his guards shared with him, was sufficient for the job. Unfortunately.

The battle-axe flashed, its blue visible over Tezi's shoulder, and she winced. She hoped the stealth device worked to hide its magic, because she had no way to tell it to knock that off. That sense of disgruntlement emanated from it again.

Thus far, it had never forced her to do anything, but at times, its magic had guided her in battle. What if it grew so disgruntled on behalf of the portal that it forced her to jump down there and attack Uthari?

Sorath glanced back, pointed upward, and raised his eyebrows.

Tovorka shook his head. *All they're doing now is focusing on keeping it up and letting their king handle the attacking. No, the portal is handling all the work. All he's doing is forcing it to.*

Sorath drew his dagger and looked up, as if he were contemplating popping the barrier.

But Tovorka gripped both of their shoulders and jerked his chin toward the portal.

"Something's coming through," a mage on the *Dread Arrow* yelled.

"Our team?" one asked.

"We're about to find out," someone else said grimly.

The portal flashed blue, and Uthari frowned and backed away, shaking his hand as if it had stung him. Tezi hoped it had.

The center came to life, stars appearing and swirling in the air. She watched, wanting it to be Jak and the others. They might not enjoy coming back in the middle of a battle, but then they would be here, and if the druids succeeded in destroying the portal, Jak and Jadora wouldn't be trapped on another world.

"Anyone remember if those are the right stars?" a mage called as a constellation formed in the center.

Sorath swore under his breath. "That's the same constellation as last time," he whispered. "The world that sent the dragon scout."

"Attack whatever flies out of there!" Uthari called, having figured out the same thing. "Before it can attack *us* this time. Pass along the message to the other ships. Dragons are coming!"

Now, Tovorka said and guided the skyboard upward. *They lowered the barrier.*

Tezi didn't know if this was the best time to try to break out a prisoner or the worst. She had no trouble envisioning their team stepping aboard the ship only to have it torn to pieces by the might of a dragon.

Within seconds, Sorath's head brushed the hull of the ship. Tovorka guided them along the bottom, then up the far side from the portal. Fortunately, when they came even with the railing, nobody stood along it. All the mages had run to the other side to prepare for dragons arriving.

After Tovorka floated the skyboard over the railing, Sorath pointed toward one of two open hatches that led belowdecks. Tezi hadn't been on this ship before but knew Sorath had. As Tovorka flew them toward the hatchway, two mages burst out.

The skyboard halted and jerked backward. If not for Tovorka's grip, Tezi would have pitched off it. They were only a couple of feet above the deck, so it wouldn't have injured her, but if the three of them didn't stay in contact…

The mages didn't see them. They ran straight for the railing overlooking the portal.

Sorath pointed at the deck and made a chopping motion with his hand. Tovorka stopped the skyboard, and they slid off.

Since Tovorka could sense the auras of people, he took the lead. He made them wait while two more mages ran out. One didn't head straight for the railing, as expected, but toward the forecastle. He ran past close to them, and they skittered back to the railing to avoid being seen, but he paused, frowning in their direction. Tezi winced. They might have let the mage get too close.

"There it is!" someone cried from the railing. "The dragon is back."

"Throw everything you've got at it!"

The mage cursed and veered toward the railing, forgetting about whatever he thought he'd seen. Sorath took the lead and hurried belowdecks, leading them down steps, through a corridor, and around a corner. He halted abruptly, dropping into a crouch with his dagger out. Another mage crewman was running straight toward them.

Tezi squeezed his shoulder, hoping to remind him that they didn't want to fight—and that it would be hard for them to remain in contact if they did. Sorath backed up quickly, almost tripping over Tezi. Her elbow clunked the wall at the corner, and Tovorka also lost his footing. Backing up all together as quickly as the mage was running was too much. He came within range and jerked to a stop as he spotted them.

Sorath surged forward, leading with the dagger. If the mage had a barrier up, the dragon-steel weapon popped it. A magical attack blasted through the corridor and Tezi gripped Tovorka, hoping her axe's protection would extend to him.

Sorath's dagger kept him from feeling the attack and he plunged the blade into the mage's chest, crunching through bone. The man tried to scream, but Sorath head butted him and rammed him into a wall. Nothing but a dying gurgle came out as the mage collapsed in his arms. Sorath kicked open the door to an empty cabin, shoved the body inside, and closed it.

Blood spattered the floor of the corridor, but there was no way to hide that. Sorath hurried on, and Tezi rushed to touch his back so he would be camouflaged again.

Sorath didn't seem to care. He strode to another set of steps and charged down them.

Yellow light glowed from mage lamps mounted on the wall. Two guards stood in front of a closed hatch ahead. The entrance to the brig? They were whispering back and forth about being stuck on guard duty instead of up there helping.

A second dragon followed the first out, Tovorka reported silently, sharing what he could sense and they could only guess at. They hadn't passed any portholes. *And a third. The mages are attacking them, but Uthari can't get the portal to cast lightning while the passageway to another world is open.*

Sorath didn't slow down. He strode forward and leaped for the guards, slashing with dagger and pickaxe. The mages cursed in surprise when he appeared out of thin air in front of them. Only one had time to loose a magical attack. It didn't matter. Sorath killed them both.

Tezi would have preferred less deadly tactics and worried about the consequences, but the arrival of the dragons compelled them to hurry. Maybe in the chaos, the prison break wouldn't be discovered until long after the event.

The hatch was locked, but Sorath jammed his dagger into the seam between it and the frame and used it like a crowbar. It worked, and he levered the hatch open but not without wrenching sounds that made Tezi wince and glance behind them.

They'll be too busy with the dragons to notice, Tovorka told her. *There are four now. No, five.*

Five dragons?

"Is it an entire *invasion*?" Tezi whispered, though there was no point to worrying about noise now, not with the hatch ripped halfway off its hinges and shouts and battle cries filtering down from above—and through the hull from the other ships.

Sorath thundered into the brig, a narrow corridor with the hull and portholes on one side and cells on the other. Most were empty, but at the far end, a cell was occupied. The prisoner was curled on the deck in the dark, his hands over his ears, as if the battle noise hurt him. Or maybe he was monitoring the chaos with his druid senses, and knowing exactly what was out there was what disturbed him.

His torso was bare, revealing raw pink flesh all over his back—deep burns left by fire. Half of his wild green hair had been singed off. The raw wounds gleamed with moisture as they wept serum.

Tezi couldn't believe his captors hadn't treated the burns. Had they planned to kill him after they finished questioning him and hadn't seen the point? She shook her head with indignation, less upset now that Sorath had killed the guards.

Grunk heard them coming, rolled over, and staggered to his feet. He wobbled, as if staying upright—and conscious—was a challenge, but he raised his fists into balls and crouched, ready to fight anyway.

His face hadn't suffered burns, but it was almost as battered as the rest of him, with his lips split and puffy and his eyes blackened. Red marks around his neck marked someone's attempt to strangle him. With magic or their bare hands? Not that it mattered.

Surprisingly, dark bars fenced Grunk in rather than the ubiquitous barriers the mages made. Sorath grabbed the gate and tried to rip it open. When it didn't budge, he attempted to use his dagger like a crowbar again. The bars flashed blue, and he grunted in surprise—or pain?—and stumbled back.

"What was *that*?" Sorath stared and shook out his arm, as if he'd been zapped with electricity.

Tezi gaped at the blue-black metal and immediately knew exactly what it was. "The dragon steel we brought back from Vran. It has to be. Their smith figured out how to work it."

"And they turned it into *cell bars*? Why waste it on *that*?" Sorath kicked the bars.

"For extra special prisoners?" Tezi smiled sadly at Grunk.

He still looked crazy, but now that they were closer, he could see her. He met her eyes, shrugged, and gave her an odd salute. Then he summoned energy from his reserves so that he could spring onto the bars, hands and bare feet gripping them, and attempt to shake them loose. It was even less effective than Sorath's kick.

"They must have wanted to test smithing it by doing something simple." Sorath grunted in exasperation and looked around. The sides of the cell were also lined with the bars.

A hatch clanged somewhere behind them.

"How many dragons now?" Tezi asked, hoping the mages were far too busy to come down here. Cannons boomed as the defenders threw everything they could at the invaders.

Tovorka shook his head in mute horror. He had stopped at one of the portholes to stare out.

His eyes widened. *Brace yourselves!*

Tezi barely had time to grab a cell bar before tremendous magical power struck the hull. The deck tilted wildly, and the ship seemed to be thrown a hundred feet.

She lost her grip and flew into the wall and then the deck—or was that the *ceiling*? Her axe slipped from her hands, and she shouted a warning to the others, afraid the deadly weapon would fly through the air and behead someone.

"Got it," Sorath called, snatching it out of the air as Tezi crashed back down to the deck.

"Get the barrier back up!" someone cried, the voice muffled by the walls.

When the ship settled back down, the scent of smoke filtered in. A huge brown-and-gray shape flew past the porthole.

Tezi hadn't doubted for a second that the invaders were the vile mottled dragons. She was glad little Shikari wasn't here to be a target.

Sorath started to return her axe but paused and spun back toward the cell. Grunk had maintained his grip on the bars, but he backed away now, watching the weapon with hope in his eyes. He pantomimed swinging the blade at the bars.

"I don't think that'll work, but I don't see any dragon steel in the ceiling above you—" Sorath eyed the deck under Grunk's feet, "—or *under* you."

He hefted the axe as high overhead as he could without

lodging it in the ceiling, then slammed it down into the wooden boards. He needn't have swung so hard. The dragon steel split the deck like water, and chunks of wood flew everywhere.

Shouts came from the last hatchway they'd run through, followed by, "Okham's dead!"

Tezi ran back to the warped hatch, trying to lever it shut. She couldn't believe the crewmen were worried about prisoners or even dead comrades in the middle of a dragon attack.

Two mages ran into view. As Tezi tried to shove the broken hatch shut, they gaped at her. No, at the hatch. The stealth device was still active, and they didn't seem to see *her,* but they had no trouble seeing the hatch moving.

One lifted a hand to attack. Tezi's first thought was that she was safe, but her heart lurched as she realized she wasn't. Sorath had her axe.

She jumped backward but only made it a couple of feet before a blast of power slammed into the hatch—and into her. It knocked her flying as pain hammered her chest. She struck Tovorka, and they tumbled to the deck together.

The mages' power tore the hatch from its hinges, and it clattered to the floor, almost landing on her feet. She jerked them out of the way just in time.

Behind her, Sorath swore and threw something. The dagger.

It spun over Tezi and pierced one of the mage's barriers, traveling through to lodge in his shoulder. He grabbed the hilt and ripped it out, but not without a scream of pain.

Tovorka launched an attack of his own, something that sent the other mage staggering back. The wounded man would have been protected from the magic, since he held Sorath's dagger, but the other mage bumped into him, and the weapon tumbled from his fingers.

Sorath leaped over Tezi, through the hatchway, and snatched up the dagger as Tovorka sent green tendrils of energy zigzagging around him to ram into the mages. But they'd gotten their barriers back up and deflected the attack.

Ducking below the tendrils, Sorath ran back into the brig. Tezi had regained her feet, and he thrust the dagger into her hand.

"I need the axe for another second. Keep them busy."

Dragon near again! Tovorka warned.

Sorath jumped through the ragged hole he'd made in the deck in front of the cell. "Follow me down!"

Tovorka gestured for Tezi to go first, but the mages didn't give them time. A gout of fire streamed through the hatchway at them.

Tezi grabbed Tovorka as the air heated and flames wrapped around them. With a dragon-steel weapon back in hand, she was protected, and its influence extended to Tovorka.

But not, she realized with a burst of fear, to Grunk. When he saw the fire, he gasped and flattened himself to the side of the cell with his stomach sucked in.

It didn't, however, breach the bars. Tezi snorted with realization. Of course it wouldn't, not if they truly were dragon steel. He was the safest of them all.

Tovorka lifted his arms, and a barrier formed, halting the fire near the hatchway and keeping the mages from advancing. For several seconds, the stream of flames continued, railing against it. Sweat dribbled down the sides of Tovorka's face.

The sound of more wood smashing came from below, and Tezi remembered Sorath's command for them to follow him.

"I'm going down," she warned Tovorka, though she was tempted to stay and help. Could he hold the mages off alone?

Tezi was halfway through the hole, legs dangling in the air, when another blast struck the ship. Again, the deck rocked fiercely, and she lost her grip.

She flew into the room below and smashed hard into a glowing panel and a tangle of power tendrils. The panel pulsed erratically, though she didn't know if it was because she'd hit it or because of the attack. Glass shattered nearby, and a power sphere went dark.

"Is this the engine room?" Tezi glanced around as she struggled to get her feet under her while the deck continued to rock.

Something slid past her, and she jumped, almost shrieking. It was a red-uniformed man with his head cleaved off. Sorath's work. She swallowed and looked away.

Sorath, while fighting for his balance, leaped up to chop at the deck under Grunk's cell.

Tovorka jumped down through the hole in the deck, the skyboard clutched under one arm. Tezi couldn't believe he'd managed to keep ahold of it, but how would all four of them fly to safety on one? They needed one more.

As soon as Tovorka landed, he lifted a hand toward the hole above. Re-forming his barrier?

Sweat ran down the sides of his face, and he was breathing heavily, exhausted from holding back two powerful mages.

"They're still coming?" Tezi asked.

He nodded and dashed sweat out of his eyes.

Tezi couldn't believe the mages' persistence, but since Grunk had killed a queen, maybe that made him an extra-desirable prisoner. Or an extra-*hated* prisoner. One they wanted to continue torturing far into the future.

"They're in the engine room!" one of the mages shouted.

"One of the power spheres went out. They're sabotaging us."

"Get help!"

"Maybe we should have gone up instead of down, Colonel." Tezi realized the crew had more reasons than their prisoner to want to capture them now.

"I don't disagree. Here, trade." Sorath thrust the axe at Tezi as Grunk squirmed down through the hole he'd made, then took the dagger back from her, though not without giving the bigger weapon a wistful look.

As Grunk landed, his knees buckled and almost gave out, but he gripped Sorath for support and managed to thump him on the shoulder. He leaned over to thump Tovorka on the shoulder as well, then peered around and spotted Tezi through the camouflage. He bowed to her.

I can't hold them indefinitely, Tovorka told them. *More are coming toward that hatch.* He jerked his chin toward the entrance to the engine room.

"I'll cut a hole in the hull so we can get out that way." Sorath glanced at Tezi's axe but must have decided the dagger would be sufficient.

Tezi was glad, because she had a lot more experience fighting with the axe, and enemies hesitated before charging at the fearsome weapon.

A *clunk-ker-thunk* came from behind the cables and equipment, and the ship shuddered. This time, Tezi didn't think it was because of the dragon.

"We're going down!" came a cry from the deck above.

A *clang* sounded at the hatch. Tovorka kept guarding the hole in the deck, but he couldn't extend his barrier to cover both entrances.

While Sorath jammed his dagger into the hull and sawed at the wood, Tezi placed herself in front of the hatch.

A humming noise that had been coming from one of the power sources stopped. A weird sinking feeling came over her. No, that was the *ship* that was sinking. Slowly, she hoped, so the crash wouldn't be deadly.

Another clang sounded. Grunk came up beside her. In the tight quarters, he must not have had trouble seeing through her camouflage. The mages likely wouldn't either.

Grunk had no weapons, and could barely stand, but he raised his fists and nodded at her, as if to say he would help.

"Do you have magic you can use against them?" Tezi asked.

He hesitated before holding up his thumb and forefinger to indicate a tiny amount.

Tezi jerked her head backward. “The axe protects me. It’ll be safer for you with Sorath.”

Grunk scowled.

The hatch swung open, slamming against the wall. Four mages stood in the corridor outside, and they snarled as they blasted magical attacks into the room.

Tezi sprang forward, hoping the sphere of protection that her axe offered would be enough to protect Grunk. And Tovorka as well. She didn’t know if he could keep a barrier around himself while he was also blocking the hole.

Magic whispered past, a wave of power that didn’t affect Tezi. Fireballs followed, blinding her with their brilliant orange light.

She wanted to run away and hide but made herself step into the hatchway instead. If the mages made it inside, they could get around her and to the others. She couldn’t allow that.

Fire crackled in the air all around her. Tezi felt its warmth, but it didn’t incinerate her.

“It’s the one with the axe!” one mage yelled.

“Get it from her!”

“I thought she was on *our* side.”

Tezi gulped, but she couldn’t worry about the consequences of being identified. Not now.

As the mages charged forward, trying to physically grab her, she swung the blade to drive them back. It flared with inner power, eager for battle, and the men in front hesitated. But others pushed them from behind and ordered them to get her.

The mages drew short swords and stabbed at her, snarling their annoyance that their magic didn’t affect her. She sliced through one of the mundane blades, leaving it in pieces on the deck. If she’d had more room to swing, she could have been more formidable, but in the narrow corridor and hatchway, she had to be careful not to get the axe lodged in a wall. They would overcome her easily then.

One of the mages threw something. Anticipating a grenade or other mundane explosive, something that the axe's magic *couldn't* protect her from, Tezi sprang back.

But it was a magical explosive, and once again, the power whispered past without harming her. The explosion blew gouges in the walls and scorched several cables near her in engineering.

"Idiot, you're doing as much damage as they are," one of the mages snarled and tried again to charge past Tezi, leading with his sword.

She sliced through the weapon and could have slashed his neck open but hesitated to land a killing blow. One of his comrades yanked him back.

"We have to—"

Something struck the side of the ship. A magical attack? A dragon's tail? Tezi had no idea, but she was smashed into the side of the hatchway as the already sinking ship lurched sideways.

Two of the mages tumbled down, but the other two once again tried to take advantage and charge past her.

"I've got a hole open," Sorath called. "Come on, you three. We're about to crash."

One of the mages cast a fireball, trying to aim over Tezi's head toward Sorath. She sprang up to block it with the axe's magic, then waded into them with the weapon, frustration and fury destroying her hesitation. She had to protect her comrades.

Her blade bit into one man's chest, and he staggered back, bumping into his comrades. She drove them farther back, swinging like a crazed logger. She destroyed another of their swords and lopped off one man's hand. Her stomach threatened to turn at the sight of the blood and his severed limb, but she had to keep the mages back, whatever it took.

"Tezi!" Sorath shouted. "Now."

She risked glancing back in time to see Tovorka leap out of the hole in the hull. Trees and the waterfall were visible beyond it—they were close to the ground.

Grunk lingered by Sorath, waiting for Tezi to come.

"Go ahead," she yelled as she backed toward them.

A mage slithered through the hole in the ceiling that Tovorka had abandoned. Tezi cursed and whipped her axe around at him before he could attack Sorath.

Sorath snarled, pushed Grunk through the hole, and reached for Tezi. "We're not being trapped in another stable."

Tezi knocked the mage aside with a swing and rushed toward Sorath, clasping his outstretched hand. Fireball after fireball roared into the engine room, lighting equipment and the walls on fire but not harming Tezi or Sorath. They hurried for the hole, but before they reached it, the ship crashed.

Great crunching and wrenching sounds thundered in their ears as the deck heaved, and the ceiling buckled, wood banging down all around them. The jolt was far greater than Tezi had expected. It threw her and Sorath into the air as mages tumbled into each other behind them.

Sorath landed first and pushed Tezi toward the hole, but an explosion blew. This time, it wasn't magical. Wood and metal and glass pelted them.

The hole disappeared as the hull crumpled and the deck above finished falling. Pain assaulted Tezi as beams and shards of wood slammed onto her. She still gripped Sorath's hand, but they were pinned together, at the mercy of the mages and the dragons.

27

Magical energy poured forth from the chief and the three men and three women linking hands with her. Jak could feel it, the tremendous power building, making him think of a pot threatening to boil over. At least his mother wasn't bent over and grabbing her head anymore. Jak was afraid he'd made a mistake in suggesting that she might be able to find a cure to their problem.

The outflow of energy drew the glowing worms. Before, they'd been all over the roof and walls of the cavern, but they now converged above the chief's litter. Their light grew brighter, bright enough to drive the shadows from even the back of the cavern, and Jak gasped as it gleamed off shiny dragon scales. Iridescent *blue* dragon scales.

Even though they'd said their ancient one was the last untainted dragon, he hadn't quite believed it.

Shikari stirred and peered over at the dragon, an uncertain peep escaping his mouth.

Light flashed, and energy surged into Jak. At first, he thought it was an attack, but it didn't hurt him. It felt *good.*

The magical power flowed through his body, energizing him,

as if he'd swilled several cups of coffee, but it didn't leave him jittery. It was soothing energy, *invigorating* energy.

The pain and worry that had marked Mother's face all day vanished, at least for a few seconds. Contented sounds came from the collected warriors, but then a low groan rumbled from the back of the cavern. The dragon was stirring.

Several moments passed, with the energy flowing into Jak, and apparently everyone in the cavern, before it faded. Before, when the dragon had slept—or maybe hibernated was the better term—her aura had been noticeable but not as powerful as that of the other dragons Jak had encountered. Now, it was stronger, though he sensed that this wasn't a dragon in her prime. If she was more than ten thousand years old, that was understandable.

Why do the guardians rouse me? the dragon asked, power ringing in the telepathic words.

She walked toward them on all fours, even more power emanating from her body as she stretched her wings for what might have been the first time in decades. Or centuries?

Even if she was old, Jak had no doubt she was formidable. He hoped she wouldn't be crabby and resentful about being woken.

The chief rose from her chair to face the dragon. To communicate with her? Whatever she said, Jak couldn't hear it.

The dragon stopped near the gathering, her bulk dwarfing the humans who gazed raptly up at her. She was far different from the frolicking dragons that the portal had shown Jak, far older, and he shifted uneasily when her gleaming blue head swung toward him and his mother.

Two horns rose up, curving back from her skull, and yellow eyes similar to but far, far older than Shikari's gazed down at him. Then she probed his mind.

Jak braced himself, expecting pain, but her touch was lighter than the chief's had been.

Hm, she rumbled into his mind. *Hm.*

We'd like to help, Jak offered, feeling he should say something. Probably not that he'd dreamed of riding on a dragon's back since he'd been a boy. She didn't look like the type to find that flattering.

Your knowledge is of no use.

Jak stifled the indignation that wanted to seep out of him. *Probably not unless you need a map drawn.*

I do not. The dragon's gaze shifted and locked on to Mother.

She drew a shaky breath but didn't look away.

Several long moments passed. Jak glanced toward the mageship and the navigation cabin porthole, wondering what the others thought of this. He assumed Harintha and Vinjo were watching, though he didn't sense Vinjo in the front of the ship. Maybe he was repairing that hole.

Shikari cheeped uncertainly. Jak resisted the urge to remind him that he sounded like a baby chicken when he did that, not a mighty predator. Shikari didn't seem to know what to think about all this any more than he did. Jak was glad it hadn't been a mottled dragon lounging back there with all these people around to serve it, but he didn't yet know if they were safe.

The dragon sat on her haunches. *I do not know if the taint can be removed by mundane means, but this one has a great deal of knowledge of herbs and alchemy.* She looked toward the chief. *It is possible she could find an answer. I fear I don't have time to wait longer for the ideal candidate to be born and find us. If a cure is not found soon... if it is not safe to hatch the dragonlings and for me to pass along the knowledge of the elders... then all will be lost. Our species will have been corrupted and the great dragons of eld no more. Only those cruel mindless husks will remain, the personalities of the first ones lost forever.*

"Does that mean you're getting the job or not?" Jak whispered to Mother.

She appeared far more worried than relieved by this discussion, so he tried a smile. As far as he was concerned, this was a more promising development than he'd expected when the guardians had taken Shikari. Of course, this didn't necessarily mean they would give him back. The dragon might have decided Mother could be useful, but what about Jak?

The blue scaled head swung back toward them—toward Mother.

Will you help us find a cure to the taint? the dragon asked. *My time is limited, so you would have to focus on this task exclusively. Of course, we would be grateful to you for your help.*

"Ah, I would be willing to do that research, but as for dedicating myself exclusively toward it, I'm..." Mother glanced toward the ship. "Someone else is in charge of this mission."

Jak scowled. Someone else was in charge of their *lives*. He couldn't help but think bitterly of Uthari.

I will share my knowledge with you, the dragon said, as if who their mission leader was wasn't a problem. *With such a mingling of memories and knowledge, yours and mine, perhaps you will find the answer. I will also share with you the location of the Orbs of Wisdom. You may find it enlightening to consult them.*

Mother looked at Jak, as if he would know how to explain their situation to a dragon.

I will also share with you some of my lingering power so others will not easily imprison you and take you from this quest.

"Power?" Mother asked warily.

"Power is good," Jak said.

Judging by the frown she turned on him, she didn't agree.

Do you accept this quest, human?

"My name is Jadora."

Jak feared the dragon would scoff and say that she didn't care.

Do you accept this quest, Jadora Freedar of Torvil, one of the first worlds that our kind visited through the portals?

Mother took a deep breath. "I'll do my best."

Then I shall grant you what I know related to this matter. The dragon reached out with a taloned forearm.

Mother hesitated, probably noting that those talons were as long as daggers, but when it grew clear the dragon wanted her to come closer, she did. Jak hoped she didn't have anything to fear from this, but he had no way to know.

The dragon rested her talons gently on Mother's head and lifted her own head, her eyes closing. The chief and all the warriors spread their arms, turned their faces toward the glowworms, and closed their own eyes, as if they were participating in the ceremony. Maybe they were.

Jak sensed magic flowing from the dragon and into Mother, but he had no idea what it would do. Transfer knowledge? More?

Jak? Vinjo spoke into his mind. *We've got a big problem and need your help.*

What is it?

A thump came from the ship, followed by a wrenching sound.

A beam of energy came through and woke everyone up, Vinjo said. *And they're—ack!*

Jak swore and lifted his hands, hoping he could get help from the guardians, but they were all still locked in the dragon's ritual. Only Shikari looked at Jak, his head tilted quizzically.

I need your help, Jak told him, then ran for the river.

He expected one of the guardians to stir and stop him, but nobody so much as yelled a warning. Shikari's talons scraped on the rocky bank as he galloped along beside Jak. More thumps came from the ship, along with a woman's scream. Harintha?

Jak had never learned to levitate himself, only others, and as he skidded to a stop at the edge of the water, he realized he didn't know how to get back aboard. The mageship hovered more than ten feet above them, and the carnivorous eels were snapping in the water.

Shikari flapped his wings, and Jak lunged for him, knowing he couldn't yet fly and afraid the eels would eat him if he ran into the water. But Shikari was too fast, and Jak only swiped at air. To his surprise, those wings, still tiny compared to those of the great female dragon, flapped furiously and carried Shikari into the air.

He wobbled and tilted so alarmingly that Jak gasped in fear for him. Shikari clipped the railing when he made it to the top of the ship, but he landed on the deck. The air stiffened under Jak's feet and Shikari's magic wrapped around him, levitating him up and over the railing.

"You're getting to be handy," Jak told him as he landed.

Shikari let out a reedy roar that was slightly fuller and more fearsome than it had been before.

"Save that." Jak ran to the hatch, sensing not only Vinjo and Harintha but Tonovan, Prolix, and Bakir in the corridor below.

Malek seemed to still be in the laboratory. Hadn't he woken up? Or—Jak swallowed—had the others killed him before he could wake up fully?

No, Jak sensed Malek's aura. He was alive. For now.

Jak threw open the hatch, though he had no idea what he would do when he reached the corridor. He didn't even have a pistol anymore.

"Let us in!" Tonovan roared as Jak descended the ladder.

"The boy's coming," Bakir warned.

"The boy is *nothing*."

Unfortunately correct. Jak wrapped a barrier around himself as he landed and called up to Shikari, who peered through the hatchway above. *Can you help me?*

"Step aside," Tonovan snarled.

To whom? Malek?

"You will not murder a zidarr," a calm voice said as Jak risked peeking into the corridor.

He barely glimpsed Prolix standing in front of the closed hatch to the laboratory. Bakir's back was in the way, and Tonovan gripped his sword as he faced Prolix.

"That bastard shoved a needle in my throat," Tonovan shouted.

"He could have killed you and did not. You will *not* kill him while he sleeps."

The hatch clanged open behind Prolix. He leaped to the side as Malek charged out, his hair as wild as his eyes. He slashed for Tonovan and might have killed him, but Bakir leaped in to help the general.

Tonovan swung at Malek, his eyes almost as enraged as Malek's. He and Prolix were to the right of the hatchway and Malek, while Bakir was to the left and closest to Jak. They had Malek flanked in the narrow corridor, but Malek was the aggressor, the madness worse than Jak had seen it. He stabbed furiously, keeping his back to the hatchway, matching the attacks that Tonovan and Bakir launched.

Prolix couldn't get around Tonovan to help, but he didn't look like he wanted to. He didn't do anything to impede Tonovan either. It was two against one, and Tonovan and Bakir battered Malek with magic as well as blades.

As he had in the past, Jak funneled his own energy into Malek, to give him more power that he could use to defend himself.

But this Malek was so different from the old Malek. He only shouted in rage at the touch of Jak's power, as if he believed it another enemy attack.

"Stay out of this, boy," Tonovan snarled. "Or you're next."

Neither man was a match for Malek when it came to blade work, but they mixed magical blows in with the sword slashes, and every time Malek's main-gauche or longsword would have cut them, they deflected the attacks with walls of power.

"Stop fighting," Jak called. "Something important is going on. There's a *dragon* out there."

They ignored him.

Jak clenched his jaw and drew upon his power as he envisioned wildfire sweeping through the tree-filled terrain in his mind.

Malek stumbled. He didn't lower his blades, but crushing magic from both of his enemies forced him to one knee.

"You're dead now!" Tonovan howled.

Jak had never wanted to throw a fireball at a person, never wanted to hurt a human being, but he blasted flames into the back of Malek's nearest foe. He wished it were Tonovan instead of Bakir, but Jak couldn't target Tonovan without risking hitting Malek. But Bakir...

At first, his flames struck a magical barrier and were deflected, heat warming his own face as fire bounced back and filled the corridor. Then Shikari channeled more power into him, just as Jak had been trying to do for Malek earlier. Jak willed the flames to continue, to melt through the barrier.

It happened so quickly that it startled him. The barrier disappeared, and flames enshrouded Bakir. Jak halted his attack as Bakir screamed, his weapons falling from his hands. The magic he'd been casting at Malek disappeared.

Malek sprang to his feet and slashed his dagger across Bakir's throat.

The admiral fell to the deck, his entire back half charred, his life's blood pouring from his throat. Jak gaped. He'd wanted to destroy Bakir's defenses, not kill him.

"You idiot!" Tonovan yelled at Jak. "Don't help the crazy insane bastard."

Though shaken, Jak managed to scowl at him. "You'd kill Malek even if he was utterly sane. You've been trying to kill him since we arrived on this world."

Malek *did* look like a crazy man as he glanced at Jak, then spun on Tonovan. Prolix formed a barrier around Tonovan, protecting him, but that didn't keep Malek from railing at it.

Jak stepped into the corridor, though he didn't know what he would do. He hadn't killed Bakir, but he'd made it possible for Malek to do so. Malek, who might turn on Jak if he defeated the others.

Stop! a voice rang in his mind.

The female dragon.

Can you help? Jak replied. *Please!*

He sensed that the dragon remained on land, but her energy flowed into the mageship. Everyone paused, even Malek, though his chest heaved, blood dripped from his blades, and he looked like he would spring for Tonovan's throat as soon as he could.

Have you no respect for the rituals of the dragons? she asked. *Never would I have helped such rude humans if the young one did not wish it.*

"Who in the slavemasters' Hell is the *young one*?" Tonovan muttered.

Jak glanced up the ladder. Shikari had changed positions to look at something else, and only his tail dangled down, but Jak was sure they were being granted this reprieve because of him.

"Who is *that*?" Vinjo asked, peeking out of navigation, though he was looking upward instead of at the others.

"I'm not sure," Tonovan mumbled, also looking up.

Jak sensed that someone powerful had arrived and stood on the deck of their ship. One of the guardians no doubt. It wasn't the dragon; he could tell that. But this person was oddly familiar.

Shikari moved out of the way, making room for Mother to climb down the ladder.

Jak's jaw dropped as he watched her descend—watched *her*. She radiated the kind of magical power that a zidarr had. *More* than a zidarr. It reminded Jak of the rulers on Vran, though even they hadn't been quite as impressive. The power of a dragon emanated from her.

"Uh," Tonovan said as Mother stepped past Jak and into the corridor.

She still wore the same clothes, still carried no weapons

besides the vials and tools bulging in her pockets, but somehow, the dragon had enrobed her in power. Was it temporary? Some gift to help her settle this fight among her own people. Or... was it permanent?

Malek crouched in the hatchway, not turning his back on Tonovan and Prolix, but he watched her approach warily, as if she were an enemy and not a friend. To him, they *all* had to seem like enemies now. He growled low in his throat like a rabid wolf.

Mother walked toward him without fear.

"Ah." Jak lifted a finger, tempted to grab her and pull her back but also daunted by that power. *Was* this still his mother? Or had the dragon changed her? "He's crazy now. You might not want to get too close."

She gazed sadly down at Bakir's body before stepping around it.

Malek growled again, and his fingers tightened around his weapons. Tonovan and Prolix backed away from Mother.

"It's me, Malek," she said softly, holding his gaze. "Let me help you. I... know how now."

Jak lifted his brows hopefully. Did she?

Mother lifted a hand toward the side of Malek's face. His grip was so tight on his weapons that his knuckles shone white through his tan skin. He was poised to snap—poised to spring. Mother rested her hand on the side of his face anyway.

Seconds passed as they stood like that. Speaking telepathically? Could Mother do that now?

Magic flowed from her fingers and into Malek. Healing magic. Or bacteria-slaying magic?

Shikari dropped down the ladder to land beside Jak, a taloned foot landing on his and making him glad he wore boots.

"Don't get cocky just because you can fly now," he whispered without taking his gaze from Mother and Malek. If he attacked her, Jak would have to do something. What, he didn't know. "You're not that graceful," he added.

Shikari whapped him in the shin as he sashayed into the corridor. He stopped and sat on his haunches, not interfering.

Malek hadn't moved for several minutes, but abruptly, he crumpled to his knees, slumping against the side of the hatchway. His weapons tumbled from his fingers, and the wildness disappeared from his eyes as his lids drooped.

In the hatchway to navigation, Tonovan stirred, as if he might take advantage of his nemesis dropping his weapons.

Shikari growled at him.

"We don't need a referee, Short and Scaled." Tonovan pointed a dagger between Shikari's eyes.

It burst into flame, as if it had been a twig rather than a weapon. Tonovan cried out, dropping it and grabbing his burned hand.

Jak would have assumed Shikari had done that, but Mother looked coolly over at Tonovan.

"Hell," he grumbled as he stepped fully into navigation and slammed the hatch shut.

"I bet Vinjo and Harintha are delighted to be trapped in there with him," Jak muttered.

Mother sank to her knees in front of Malek and gripped his shoulders. "I believe I got all of the bacteria, but you might want to double-check. I'm new to this."

Malek opened his eyes and focused on her face. The wildness had faded, but he appeared weary. And confused. Jak understood perfectly.

"You have power," he whispered.

"Apparently." She shook her head sadly.

Jak knew she was the last one who would have wanted power. He could already envision her pushing her hands through her hair and trying to figure out how to tell Grandfather—Grandfather, who detested mages and anyone else who didn't do honest work through body-wrenching labor.

"Let's get you onto one of the cots to rest." Mother used a trickle of magic to help Malek to his feet.

He looked like a man with questions, but also one who was stiff after battling multiple mages and being hurled around the ship. He let her guide him into the laboratory.

Jak eyed Bakir's body, feeling renewed chagrin for having been partially responsible for his death. What was the procedure for burying him? Or were funeral pyres or something else the norm in the Jutokor Islands? Maybe they were supposed to take the body back so that his kin could handle the arrangements. Jak shook his head, not ready for this kind of adult responsibility. But would Malek be up to it any time soon?

Jakstor Freedar, the dragon's voice boomed in his head.

Yes? Huh. She'd learned his name. From the knowledge in Mother's head? He still didn't know hers. *Uhm, yes, ma'am?*

I am Zelonsera. The dragonling has grown attached to you.

Yeah, I'm fun to hit with a tail. And I have a hat that's delicious.

You aren't powerful enough to protect him from all those who would threaten him.

Jak shook his head glumly. *I know.*

But he wishes to continue to travel with you.

Hope stirred. *Is that... permitted?*

Normally, I would say no, but you travel with mages of reasonable power. Malek's image flashed into his mind—Zelonsera didn't think of Tonovan. *Also, your mother will gradually learn to use the power I've given her.*

Uhm, yes, about that... Is it permanent? She's more powerful than I am now. Than even Malek, I think.

A female should *have more power than a male.* Her telepathic tone conveyed dryness.

Jak didn't know if that was a joke or if that was how it worked with dragons.

I have transferred some of the knowledge of our ancestors into the dragonling's mind, she continued. *His brain is still growing and can't absorb it all, but he may be more helpful now in your quest. He has more memories of that which went before.*

What did *go before? How did that parasite come into existence and take over your kind?*

Nature likes balance. It never creates beings of great power without creating something that can slay them, thus to ensure populations do not grow out of control and no one species overruns all others. At first, the parasites simply shortened our lives, acting as a disease, eating away at our power and our longevity. Our scientists attempted to eradicate them, but as is often the case in such matters, some survived, mutating to resist our magic. They even came to thrive on our magic, absorbing it into themselves and becoming more resilient. The altered parasites were impossible for us to kill, and they spread with great fecundity, turning those they took as hosts into slaves that would not seek to eradicate them.

Jak shivered, remembering how the dragons at the ziggurat on Vran hadn't wanted to kill Shikari but to make him one of them.

Perhaps, Zelonsera continued, *it was the punishment for our hubris, in believing we could destroy another species, however minuscule a species. Unaltered dragons grew rarer and rarer. I and a few others acted out of desperation, gathering all the unhatched eggs of our kind and using our power to pause their development until such a time as it was safe for untainted dragons to return to the world. And we taught and trained human guards to help protect us and the eggs as we sought answers. But those of us who went out were constantly in danger of being caught and tainted by the others. Soon, only I remained.*

One night, as I worked the dragon steel into weapons for the guardians, I had a flash of insight. I saw a dragon being born in the future who would have the knowledge to save our kind. I also saw that the tainted dragons became sterile and could not give birth. I thought if I waited long enough, they would all die out, and it would be safe for me to hatch the eggs and repopulate our species. But the parasites also granted long life, and as I grew older, I realized the tainted dragons were not dying quickly. Worse, they'd found out about the eggs and launched raids into this place to try to get them and destroy them. My guardians took them and hid them on another world, one that our religion teaches is cursed and that dragons rarely visit.

Except the killer dragon who'd been hunkering there in that fortress... Jak admitted that had been the only sign of a dragon there that they'd seen.

The guardians encased the eggs in ice to hide their auras, and I went into hibernation to preserve my life until such time as it was safe, safe to hatch the eggs and safe to share our knowledge and teach the young our ways. But I have been waiting so long. So very long.

I'm sorry.

Now there is hope again. You and the dragonling will assist your mother and find a solution so that our kind may return to the world without worrying about being turned into monsters.

I want that very much. Jak hoped it was possible.

Return when you have found the solution, and we will reward you.

Jak thought of his dream of removing the wizard rulers that lorded over Torvil and mundane humans, and how he and his father had always believed that dragons could be key in doing that, but he didn't want to try to make a deal with the old dragon. At that moment, all he wanted was to see the fun, frolicking dragons from the visions the portals had shared return to the world—the universe. If they were the creatures he believed they'd been in millennia past, perhaps they would see the injustice and act upon it of their own accord.

We'll do our best, Jak replied.

"Jak," Vinjo called from navigation. "Your dragon is chewing on the aersubsisto."

"Is that something important?" Jak headed up the corridor. He hadn't noticed the hatch opening and Shikari slipping into navigation.

"If we want the ship to keep flying and not sink into the river where eels will eat us, yes."

Jak stepped into navigation to find Tonovan and Prolix in the corner, muttering to each other. Harintha had turned the ship around and was piloting them back down the river while Shikari sniffed at things on the console. How had he gotten up there? By jumping? *Flying*? Jak didn't see anything that appeared chewed, but Shikari did bump a few levers with his tail.

The ship rocked, nearly dumping Jak in Vinjo's lap.

"Your dragon is a menace, kid," Tonovan growled.

"I hope not," Jak told Tonovan.

Prolix slipped out of navigation, pausing in the corridor to heft his fallen comrade over his shoulder. Tonovan was glaring at Jak, and Jak expected the same from Prolix, maybe with the addition of a promise of vengeance, but he only took the body to a cabin. He'd tried to keep the others from ganging up on Malek, Jak remembered. Maybe Prolix was all right. Zidarr honor and all that.

"Shikari is supposed to work with my mother to save all of dragonkind," Jak added.

"What happened to her?" Tonovan's sneer suggested he didn't believe the change was an improvement.

And why would he? It might mean she could beat the snot out of him now. Jak smiled to himself, *hoping* that she could. And that she wouldn't be too mature and refined to do so.

Tonovan squinted at him, but he was either too rattled to respond to Jak's thoughts, or Jak had finally gotten good enough to keep other mages from reading them.

"She was blessed by a dragon," was all he said.

"Shit." Tonovan walked out.

Vinjo peered around his chair, watching his back until

Tonovan stepped into his cabin and slammed the hatch shut. “What really happened, Jak?”

Jak sighed. “My mother was just assigned a mission far more daunting than the one Uthari gave her.”

“What happens if she fails?”

“The dragons die out forever.”

28

Neither the crash nor the decks slamming down on Sorath knocked him unconscious, but it hurt like a torture session with a blacksmith. Muffled screams reached his ears, but he didn't think they came from within the wrecked ship. Those dragons were still out there, destroying everyone and everything they came across.

He groaned and attempted to shove himself up to his hands and knees. Broken wood and the shattered remains of one of the spherical power supplies hemmed him in from either side, and a beam lay across his back. But when he pushed, he managed to shove enough of the wreckage aside to move. More tumbled down from above and hit him on the head.

"At least my hair's gotten thick enough to cushion my skull," he muttered.

Reminded of the stable that Yidar had brought down on him, he was tempted to lie down and play dead until all this ended, but if a dragon landed atop the rubble, it might accidentally crush him to death.

"Sir?" came Tezi's pained voice.

Sorath swore, reminded that she also hadn't gotten out before the crash.

"Yes," he said. "Where are you?"

A faint grunt sounded. "Trapped."

Everything was dark, all the lamps and power supplies dead or smothered.

Knowing someone else was hurt gave Sorath the strength to push aside his own pain—and all the wreckage piled on top of him. As he shoved pieces to the side, maneuvering in the dark toward Tezi's voice, something clunked off to the right and blue light seeped in.

His first thought was that it belonged to Tezi's axe and that he was heading in the wrong direction, but the screams came through more clearly now, as well as the scent of crushed foliage and jungle air. It had to be coming through the hole he'd cut in the hull, and the blue light... Was it from the portal? Had they crashed close to it?

If so, he didn't know if that was a good thing or not. Booms, yells, and cries of pain suggested the fighting was centered nearby.

"I've still got my axe," Tezi whispered from in front of him.

"Good." Sorath had sheathed his dagger right before the crash to keep from losing it. "I'm reaching out to find you. Don't let it slice off my hand."

"Yes, sir." Rubble shifted, and Tezi's hand extended out of some wreckage toward him.

He caught her wrist and pulled gently, not wanting to yank if she was pinned. She grunted and shoved something aside, then scrambled out with his help.

"This way." He led her toward the hole.

An inhuman screech ripped through the night, and he halted. That had sounded like a dragon, and it had been nearby. *Very* nearby. The image of one perched atop the wrecked ship returned to his mind.

"Are we sure we want to go out there?" Tezi whispered.

She'd been fearless facing the mages in the hatchway, buying time for him to cut the hole, and if he ever managed to reunite with Thorn Company, he would praise her to her superiors. He couldn't blame her for being daunted at the thought of facing a dragon.

"No," he said, "but we will anyway."

"Yes, sir."

"Once we're on solid ground, it'll be easier to sprint away from the battle and hide in the jungle." Sorath reached the hole but had to shove aside more wreckage to widen it enough for them to fit.

"I don't think you'd ever do that, sir."

"Probably not. I'm not that smart." Sorath wished he were joking. "I just hope Grunk and Tovorka got away. It's tedious when you risk your life rescuing prisoners only to have them die smashed under the ship."

"That's grisly."

"Sorry." As Sorath widened the hole further, the inhuman screech sounded again.

"Kill that bastard!" someone cried. "He's guarding the portal so we can't keep the others from coming out."

Was that Uthari? Sorath couldn't keep from rolling his eyes. Why couldn't *that* bastard be smashed under a ship?

Sorath drew the dagger, clenched it between his teeth, and crawled through the hole. It was a five-foot drop, and he landed in the dirt behind the portal, with the waterfall roaring down nearby, unperturbed by the invasion. Sorath twisted and looked up.

The dragon that kept screeching wasn't on top of the ship. It was on the portal, casting waves of power that flattened mages lined up on the ground attacking it. More mages swept around on skyboards, wielding lesser-dragon-steel weapons and trying to get close enough to physically attack the dragon. It wasn't going well.

As Sorath watched, another dragon flew out of the portal. How many was that? Sorath half expected to see an armada of the winged beasts in the skies, but the new one flapped its powerful wings, impervious as fireballs struck it, and disappeared over the trees. Maybe to attack the mageships. Few remained in the area, though Tonovan's *Dread Arrow* wasn't the only one that had wrecked. Another smashed vessel lay halfway in the pool, with men and women swimming for the bank.

Sorath pulled the dagger from between his teeth and debated his options. For now, the dragon wasn't focused on him. He and Tezi had crawled out of the crash behind the portal. The weapon was ridiculously small next to the creature's bulk, but would dragon steel pierce its defenses? He eyed the blade doubtfully. Even if it did, even if he could lodge it up to its hilt, he would hit nothing but muscle and scale. Hardly a killing blow.

I'm going to try to close the portal, Uthari spoke into Sorath's mind, startling him. He'd forgotten he'd given the stealth device to Tezi, even though she was blurry as she stood next to him a few feet away.

Then he realized Uthari wasn't singling him out. He didn't even appear to have noticed Sorath. He was speaking telepathically to everyone.

We have to keep more dragons from coming through, Uthari added. *Cover me!*

As much as Sorath hated Uthari and wished he'd managed to kill him the other night, he had to admit the old wizard had balls. With his own magic crackling in the air around him, Uthari strode toward the portal—and the dragon perched atop it. As powerful as Uthari's magic was, it had to be minuscule compared to what that great scaled creature possessed.

The dragon's head turned on its long, sinewy neck, and yellow reptilian eyes focused on Uthari. Sorath sensed a magical attack roiling from it, battering Uthari's defenses. Behind him, his fellow mages reinforced his barrier, helping to stave off the assault.

Uthari clenched his jaw and kept walking, though it was as if he was striding up a steep hill in a windstorm.

If the portal had a way to help him—if it *wanted* to help him—it wasn't evident. It wasn't pulsing blue or shooting lightning or doing anything else that Sorath had seen Jak convince it to do. It merely held the gateway open, allowing more dragons through into the world.

"Do we try to help?" Tezi asked over the cacophony of cannons firing, men yelling, and another ship crashing into the trees. She glanced at Sorath. "Or hope he dies?"

Sorath grimaced. "These dragons are going to be trouble for everyone here, including—" He paused as he glimpsed another black-hulled ship flying into view over the trees from the south. It was the *Star Flyer*, the ship Rivlen commanded, the ship that held Ferroki and the rest of Thorn Company.

And there they were. Ferroki, Sasko, and the rest were stationed at the railing with their rifles pointed at the dragons, the women interspersed with red-uniformed mages preparing to add their might to the battle. Rivlen stood in the forecastle, her arms raised, and she cast a wall of fire toward the dragon on the portal.

Her target twitched its tail, like a cat perched on the back of a chair and mildly annoyed by a fly buzzing around it. The fire never reached it, for a barrier even stronger than the one around Uthari deflected the flames. The attack *did* get its attention, and the dragon focused on the *Star Flyer*. Sorath swallowed. On Thorn Company.

"We help," he rasped.

He considered climbing up the portal to try to stab the dragon in the foot, but even if he'd still had both hands, he would have found that climb challenging. And even if the dagger protected him from magic, if Sorath got close, the dragon could lunge down and bite him.

"I'm going to throw the dagger and try to find a vulnerable

spot. Let's not risk losing your axe until we see if our blades can hurt it." Sorath could easily envision the dagger and axe lodging between its scales only for the dragon to fly off, taking the weapons with it.

"All right." Tezi glanced to the right as Grunk limped over to stand beside her.

"Help her stay alive, killer," Sorath told him, though he was tempted to order him to flee into the jungle. The kid was so injured, he could barely stand.

Grunk nodded, his green hair hanging limply into his eyes.

"Wait." Tezi lunged after Sorath, removing the stealth device from her wrist.

He shook his head, wanting her to have it, though he doubted it would be effective against a dragon.

"It's yours." Tezi thrust it at him and glanced at Uthari. "You may need it."

Though reluctant, Sorath accepted the wisdom—and the tool. Uthari might loathe him enough to risk stopping in the middle of a dragon battle to kill him on sight.

Sorath fastened it around his arm above his pickaxe, gripped the dagger, and circled the portal to look for a vulnerable spot on the dragon.

It still perched atop it, its tail dangling down to the ground below. Sorath almost picked that target, since it would be easy to reach, but it wouldn't be fatal. If a dragon was like a lizard, Sorath could cut the whole thing off and the tail would grow back. He had to strike it in the head. Ideally an eye.

As Sorath circled, the dragon returned Rivlen's attack. It roared, and power pulsed, the air shivering as if with a mirage as raw energy poured toward the *Star Flyer*.

Rivlen and every mage onboard must have combined forces to create a barrier. The attack didn't obliterate the ship, but even with their protection, it rocked ominously. The Thorn Company women gripped the railing to keep from flying backward.

Sorath skirted the pool and stopped to the side but in front of the dragon. From below, he couldn't see its eyes, not when it was focused on the ships above. But when it roared, the pink roof of its mouth was visible. The jaw snapped shut again before Sorath could throw the dagger, but he readied himself for the next opportunity. He would only get one chance.

Soldiers on another black-hulled mageship fired at the dragon, unleashing their magical and mundane weapons. Sorath almost laughed at the crack of a black-powder rifle. His favored weapon. As expected, none of the projectiles reached the dragon. It didn't take its focus from the *Star Flyer*.

Uthari reached the portal and pressed both hands to it. Sorath had no idea how many dragons had come through, but he hoped the old wizard could shut it down. Maybe after this, the rulers and fleet commanders would finally realize it was too dangerous to leave the portal up.

The dragon roared, the pink of its mouth showing. There was his chance.

Sorath threw the knife, glad for all the practice he'd had over the years. The beautifully weighted weapon sailed true, but before it hit, the dragon noticed that Uthari was doing something—something it didn't like. It snapped its jaw shut, and the dagger clanked off its scaled snout. It didn't even seem to notice. Its head whipped around on its long neck, and it snapped down toward Uthari.

The mages' collective barrier kept the dragon from reaching him, but it roared in fury and must have launched another attack. Two of Uthari's mages wilted under the mental pressure, stumbling and falling to their knees.

"Look out, Your Majesty!" someone cried.

"His barrier's down!"

Uthari had to be as aware of that as anyone, for he sprang back, but he was too ancient to manage much alacrity. The dragon snapped for his head, no barrier left to deter it. Sorath sprinted to pick up the dagger but knew he wouldn't be fast enough to help.

Then he saw Tezi. She'd been creeping closer to the portal, and as the dragon lunged for Uthari, she sprinted at it. The tail still hung down within reach, and she chopped the axe into it, as if she'd practiced the move a hundred times and had no doubt that it would work.

And it did. The big axe flared brilliant blue as it pierced the dragon's defenses and sliced deeply into its tail. The pain derailed it, and its snout missed Uthari and smacked into the ground two feet to his side.

It startled Uthari, but he was still able to react quickly enough to fire off an attack. He blasted that snout with power as the dragon pulled it back up, roaring its fury and pain. Thanks to the axe, its barrier was still down, but the dragon jerked its tail away.

As Sorath had feared, the blade was lodged in deeply and didn't come free. The tail whipped away, tearing the axe from Tezi's hands. The dragon spun to focus on the one who'd hurt it the most. Not Uthari but Tezi.

Sorath lifted his dagger, again searching for a vital target. Since the dragon had turned, its back was to him now. It wouldn't be vulnerable, but he couldn't wait.

He aimed and threw the dagger at the back of its neck. A wall of fire roared down from the *Star Flyer*—Captain Rivlen's work—and Sorath didn't see if his weapon struck. Thorn Company also opened up, charges from magelock rifles pummeling the dragon.

All the attacks distracted it from Tezi, and she scrambled away before it could snatch her up. The dragon gave up on its perch and sprang into the air, powerful wings creating wind that battered at Sorath's chest. He glimpsed his dagger lodged in the back of the dragon's neck. It had sunk in deep between the scales, but as he'd feared, it was far from a killing blow. He might as well have jammed a sliver into its foot.

The dragon flew straight toward the *Star Flyer*, and he had nothing left to throw at it.

Jadora found that she could use magic to melt a few metal cabinet doors into a patch that sealed the hull and the deck and made it safe to walk around the laboratory. She also created a breeze that swept up the shattered glass and equipment, pushing it into a pile that she could bag up later. Sadly, fixing the microscope was beyond the magic and knowledge the dragon had shared with her, but maybe Vinjo could help her with that later.

It surprised her that she'd been given the knowledge to do things with her new power, not only the power itself. It didn't seem fair, since Jak had been forced to practice and sweat and pledge his fealty to mages to get them to teach him. But Jadora was glad she'd been able to heal Malek immediately and hadn't needed to spend time rehearsing. Malek hadn't had much time left.

She swallowed, the memory of him as a wild killer making her throat tighten again, and she glanced at him on the cot to remind herself that he was better now. Better but tired. He'd fallen asleep as soon as she'd helped him onto the cot. Zethron was out too and had been since she returned, knocked out by Malek or one of the other mages when the fight had started. Fortunately, that had made it easier to heal him.

Even though she'd tried to be brave as she'd walked forward to touch Malek and use her magic on him, she'd been scared. He'd been like a predator, a rabid, starving predator, poised to leap on its prey. Now, as he breathed evenly, his body was relaxed. Thankfully.

Jak walked down the corridor with Shikari trailing behind—she *sensed* them approaching before he stepped through the hatchway. She sensed all the mages on the ship, as well as everyone's magical weapons and all Vinjo's gewgaws that powered the craft.

"Can I leave him in here for a few minutes?" Jak waved for his charge to come in.

Shikari whacked him on the leg with his tail as he sauntered past, pausing to sniff at and then chew on one of the cot legs. It was metal, so Jadora couldn't imagine it tasted good, but maybe he was going through the dragon equivalent of teething and needed things to gnash on.

"Vinjo is trying to teach me a few things, and someone is getting in the way." Jak widened his eyes with significance, and she remembered the *kerzor* he wanted to learn to make.

"You don't think he'll be in the way in here? Malek might not be pleased if his cot collapses and he ends up on the deck."

"I trust that thanks to your healing, Malek will be a calmer and more serene person again."

"I'm not sure he was ever serene enough not to react to a dragon dumping him on the deck."

Jak shrugged and turned to leave.

"Wait." Jadora stepped forward and checked with her senses—it was strange how quickly that had become automatic—to make sure none of the other mages were near or seemed to be paying attention to them. Nonetheless, she lowered her voice. "Are you sure you want to work on that now? We have another task that has to take priority, and I doubt Uthari is going to be happy about this, unless he somehow thinks the dragons could become allies to him." She frowned darkly at that thought and hoped it wouldn't be possible. "He *definitely* won't be happy if he catches us thinking about stabbing mages with those needles and stealing their power."

How odd that she would have to worry about that happening to *her* now.

Jak shrugged. "I'm getting a lot better at protecting my thoughts around them, and I can't read *you* at all anymore."

"Oh?" Jadora hadn't expected that. She wasn't doing any of the exercises from *The Mind Way*, not that they'd ever helped that much.

"Nope."

Shikari abandoned the cot leg, instead pulling the blanket off Zethron and chomping on the corner.

"To my senses, you seem like one of them," Jak added. "As powerful as a zidarr. Or *more* powerful."

"Oh," she repeated, not able to keep the glumness out of her tone.

She never would have asked for this. What if it changed her? Her *personality*. What if she became indifferent to the plight of terrene humans? What if she became cold and cruel? Like one of *them*.

"It'll be all right, Mother." Jak smiled encouragingly.

Even if he couldn't read her thoughts, he knew her well.

"I hope so," she whispered. "I hope we can do what they want. What *she* wants."

"If you can figure out how to help them, you'll be a hero to all dragonkind. Untainted dragonkind, anyway."

"Which is currently an extremely old grandmother dragon and a toddler dragon working on digesting a blanket."

Jak eyed Shikari, then bent and extricated the chewed corner from his mouth. "Maybe I should take him to Tonovan's cabin."

"That would be cruel."

"To Shikari? Or Tonovan?"

"I'm not sure."

"Shikari, how about we go up on deck?" Jak offered. "You look hungry. Maybe we can pull down some giant glowworms for you to eat."

As if he understood perfectly, Shikari galloped out ahead of Jak.

"Are giant glowworms edible?" a soft voice croaked.

Malek. Jadora spun and knelt beside his cot. He hadn't lifted his head, but his eyes were open.

"I think everything is edible to a dragon. Don't lean too heavily toward your bottom left."

"I'll try to refrain." Malek gazed blearily at her. "I can't read your thoughts anymore."

"Well, it was worth it for that anyway." She smiled at him, though it was more Uthari and Tonovan and the rest of the mages that she wanted to keep out of her head. Oh, Malek could be dangerous to her too—in some ways, more dangerous than all the others—but after a while, she hadn't minded sharing that intimacy with him.

He didn't return the smile, instead gazing at her with puzzlement. Or was that wariness?

An uneasy feeling washed over her. What if her new power disturbed him? She'd never been a threat to him—or to his king—before. What if he saw her as one now?

"Does it bother you?" she asked quietly.

"It's... different."

A statement which did not answer her question. Jadora watched him sadly while he pondered this new development.

"I'm still the same person," she said, though she had a feeling they wouldn't be sharing any more kisses. Maybe that was for the best. At the least, it was safest for Malek. And for her.

A thought that didn't keep moisture from threatening to film her eyes. She looked away.

"Are you?" Malek asked. "I'm going to need proof."

"What kind of proof?"

He smiled slightly for the first time. "Empty your pockets."

"*All* of them?"

"You didn't clink as you knelt down. I'm not convinced you're the same person."

"I am."

His eyebrows rose in skepticism.

Jadora stood up, loosened her jacket, and jumped up and down. Not only did she clink, but she also jangled. And dirt flew out of one pocket and landed on his chest.

He picked up the clump and examined it. "You're collecting dirt now?"

"Not exactly." She withdrew a sample of the Jitaruvak that she'd retrieved, with permission, from the guardians before hurrying back to the ship. "If you mage people hadn't been in here trying to kill each other, I might have been able to get more than a few roots and leaves."

"Oh?" Malek eyed her pocket. "Can you fit a whole shrub in there?"

"I'd have to use your special backpack for that. I'm sure it can fit a whole nursery."

"Maybe only half of one. I'm not *that* good of a crafter."

"You're fortunate that I have low standards when it comes to men."

"*Low standards*?" He lifted his chin, oozed zidarr pomposity, and pulled her down into his lap.

The cot creaked ominously.

"This is dangerous," she whispered as he sat up, wrapping an arm around her. Maybe he *did* still want to kiss her… Something that wouldn't be wise with Zethron sleeping five feet away. He could wake up at any moment, and just because Uthari wouldn't be able to read her mind anymore didn't mean he couldn't poke into the minds of those around her.

"Because your low standards have led you to believe I'm appealing and irresistible?" Malek asked.

"Because a dragon was chewing on one of the cot legs earlier, and I'm not that confident about the patch job I did over that hole in the deck."

Malek peered down at the indicated spot. "It is rough. It's possible you won't be a high-level crafter either."

"So long as I can find another microscope. Some mages having a temper tantrum destroyed mine."

He tucked a strand of her hair behind her ear, the simple touch sending a tingle of pleasure through her. "That was rude of them."

"I thought so."

Malek switched to telepathy to say, *If I kissed you, I would regret it when I'm standing in front of the king and attempting to explain this mission to him.*

You could leave out any parts involving kissing.

The Zidarr Code compels me to honesty. I'm also not a good liar.

I'm sorry to hear that. Especially since his lips were already looking much better than they had during his wild-man period. She leaned against his chest and rested her forehead on his shoulder so that she wouldn't see them, but that only made her aware of his hard body and the muscular arm wrapped around her.

You did save my life, Malek mused. *One should reward a woman who saves his life, thus to encourage such behavior again in the future.*

Logical.

Indeed. Uthari would have to see it that way.

Jadora doubted that, and she hated the thought of Malek being punished again. She kissed him on the neck but squirmed out of his grip before she could be tempted to do more.

He released her, though she sensed his reluctance to do so, and a part of her wanted to rush back into his arms.

But Zethron stirred, saving her from such impulsiveness.

"I'll prepare some food and water for you two," she said, hurrying to one of the doorless cabinets.

"Thank you," Malek said aloud as Zethron rubbed his eyes and peered around. Silently, Malek added, *Jadora?*

Yes? She looked back at him.

I care for you too.

She nodded sadly at him. That was the problem.

29

All Rivlen had been thinking when she attacked the dragon was that she had to keep it from killing King Uthari. She hadn't intended to draw its ire. As it flew toward the *Star Flyer,* hatred in the cold yellow eyes that pierced her soul, she couldn't regret the choice. Behind it, Uthari was able to get back to the portal. If he succeeded in shutting it down and keeping more dragons from coming through, it would be worth her life.

But she didn't *want* to die, nor sacrifice her ship and crew. Not when there were battles left to fight—and so much more she wanted to prove. Besides, she saw other dragons flying off over the jungle. She couldn't let the ship fall when so many threats remained.

Put all your energy into our barrier! Rivlen cried the order into everyone's minds as she did the same.

The dragon blasted them with a magical attack as it flew close, its jaws snapping toward Rivlen. She was an easy target on the forecastle, but so be it. Better it target her than the others.

Their barrier held under its magical and physical assault, but it drained their power and left the mages on deck gasping. Rivlen locked her knees, willing her power to remain strong and wishing Jak were there to funnel some of his into her. He would have been useful in this battle.

The dragon hissed in irritation as it flew past and banked. It flicked its tail, and something flew free. Rivlen blinked. Tezi's axe.

Rivlen had seen her drive the weapon into its tail and save Uthari's life. She hoped the king had seen it too and rewarded the girl—or at least kept her safe. Should they all survive this.

As the axe splashed into the pool below, the dragon banked to come around again.

"Where's *our* axe?" Rivlen demanded.

"Here!" Sergeant Tinder stood on the deck and raised the weapon.

Rivlen was tempted to run down and snatch it from her, certain she could do more with it than the mercenary, but the dragon cast a wall of fire at the *Star Flyer*, and she didn't have time to focus on anything except maintaining the barrier.

"You'll have to throw it," Captain Ferroki yelled to her sergeant. "It's not coming close enough for a duel."

The flames poured against the barrier with staggering force, and Rivlen gritted her teeth as sweat trickled down her spine. She could see the dragon's yellow eyes through the flames. They kept staring at her, and she knew it had chosen her own favorite form of attack on purpose, showing her how a *dragon* cast a wall of flames.

A ragged cheer went up from below.

Rivlen glanced down, hoping Uthari had convinced the portal to shoot lightning at the dragon, but the ancient artifact had gone dark. At first, that filled her with disappointment, but then she realized he'd done what he'd wanted. He'd closed the gateway to whatever world the dragons were coming from.

"Too bad a zillion of them are already *here*," Rivlen panted, drawing upon her reserves to keep the barrier up.

She could feel the other mages in her crew running out of energy, their contributions falling away.

"Throw that axe!" Rivlen yelled as the dragon skimmed past above, then added a silent order to the mages to drop the barrier.

Tinder hurled the weapon. With the dragon so close, she couldn't have missed, but it only grazed the inside of its leg, barely cutting through scale and drawing blood, before tumbling back to the deck. At least it didn't fall into the pool with the other one.

So puny, the dragon drawled into their minds. *It will be a simple matter to take this world for our own, to eat or enslave your kind, and to rule for all eternity.*

Barrier up, Rivlen ordered as Tinder ran to collect the axe.

Rivlen and the weary mages weren't fast enough, and the dragon's tail smashed down. It struck Tinder from above as she tried to pick up the weapon. With a flick, the tail sent the axe skittering through the railing and overboard.

Rivlen groaned. The *one* weapon that had been useful.

"No!" Dr. Fret yelled and rushed toward her fallen comrade.

Snarling, Rivlen threw the last of her energy into reestablishing the barrier as she telepathically urged everyone capable of helping her to do so. *Now.*

Down below, someone was swimming in the pool. Someone invisible. Was that Colonel Sorath again? That man kept showing up *everywhere.* Rivlen hoped he could get Tezi's axe off the bottom and do something.

Tinder's axe clanked down on the portal and bounced off. Uthari, who still had his hands planted on the artifact and was either chanting or cursing at it, didn't stir. But Tezi and a green-haired druid kid ran to pick it up. In the water, splashes suggested Sorath had come up, but Rivlen couldn't see him and didn't know if he'd found the other axe.

The dragon was flying a hundred feet up now, and Rivlen

doubted any of them could throw a weapon and hit it. They needed more help. They needed—

Red lightning streaked from the portal.

Rivlen clenched her fist. Uthari had done it.

The branches arced up and struck the dragon on either flank. It had a barrier up, and the lightning didn't hurt it immediately, but the power emitted by the portal was so great that Rivlen could feel it from the deck of her ship. Surely, even a dragon had to wilt under that assault.

But just in case…

"Barrier down!" she yelled. "Join in the attack!"

Tezi crouched by the pond below, Tinder's axe ready. A puddle next to her suggested Sorath was at her side, hopefully with the other axe.

Rivlen summoned her dwindling reserves, again wishing Jak were there to support her, and sent a wave of fire at the dragon. The other ships, many of which had stayed back, afraid to risk the dragon's ire, now sailed closer. Their mages unleashed fireballs and other attacks at the dragon. Its wingbeats faltered, and Rivlen sensed its power waning.

The dragon's barrier dissolved, and the lightning streaked through to hit it. It roared in pain.

Rivlen resisted the urge to call *it* puny. It was far from true, and its allies might come back at any time, so goading it would be stupid. Instead, she threw more fire at it, pouring on with the others.

The dragon dropped to the ground, landing on all fours. It roared again and charged at the portal—and Uthari.

Sorath and Tezi ran in from the side and intercepted it. They leaped, swinging at its belly, its legs, its tail—any target they could reach. The dragon-steel blades bit in when few other weapons could, and blood soon dripped from a dozen wounds.

The portal flashed, as if the dragon were trying to activate it, and the lightning faltered and went out. Uthari scowled and shouted something at the portal. Some ancient command? Or curse?

It didn't matter. The dragon bled freely, the axes biting in as attacks from Rivlen and the other mages took their toll.

The tail smashed to the ground, trying to strike down Tezi, but she rolled away in time to escape being smashed. She sprang up immediately and ran in, her axe raised, as if she would chop into that tail again. But instead, she borrowed one of Malek's tactics. She jumped *onto* the tail and scrambled up it to the dragon's scaled back.

She wasn't as agile as Malek, and she slipped and flopped down before reaching the neck and head, but she caught herself before falling off and ended up astride the dragon, as if it were a horse. As the invisible Sorath harried it from the side, Tezi drove the axe downward, the blade biting into its flesh and—Rivlen hoped—its spine.

Since she'd helped Tezi learn to use the weapon, Rivlen beamed with pride. It was all she had left to send down to the battle. With her energy drained, her knees threatened to give out, and she had to grip the railing for support.

It didn't matter. Tezi landed blow after blow to that spine, and the head finally flopped down into the dirt in front of the portal. The invisible Sorath jumped in, and wounds appeared as he pounded his axe down on the vulnerable neck. The dragon twitched but didn't rise again. The gleam left its eyes, and it didn't issue any more threats about what it would do to the world and humanity.

Uthari stepped away from the portal and walked toward them. But when his back was turned, it pulsed blue.

Rivlen tensed, afraid that meant the dragons who hadn't made it through had activated another gateway, but the stars didn't form in the middle of the portal. Instead, a single branch of red lightning lashed out.

She expected it to hit the dragon, one final blow for good measure, but it slammed into Uthari's back. Rivlen gaped as it sent him flying through the air and rolling across the dirt.

Every shout, cheer, and even cry of pain fell silent as hundreds of mages stared in shock. The attack hadn't lasted long, but Uthari lay still, the back of his tunic charred—his *skin* charred.

Rivlen could sense his power and knew he wasn't dead, but she realized abruptly that he was vulnerable.

Tezi slid off the dragon's back and stared at Uthari, the deadly axe in her hand. Rivlen didn't think she would attack him, especially not with everyone watching, but Sorath? Oh, he absolutely would.

Rivlen drew upon the last of her energy to jump over the railing and cushion her fall as she plummeted downward. Even with her magic helping, her exhausted legs and rubbery muscles nearly buckled when she landed. She forced them into a run anyway.

Since he still wore that stealth device, Rivlen couldn't see Sorath, but she knew he was there—and that Uthari was in danger. Uthari groaned, proving he was alive, but he couldn't have mustered so much as a candle's worth of flame at that moment, and he wasn't protecting himself with a barrier.

Rivlen sprinted the last twenty feet and jumped to land with one foot on either side of him.

A shadow moved to her left, and she spun, hands raised to fling fire. Sorath loomed out of the shadows, Tezi's axe raised over his head.

Rivlen swore. Her magic wouldn't affect him, she didn't have another weapon with her, and the mercenary colonel had no reason to love her. Her impulsive move might get her killed, especially since nobody else could see Sorath. Nobody else knew of the threat.

Clenching her jaw, Rivlen lifted her chin and stared him in the eyes. Instinctively, she wrapped a barrier around herself, extending it down to Uthari, but the axe would pop it like a soap bubble if Sorath swung.

And he wanted to. The frustration in his eyes promised that she hadn't misinterpreted his intent.

But would he cut her down to kill Uthari?

Long seconds passed with their eyes locked.

"Colonel?" Tezi asked uncertainly from the side.

Sorath stepped back, fading from Rivlen's sight. Did that mean he wouldn't attack? Or that he planned to come in from another angle and try to get behind her?

A thud came from the side, and the axe appeared at Tezi's feet.

"That's your axe, killer," Sorath said from ten feet away, his voice weary. "See to it that Sergeant Tinder gets hers back."

"Yes, sir," Tezi said.

Thanks to the ever-present roar of the waterfall, Rivlen couldn't hear his footsteps and didn't know for certain if he'd walked away.

Below her, Uthari groaned, recovering his senses. Rivlen lowered her hands and stepped to the side. Uthari pushed himself into a sitting position, his hands shaky. Smoke still wafted from his back.

"Do you know what happened, Your Majesty?" Rivlen asked as one of his healers jogged over.

Uthari looked toward the portal, now dark and quiet, as if the attack had never happened. But he only studied it for a moment. His gaze grew unfocused as he looked toward the north, toward the Forked Sea and the continents beyond it. Perhaps toward their own kingdom of Uth.

Because of their mighty auras, Rivlen could still sense many of the dragons that had flown into their world. She had no idea where they were going or who they would target. All she knew was that all of Torvil was in trouble.

Judging by Uthari's face, he knew it too. All he did was shake his head and let his healer shoo everyone away so he could be tended.

Rivlen joined Tezi and picked up the spare axe to return to its owner, as soon as she could summon the magic to carry her back up to the *Star Flyer*. Maybe she would curl up by the pool and take a long nap first. Her stomach growled with the need to replenish her body's reserves.

Thank you for your help, Captain Rivlen, Uthari spoke into her mind.

You're welcome, Your Majesty, she replied, not certain whether to be pleased he'd noticed or uneasy about the direct contact. She hadn't succeeded in destroying the druids, and she'd let Sorath go without trying to kill him. She'd also helped him kill Yidar. Sooner or later, Uthari would find out about everything. Would her act today prompt him to forgive her for any disappointment he might feel in her?

Finish repairs to your ship, and tell the other captains to do the same. As soon as I figure out what to do with this... obstinate artifact, we'll have to go after those dragons. I can't let the world be enslaved because of my hubris.

His honesty and openness surprised her. *Yes, Your Majesty.*

Maybe she would yet have her opportunity to prove herself.

Jak tugged on his skullcap as the ship descended below the canopy and the buzz of insects reached his ears. Even though his mother could cure the parasitic disease caused by those death darters now, he didn't want to risk being stabbed in the back of his head if a swarm showed up.

"My skin isn't anything like your scales," Jak said to his lone comrade on the deck.

While he sat, Shikari lay on his belly, swishing his tail as he peered into the perpetual twilight of the swamp. A pair of bat-like creatures flew past, and he roared at them. One chittered like a nagging squirrel, and neither appeared alarmed. Shikari pushed up to his feet, his tail still swishing, and crouched, as if he was going to spring into the air and chase them down.

"Are you sure?" Jak peered over the side. "We're still a couple hundred feet from the ground, and you've only flown once, and it's possible that was by accident."

Shikari looked at him, as if he understood. And maybe he did. They'd only spent a short time with the ancient blue dragon, but she'd imparted knowledge to him as well as to Mother. Shikari seemed to grasp more now. Though maybe he was just maturing.

Shikari opened his maw and roared at Jak. One day, it would be the kind of roar that made men wet themselves. For now, it sounded like a rooster strangling itself, and the only moisture Jak noticed was the spittle that hit his cheek.

"Gross." He wiped it off. "To make matters worse, you have insect breath. How do dragons feel about toothbrushes?"

He remembered his mother trying to swab saliva out of Shikari's mouth with a sample spatula, and how it had ended up chewed into pieces and dribbled down his jacket. Most likely, a toothbrush would come to the same gruesome end.

Shikari returned to contemplating the flying wildlife, but the swishing tail occasionally curled up to thump Jak on the back.

"There's the portal." Jak spotted it on the island in the distance, the dark monolith still draped with vines.

Would it work this time? It seemed like they'd been gone for months, but it had only been a few days. Still, that ought to have been long enough for it to work out whatever kinks had perturbed it, right? The portal network had been around for millennia, with all the nodes Jak had visited still working. They had to be capable of self-repair.

The image of a portal popped into his mind, along with a toolbox on the ground next to it and a human wearing greasy coveralls banging a wrench on its side. A sense of dry amusement came with the vision.

"That wasn't you, was it?" Jak squinted at Shikari, but it reminded him more of the communications he'd had with the portals.

The distant artifact flashed blue at him.

Jak rose to his feet and gripped the railing. That meant it was working, didn't it? He touched his hat, the reassuring medallion nestled in the band. Earlier, Mother had tried to return the key to Malek, but Malek had given it to Jak, saying the portal would be more likely to respond to him.

The next image Jak received showed Mother bent over a microscope, her hands darting about at impossible speed as she moved slides in and out of it while stirring concoctions in beakers. It looked more like someone's imagination of all the things a chemist might do than something actually happening. Jak *knew* it wasn't happening, because that microscope was broken. This time, a sense of smugness accompanied the vision.

It seemed the portal was both amused and pleased with itself. Given that it had been aloof and condescending the last time Jak had communicated with it, he supposed that was an improvement.

He scratched his jaw and directed a telepathic message toward it. *Did you change your mind about believing we could be helpful and arrange all this? Did you trap us here on purpose so that we would find the guardians and the ancient dragon?*

Blue flashed, more noticeable now as the ship flew closer, and the smugness kept radiating from the portal.

When last Jak had communicated with it, it had spoken to him with words, but this time, it stuck to images. The next one was something that had been plucked from Jak's mind, him riding a dragon in the skies of his own world, of becoming good friends with that dragon. Jak looked at Shikari, but he was too busy watching for bats and bugs to glance back at him.

As the ship flew lower and closer to the portal, the symbol for Torvil flared to life, and stars swirled inside its frame of intertwined dragons.

"Uh." Jak removed his hat and looked at the key seated snugly in the headband.

The stars stopped swirling and formed the Dragon's Tail constellation of their home world.

How did you do that, Jak? Malek asked from the navigation cabin.

I didn't. The portal did. I guess it's time for us to go home.

Jak and Shikari headed below to join the others in navigation. Jak wondered what kind of mess they would return to this time. The memory of those dragons trying to reach Torvil came to mind. Had they succeeded?

Mother squeezed into navigation behind him and rested a hand on his shoulder. Vinjo, Malek, and Prolix were already in there, along with Harintha and Zethron, who, like Malek, was run-down from the infection but had recovered well enough to walk around. The servants Yira and Idora were in the corridor, peeking past everyone and toward the portal as well. Only Tonovan was ensconced in his cabin, ignoring them all. That suited Jak fine.

He closed his eyes as they sailed through the portal, sensing when they crossed into the passageway, its magic streaming past him, foreign and yet growing more familiar. It reminded him of the ancient dragon Zelonsera in the cavern.

"Huh," Vinjo said, the first to speak when they flew out of the portal on the far side.

Harintha had to steer the craft to the side quickly to avoid smacking into the corpse of a mottled dragon. Uthari and more than a dozen mages stood nearby, and a wrecked ship lay halfway in the pool. Mercenaries were dragging bodies into a communal pile for a funeral pyre. Jak stared bleakly at the carnage and barely kept himself from glowering openly at Uthari when he looked toward them with a puzzled crease to his brow. Did he sense Mother's aura?

As Harintha maneuvered the ship, looking for a place where they could set down or perhaps hover out of the way, they had a view of more carnage. The tents were all flattened, other ships hung wrecked in the treetops—what treetops remained. It looked like a logger the size of a mountain had stalked through, swinging an axe of corresponding size.

"The portal continues to be a source of death and devastation," Mother murmured. "As the druids warned us."

Malek looked at her but didn't reply. Jak hoped Malek didn't begrudge her for making observations that hinted that Uthari was a selfish idiot. He also hoped Malek would one day realize that himself and walk away from the wizard, but he feared that would never happen. Even if he *did* realize it, he was married to the old man in a sense; he owed Uthari too much to ever betray him. That saddened Jak almost as much as all the death they'd come back to.

"Is that General Tonovan's ship?" Harintha pointed at a wreck behind the portal, the color of the black hull—what was left of it—the only thing recognizable about it. "The *Dread Arrow*?"

Jak kept himself from saying he hoped so and smiling at the idea of Tonovan losing his flagship.

"It is," Malek said.

Harintha opted to land. As soon as the ship touched down, Tonovan sprang out of his cabin and up the hatchway, eager to be the first to report in to his king. To tattle on Malek and complain about Jak and Mother and who knew what else. Jak knew it was awful, but he couldn't help but wish Tonovan had been killed, not Bakir. The admiral hadn't been a paragon of pleasantness, but he would have returned to his own fleet and wouldn't likely have troubled them again.

Shikari scrambled up the ladder as well. With his wings folded to his sides, he barely made it out. He'd grown in the short time they'd been gone, and Jak realized it would be difficult to continue to take him along on the ship unless he rode on top the whole time. Or flew after them.

"At least my bunk will be less crowded," he muttered.

Mother lifted her eyebrows.

"Just musing about the future."

After Jak, Mother, and Malek disembarked and stood on the ground outside, Jak peered around, hoping to spot Rivlen—and hoping the *Star Flyer* wasn't among all the wrecked ships. Had she and Thorn Company survived? And Tezi? With her axe, Jak could envision her having been thrust into the middle of the fray. A number of gashes in the dragon's body looked a lot like axe wounds.

Jak spotted Uthari's *Serene Waters* in the sky and hoped that meant Grandfather was all right. He never should have been caught up in all of this.

Shikari sniffed the air and started toward the dead dragon, as if he might investigate.

Jak caught him. "Don't even think about it. Remember that parasite that floated out of the other dead dragon?"

The memory of that encounter made Jak want to stuff Shikari back in the ship and shut the hatch. He didn't sense anything living or magical about the dead dragon, not the way he had last time, but that didn't mean the parasite couldn't be in there, lying in wait for a potential new host to infest.

Shikari cheeped uncertainly.

"That's right," Jak said. "We don't want you to turn into a vile man-eating dragon."

Shikari wandered a few feet to the side and relieved himself. Jak rubbed his face. Fortunately, Shikari seemed to have heeded his warning, and he headed toward the portal for his investigations while giving the deceased dragon a wide berth.

"I don't sense anything magical inside that one," Malek said. "It's possible it's been dead long enough for the parasites to also die."

"Maybe," Jak said, "but I still want Shikari to stay far away from it."

"Wise. I will report to King Uthari and find out what is to be done..." Malek looked at Mother but finished only with, "next."

Her expression turned bleak as she watched him walk toward Uthari and Tonovan. Tonovan was gesticulating and quite obviously complaining, but he happened to glance toward the wreck behind the portal and halted abruptly.

"Is that my *ship*?" he roared. "What *happened*?"

Uthari, who'd doubtless been there for the battle, only watched as his general stalked off without asking for permission. The king's face was harder to read. He didn't appear pleased by anything, but he wasn't stomping around and throwing tantrums like Tonovan.

His gaze fell upon Mother, and he considered her for a long assessing moment. Jak had the urge to step protectively in front of her. Uthari wouldn't *attack* her, would he? Or try to test her and prove that he was more powerful or something ludicrous?

Malek stopped in front of Uthari and saluted, drawing his attention away from Mother. They spoke telepathically, with a lot of gestures toward her, then walked off side by side.

Surprisingly, there was a large hole in the back of Uthari's tunic, the edges charred. His back wasn't burned, but maybe it had been and someone had healed him. Jak wondered what mage had dared take a shot at him. Maybe it had been the dragon.

Uthari gripped Malek's shoulder as they walked, their heads together in what was doubtless a serious telepathic conversation.

"That's not at all ominous," Mother murmured.

"It'll be all right." Jak was concerned but wanted to reassure his mother. After all, it was possible they weren't talking about her at all.

"I'm worried he'll see me as a threat now and want to get rid of me."

"He would be foolish to try to. You're going to be the savior of all the dragons."

As one, they looked at the great scaled corpse in the middle of the camp.

"All the *other* dragons," Jak amended.

"I don't know if that's possible. Even if one could eradicate the parasite, after thousands of years of living with the infestation, the effects might be permanent."

"They won't be," Jak said with determination. "Dragons are inherently good. Look at how amiable and wholesome Shikari is, frolicking in the grass over there."

Actually, Shikari was chasing a butterfly, but one could interpret the bounding as frolicking. He sprang into the air, his wings flapping, and caught and chomped down his prey.

"He's not amiable and wholesome to insects," Mother said.

"Well, they're obnoxious anyway."

"Yes, many poems have been written about the loathsomeness of butterflies."

Zethron joined Jak and Mother, looking uncertainly around at the carnage.

"Do you know what will happen to me now?" he asked quietly, glancing at the cargo hatch.

Harintha, who'd originally been sent along to guard Zethron

for her queen as well as pilot the ship, had walked out with her pack over her shoulder. She wasn't paying any attention to Zethron. She looked like she'd had enough of the adventure and wanted to beeline back to her ship, but Jak didn't see any green-hulled vessels in the sky.

"I think if you wanted to disappear again," Jak said to Zethron, "this might be a good time."

"If you wait until nightfall and things have quieted down," Mother said, "I might be able to help you go through the portal and back to Vran."

"That would probably be the wisest thing I could do, but I've only seen five square miles of this world so far and not a single ancient ruin." Zethron looked wistfully at Mother.

She was gazing up at the ships, and Jak had the strange certainty that she was using her new power to read minds and gather information. Or maybe she could simply absorb it from the world around her now.

Her eyes were haunted when she replied. "This isn't a good time for sightseeing on Torvil, my friend."

"Ah," Zethron said with disappointment.

"We are thankful for your help on this mission," Jak said. "Even if you didn't want to come along."

"I didn't object so much to coming as being tortured and *forced* to come."

"Tell me about it," Jak muttered.

Vinjo, who'd also disembarked from the ship, jumped up and down and waved at something. There was nothing haunted about *his* eyes.

The *Star Flyer* was sailing into view over the waterfall, and several of the mercenaries were visible at the railing, including Tezi, Ferroki, and Sasko. A little surprisingly, Sasko smiled and waved back at Vinjo. She'd always struck Jak as gruff and sarcastic, not at all the kind of woman to be wooed by an exuberant but slightly goofy mage engineer, but maybe he was wrong. Or maybe Vinjo had tenacity that could wear down a woman's initial standoffishness.

Jak looked for and spotted Rivlen—she was up in the forecastle—who looked fierce and competent in her red captain's uniform, her dark hair swept back in a tidy bun. He would have waved to her, but she was looking at Uthari and Malek. Jak wondered if she had noticed he was gone or thought of him at all, then snorted at himself. Why would she have? He wasn't part of her crew or a colleague, just someone she'd been on an adventure with and had given a couple of lessons.

When she did look toward him, her first words were, *What the cursed dragon's fang happened to your mother?*

It's good to see you too, Rivlen, Jak replied. *I'm glad you survived what must have been a harrowing battle.*

Uh huh. She's beaming power like the sun. Did she swallow a dragon?

Not exactly. Jak wondered if Tezi would be more excited by his return. Or even Captain Ferroki. It would be nice to have a woman who wasn't his mother pleased to see him alive and well.

Come up to my cabin later, and give me the details.

Is that an order? I'm not in your chain-of-command, you know. Besides, Uthari might be dragging them to *his* cabin.

Sorry, did you want it to be a request? An invitation to a dinner date?

Naturally. A promise of food would woo me and make me eager to appear at your door. I might even shave and wash under my armpits.

Shave what? Those three chin hairs?

There are five. And they're manly.

Like your copious chest hair?

Even more so.

"Are you getting an update from her on the battle?" Mother murmured, catching them looking at each other. "I hope all of the mercenaries survived. I'm relieved to see Tezi and that she's managed to retain her axe."

"Actually," Jak said, "I believe Captain Rivlen and I are flirting."

Mother's eyebrows rose. "Are you sure? She looks fearsome."

"She always looks like that when she's in uniform and on duty. But she invited me up to her cabin for dinner."

"Oh?"

"It was more of an order. And she forgot to mention food. Or how we would lounge together on settees and she would feed me grapes."

"Your mind is an interesting place, my son."

"Yes, it entertains me vastly."

Lieutenant Sasko found a skyboard, and Rivlen or another mage guided her to the ground on it. Jak assumed she was being sent to report in to Malek or someone else, but she strode straight to the still waving, and now grinning, Vinjo. He sprang for her, arms wide, but hesitated. Not certain if she would allow a hug? Most of the Thorn Company mercenaries were almost as fearsome and intimidating as Rivlen in their military uniforms, and Sasko was no exception.

But she stepped into Vinjo's offered arms and kissed him soundly on the mouth.

Vinjo seemed as surprised as Jak, but he responded quickly, hugging her and kissing her back.

"That was because of your magical bulwarks," Sasko said when they broke apart.

"They wanted you to kiss me?" Vinjo asked.

"Yes."

"I didn't realize I'd built that desire into them."

"They were very useful on our mission," Sasko said. "Did you know they could protect nearby mercenaries from sleep gas floating on a fog bank as well as direct magical attacks?"

"Oh, yes. I tried to make them as handy as possible. Terrene humans are fragile and need a great deal of protection from mages."

"You're calling me fragile? My arms are more muscular than yours."

"I know. Engineers are fragile too. It's how we know what people need built."

"Hm. Let's chat somewhere in private." Sasko looped an arm around his waist, and they walked off, though Jak couldn't imagine what quiet, private place they might find for their reunion when even the pool was currently in disarray with wreckage floating about, being pounded by the waterfall.

"Malek's coming back," Mother said quietly.

Jak was relieved that Uthari wasn't with him. He'd grabbed a skyboard and was heading up to his yacht.

Jak spotted Grandfather at the railing, a guard standing beside him, and waved. Grandfather's fingers lifted in acknowledgment, but he was frowning with concern as he looked at Mother. Had word already gotten around about her new power? Jak hoped they wouldn't end up arguing. It wasn't as if Mother *wanted* to be a mage.

"We have a lot of problems to deal with," Malek said, stopping in front of them.

"We, as in you, or we, as in us?" Jak waved at himself and his mother.

"All of humanity, but it will fall to the mages to address it. Terrene humans won't be capable of it."

"Are mages the reason it exists?" Mother asked coolly.

"Yes," Malek said.

His honest answer surprised Jak, though it shouldn't have. Malek wasn't one to prevaricate.

He faced Mother. "Uthari invites you up to his yacht as soon as it's sufficiently repaired. The suite you and Jak were occupying was damaged." Malek glanced toward a gaping hole in the hull, where two mages floated on skyboards repairing it. "He'll find another one for you that's suitable for your work as well as dwelling in. Uthari trusts you intend to make good on your promise and synthesize the drug for him. Also, that you won't prove yourself a… problem."

Mother lifted her chin but didn't dignify that with an answer.

Even if that dragon had given her the power and knowledge to cast fireballs, Jak couldn't imagine her doing so. He could barely stomach the idea himself, and he wasn't as pacifistic as Mother.

Reminded of his success with fire on the paddleboat, he hoped he got a chance to tell Rivlen about that. What if the only *details* she wanted from him were on Mother's new power?

"I promised him you hadn't changed," Malek continued when she didn't speak. "As evinced by your clinking pockets full of vials."

Mother smiled slightly but only for a second before saying, "I do have a new mission, one I promised that dragon and all of her guardians that I would pursue. But both will require lab time, so I should be able to work on them concurrently." She watched his face, her eyes wary.

She had to be worried that Uthari would believe his desires should supersede those of the ancient dragon. Jak couldn't have cared less about whether Uthari got a drug that would make him immortal. He wished there were a way that he and Mother and Shikari could leave through the portal and find a place where they could research the dragon problem exclusively. But that wasn't realistic, not when she would likely need access to libraries and resources on Torvil. Uthari could provide a better laboratory and research equipment than they'd seen evidence of on other worlds.

Malek spread a hand. "It's not as if he'll be able to read your thoughts now and know which task you're prioritizing. As long as you're making some progress on his, he shouldn't object to the other."

"I would hope that even he realizes a three-hundred-year-old man's quest for immortality—*further* immortality—shouldn't take precedence over saving an entire species from extinction."

Malek gazed at her, and Jak couldn't keep from wincing at Mother's bluntness. Even if he served Uthari, Malek was their ally. At least, Jak hoped he still was. It wouldn't be wise to be snippy and sarcastic with him and risk driving him away.

"Gather your belongings from the mageship," was all Malek said, "and I'll have them taken up to the yacht. We'll be leaving soon."

"Leaving?" Jak asked.

"This dragon—" Malek gestured to the body, "—held the gateway open while forty other dragons entered our world. They flew off to the north. Our kingdom is now at risk. *All* of the kingdoms are at risk."

"Forty?" Mother mouthed.

Jak thought of the dragons they'd fought and how difficult it had been to battle one or two at a time. They never would have defeated the pair on Vran without the help of the dragon-steel ziggurat, and as far as he knew, such ancient structures did not exist in their world. Even though they'd brought back a chest of dragon steel, it wouldn't be enough to build anything like that.

"Forty," Malek said. "Jak, we'll continue your training on the way back to Uth. We'll all need to be at our best to keep our world from being taken over by dragons."

Malek nodded at them and headed up to the yacht to join Uthari.

Jak stared bleakly at the frolicking Shikari. With so many of the infested dragons in the world, how would he be able to keep his charge from being infected?

"When I envisioned enemies coming through the portal and threatening people," Mother whispered, her gaze toward the northern sky, "it didn't occur to me that they might leave the area and threaten everyone back home."

"We'll find a way to deal with the dragons and protect everyone we care about," Jak said, trying to sound reassuring. He didn't point out that the best way to do that would be to figure out how to cure the dragons of their affliction. Mother's eyes had been daunted when she'd pointed out that might not be possible.

Zelonsera had given her the power to try. Jak had to believe she could do it. The alternative was too dark to contemplate.

EPILOGUE

As the sun set over the jungle, Captain Ferroki called the company into a formation.

Tezi fought off a yawn as she took her spot at the end of the last row. Between the battle and sleeping so little the previous nights, she longed to curl up in a blanket and snooze for hours, even if it was on the deck of the *Star Flyer* instead of in a bunk. She would take anything, as long as she could close her eyes.

After the battle, Thorn Company had been pressed into helping with repairs, here and on other mageships. Soon, all of Uthari's ships would leave the area and head north to protect their kingdom. The last Tezi had heard, Thorn Company was being retained and would go with them. She didn't know if Captain Ferroki had been given the option to decline.

Most of the fleets had broken apart, their skirmish over Queen Vorsha's death forgotten in the face of the new threat, and some had already left, those who hadn't been close for the dragon battle and hadn't taken as much damage. The other mercenary units, including the roamers, had also been swooped up onto ships. The mages believed they would need a *lot* of troops for what lay ahead.

Tezi had heard that dragons had already been reported doing damage to the cities along the coast of Zewnath and that some had been spotted flying over the continents to the north.

Corporal Basher, who stood next to Tezi in the formation, dug an elbow into her ribs. "Good fighting down there, Rookie," she drawled around the stub of a cigar dangling from her lips.

"Thank you, Corporal."

"That was Sorath down there with you, right?"

Tezi nodded. She hadn't seen the colonel since his stand-off with Captain Rivlen, and in truth, she hadn't even seen him then, thanks to the stealth device. She'd only gathered the gist of that moment by watching Rivlen's reactions. Wherever Sorath had gone, Tezi hoped he would be all right and that he wasn't in need of medical attention. She'd caught Ferroki gazing sadly into the jungle more than once and knew the captain cared for and worried about him.

Tezi wished she knew what had happened to Grunk. She'd risked much to help rescue him and then hadn't even gotten to say goodbye. Since she barely knew him, and he was crazy, she didn't know why that bothered her. Maybe because he'd seemed broken, and after losing her parents and watching her brother be taken into slavery, she often felt that way too.

"I figured. I knew he'd never leave the company. The *captain*." Basher winked.

"We'll be leaving *him*, if he can't find a ride north," Tinder said over her shoulder from the row ahead.

"Is this supposed to be a *chatty* formation?" Sasko demanded from the front. "Captain, you didn't ask me to order a *chatty* formation, did you?"

"Carry on, Lieutenant," Ferroki said dryly.

"Yes, Captain." Sasko clasped her hands behind her back and prowled around the troops, eyeing them up and down.

Were they doing an inspection? *Now*?

Tezi grimaced at her stained and rumpled clothing—she even had dragon blood spattered on her sleeve—but did her best to stand straight, facing forward and not letting herself glance at Sasko when she paused. Her gaze descended down Tezi's dirty uniform to her mud-spattered boots. She clucked a few times before focusing on Basher.

"Did someone say you could smoke in formation, Corporal?"

"No, ma'am." Basher put her cigar out by smashing the tip against her ammo pouch, then slipped it into a pocket, which proceeded to waft smoke into the air.

Sasko rolled her eyes and continued walking around the formation. "Just because it's been a long day isn't an excuse for slovenly behavior. Is that understood?"

"Yes, ma'am," came the united reply.

Out of the corner of her eye, Tezi caught Captain Rivlen leaning against the railing with her arms crossed as she watched. She was smirking, though Tezi didn't know if it was because she was amused by Thorn Company being reprimanded or if she was sympathetic because she'd endured such treatment in her own military career. The smirk didn't seem malicious.

You should have wiped the dragon guts off your boots before this, Rivlen spoke into Tezi's mind.

Given the day's events, I didn't think it was a priority. And they're not guts. That's just mud and blood. Tezi glanced down. *And some kind of smashed fruit. It might have been a mango.*

Classy.

Is there a reason you're mocking me, ma'am? After all we've been through?

Because I know something you don't know and enjoy being smugly superior. Rivlen's smirk widened, and she glanced at Sasko and Ferroki, who were conferring quietly at the front of the formation.

Mages are good at that, ma'am.

We practice a lot.

"Rookie Tezi," Sasko bellowed. "Front and center."

Though startled, Tezi broke ranks and hurried to obey. Her axe was in its sling on her back and bounced as she ran.

She stopped in front of Sasko and Ferroki and stood in a rigid attention stance, her back to the others, though she could feel their curious gazes upon her. Since she wasn't officially in the company anymore, Tezi hadn't been certain she should join the formation. But surely Sasko would have asked her to step aside if she'd felt that way.

"Aside from an unannounced departure to go on a mission with *druids*," Sasko said, "we believe you've performed adequately of late."

"Since she wasn't in the company then," Ferroki murmured, "she didn't need to ask permission to leave."

"I believe Captain Rivlen feels differently, ma'am, but I understand that the brutal and effective slaying of a dragon is considered a mitigating circumstance, and that all has essentially been forgiven."

"That is my understanding too." Ferroki inclined her head toward Rivlen, who mirrored the gesture back. Rivlen still stood with her arms crossed as she leaned against the railing and observed. "I believe that Rookie Tezi has performed well and continued to work with the company in body and spirit even though we sought to protect her by asking her to leave."

"Do you think she wants back in?" Sasko asked.

Tezi arched her eyebrows. Before, she hadn't had the foggiest idea what this was all about, but the light began to dawn. Now that she had the dragon-steel axe, and zidarr and mages couldn't read her mind and learn about her dubious past, she wasn't a threat to the company. And the officers saw that. They meant to ask her back.

She bit her lip, more relieved than she had been when the dragon had died.

Ferroki smiled. "I don't think you need to ask, Lieutenant."

"No, you're right. We're delightful people and she must see that it's an honor to serve with Thorn Company."

"She must," Ferroki agreed.

Tezi grinned. "Yes, ma'am. *Ma'ams.*"

"I officially reinstate Rookie Tezi into the company and onto the payroll," Ferroki said.

Cheers went up in the unit, but Sasko frowned and tapped a finger to her chin. "That doesn't sound right, Captain."

"No?"

Tezi's grin faltered. What was wrong?

"The Rookie Tezi part," Sasko said.

"Oh, yes, I see," Ferroki said. "Given how much she's learned and all that she's done these past months, I believe a promotion is in order."

Sasko nodded. "Indeed so."

Tezi's grin returned. A promotion? She would no longer be a rookie?

"Also, the size of her axe suggests those who've razzed her hardest might want to watch themselves going forward," Sasko said, sending a warning look over the company.

"It *is* a substantial axe, a large weapon for a corporal to carry," Ferroki said, "but these are extenuating times."

"They are. Very well, Captain. Will you do the honors?"

Ferroki withdrew a fresh armband from one of her pockets, one that showed the company's insignia and sported two thorns instead of one. She wrapped it around Tezi's sleeve and tied it on.

"I trust you can scrounge a needle and thread from someone in this jungle to sew that on permanently," Ferroki said.

"Yes, ma'am," Tezi whispered.

Ferroki stepped back, faced the company, lifted an arm and announced, "Corporal Tezi."

Another round of cheers broke out.

"Company, dismissed," Sasko said.

Everyone came forward, swarming Tezi to welcome her back and congratulate her. Somehow, Corporal Basher had already relit her cigar, and she offered Tezi a puff. Tezi shook her head, certain it tasted as awful as it smelled, if not worse.

Several people wandered off, promising to locate some alcohol even if they had to ferment the fruit themselves. Tezi glanced down at the smashed mango on her boot and hoped something already prepared could be found.

"Good going, kid." Tinder clapped her on the shoulder. "I'm not sure how you keep coming out of these dragon battles unscathed, but I guess it's not just luck."

"I wasn't unscathed, Sergeant. I have wounds."

"A dragon tail smashed me into the deck and broke two of my ribs." Tinder touched her side and winced. "I'm going to have Dr. Fret rub me all over tonight."

"Doesn't she do that anyway?" Sasko asked.

"Only if I bribe her with favors." Tinder winked, then clapped Tezi on the shoulder again. "Keep it up, *Corporal*, and you'll get another promotion in no time. You might even take Sasko's job."

"She's not quite ready for *that*," Sasko said, though she looked a little wistful as she looked out toward the portal.

Lieutenant Vinjo was down there with one of Uthari's red-uniformed officers, circling it and pointing, as if they were making some plans for it. Engineering plans? Tezi couldn't imagine what that might involve.

"But maybe one day," Sasko added. "When I retire."

"My job might be available soon. If we keep having to fight dragons. I'm not sturdy enough for that." Tinder smiled but touched her side again and winced.

Sasko sighed. "I'd like to say we're done with that, but..."

"We heard about how many came through the portal," Tinder said.

"At least you have an axe that protects you from magical attacks."

"And that's perfectly useless against dragon tails falling out of the sky on top of you."

"You should probably avoid letting that happen," Sasko said.

"Funny how I didn't think of that on my own."

"I'm going to ask Vinjo if he can build us some more stealth devices."

"Enough for the whole company." Tinder nodded with enthusiasm. "Do they work against dragons?"

They looked at Tezi, as if she were the expert on dragon battles now.

"I don't think so." She'd heard a number of pained grunts from Sorath and was positive he'd also taken a tail in the chest at one point.

"Damn," Tinder said.

Someone thrust a wooden mug of something alcoholic into Tezi's hand. It smelled like rotten bananas, but she took a sip anyway. Tomorrow, she could worry about dragons. For tonight, she intended to bask in her promotion and enjoy being back in the company, where she was coming to realize she belonged.

Sorath limped into the jungle with an arm wrapped around Grunk's waist, doing his best to support the kid even as he wished he had someone to support him. Battling dragons was *not* good for one's health.

Two mercenaries on patrol passed through the trees ahead and glanced in their direction. Sorath looked at the stealth device active on his wrist, relieved that it still worked. He'd been thrown to the ground more than once as he'd fought the dragon and cracked it on a rock at one point.

He'd cracked *himself* on the rocks too, as his aching ribs attested.

"Any idea how to find your people?" Sorath asked.

Grunk barely seemed conscious, but he kept walking. He mumbled something in a language Sorath couldn't understand.

"I hope that was that you and your powerful magic are taking care of it." Otherwise, Sorath didn't know where to go.

If Thorn Company hadn't been staying on the *Star Flyer*, he would have been tempted to sneak into their camp and pay Dr. Fret a visit. But when he'd left, they'd been fifty feet up in the air and surrounded by mages. He wished he'd had a chance to see Ferroki and make sure that she was well. All he knew for sure was that she and the company were still alive. That would have to be enough for now.

A couple of miles passed underfoot, and Sorath lost the faint animal trail he'd been following. He was debating stopping and waiting until morning to figure out where to go and what to do when a wolf padded into view ahead.

It turned to stare at them. Sorath halted, remembering his last encounter with one of the creatures. This might be the same one, some druid's furry assistant who could see—or smell—through his magical camouflage.

Two male druids stepped out of the trees after the wolf, each carrying staffs. Neither man was familiar to Sorath. If he hadn't had Grunk with him, he wouldn't have announced his presence, but the kid needed treatment.

Sorath tapped the stealth device to turn it off. The wolf sat on his haunches and glanced up at one of the druids, as if to say *I told you so.*

A third druid stepped into view. Kywatha.

"He needs help." Sorath tilted his head toward Grunk, but the two men were already coming forward.

One unfolded a stretcher, twitched a finger, and it floated of its own accord. They levered Grunk onto it, and Sorath patted the kid on the chest, doubting he was coherent but hoping he knew he was in good hands now, that his people would take care of him.

Grunk surprised him by gripping his wrist. *We fought well together, Colonel. Queen Vorsha is dead. May her slaves be freed.*

Though Sorath's mind was occupied with dragons now, and he couldn't care less about Vorsha's passing, he nodded and returned the grip. *Yes, she is. You got her.*

Yes. We'll fight again together.

I'm sure we will.

What is the girl's name?

Sorath blinked in confusion.

She who helped rescue me.

Oh. Tezi. She's a mercenary in Thorn Company.

Tell her thank you.

Sorath didn't know if or when he would see Tezi again, but he nodded. *I will.*

Grunk released him, and the druids carried him away.

Kywatha remained. "Come with me, please, Colonel."

She gestured toward a trail that he would have walked past without noticing. He wasn't positive it had even been visible a minute before.

Though he wanted to wrap a bandage around his ribs, find something to eat, and sleep for twelve hours, Sorath followed Kywatha.

"I've spoken to the elders," she said as they walked. "I regret —*we* regret—our decision not to join the mages and fight against the dragons as they came out of the portal. You were right. We needed to work together."

"Yes." Sorath was too tired to feel smug. Given the gravity of the situation and what their world now faced, maybe it wouldn't have been appropriate anyway.

"Our people will be threatened, the same as yours. It's the

mages' fault—your rulers' faults—but..." Kywatha sighed as the trail ran up a slope. They climbed in silence through the darkening jungle, guided by a light that she'd conjured to bob along ahead of them. "We didn't want to die because of their choice to erect the portal," she added after a time. "Many of us were afraid. Dragons once were friends to humans, and even worshipped by some, but that changed long ago. Our people fear them now."

"With good reason." Sorath touched his ribs again.

"But if we, with the power of magic, do not fight them, who will? We are already hearing about incidents—*deaths*—from the innocent people of Zewnath."

"I'm not surprised. And that's unfortunate."

The trail steepened, and Sorath grimaced. He was on the verge of saying he wouldn't go farther when they came to a break in the trees. They were on the same mountain that he and Kywatha had stood upon a week earlier—it seemed like it had been months—and he could see the camp. There were fewer mageships floating above the area now. Maybe the fleets were heading to their homelands, called back to help deal with the dragons.

To his surprise, Uthari's yacht and one of his mageships hovered low over the portal. A group of red-uniformed mages that looked like ants from this distance stood around it, their hands raised. They were levitating it up to the deck of the larger ship.

"One good thing has come of all this," Kywatha said. "No further enemies will be able to come through. But we have a saying that there's little point in closing one's tent flap after the mosquitoes have already entered."

"In the desert, our saying involves camels getting away and paddock gates being closed afterward."

"Yes."

Sorath pointed to the yacht—was that Uthari at the railing? "That's ballsy of him to take it onboard his ship."

The memory of the portal blasting Uthari in the back with

lightning came to mind. Sorath remembered his awe and delight when he'd believed it a mortal blow. He'd stalked in with his axe, intending to make *sure* Uthari didn't rise again, but Captain Rivlen had jumped down out of nowhere to guard her king.

He shook his head. He'd been so close to shoving her aside, especially when he'd realized the axe would make him impervious to her magic, but Tezi had also been nearby, and he'd envisioned Rivlen barking an order for *her* to attack him. When he'd seen them together after killing Yidar, they'd seemed to feel some loyalty toward each other, and he hadn't wanted to put Tezi in the position of being forced to choose between them. He also didn't have anything against Rivlen, other than frustration for her loyalty to that odious wizard, and hadn't truly wanted to fight her. But, oh, how he wished Uthari were dead. He *deserved* to be dead. The dragons had only been allowed to invade Torvil because of him and his obsession with the portal and finding resources on other worlds.

"The one whom the gateway likes is also on board." Kywatha's tone was bitter. Maybe she knew about the portal's attack and wished, as he did, that it had killed Uthari. "He who convinced it to attack our people."

"Jak," Sorath said. "He's not a bad kid. Even if they're teaching him how to be a mage."

Sorath hoped Jak was still a good kid. They hadn't interacted in a while. It would be distressing to see him adopt their ways and become one of them.

"Will you work with us again, Colonel?"

"Who do you want me to assassinate now?" His body ached at the thought of trying to get to Uthari again. And Malek would be even worse.

"Nobody. We have a new problem now."

"The dragons."

"The dragons," Kywatha agreed. "Somehow, they must be

stopped before they can destroy our cities, enslave our people, and take over our world."

"No argument there. You know we'll all have to work together to have a chance at defeating them, right?" Sorath waved at her and then toward the distant mageships.

"Yes, but I'm terrified that we won't be capable of that."

"Of defeating dragons?" Sorath asked. "Or of working together?"

"Both," she said sadly.

"It *attacked* you?" Malek stared at Uthari across his desk.

They were alone in his office as the yacht flew northward, leaving Zewnath and heading home. The *Serene Waters* had taken damage during the battle, but this part of his suite hadn't been disturbed. A tray of drinks and biscuits rested on his desk, as if all were normal in the world, though Uthari's uncharacteristically haunted expression would have ensured it wasn't, even if Malek hadn't already been briefed about the dragon invasion.

"You didn't notice the scorch hole in the back of my shirt when you returned?"

"I didn't think the portal did it." Malek had been standing, as he usually did, with his hands clasped behind his back. He dropped them and sat in one of the chairs.

"Yes. When I found the ancient text that allowed me to force the portal to attack others, the book warned me that there could be repercussions, that the soul residing within it might not appreciate being manipulated against its will. I scoffed at the idea that an ancient artifact might have a *soul*."

"And now?" Malek arched his eyebrows.

"I acknowledge that I made a mistake."

He'd made *many* mistakes, but Malek kept that opinion to himself. After all, he'd made plenty too.

"There are ancient magics that even well-educated, modern mages don't entirely understand." Uthari extended a hand toward him, as if to bring up the rituals they'd once shared that had infused Malek with zidarr power and altered his body, made him something not entirely human.

"Perhaps you shouldn't attempt to use it as a tool again." Malek could sense the portal lying flat on the deck of the *King's Courage,* the large mageship flying in parallel with the *Serene Waters*. He'd assumed that Uthari had ordered it stowed on the other ship because it wouldn't fit on the yacht, but maybe it had been because he hadn't wanted it on the deck right outside his suite.

"That would be wise, but given the danger ahead…"

"We're here now," Malek said. "If necessary, Jak can ask it to shoot lightning at the dragons."

Uthari's lips thinned. Maybe Malek shouldn't have mentioned Jak. If the portal had *attacked* Uthari, he might be resentful that their young student had a far different—a far better—relationship with it. Or the soul within.

"Yes. It's always favored him." Uthari smiled. It seemed forced, but at least he wasn't stomping around, throwing tantrums like Tonovan. "We're fortunate that he and his mother returned safely and are back with us, especially since there were other deaths on your sojourn."

"Just one," Malek said quietly, wondering why Uthari was bringing up Bakir's death. He'd already given a full report of the events on Nargnoth, and Uthari had seemed indifferent to the loss of the admiral. As Malek recalled, Uthari hadn't wanted to let Bakir and Prolix—or officers from any other kingdom—go along in the first place. "I barely remember it, since I wasn't in my right mind at the time. I just know I was responsible." Malek remembered Jak's contribution, and how it might have saved his life, but he hadn't wanted any onus to fall upon Jak, so he'd left it out of his report. It disturbed him how often he felt compelled to omit details in reports these days. It wasn't out of a sense of disloyalty to his king but a desire to keep Jak and especially Jadora safe. "If there are repercussions, they must fall on my shoulders."

"I will not allow King Jutuk to punish you in any way," Uthari said. "When he decided to send those two along, he knew the mission would be dangerous. Though I don't think anyone could have foreseen bacteria taking over my zidarr."

Malek grimaced, not wanting to dwell on the memory, though he was intensely relieved that Jadora had been able to cure him.

"I've made a note," Malek said, "to don whatever attire the natives wear, should I have the opportunity to visit other worlds again."

Would he have that opportunity? They'd found what Uthari wanted, and the portal was en route to Uth to be locked away in a vault. It might be another ten thousand years before someone used it to leave Torvil. Those other worlds had caused Malek a lot of pain, but he couldn't help but admit being curious about the rest of them. He would enjoy the challenge of exploring them, perhaps with Jak at his side to map the way and to continue to learn magic from him.

"Isn't that how you ended up wearing nothing but studded leather underwear in an arena?" Uthari asked.

"I don't recall mentioning that gladiator costume—" Malek curled his lip at the memory of the dreadful thing, "—in my report to you."

"I saw it in the professor's mind. I believe she found you fetching in it."

Uthari smiled, but Malek took care to make his own face a neutral mask. He'd kissed Jadora on their mission, and he couldn't blame it on drugged juice. It had also been before he'd taken in the brain-altering bacteria. He'd been fully aware of his choice, and that Uthari would have forbidden it if he'd been there, and he'd done it anyway.

Uthari's smile faded. "I can't read her mind now. I suppose you know that."

"Yes."

"You said in your report that the dragon gave her that power." Uthari propped his elbow on the arm of his chair and rested his chin on his fist.

"That's what I was told," Malek said. "I was at first sedated and then trying to kill everyone on the ship, so I missed meeting the dragon."

"I knew the dragons made dragon steel and that *they* had great power. I wouldn't have believed they could flick a wingtip and instantly change a human forever. Or *is* it forever? Do you know?"

"I don't."

Since before they'd returned, Malek had worried about how Uthari would respond to Jadora's new power. He'd been stunned when he first saw her—*sensed* her—but he hadn't said much since then. Malek intentionally kept his answers short, hoping his king wouldn't dwell too long on the possible ramifications of their prisoner having power greater than his. It had been a long time since Malek had thought of Jadora as a prisoner. He hoped Uthari no longer did, as well.

"She's more of a threat now. I'm sure you're aware of that." Uthari watched him intently.

"I don't believe she is."

"With all that power?"

"She seems to have also been given the knowledge of how to use it."

"That's *more* alarming, not less."

"I only meant to say that she's unlikely to accidentally hurl one of your officers over a railing and to his death." Malek thought of Tonovan, but he didn't believe Jadora would do that, even to him.

"She might not-so-accidentally hurl *me* over the railing."

"She's not a murderer. Even when she had the opportunity to..." Malek stopped, belatedly realizing he shouldn't have brought up the subject. Even though his king understood that Malek deeply disliked Tonovan and accepted that they might one day end up dueling to the death, Uthari wouldn't like it if Malek admitted he had been willing to kill Tonovan to protect Jadora. If she'd asked for it, Tonovan would have come back in the same condition as Bakir.

"To kill Tonovan when she was gifted that power?" Uthari guessed.

"Yes."

Uthari watched his face, as if he knew there might be more. Malek sighed and looked toward the porthole, not pleased with himself for disobeying Uthari's wishes and allowing himself to develop feelings for Jadora. Those who'd written the Zidarr Code had been wise to forbid the zidarr to have lovers. It *did* complicate one's relationship with one's liege.

But Malek's attempts to distance himself from Jadora and retract his feelings for her hadn't worked. He wanted to be with her and to protect her, not wall himself off from her.

"She won't be a threat to you," Malek said, willing Uthari to believe him. *He* believed it.

If Jadora hadn't been willing to order him to kill Tonovan, or to do it herself once she had the power, she wouldn't assassinate Uthari either.

"What about to mages in general? To our way of life? To the very way we've structured our society? You know what she and her son want. You've seen their thoughts. It'll be more dangerous now that she has that power and that we can't read their minds."

"She's a scientist, not an assassin. Just give her a new lab and the freedom to work, and she'll be happy. She won't plot an uprising, and she won't be a threat to anyone."

"Would you kill her if you were wrong?" Uthari asked. "If she became a threat to our kind and our way of life? To everyone in the kingdom you're sworn to protect?"

Malek exhaled a long slow breath. "I don't know."

"Well, at least you're honest about that."

Did that imply Uthari didn't believe Malek had been honest about everything? Maybe he sensed the omissions in Malek's reports.

"I would like to think there would be alternatives," Malek murmured.

"Such as what? Taking their key to the portal and exiling her on another world?"

"I suppose that would be better than death," Malek said, though it was hard to imagine being so cruel. Thus far, those other worlds had proven themselves deadly. He supposed Jadora might survive on Vran. If she went back with Zethron, she might even be accepted by the people there.

But Malek would never see her again.

"I'm glad you agree," Uthari said.

Malek frowned at him. Why did he have the feeling that Uthari had been thinking about this since well before Malek had walked into the office? That he wasn't musing so much as finalizing a plan for Jadora, one he planned to enact if she proved too dangerous to their people?

"Why? Because you'll ask me to do it?" Malek should have remained calm and kept his neutral expression in place, but he couldn't keep the bitterness out of his voice.

"Because, with the power she now has, you're likely the only one who *could* do it." Uthari lowered his voice. "Who she would allow to do it."

Malek closed his eyes.

"I believe I've been lenient about your relationship with her," Uthari said, "since I feel some responsibility for having first encouraged you to spend time with her, but if she becomes a threat not only to me but to mages everywhere… we can't allow that. I want your word, Malek. I won't ask you to kill her, but I *will* ask you to force her into exile, to leave her somewhere from whence she can't ever return."

Malek's insides churned, both at the idea of doing that to Jadora and of never seeing her again.

But Uthari held his gaze, his eyes intent. This wasn't a hypothetical question. He wanted confirmation.

"Will you give me your word, Malek?" he asked softly.

"You would force her into exile and leave her son here?" Malek asked, more to buy himself time to think than because he wanted Uthari to realize he should also exile Jak.

"He is your pupil, and he doesn't have the power she now has. She's the larger threat."

Malek didn't think that was true, but he didn't want to argue it. He didn't want Uthari to believe *either* of them was a threat.

"If she becomes dangerous to us and can't be exiled…" Uthari spread his palm toward the ceiling. "She would have to die."

Malek dropped his chin to his chest.

"I wouldn't be so cruel as to ask you to do that," Uthari said, "but it would have to be done."

No, Uthari would only be cruel enough to take someone Malek cared about from him.

He closed his eyes again. "She *won't* be a threat. She's done what you asked and brought back your plant. She's found the secret of working the dragon steel, and she'll synthesize your drug for you. There's no need to have this discussion."

"And yet, I feel the need to elicit this promise from you. And it concerns me that you won't give me your word on the matter."

"*If* she threatens the mages in our kingdom, and *if* it is the only way you'll refrain from assassinating her—" Malek could hear the bitterness in his voice again, but he couldn't tamp it down, "—I will deliver her into exile myself."

"Thank you, my son. I shall hope for your sake that it isn't necessary, but we dare not underestimate those two. Especially now."

"I understand."

And Malek did. He just didn't want to acknowledge that Jadora could be dangerous to the mages of the world. Not when he loved her.

THE END

Printed in Great Britain
by Amazon

78856552R00345